(Imagined) Advance Praise for *The Time Flies*

*"This book completely changed my life! I guess I was a little better off before, but still. You should read it!"**

J.K., IOWA CITY, PA

*"I stopped doing crimes when I read this book! Then I started again. But I might stop again, a little! Read it!"**

L.B. III, SEATTLE, RI

"I thought it was going to be about something else. But you can read it if you want."

D.R., CHEYENNE, NC

*"This is a real book, with pages. First time I've done this. Please read!"**

P.F., PHILLY, NV

"The parts I read were really okay."

Y.G., FARGO, FL

*"I couldn't put it down until I had something else to do!"**

J.M., TRENTON, NM

"How many people can get away with stuff like this?"

G.Y., JUMBOLAND, DE

"This book is more serious than you'd think. Not much, but some."

ROLAND GODIVA
THE GAROGS INSTITUTE

*Exclamation points added by author for visual enticement.

Other Stories by George Ciardi

Moving Day

Unhanging Ol' Cyrus

Common Man Stories Volume 1

The

Time Flies

George Ciardi

To my family
for putting up with my eccentricities and crabbiness for the (too
many) years that it took to get to this stage, especially my amazing
wife, Sharon Elise Dunn, whose patience and understanding
for the insanity of others is almost unforgivably noble.

Author's Note

Note: The character of Arturo Bandini is based on the character of the same name from John Fante's superb novel, *Ask the Dust*, set in the Bunker Hill section of late 1930s Los Angeles, and from which I learned so much.

The

Time Flies

The First Consideration

For most of their history, the Time Flies had made it a rule never to contact their prisoners. Their limited obligation was to provide invisible guidance, a watchful eye, to act as anchors to the time period into which those they'd sentenced had been imprisoned. So immutable was this rule to avoid contact that Professor Cyril T. Rocklidge had made it one of the *Ten Rules to Consider* when he wrote about the Time Flies back in 1923. So, when Bob and Lenora began getting contacted by the Time Flies through Bob's typewriter, long after they'd lost most of their memories and with only a few years left on their sentences, it came as quite a shock. They had tried repeatedly over the years to ask why they had been sentenced in the first place and to find reasons for their frozen emotional states and the fact that they'd stopped aging. All requests up to that point had been answered with silence from the Time Flies, with the exception of the paper copy of the *Time Fly Law*, which the Flies had surreptitiously stuffed into the back pocket of Bob's pants upon the commencement of their sentence. A law that, due to its poor translation from the Time Fly language, told them virtually nothing about why they had been convicted or what to expect in the way of punishment.

But the story of Bob and Lenora does not start with Bob's typewriter, or with the *Ten Rules to Consider* by Professor Rocklidge, or even with the copy of the *Time Fly Law* in Bob's pocket.

It does start with the aftermath of the crime that Bob and Lenora didn't know they'd committed, against a species they did not know existed.

Start Here

Bob was standing on the sidewalk in front of the office building where he had worked for more than eleven years, with a bag containing his things in one hand and his other hand down the back of his pants. He was looking at clouds, watching as tons of water, held in suspension, were being pulled across the sky. It was warm today, but rain was coming.

A homeless man, his radar detecting the glint of disorientation on Bob's face, stopped and asked him for some money. He needed it for bus fare, or to fix his car, or to fund an art project, or something. But Bob didn't hear him; he was drifting.

"It's not easy being like this, you know," the homeless man said, as he muddled away.

.   .   .

The day was Friday. The month was April. This was the last day of school for his wife, Lenora, before spring break in the year 2015. Lenora was a high school teacher. History, mostly.

Bob usually requested vacation time to coincide with Lenora's break. On that Friday, he would take off from work a little early to stop by the bank and fill his pocket with cash. He and Lenora liked to use cash on their vacations because it made them feel rustic and because it didn't leave a trail of information the way plastic did. It also provided them with a self-imposed limit. They would spend only what was in Bob's pocket, and only where American money was expected. Like latter day isolationists, they had rarely strayed beyond the star-spangled shores, content with road trips where the gasoline was measured in gallons and the distances in miles.

But this particular Friday had turned out differently than Bob had expected. He had been sitting at his desk in his windowless office, piddling, his mind elsewhere, looking forward to a lovely week on the Oregon Coast, when his boss, a new man nearly half his age, had called him into his office and told him that it wasn't all that necessary for him to return to work following his vacation.

"There's just not a lot going forward right now," he'd said, his hands folded on his desk in what Bob assumed his boss thought was a commiserating manner, the bluish Seattle skyline outside the window behind him seeming to rise from his shoulders. "We have to make some changes for the good of the company."

He smiled at Bob to show that he meant no harm, then stood and extended his hand. Bob looked at it, speechless. "Good luck," said his ex-boss. "I envy your opportunity."

Ordinarily, Bob would have emailed Lenora if anything unusual happened at work, but the access to his computer had been disabled before he'd left his boss's office. He gathered a few things from his desk and put them in his bag while Ricardo, the security guard he'd known since the beginning, waited patiently for his allotted five minutes of packing time to transpire before escorting him out of the building. This was a precaution in case Bob decided to go crazy and attack innocent, employed people. He didn't, and Ricardo was thankful, bidding Bob farewell at the lobby door.

"That's a lot of years," Ricardo had said to him, shaking his head.

Now Bob stood on the sidewalk, with one hand in his pants, outside of his newly former place of employment. He didn't know what to do. It had happened too fast. He thought that maybe people didn't like him anymore or that he was some kind of an idiot for losing his job. It hadn't been a great job—managing a small department that created spreadsheets that nobody read for a company that made things that people didn't really need—but it had been eleven years of his life. That did seem like a lot, although it hadn't seemed like much while he was living them. He thought of texting Lenora about it, but they'd just purchased new phones the evening before, at Lenora's insistence, and he didn't know how to use the text function yet.

He took the smart phone from his pocket and swiped his finger across it. Mysterious icons lit up the screen. He looked up at the clouds one last time then crossed the street to the bank, filled his pocket with cash and headed home to deal with the cluster flies before leaving for a lovely week on the Oregon Coast.

.   .   .

He rode the light rail in a daze, his face pressed to the window, the tunnel wall rushing past, inches away, with a sound like the wailing of ghosts, while everyone else looked at the screens in their hands.

"World of screens," he muttered, slouching lower in his seat. Bob had little patience with the technological slavery of the twenty-first century. There had been that guy at the urinal next to him, checking his messages while taking a leak, and it had amazed him. That had been just yesterday, when he still had a job and no detectable horizon of unemployment. That guy was probably still working.

When he arrived home, he stood on the deck out back trying to get his bearings before going in, looking across the dense tangle of garden to where the clematis was wrapping itself around the plum tree, climbing ever higher. He was supposed to have taken care of that. Paul, Dave's dog from next door, was lying on the grass, twitching in a dream, oblivious to the coagulated whoosh of traffic noise coming from the interstate. Bob glanced at the teeth marks on his arm. He'd had an altercation with Paul just that morning, the result of differing opinions on digging under his front porch. That seemed so long ago now. He watched as Paul fluttered awake, yawned, sniffed, scratched, got to his feet and dragged himself around to the front to sleep under the porch.

Inside, he could hear Lenora lightly cursing the cluster flies.

.   .   .

Bob and Lenora had begun their legal union in Seattle at the birth of the twenty-first century. They bore no children together and never would, instead hauling cargo from previous failures, Lenora adding one daughter from 'before' and Bob slipping in two, all adults now, all living mostly at home, with brief boomerangs into the world at large, depending on job or relationship status. None of the daughters were at home right now and for that Bob was grateful.

He found Lenora in the living room, barefoot and in garden-stained sweats, opening windows. Hundreds of flies that she thought were cluster flies—but weren't—blimped sleepily about the room. The flies were big and fat and lazy, making farty buzzing sounds. They landed on the furniture, polka-dotted the walls and windows. Lenora turned, her smile glittering with a freshly installed freedom that prevented her, for the moment, from picking up on Bob's distress.

"Vacation!"

He forced it. "Vacation!"

These were the times when he loved her most, when she was temporarily released from the responsibilities of teaching, when her exhaustion lifted and she stopped ranting endlessly about her students and their resistance to having their young minds molded. She appeared so happy now, standing there with flies buzzing about her, so secure and relaxed. And he was going to have to ruin it by telling her that he'd just lost his damn job.

Lenora finished opening the windows and doors, then stood next to Bob and waited for the flies to leave. That's what was supposed to happen. It always had. The cluster flies had been an unwavering seasonal presence at their home, whether inside the house, or outside in the garden. Cluster flies weren't like regular flies, the common houseflies swatted by the millions, although they were quite common as flies go. Cluster flies didn't eat garbage and weren't attracted to open wounds or the crusty eyes of the impoverished. They ate flowers. But in the autumn, when the flowers passed on and the weather cooled, the cluster flies would move en masse, through cracks and gaps, to winter inside the south wall of the house, clustered against the cold between siding and drywall. The house was one hundred and four years old. It had many cracks and gaps through which the flies could seek refuge. When the spring warmth arrived, the flies would come into the house, seeking escape by the light of the windows. Why they didn't go out the way they had come in was baffling, but that's the way it was. It had been the same every year: spring break and cluster flies. They were used to it.

"What's wrong?" she said, looking up at his face.

"Nothing. Why?" He avoided looking at her, keeping his attention on the flies.

"You have your hands in your pants." This was a bad habit of Bob's when he got nervous or stressed—he put his hands in his pants. Always the back, never the front. And not his whole hands, mostly just the fingers. The thumbs remained in the safety zone above the belt line. But there was something about the warm roundish comfort of his buttocks against his palms that helped calm him.

"So, what's wrong?" she said again.

He took his hands out of his pants and continued watching the flies. He didn't want to tell her just yet. "Have you noticed that they're not leaving?"

"What?"

"The flies. They're not leaving."

Lenora looked around the room. He was right. The flies weren't leaving. Something *was* wrong. These weren't behaving like cluster flies were supposed to behave. These flies didn't want to go outside and munch flowers. They simply buzzed about the room, landing where they pleased and mostly staying put. They didn't even look like cluster flies, really. An extra wing poked from their thoraxes, sticking straight up, which made them look a bit like a sundial. On occasion, they seemed to disappear in midair and reappear a few feet away.

"How strange," she said. "I'll be right back."

She left Bob standing in the middle of the living room. A fly landed on his bald spot and he could feel its feet jittering around on his scalp. He imagined the feet tapping out a Morse code: *Tell her, tell her.* But when Lenora returned from the bedroom clutching her laptop, and perched herself on the living room floor, he again demurred.

"Oh, come on," he said, when he saw the laptop in her hand. "Why don't we just go?"

"Stop whining. Do you want to know what's wrong or don't you?"

"Not really. I want to go. Where's the suitcase?"

"Already in the car."

She opened the laptop and it musically introduced itself. Bob sighed so she could hear it and sank onto the couch. He listened to her mumble at the sporadic Internet connection—"goddamnitshitstupidpayingfor-fuckingnothing....."—as she got up and began pacing around the living room trying to catch the signal. *Here we go*, he thought. Panic mode. Bob said her problem was due to her being a vegetarian; that a little meat could calm her nerves and keep her from stressing so much, a ludicrous claim that she didn't even bother to acknowledge.

Connection made, she sat on the floor again and began typing, her bony cheeks resting uneasily on the hardwood, ready to spring her into action should she lose the signal again. Bob watched her search, her eyes molesting the screen with their need for information.

He was going to have to tell her.

And then it happened. He could always tell by the change in intensity of her typing. The way her pounding fingers caused her long silver mane to vibrate.

"You're answering emails?"

"Shh! Just one."

"I thought you were looking up the flies."

"Shhh!"

Bob grumbled and got up from the couch, tromping with audible vexation over to the bookshelves that lined the north wall of the living room and the entire entryway. Most of them were crammed with Lenora's books, all profusely flagged and highlighted for use, or intended use, in her lesson plans. There were books on multiple versions of history, both civilized and uncivilized, from all periods and geographies; from ancient China through the Russian Revolution; from the Civil War through Civil Rights. Suffragettes to Astronauts. Waterloo to Watergate. Vietnam. A whole section on WWII. An awful lot of Lincoln. Books on as many versions and races of oppressed peoples as she had room for (none of which she actually belonged to). On the floor, a jagged palisade ran the length of the shelves, the stacks growing for more than two years now, since she'd run out of shelf space.

Bob's smaller portion of the shelves, the ones closest to the fifty-inch TV—the other love of his life—were stocked with movies from the mid-twentieth century, from Hollywood's Golden Age to its wide screen, fear-of-television phase, to its rebirth in the late sixties after the death of the Production Code. He began thumbing through the film noir section, the cream of his collection, pulling out some of his favorite titles: *On Dangerous Ground; The Man Who Cheated Himself; Detour; Out of the Past.* He gazed at the actors on the covers, caught in dramatic poses of apprehension and violence and fear and death. These were the friends he understood today. He was one of them now; a man with nowhere to turn, aging and unwanted, cast off to starve in the gutter, to fight and claw and kill for what he needed.

A fly landed on the picture of Robert Mitchum's lip-dangling cigarette and he brushed it away. Lenora caught his movement peripherally while keeping her eyes on the screen.

"You're taking movies?"

"Uh, no. Just a few. They might have a DVD player at the hotel."

"I thought we were going to walk on the beach."

"Not at night."

"Why not?" she said.

"Fine. I won't take them, but you can't take your laptop either."

"I already said I wouldn't. Did you remember to get cash from the bank?"

A wave of sickness flushed through him as he replaced the movies on the shelf.

"Are you hyperventilating?" Lenora asked almost matter-of-factly, still typing.

He spun to face her. "Just look up the goddamn flies, will you?"

She stopped typing and raised her head, a piqued flicker in her eyes as they met his. All that could be heard was the farty buzzing of the flies. "Okay, Bob. I will. But eventually, you're going to have to tell me what's wrong."

Bob looked away. Maybe he didn't need to tell her. What did it matter now? In an odd sense, those eleven years were already growing distant for him, already consigned to the memories of who he used to be, and submerging beneath the uncertainties of who he would have to be next. He became faintly aware of her typing again as he slumped back onto the couch, wringing his hands. *Tell her now. Tell her later. Don't tell her.* He couldn't decide. His stomach flopped and twisted. Trickles of sweat ran down the insides of his arms.

"Okay," he said at last. "Okay, okay. I'll tell you."

"Wait. Here it is." And before he could muster the courage to let it all out, another truth revealed itself first. Lenora looked up from her screen, kicked out two beats of laughter, and announced: "Hey, these aren't cluster flies—they're Time Flies."

And Time Flies they were. And they had a job to do. They were there to send two fairly average people back in time. Now.

The Missing Freeway

The transference from Spring Break 2015 to December 1938 passed without incident. There were no switches thrown, no electrical arcs or bright flashes, no falling through mirrors, and no helpless spinning around in a zero gravity void. The Time Flies did not deal in theatrics.

Bob had simply found himself on a different couch, stiffer and scratchier than the one he'd just come from, feeling exactly as he'd felt a moment ago, lost and confused and ashamed.

Lenora was sitting in the same spot on the same hardwood floor, the tail end of the word "flies" still dying on her lips, the tense ligaments and bone and fatless skin of her fingers hovering above the spot where her laptop had been. She wondered briefly how Bob had been able to get it away from her without her noticing.

"What the … ?"

Now, Bob and Lenora were not the type of people to believe in time travel. They'd seen some movies, read a few novels about it, had watched *Doctor Who* in their early years while partying with friends, but it had always struck them as nothing more than fanciful. Something to ponder, but nothing to plan for. So, when Bob suddenly saw the TV disappear, he didn't think much of it. He thought it must have something to do with his becoming jobless, or, more accurately, with the state of stress he was in as a result of it. He'd lost his job, and with it, his self-confidence, his security, his sense of structure. Why not lose the TV? He was willing to think of it as a hallucination. But one thing did strike him as odd: the gauzy curtains over the windows that now occupied his field of vision were not something he recognized. Neither were the ghostly images of the houses across the street that he could see through them.

Houses?

He sprang from the couch and threw open the curtains. The loss of his TV he could understand, but not the addition of houses.

"Where'd the freeway go? And who are all those kids out front?"

Lenora jumped up from the floor and pushed her face to the window, joining him, and saw that Interstate Five, the bi-directional river that had roared two hundred feet from the front door of this house since 1963, had indeed disappeared. In its place were rows of rugged craftsman houses. The traffic from the off ramp had been replaced by a mob of woolen-bundled kids playing on a narrow icy street.

"I don't…I don't understand," Lenora said, joggling her head in disbelief, her voice tremulous, almost irritated. "No, I really don't understand. The freeway was right there. Where the hell is the freeway, Bob?"

"I don't know. Why ask me?"

They appraised each other fearfully, hyperventilating in unison, looked back out the window, and then back at each other again. Lenora surveyed the room. "The flies are gone," she said. "The goddamn flies are gone, Bob, and this isn't our house." The room was the right shape but she didn't understand the furniture, which was more like some great grandmother's house, small round tables with doilies and sepia photographs of unsmiling people in oval frames. In a corner stood a short Christmas tree draped with tinsel. The air held the pinched aromas of burnt coal and chlorine bleach.

Bob said, "Isn't that our fireplace?"

She turned. "Those ugly bricks? They're not even white. I painted them white years ago." Then, as if receiving a sudden message, she whirled around, and upon seeing the nearly blank walls of the entryway, gasped and covered her mouth.

"My books!"

Bob put his hands in his pants.

The Stenographer

It was disorienting, to say the least, and they found themselves behaving like gape-mouthed actors in an underwritten *Twilight Zone* episode. There were the expected *"Where are we?"*s, and *"Oh, my God!"*s and such, some aimless running around the house, and even an accusation or two brought on by the stress. Suffice it to say, they were shocked, confused, cried some, got a bit snappy with each other, went on and on about their daughters and friends, and—since there seemed to be no other alternative—decided to deal with it.

"Look at this," said Bob, picking up a piece of paper from the table. They were standing in the kitchen, which looked very different from the kitchen they remembered from an hour ago, even though it was, geographically, the same kitchen. "It's a letter."

Lenora's eyes flicked nervously around the room, still swollen but mostly dried of tears. She had passed through shock and had entered a stage that could best be described as unamused bafflement. She rubbed her bare feet alternately on her calves. "It's freezing in here," she said.

"It's to someone named Minnie," said Bob.

That was Minnie Beckback, a previous—now present—owner of their house. Minnie, a stenographer for the local police precinct, was on her way home from work now, having stopped off at the grocery store for a few things. The letter was from her husband, Burt. He was leaving her for a logger's widow. The letter began with 'Minnie'; not 'Dear Minnie,' just 'Minnie.' It ended with the beginning of her new life alone.

"I don't think you should be reading that," Lenora said, reading over his shoulder.

"How do we know what we should be doing?" He put the letter down and pulled that morning's *Seattle Daily Times* toward him. His voice rose as he read, so that by the end of his sentence he was nearly shouting. "Friday, December 16, 1938?"

From outside: the clomping of shoes on porch wood and the rattle of keys.

The Broken Glass

Footsteps clacked across the kitchen floor above their heads. They heard the crinkly thud of grocery bags on the counter, felt the pause as Minnie picked up the letter from the table.

Bob and Lenora huddled together in the basement, hidden beside the coal stoker. In twenty years, the stoker would be replaced with a gas furnace. Now the floor was still dirt. The rest was wood and bricks and spider webs. A gas meter with a coin slot was bolted to a wall, a small stack of coins on top of it.

Above them, a chair was slid out from the table. Its legs adjusted slightly under Minnie's weight. She cried. The crying had history and anger in it.

A glass smashed on the floor.

Minnie stood and her footsteps traced a path to the opening and slamming of drawers and closet doors. They heard a phone being dialed. It was a sound they had not heard since childhood, except in old movies.

Another pause, then—

"He's done it, the bastard ... Yes, Burt. Who else? He left me for that tramp ... I know ... yes, I know. Merry damned Christmas ... He left most of his clothes—can you believe it? He didn't even take his precious coat ... Yes! That cheviot I got him last Christmas on layaway. The bastard. Can you imagine? He'd better not try coming back for it ... Huh? Oh, not yet. Where would I go? ... Can we come over tonight? I just can't bear it here ... Thanks. Tell Stevie to make some room for Freddie ... Yes, I'm sure it will be fun for them. Bye."

While Minnie sobbed and swept broken glass, Lenora and Bob stayed curled beneath the stairs, up against the stoker, cramping. Bob placed his hand on Lenora's knee, which had begun to twitch.

When Minnie's son, Freddie, roared in, she stopped him with a poke of the broom handle.

"Ow!"

"Be careful!"

"It's really icy outside." He saw the broken glass. "What happened?" He saw her tears. "What's the matter? Was that your favorite glass?"

"Go to your room and get your pajamas. We're spending the night with Aunt Betty."

"Oh, boy! Are we gonna stay the whole weekend?"

"No ... I don't know. The weather might get worse. Bring a change of underwear just in case."

"Should I bank the coal before we go?"

"No. We're going to be gone too long. Leave it out. And hurry. I don't want to be driving on this ice after dark."

The last thing they heard before the door closed for the evening: "What about dad?"

Nazis Again

Bob washed off the coal dust in Minnie's bathroom sink, moving his hands back and forth between the cold water and hot water faucets. Lenora studied herself in Minnie's mirror.

"My feet are so freezing," she said. Through the tiny bathroom window she could see a bit of the house next door, the house that she had known as Dave's, and the park across the alley, where the trees were so much smaller than she remembered. A thick fog hung in the air.

In a way, they had Burt the Bastard to thank for this brief opportunity to adjust to their new surroundings. If he hadn't buzzed his chainsaw into the lonely clear cut of a logger's widow, the whole family might have been at home; Burt reading his newspaper; Minnie sending Freddie to the basement to put a coin in the gas meter so she could make dinner—"Don't forget to light the furnace!"—and Freddie running back up the stairs to report on the two people in funny clothes hiding by the stoker.

A lucky break.

They had the whole night to figure out what to do. Bob went into Minnie and Burt's bedroom and got a pair of thick socks from a dresser drawer and handed them to Lenora.

"That's stealing," she said.

"It's borrowing. Minnie didn't seem like the kind of person who would refuse you warm feet."

"You went through somebody's drawers," she said as she sat at the kitchen table and put them on.

"Just before your laptop disappeared you said something. What was it?"

"I said … 'These aren't cluster flies, they're Time Flies.'"

They sat together as the light of December 16, 1938 faded. Due to fog and season, darkness was settling at around four pm. Above Bob's head, a cuckoo clock announced itself, startling them. They had been trained to respond to electronic beeps. Now they would learn to respond to bells and whistles and cuckoo clocks again.

"What are Time Flies?"

"I don't know. That's what the website called them."

"What else?"

"There was a counter. I think I was the first visitor to the site."

"What else?"

"I don't remember." Lenora rested her hand against her head. "Wait. There were drawings. And something about time travel."

"Yes?"

She sighed. "I don't know. That's when it disappeared. When *we* disappeared. I guess the laptop is still there." She picked up the newspaper and held it to the fading window light. Page one had an article about the United States hinting at reprisals if the Nazis didn't guarantee property rights for American Jews and Catholics living in Germany.

"I'm hungry," said Bob.

"I can't believe this," said Lenora, shaking her head.

"What?"

"Nazis. Does this mean it has to happen again? Are we really going to be here for that? I mean, if the date on this newspaper is correct then they've already teamed up with Austria. *Kristallnacht* was just last month."

The Professor and the Internet

Little was known about The Time Flies. There had been rumors, dismissals of those rumors, and a few who believed. Someone even wrote about them. While searching the Internet for fly information, Lenora had stumbled upon an obscure website containing the private papers of Professor Cyril T. Rocklidge, a former professor of mathematics at Princetown University in Cleveland, Indiana, beginning in 1910 and ending abruptly in 1923, the year he became a Time Fly prisoner and began writing about them.

His unfinished papers had been discovered in the attic of a pastry chef's home in France, while preparing the home for sale in early 2015. The pastry chef had shown the papers to a friend who thought they were funny and suggested that he scan them and post them online. A good joke. He did, and a few days later Lenora became the website's first visitor.

Professor Rocklidge had not had an easy time of it after his experience with the Time Flies. One moment he had been a respected mathematics professor with a distinguished beard and rimless spectacles, and the next he didn't seem to know who anybody was. His family and friends, all strangers. He had developed a French accent overnight. He talked about being abducted by the Time Flies, claimed he had written about them in France, and blamed them for his memory loss. Everyone thought he'd gone wacko. He moved to France shortly thereafter, took up with old friends, and was never seen by his family or the university again. He would be gunned down by Nazis during the 1940 invasion.

The website would be discovered by descendants of the Professor in 2016. They were embarrassed about it. It was a painful chapter in their family history. They would manage to contact the pastry chef and request that he shut the site down and return the papers to them, the rightful owners. After an agreement had been reached on the pastry chef's fee, the papers would be returned and the website dismantled. All would be forgotten.

Professor Rocklidge's papers on the Time Flies were incomplete, as he had died before finishing them. They were never published and no one had ever read them until the pastry chef had discovered them and posted them on the Internet, the great repository for unknowns. But Rocklidge got some things right and they could have been helpful to Lenora and Bob if Lenora had had more time to read them before being sent into the past. She did have time to read this:

```
-Time Flies are everywhere, in every home and building,
in every wild landscape on Earth, traveling through all
periods of time. They are mostly out of sight, hidden,
or 'disappeared' from view. On the rare occasion they
are sighted they are usually mistaken for common houseflies
(Musca Domestica) or cluster flies (Pollenia Rudis).
```

and this:

```
-On the issue of emotional states------
```

before she disappeared.

Recognition

"Well, whatever they are," said Lenora, across the darkness of the kitchen table, "if they're responsible for this, I hope they let us in on it. It would be nice to know what the hell is going on." They discussed possible scenarios for how they should handle themselves. They had no idea how long they would be here, wherever *here* was, but it seemed prudent to be prepared. They certainly couldn't stay in this house—their house—for long. Minnie would be back. They needed food and clothing, some of which they would have to take from Minnie and Burt. This time it would be stealing. Then what? They cried, rattled their heads in disbelief.

"I have money," Bob said, putting his wad of vacation cash on the table. "That should help for a while.

Lenora pushed it away. "It's the wrong kind of money."

She was right. Their money would not work well in 1938. Bob scooped up the wad, the tens and twenties with their enlarged off-center portraits and faint washes of color, and put it back in his pocket.

"We can try."

Lenora thought it unethical of them to be in someone's home without the legal occupant's knowledge and said so. True, they hadn't had much choice in being sent here, but they were now in a position to leave if they so chose and it bothered her that they weren't. Ethical dilemmas were the cornerstone of Lenora's teaching style. History was filled with them. They were what made history interesting and worth studying in the first place. She had a great interest in the violation of ethics in the past, but little patience for it in the present. "We are who we are because of who we were," she reminded her students regularly. These were high school kids. Not all of them understood, but many of them wanted to. And although she was essentially a teacher of history, she took it upon herself to act as a rudder to her students' moral lives as they navigated the muddy deltas of adolescence, their minds cluttered with digital distractions. It could be said that her largest muscle group was the strength of her convictions. And though she appreciated the need for her students to explore and experiment, she had been remarkably consistent in her own life up to this point. She didn't care much for spontaneity or change any more than Bob did. Thrills, to her, were found in books and in teaching about the lives of other, more spontaneous people.

"I think we should go," she said again. She was feeling a tremendous desire to walk.

Bob tilted his head, doubtful. They had to be careful here, not do anything rash. He tried to think, but wasn't having much luck. "Not yet. We'll need a plan."

"What's your plan?"

"I don't know." His head was spinning. He couldn't seem to hold onto thoughts long enough to assemble them. He felt the same sense of confusion he'd felt just before they were sent here, when he had been about to tell Lenora he'd been laid off from his job. "Do you feel alright?"

"Given the circumstances, I'm okay. Aren't you?"

"I don't know. I don't think so. Maybe I'm just hungry."

Minnie had food. They'd caught her on shopping day. Still, they were too nervous to eat much and didn't want to steal any more than was necessary.

Bob went to the basement and put a coin in the gas meter so they could cook. They split a can of Franco-American spaghetti that he ladled into small ceramic bowls and served to her with a homey flourish along with some white bread. He'd suggested the one with meatballs but Lenora just looked at him and he put it back. They ate in darkness so as not to alert the neighbors to the presence of strangers in the home.

They were afraid of everything. They didn't want to leave the house, ever.

Around two in the morning they fell asleep in their clothes on Minnie's bed, pulling the bedspread around them for warmth. Occasionally, they were awakened by a dog barking outside. The barking sounded familiar. Sometime near dawn, Bob said:

"Doesn't World War II start soon?"

Lenora rolled over. "If the date on the newspaper is correct, then three days ago Göring took charge of resolving the 'Jewish Question.'"

"Do you think anyone around here knows that?"

"I doubt it. A few, maybe. We are close to the university."

They lay in silence a moment.

"What about Poland?"

"Not for about nine more months."

Bob drifted off to sleep again. Lenora watched the dawn light grow into early morning light. The light was pressure to her. As it grew brighter, filling the room, she felt more constricted, fearful. It represented the passage of time. Decisions needed to be made.

There are new people living in our old house.

As she lay there, her legs began to twitch again. It had woken her a number of times during the night, accompanied with the intense desires to walk and read. She rolled onto her back to try and calm her legs and stared at the ceiling. Minnie's bed, noisier and with more topography than theirs, was in the same spot that theirs had been in. The shape of the room—the door, the closet, the drafty windows—allowed for pretty much only one spot for the bed.

I know this ceiling.

It was discolored, needed paint, but she recognized the texture, the tiny bumps on the plaster in the same patterns she'd been looking at for nearly fourteen years. The light from the window, kept low by the fog, cast faint shadows from the bumps. The ceiling light fixture was the very same one that she'd used, but much newer looking now.

December 17, 1938. Her father had turned twenty-four years old two weeks ago. Her mother was nineteen. They hadn't even met yet.

Her legs had stopped twitching and she had just about dozed off again when she was startled awake by the thud of the morning newspaper hitting the front door.

The Discovery

Bob was not alone in carrying a secret into the past that may have been of interest to his spouse. Lenora was reminded of hers as she was hunting for a belt to cinch the dress that she was stealing from Minnie's closet. As she pulled the belt from its hanger, her hand brushed against the lump in the southeast corner of her left breast, causing her to flush with the anxiety of an important, but nearly forgotten, memory. She had discovered the lump, a tiny thing, as small and hard as a polished pebble, while putting on her bra before leaving for school on the morning of the day they went back in time. Yesterday. There had been no opportunity to have it checked by a professional, and in all the craziness that followed she had forgotten about it. She hadn't told Bob yet and didn't think she was going to for quite a while now. She turned her back to him and felt the lump again. It hadn't changed. A good sign, but what was she going to do about it now?

She forced a smile as she tried on some of Minnie's hats—one that looked like a tall lawn gnome's hat and another that was shaped like a flying saucer.

"It's like wearing costumes," she said, putting on a ribbed felt hat with a feather in it.

"Everything we wear is a costume."

"Mr. Social Philosopher." She took the hat off and put it carefully back on the closet shelf. She settled for a pillbox with a net windshield.

They felt sorry for Minnie—she had enough troubles—but it had to be done. Their own clothes would be too strange looking. They didn't even have coats or proper footwear.

"You'll have to give up your shoes," Lenora said.

Bob's shoes were of the hyper-athletic style, with plastics and fabrics and random splashes of color. The soles were like the tracks on a tank. They would have looked like space boots in 1938. He did not want to give them up. They had strong arch support. He had sore feet. They were a good match for each other. He sagged on the edge of the bed as Lenora stroked his bald spot.

"You still have your exercises. You'll just have to keep up with them better."

"I keep up with them. It still hurts."

Lenora nodded but Bob could tell she was just being polite. He didn't keep up with his exercises. He thought that since he had paid a lot of money for his shoes, and for the orthotic inserts that he'd shoved into them, that the shoes should do the work for him. He'd always considered it unfair that Lenora had the foot mechanics of a nomad and could walk forever when he had been plagued for the past eight years, for no seemingly good reason, with bullheaded flare-ups of plantar fasciitis. His arches were like old rubber bands. It was a source of embarrassment for him. It had even occurred to him during moments of marital weakness that Lenora might leave him for it because he couldn't keep up. He looked at Burt's shoes with their flat leather soles and rubbed his fingers along the inside. The arch support was pitiful.

"I will," he said, meaning he would do his exercises. When she wasn't looking, he took the orthotics out of his space boots and put them in Burt's shoes.

They had no problem stealing from Burt. Burt was a bastard. Bob had just taken off Burt's cheviot coat and was preparing to try on the pants from a blue tweed suit when he pulled something out of his back pocket.

He unfolded it. It was the poorly translated copy of the Time Fly Law that they had violated. The Time Flies had placed it in Bob's pocket to assist them on their journey.

"Uh-oh."

In the top right corner of the page was an official looking stamp, oblique in angle, red in color that said—Convicted and Sentenced—with two lines beneath for the names of the convicted.

Line one said: Lenora
Line two said: Bob
"What?" said Lenora.
"I think we may be in jail."
They would not leave Minnie's house that day.

The Law

Time Fly Law
Relative Order

Section 436 Documents 11 and six-6

_____721.67+4rtt

Unauthorzed Movement of Projected Matereals
by sub-species

Insofar as one expected, alongside, or otherwise // determined:

Anyone, of any known or questionalbe species, who knowingly, wilfully and/or supposedly, removes a legally and properly projected item from its exact place and brings it, places it, or disposes of it in any place(s) less than, equal to, or other than, its said exact place(ment) shall be punished for a period, unquestioningly, and deservedly, of not less than and exactly to

25 years, not exceeded.

THUS
EXECUTION OF LAW:

This law, pursuant to, as/to therefore, shall be enforced and remained whole by exactly the number of flies to not improperly guide the convicted throo the sentence, entirety. Each fly present at time of said infrakshun, with equal presence upon original projection, shall be counted, divided and averaged to determine time of service to convicted rendered.

Egxample:

nOmber of flies present at infriction: 1000
length of sentence: 25 yrs
in hours: 219,145.319
guidance time for each Fly: 219.145319 hrs

Illustration:

Each Time Fly pursuant to example above, and as example only, bears responsibility for guidance and protection (minimal) of convicted through 219,145319 consecutive hours of time, after which time is exhausted shall not remain unrelieved by next assigned Fly.

Questions of volume - negated. Flies may guide suspects
convicted in any knumber greater than zero and less than ☞ ⊗

Conditions and Allouwances

Convicted are free to travel at will. No expenses are t^ be cuvered. No per diem is allouwed.
Convicted will not age for duration ov sententse but may retain marks, scars and disabilities purchased during =__*
Guidance is limited to the consecutiv passage of ℤ. Assistance by guiding Time Fly is not perm‡✔__ does not exist
Protection is limited to said consecutive passidge of time. Injuries - physical, spiritual, psychologikul - as allowed to happ℞; events dictated.
Although ev⌐ℓy effort is made to guide convicted less than unsafely while incurring no effort_1♦ OR as to   .
Time Flies bear no liability for ruptured (ors), psychological trauma, limb damage, intelectual reduction, scarring, burns, breakage, punctures, emotional distress, loss of laughter, or any and all conditions of adjustment from original ↘①↙ℯ arising and therefore experiencing (gup)(gup)   cannot be held liable.

Upon satisfactory completion of sentence, convicted will return to exact time and place of departure at commencemint &^ ___ ⊛.

Other ap7lied conditions for suksessful return include   ⁊∠↑↖, as well as (construct)‡‡‡ all original IMPORTANT)) must be inTact or return will/can be (complicated by death) extraction   ⊕④   failure   dElay!

The Rules According to
Professor Cyril T. Rocklidge

The translation of The Time Fly Law in Bob's pocket was rudimentary. There had been difficulties translating from the Time Fly language; the translators' capabilities had been limited. The best that could have been done had been done.

In some respects, The Law was quite clear. They had been sentenced to a period of twenty-five years. But the document was incomplete. There were omissions. Gaps. It didn't even clearly state their crime.

Professor Rocklidge had received a translation of his own in 1923 at the start of his sentence of fifteen years for getting a Time Fly briefly caught in his beard. The Time Flies had called it assault. But it had been a better translation than the one Bob got stuck with and from it he fleshed out a set of rules for all Time Fly prisoners to follow, most of which Lenora would have to figure out on her own since she hadn't had the opportunity to read it on the website:

Ten Rules to Consider

-The Prisoner will not age for the duration of his sentence.
Most parts of the body will stop progressing, but not all.
Ex: Hair will continue to grow; fingernails will not.

-The Prisoner will almost always feel tired and may fall
asleep at odd moments.

-The Prisoner is allowed to move freely about the planet.
He can do whatever he pleases. He can experience joy,
frustration, pain, anger, disappointments, orgasms, injury
and even death. Death should avoided as it will complicate
the return process at the completion of the sentence.

-There is no interference allowed on the part of The Time
Flies assigned to guide the Prisoner through his sentence.
The Prisoner will never meet his jailers. Guidance Flies
are simply there to ensure that the Prisoner does not fall
out of time or start jumping around from place to place

against his will.

-The number of Time Flies assigned guidance is equal to
the number of Time Flies present at the time of the
infraction.

-It is essential that all Guidance Flies be present at the
moment of their appointed rounds. Should a Fly prove missing
during its period of assigned guidance, there will be
serious consequences for the Prisoner.

-At the completion of the sentence the Prisoner must return
to the exact spot at which they began their sentence in
order for transfer to the former life to be successful.

-The Prisoner will return to his former life at the exact
moment he began his sentence, with no loss of years from
that life. No person shall have missed the Prisoner in his
absence.

-The Prisoner will have little or no memory left of this
former life and will remember only his life as a Prisoner.

-The Time Flies are never wrong.

There had been 2976 Time Flies present at the time of the infraction for
which Bob and Lenora were convicted and sentenced, an infraction that
would remain essentially a mystery to them. Two thousand nine hundred
and seventy-six. They would have been appalled if they'd known there had
been that many flies in their house. All of these Flies would be assigned

the duty of guiding Bob and Lenora, unseen and unaided, through their twenty-five-year sentence. Using the formula as stated in The Law, each of the 2976 Guidance Flies would be responsible for 73.63754 hours of guidance before handing the duty off to the next Guidance Fly in line. If Bob and Lenora had been able to meet their jailers, they might have seen something like this:

**Artist Rendering of Time Flies Performing Guidance
(Based on the drawings of Prof. Cyril T. Rocklidge)**

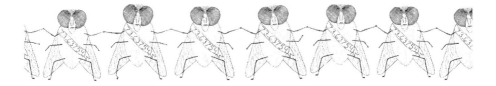

Weekend At Minnie's

"This is absolutely the dumbest thing I've ever seen in my life," Lenora said, handing the Law back to Bob. She was tempted to not take it seriously. Bob scanned the document, but it made little sense to him.

"I don't understand," he said. "I can't even read this." He tossed the Law on the bed in frustration. "What did we do? Twenty-five years for what?"

Lenora smirked as she squeezed into a pair of Minnie's waterproof patent leather pumps. "Apparently, we stole something."

"Stole something? I didn't steal anything. Did you?"

"You know better than that," she said, testing the walk-ability of the Cuban heels.

"Well, what was it then?"

She picked up the Law again, pinching her lower lip as she read. She didn't know whether to laugh or cry. "It doesn't say."

"What *does* it say?"

"We've stopped aging."

"That's stupid. How can we not age? Vampires don't age. Can I see it?"

She handed him the Law. "I told you it was dumb."

"What does it mean 'guidance time for each fly'? And what about these injury clauses? Do you understand any of this?"

"I think we're on our own for twenty-five years."

"Man, my head is really spinning," he said, sitting back down on the bed. "Still, I don't remember leaving the house with anything that wasn't mine."

And then Lenora's face went white. Her head began to bob forward, shaking her hair down the sides of her face like silver blinders, something she always did whenever she felt herself potentially responsible for an act of dishonesty.

"What is it?" said Bob, noticing.

"What's what?" feinted Lenora, her face shaded by her hair.

"You know what. What did you just think of?"

She took a breath and composed herself. "Nothing. It's ridiculous."

"What's ridiculous?"

"I refuse to believe that it could have been the rat traps."

Bob's eyes grew wide. "The rat traps! Oh my god! Those two rat traps that you took to school yesterday morning to show your students."

"Oh, please. Really? Twenty-five years for stealing rat traps?"

But they had been no ordinary rat traps and she'd known it from the start. She had been in the attic looking for the camping lantern to add to their Earthquake Emergency Preparedness Kit when she came across the two traps. They immediately struck her as odd. The 4x8 inch plastic trays were filled with a sweet smelling gluey substance designed to stop rats in their tracks, horrible La Brea-like death machines that killed without killing. The first tray featured the beautifully decayed carcass of a rat caught in mid-stride. It was like a museum piece. Its ribs were visible through its collapsed layer of hair and there were holes rotted through its stomach. The eyes had disappeared. The other tray contained the corpse of a mom fly—not a Time Fly, but an ordinary housefly—that had given birth shortly after becoming stuck in the glop. (The rat had witnessed the creation of this nativity scene, as it had not yet been all the way dead.) The mom fly was lying on her back, feet in the air, with her dead maggot offspring peppered about her body. It looked like a diorama of a fly family picnic disaster. Lenora experienced a profound, but momentary, sense of sadness for their loss.

"I don't remember seeing these before," she'd said, thrusting the traps at Bob and causing the rat to wobble on its spindly legs. "Did you put them there?"

"Gross! No. Where?"

"Such cruelty. The poor things starved to death."

"I said it wasn't me."

The next morning, on the Friday that would mark the beginning of Spring Break, the end of Bob's employment and the beginning of their prison sentence in the past, she had taken the specimens to school for study by her students.

"They must have been trapped for at least six months," she had told them, "given their states of decay. But we've lived in the house for almost fourteen years and we didn't put the traps there. I would never kill anything this way. We're not sure where they came from." She had used the traps as writing prompts for that day's history lesson. They were studying World War II.

Could this have been their crime? They could never be sure, for there was nothing in the Law stating that the traps Lenora had taken had come from this very house in 1938 just minutes before she had stumbled upon them in 2015; or that the vermin snagged by them had been 1938 vermin and that the traps had been in use as educational tools for training Time Fly youth in the art of time projection.

Removing Time Fly projected items by a non-Time Fly species while the items were considered still in use was a violation of Time Fly Law. When Lenora had removed the traps from the house, the Time Flies had been jostled into imbalance and disorientation. Once they had shaken the dust of thievery from their wings and regained their composure, they waited for Lenora and Bob to return home, then set about arranging a restorative exchange: the two traps taken for the two people most closely associated with absconding with them. Lenora and Bob had become suspects, and had moved assuredly into becoming convicts.

"Utterly ridiculous," Lenora said to Bob now. "I refuse to believe it." And she never really would.

The fog and ice continued all day Saturday. They were exhausted. They'd never felt so tired. They slept in shifts during the day in case Minnie or Burt showed up, or in case they were suddenly flung into some other time period in their house. They trusted nothing.

While Bob slept, Lenora tried to make more sense of the Time Fly Law. The house was freezing, but they kept the heat off so as not to attract attention with chimney smoke.

We've been convicted of stealing.

She paced restlessly from room to room, the Law clutched in her fingers, bundled in layers of Minnie's clothing, searching for signs of her future life. She lamented the loss of her library. Where the bookshelves had been, stuffed with more than five hundred books, there were now just walls. One of the walls had a large clock on it. The numbers on the clock were as big as English muffins.

We're being guided by flies.

Next to the Christmas tree was a table with a radio on it shaped like a tiny cathedral.

We can be killed.

The house was so different and yet there were pockets of familiarity; corners and window frames, the hardwood floor of the living room.

We will return at the end of our sentence to the exact moment we left. No one will know we've been gone. What will that be like?

Her fingertips prodded at the lump in her breast. If they weren't aging, did that mean that the lump would stop growing?

She held the newspaper that she had picked up earlier from in front of the house. She had wanted to go all the way outside, snatch glances of the houses across the street, but hadn't dared, peeking through the curtains instead. All those unfamiliar houses. By 1963 they would be gone and freeway traffic would begin sprinkling grime all over the front porch. It was cold enough in the house that she could see her breath, but it looked much colder outside. Once they left the protection of Minnie's house, they had nowhere else to go. A '36 Ford crept by, sliding precariously from side to side. Children stomped a frozen puddle. Were they younger versions of people she knew? Lloyd had lived three houses down since 1929. Was he one of them?

Front page weather report: The fog and icy conditions were going to continue, as well as the record low temperatures. Driving was discouraged. She confirmed the date on the newspaper, *December 17, 1938*—Only 6 shopping days to Christmas!—and curled up on the couch.

And then it struck her again: the intense desires to both read and walk. Her thighs began to twitch. Where was this coming from? She had always loved reading, since the days when, as a girl, she used to read the obituaries aloud to her mother as she prepared dinner (a practice that Mom put a stop to after overhearing little Lenora say to a friend, "Your daddy is really interesting. I can't wait to read his obituary.") And as a teacher, without much else in the way of hobbies, it seemed to her that her primary purpose on the planet had been to absorb vast amounts of information and then regurgitate it on her students. But this was different, as if she didn't care about anything else other than reading and walking for her own sake and for no one else's. Within minutes, she had burned through the newspaper and was up and pacing again, on the hunt for more.

There weren't many books in the house, but with minimal ransacking and a trip to the basement, she uncovered stashes of periodicals, both recent and outdated, which she gathered and carried to the couch. She devoured everything with words or symbols on it; seventeen copies of *Life* magazine, six of *Vanity Fair*, three issues of *Literary Digest* (noting, with embarrassed glee, the article on food shortages within the Third Reich), a small stack of *Harper's Weekly, Weird Tales, Spicy Detective* (heavily dog-eared), *Colliers, Amazing Stories, The Saturday Evening Post* and *Ladies Home Journal*. She even found two worn copies of *June Bride* and one of *Romantic Movie Stories* salted away in the bottom of Minnie's underwear drawer, which she felt guilty about having read so compulsively. When she ran out of proper material, she moved on to food packaging labels and cleaning products instructions. She even read the numbers on the clock then took it off the wall to see if there were any words on the back. After attempting to hang it back on the wall, and failing, she set it on the floor, stumbled to the couch, bloated with more information than she could make logical sense of, and was deeply asleep in seconds atop the piles of magazines and newspapers.

As Lenora snored away in the parlor, Bob wandered nervously from room to room with his hands in Burt's pants. The pants were high-waisted, coming halfway up his belly, adding some challenge to his habit, his elbows jutting to the sides like chicken wings. He went upstairs to Freddie's room, the only room Lenora had not violated during her reading frenzy. Pinned to the wall above the dresser was a fresh American flag with forty-eight stars. He thumbed through some comic books by the bed, and pulled a copy of *Stage and Screen* from beneath the mattress, the cover of which featured a painting of a naked starlet in a bathtub with many male hands holding microphones and reaching for her. He brought it downstairs to show Lenora, but she was still passed out on the couch atop layers of slick printed material, Minnie's dress hiked up around her scrawny thighs as she slid slowly toward the edge.

As he was hanging the clock back on the wall, he heard the dog next door barking again, the same familiar bark that had kept him awake last night. He went to the kitchen to look out back. There was no deck, only a small staircase leading to the backyard. All lawn, no garden. The dog barked again and he looked over at the neighbor's yard. And there, through the fog, standing on the frosty grass, whimpering—was Paul.

Bob shouted.

Lenora's butt crested the edge of the couch, sending her to the floor and springing her awake. "What!? What is it?"

"It's Paul!"

"Paul who?"

"Paul! Dave's dog."

"It can't be."

It was.

Why Paul?

Paul had no idea what was happening to him. One minute he had been sleeping beneath Bob and Lenora's front porch on a beautiful twenty-first century April afternoon, and the next he was spread across icy needles of grass during a freezing fog in the winter of 1938. It was still his grass—or was it? The yard was uncharacteristically clean and well mowed, the house in a lot better shape than it should have been. Paul was a rather indifferent mutt of no particular bloodline, stout, but flexible, with black hair that was 'low shedding', but constantly matted from lack of servicing. His caretaker, a malfunctioning human by the name of Dave, had the wild straw hair, boopic crimson eyes, and snot storage beard of a classic Bukowski-esque alcoholic. A photograph of FDR graced his front window, next to a much newer one of Obama. He somehow owned his falling down house outright.

Paul was terrified to move. He wanted Dave. He barked and barked, calling to him. Every once in a while, an old lady, who looked and smelled nothing like Dave, would open the door and try to shoo the strange dog away. Poor Paul would walk a few steps across the lawn with his head down, and when the old lady closed the door, he would turn around and start barking again. There really wasn't anything else he could do.

"That's just not right," Lenora said as she stood next to Bob, watching Paul shiver and bark. "It's bad enough sentencing two people for a mysterious crime they didn't know they'd committed. Everyone is guilty of something. But a dog? How could a dog commit a crime?"

Paul had not committed a crime. The Time Flies had not accused him of anything. It had been a mistake. He had been sleeping in his backyard when he got too hot and had crawled under the shadow of Bob and Lenora's porch just moments before the Time Flies had sent all occupants of the property into the past. They didn't even know they'd included Paul until it was too late. But the Time Flies did not rectify their mistakes. They were never wrong.

Lenora and Bob grew furious with the Time Flies.

"And who else is here?" said Bob, flailing his arms. "Do we need to go around knocking on doors to see if any of our old neighbors are having trouble adjusting to their home's new owners? Maybe I could get some shoes that fit."

"I want to be warm," said Lenora.

"Then you shall be warm." And with that, Bob rumbled to the basement to crank up the coal stoker. They were Americans, and no Time Flies were going to make them afraid. They didn't have to put up with being cold or hungry. They could put up with being tired—Americans would always be tired. They could put up with being poor—no matter the shame bred into them they could still be poor and get by. But food had to be eaten every day. And being warm was just a god-given right. So, after only sixty-seven minutes of profanity laden fiddling, Bob had the stoker pushing heat through the ventilation system and they were shedding layers of clothing until they were comfortable wearing nearly nothing at all. Smoke guzzled up the chimney.

"Let's invite Paul in," said Bob.

But when they looked out back again, Paul was gone.

As the stoker roared, and the light left another day, they stole a bottle of brandy from Minnie, got buzzed, and ate her into empty shelves and a cavernous, echoing refrigerator. They gorged on salmon and baked potatoes, frozen spinach and biscuits from a tube, throwing the leftovers out back for Paul, should he return.

"How stupid is it to send a dog back in time?" said Bob, with butter on his lips.

"The Soviets sent one into space in 1957," countered Lenora, one cheek bulging with salmon. (Technically, Lenora was a pescatarian—she ate fish.)

"Gee, I guess we'll get to see that again, huh?" Bob laughed.

It became their latest conviction that none of this was actually happening and that anything they did wouldn't matter to anyone. Time travel was stupid. Flies were just flies. And dogs don't stop aging. How could they have fallen for it? The Law. Ha!

It was a foolish way for them to think, given the incredible task before them, but it was how they decided to approach the evening. Professor Rocklidge would have advised against it.

After dinner, they took hot fragrant baths and wore Burt and Minnie's pajamas. Bob had an amusing, nick-filled session with Burt's straight razor. Lenora tried some of Minnie's perfume.

They drank more brandy, luxuriating in its warming effects while snuggled together on the couch listening to Orson Welles on the radio: *The Shadow—The Man Who Murdered Time*, the story of a time machine. They drifted without concern or seriousness in a brandy infused haze, listening, just listening, imagining the scenes in black and white. Nothing seemed real.

The local news warned against travel in the icy conditions. Many accidents had been reported. They felt assured that Minnie would not return that night, or even on Sunday, if she even existed.

They finished the brandy. Bob pretended to be a rat frozen in a trap and Lenora laughed her ass off. They had sex on the couch with the lights on and the curtains open, experiencing tremendous orgasms that they hoped were a side effect of not aging (they were). They danced naked to swing music, jumped on the furniture and accidentally knocked over the Christmas tree.

The End of Minnie's Hospitality

They awoke on the couch early Sunday morning, cobwebbed with hangover. Their heads pounded. The coal was exhausted, the heat vents reduced to an asthmatic sigh of cooling air. They didn't want to talk. Bob wanted to drift. Lenora had an urgent need to check her email. "I need to find out what's going on," she groaned.

As they spooned oatmeal with frozen strawberries that tasted rusty, it dawned on them what a dangerous experiment the evening before had been. They really were in someone else's house. They really were back in time and they were going to have to address that soon. But it was freezing outside and they couldn't imagine leaving without a plan. The Internet could have helped them. The Internet could have shown them the way with maps and emergency supply lists, information on local customs, suggestions on restaurants and interesting things to do and purchase in the area. But it was nowhere to be found. Two days ago, they could look up anything they'd wanted to from this time period by looking at a screen. Now they couldn't.

Now they would have to try to remember what was going to happen.

But rather than begin their preparations, they retreated, at least until their hangovers lifted—Bob into Freddie's comic books, Lenora into the Sunday morning paper, stacking the crushed periodicals littering the couch on the coffee table before curling up to read.

Page one—a guy arrested in Los Angeles in the cockpit of a bomber, claiming to be a spy.

Page four—a suicide in a car. The note left said to notify his boss. Mrs. Jennings said her husband had been despondent.

Page five—a warning to local merchants to be on the lookout for counterfeiters during the holiday season, stating that counterfeit money is usually dull and lifeless in appearance.

When she finished the paper, she began rereading the magazines before dozing off.

"I think we need to change our names," said Bob. He was standing before her, his head slightly bowed, looking very much like a lost little boy.

Lenora yawned, squinting up at him from the couch. "What names?"

"You know. Our names." He was holding a comic book called *Crackajack*. The cover showed cartoon drawings of four comic strip heroes of the time—*Detective Dan Dunn, Captain Don Winslow of the Navy, Myra North: Special Nurse* and silent movie star cowboy *Tom Mix*.

What are you talking about?" said Lenora, sliding the newspaper off her lap. It was now late morning. The fog was finally lifting.

"I want to change my name."

"Oh, god." Her head throbbed as she sat up. She kneaded her face and scratched at her skull. "Change your name. What for?"

"I don't feel right just being me. Not here."

She squinted up at him. "Huh? Are you serious? What about identification?" she said, trying to be logical.

"We don't have any anyway," he said, remembering that he'd left his wallet on the kitchen table in 2015. "At least I don't. Do you?"

"No, I guess not." The light was growing stronger, the shadows more defined. She yawned again and pulled the curtain shut. "I feel awful."

"I'm serious," Bob said. "Legally, we're not even who we are. We haven't been born yet. You said so yourself, yesterday. That's what gave me the idea."

Lenora sighed heavily. The combination of hangover and having the entire contents of the Seattle Sunday Times injected into her brain in under ten minutes had left her a little loopy. She had no counter argument, nor the energy to make one if she did. The idea even made a little sense to her. They could be other people.

"What did you have in mind?"

Bob showed her. "See these four people on the cover? We could use these. I thought I could use the 'Tom' from *Tom Mix* and the 'Winslow' from *Captain Don Winslow of the Navy*. Tom Winslow."

She held out her hand for the comic book. "You want me to call you Tom?"

"Sure. Why not?"

Her head pounded.

"Tom Winslow could work, you know," he said.

She scanned the cover. "Why do we have to pick from this one? There's only one female."

"Well…"

"Never mind." She realized as soon as she said it that she wasn't ready for the explanation. It didn't matter anyway, really. She liked the drawing of *Myra North: Special Nurse*, with her yellow hair, white nurse's cap and cynical, knowing eyebrows. Bob pointed out the pictures of the other heroes.

"You can't pick the exact name. You'll have to mix it up."

Lenora sighed with attitude. "Thanks."

"Tom Winslow, Tom Winslow," Bob whispered to himself. Lenora heard him. She didn't want to hear him, but she did.

She handed the comic book back to him. "Myra Mix."

"Myra Mix?"

"Myra Mix. Take Tom Mix and Myra North. Myra Mix. By your rules."

"It's not the same as my last name."

"And?"

"I don't know. Nothing, I guess. Are you sure?"

"Yes, Tom."

"That's kind of quick for such an important decision, don't you think?"

"I was inspired. Tom."

He looked at her nervously. "Are you really going to do this?"

She stared at him for a long moment, digging through the worry in his eyes. He was frightened, yes, but so was she. That wasn't it. Something else. Something was different about her husband, something that seemed somehow permanent, as if he was no longer the same man.

"Okay. But not until we leave the house, which needs to be very soon." She was still drowsy, still not moving. "And I'm staying a vegetarian."

Then, as if sensing that the tension needed to be turned in another direction, there came a small shy knock on the front door.

"What's that?" they said, in unison.

KNOCK! KNOCK! KNOCK! came the second round, louder, along with a man's voice. "Minnie?"

Bob bolted to the window and peeked around the curtain. "It's a guy with a suitcase."

Keys rattled next. One began getting intimate with the door lock. Bob and Lenora hightailed it for the bedroom and dove under the bed, not quite believing their lame choice of hiding place.

The front door opened and the voice became more cautious. "Minnie?" The voice sounded like it didn't really want Minnie to hear it.

Bob and Lenora lay still beneath the mussed bed. They heard the door close, the footsteps coming through the entry, the voice saying, "What the hell is this?" to the mess in the living room. They had made a shambles of Minnie's place and now someone was inspecting it.

The feet that went past the bed were the same size as the shoes Bob was wearing. The suitcase landed on the bed above them. The closet door opened and an urping of profanity followed.

"Where the hell is my coat? Where are my goddamn shoes?" He would not find the coat because Bob had pushed it beneath the couch after they'd had drunken sex on it the night before.

"Dammit!" shouted the man as his feet went in the other direction past the bed and out of the room. They heard more cursing and things being thrown about. As the energy in his cursing began to wane, he came back into the bedroom, scooped what he could from the closet and drawers, and stuffed it all into the suitcase. A minute later the front door slammed shut and it was quiet again.

"I'm guessing Burt," said Lenora.

"He took the radio."

"We need to leave. Now."

A copy of *Life* magazine was on the living room floor where Burt had thrown it, flapped open to an advertisement for Studebaker automobiles. The ad attested to the non-destitute nature of its employees. Bob bent over to read it.

> *Studebaker employs no transients. The average Stude-*
> *baker craftsman is a solid citizen, 40 years of age*

"Are we transients?"

"If Burt was able to get around, Minnie could be coming home any minute. And she won't leave."

The ad had a picture of two solid citizen craftsmen, a father and son team, smiling with wrenches in their hands. The son's name was Edison. Something about it appealed to Bob. It sounded smart. It had three syllables.

"I'm changing my mind."

"Should we take food?"

"I want to be Edison, not Tom."

"We don't have a plan."

"Edison Winslow is my name."

Edison and Myra

The Truth About Frozen Emotional States

The bodies of Bob and Lenora were not aging, their twenty-first century lives dangling in time, awaiting their return. As a side effect, byproduct, or added value of this condition, their emotions, for the most part, were also not moving forward, an unintended consequence for which the Time Flies had provided no explanations or justifications. It was not mentioned in the Law. Bob and Lenora knew nothing about it. But Professor Rock-lidge did offer this conspectus based on his own emotional state during his incarceration:

```
-The Prisoner will spend his entire sentence suspended
in the emotional state that he had been experiencing in
the moment just before his sentence began. This stagnation
may come with side effects which include, but are by no
means limited to, episodes of mania, delusions of grandeur,
immaturity, a gradual disintegration of self confidence,
and a decrease in logical thinking. These side effects can
be more pronounced in prisoners frozen in a state of
negative emotions. Only upon the return to his former, and
largely forgotten, life will the Prisoner's emotions resume
their rich and varied nature.
```

Professor Rocklidge had intended this to be part of his *Ten Rules to Consider* and would have added it, changing the title to *Eleven Rules to Consider*, if a German Stuka hadn't filled him full of bullets as it strafed the French road on which he was fleeing with other refugees, leaving his body riddled and his papers on the Time Flies unfinished in the attic of his abandoned home.

Accordingly, the moods that Bob and Lenora had been in at the time of their projection into the past would be the same moods, more or less, that would carry them along through their entire twenty-five-year sentence. Not that they were unable to experience a variety of emotions, but that the one they were stuck in would serve as the default and provide the stage upon which all other emotions would perform. For Lenora, that had a few advantages. At the moment of incarceration, she had been searching the Internet for a solution to a problem. Her last line had been "Hey, these aren't cluster flies, they're Time Flies!" A discovery. A mild epiphany. A sense of accomplishment. Her drawbacks, which would prove significant, would be a compulsion to visually ingest mountains of printed information that she didn't need, coupled with a tendency to waste vast amounts of time walking, a consequence of the intermittent Internet connection that had caused her to pace around the living room while searching for information on the flies. But her mood had been largely positive, albeit lightly seasoned with the pinch of irritation she'd felt when Bob had snapped at her, the half-teaspoonful of worry she held in reserve for the lump in her breast and a dollop of intolerance for idiocy. She would be mostly all right. She would be driven. A problem solver, when she wasn't wasting time.

Bob would not be as lucky. What this freezing of emotions meant for him was that the disorientation and shame that had been submerging him upon the commencement of their sentence, due to the very recent loss of his job and his near confession of this to his wife, would be pretty much what he could expect for the duration. A kind of numbness was setting in, stirred into a chronic feeling that he had done something terribly wrong, that he was unworthy, causing him to vacillate between worrying too much and not giving a shit. He would be constantly confused, unable to think clearly, or to make wise decisions, and would be prone to engaging in outrageous, even chimerical, schemes, qualities that would deepen as the difficulties ahead of them mounted, transforming him into a sort of man-child. In time, he would discover coping mechanisms to assist in moderating his behavior.

The Christening

They left Minnie Beckback's house as Myra Mix and Edison Winslow, leaving their real names and their future past lives safely inside until their return in 1963. They left as new people, unsure of where they were going, how they were going to get there and whether or not they would arrive hungry and willing to compromise themselves.

The underbelly of the clouds reflected amber as the city lights came on. The ice that had begun melting during the last few hours of daylight was now freezing again.

Edison turned to appraise the house as they walked away. He tilted Burt's fedora back to get a better look in the creeping darkness. "The siding looks good."

Two young brothers playing in the alley had seen the strangers leaving Minnie's house.

"Who are you?" said the older brother.

"My name is Edison Winslow."

"Come on," Myra said, pulling him along.

"Mom!" called the younger one to an unseen authority figure.

Edison and Myra quickened their pace, their feet making potato-chippy sounds on the ice that echoed off the other houses.

They'd left Minnie's house much as it had been before their arrival. They had cleaned and straightened and done the dishes. They made the bed. But they had done no laundry because they couldn't figure out the machine. And there were things missing.

For Minnie's troubles, for the empty cupboards, the diminished clothing inventory and the soiled bed sheets, the stolen brandy and the exhausted coal supply, Edison had left her one hundred and fifty dollars in twenty-first century bills that were worth essentially nothing. He might as well have drawn them with crayon.

They turned the corner at the end of the alley to be out of the brothers' line of sight and stopped on the sidewalk. The neighborhood was quiet. Streetlights cast weak cones of light on the glittering ice. No one was driving. They stood with steaming breath, not knowing which way to go. The apartment building that had been at the end of their alley was now four houses. Some of the other houses around looked almost as they remembered them, their windows glowing warmly. Peeking out from their costumes, they felt like fugitives, although they were legally serving their sentences. Edison wore Burt's fedora pulled down to shade his eyes. The cheviot stopped just above his knees. The pants showed a bit of ankle. Myra saw the street strained through the net waterfalling from Minnie's hat, her silver hair stuffed up under. Minnie's deep red wool coat was a little large but warm.

"I think we should go left," said Myra.

More potato-chippy sounds, lighter in tone than their own, approached from behind. Paul sidled up to Myra and leaned against her leg, casting wary eyes at Edison.

"We're not changing his name, too, are we?" said Myra.

"I don't think so."

She grabbed hold of Edison's arm. "Let's walk."

Paul followed. Time passed.

They came upon an odd scene of firemen adding the final extinguishing touches to a house that had just finished burning to the ground. Most of the roof had collapsed and two walls were nearly gone. Blackened boards jutted up like haunted fence posts. The last straggling remnants of an earlier crowd watched. The homeowners wept nearby, their Christmas ruined. Two of the firemen were carrying charred furniture and stacks of scorched books to the curb, great huffs of steam billowing from their workingman's lungs. A fire hydrant gurgled onto the street. A sheen of fresh ice was forming on everything wet that had cooled off enough to accept it.

No one paid them any attention.

"Maybe they're all prisoners, too," whispered Edison.

Myra studied the faces in the faint glow. "I don't think so," she said, turning until her eyes landed on Paul, hind legs forward, back arched and tail up, leaving his calling card on the strip of grass between the sidewalk and the street. She elbowed Edison and pointed. They watched, not because they were into that sort of thing, but because due to the training they'd received even as non-dog owners in the future, they felt they had to pick it up.

With no thoughts of the social mores regarding canine feces in 1938, Myra looked around for a proper scoop, her only consideration the nagging embarrassment she would carry with her if this pile was left in its present spot to be frozen, thawed and ultimately stepped in by one of the neighbors. At the edge of the fire she saw a Sanka coffee tin that was not too wet, too icy or too scorched and bent to pick it up, handing it to Edison.

"This one's yours."

Edison looked at the tin in his hand. He looked at Paul's cargo and at Paul. Paul gave a slight bow of his head. As Edison bent to scoop it up, his action caught the attention of a fireman, who stopped what he was doing to laugh.

"Hey, buddy. What're you going to do with that?"

The stragglers, along with the other firemen, turned toward Edison. Even the homeowners paused in their weeping to see. Suddenly, the anonymity they had hoped to retain seemed vanished. Edison stared dumbly at the fireman, a tin of steaming poop in his hand. "We're scientists," he said weakly.

The fireman stared at him, trying to imagine Edison in a lab coat and thick glasses, surrounded by vials and knobs and throwing a huge switch with mad wild-haired laughter.

"It's an experiment," Edison said, almost as a question, then added, "for the government."

Oddly, this seemed to be an acceptable scenario. The fireman raised his eyebrows, guffawed again and went about his business. Everyone returned to what they had been doing, either working on the fire, watching it or crying about it. It was another few blocks before they located a proper trash can in which to dispose of the tin.

When Minnie phoned the local precinct where she worked and asked to speak with the desk Sergeant, Mickey McBluffo, she did so more out of perplexity than anger. She knew Burt might drop by the house, but she hadn't expected this.

"Was there any sign of forced entry?" said Sergeant McBluffo.

"No. Burt has a key," said Minnie. "He took some of his clothes … and some of mine," she added uneasily. "And some food. Quite a lot of food, actually."

"Hmmm … "

"But the reason I'm calling, Mickey, is that he left me some money. A hundred and fifty dollars worth."

"That's a lot money, Minnie." Sergeant McBluffo had been a friend of Burt's before the affair with the logger's wife had started. He wanted to believe that Burt was doing something right by Minnie.

"Yes, but the money doesn't look quite right. It has colors on it."

"Colors?"

"Uh-huh. And the president's pictures are too big and not exactly in the middle."

There was a pause.

"And you think Burt left it?"

"Well, I don't know for sure. But who else could it be? Do you want me to bring it in?"

"No, I'll send someone right over, Minnie. Just sit tight. and Minnie?"

"Yes?"

"I'm sorry about this. If you need a few days … "

"Thank you, Mickey."

The cops took the money, as well as Minnie's statement, and asked around the neighborhood. They spoke with the brothers who had seen Burt going in and coming out.

"Mister Beckback looked real mad when he came out," said one of them.

"He had a suitcase," said his brother.

And shortly after, they had seen a man and a woman come out.

"Was it someone you knew?" said the officer.

"Nope."

"Did you see when they went in?" He had a notepad to record the boys' responses.

"Didn't see them go in," said the first kid.

The cop nodded and wrote it down.

"The man's name is … Ed Slow," said the younger brother.

"It is not, stupid," his brother admonished him, punching his arm.

"Shutup. What is it then?"

"I don't know, but it's not that. There was more. Stupid."

"Boys," said the officer sternly, restoring order.

"How about here?" Edison stood next to a 1938 Plymouth Sedan.

Myra surveyed the darkened houses around them. "You want to sleep in someone's car?"

At first, it had been nice to walk along University Way, enjoying the sparkly Christmas displays. Edison shuffled along in a daze, trying to keep up, while Myra scanned the store windows, reading the Christmas sale advertisements. "These ads have so many words. They're marvelous." The stores looked warm inside, but the few places that were still open didn't have many shoppers left and they'd felt too self-conscious to go in. They wandered their neighborhood, gawking at sights both familiar and semi-familiar, places still standing and places not yet replaced.

But by eleven pm, with the streets tucked under a thin sheet of ice for the night, they needed a way to end their day. They'd thought, or were hoping, as most comfortable people do, that something sufferable would present itself if they just wandered around enough. But in time they surrendered to the truth that their sleeping arrangements for the evening were to be alfresco. They nosed around in alleys, rejected doorways and heating grates, looking for a cradle where they could lay their bodies without scaring the hell out of themselves. As the evening progressed their standards dropped, but still not low enough to lie on the ground.

Edison ran his hand along the back fender, caressing the heavy smooth curve. He opened the back door slowly. "It's unlocked. Look at the size of the seat. Both of us could fit."

Spooned together, shivering, with Paul on the floor below them, Myra wept uncontrollably. Edison stroked her hair and tried not to get irritated when she didn't stop soon enough. The windows steamed up and hoarfrost formed in beautiful patterns as they drifted and snoozed through uneasy dreams that carried and pushed them through the night.

In the morning, they were awakened by footsteps outside the car. A few seconds later, the back passenger door opened and a little girl in a green wool coat, scarf and a cute knit hat gaped at the contents of the back seat, then turned and ran back toward her house yelling "Daddy! Mommy!" and disappeared inside.

Time to go.

They scrambled out of the car as the house door was re-opened.

"Hey, you!" yelled an adult male in shirtsleeves and a tie. "Stop right there!" He made his way threateningly down the first few steps of his porch. An adult female appeared in a window, clutching her daughter to her breast.

Myra and Edison shuffled briskly across the icy street, Paul skittering in tow, burying their faces in their coats.

"I saw them!" said the little girl. "They were old! The lady had silver hair!"

The First Things They Noticed
Were the Blondes

As they made their way back toward University Way the sun came out to play and Myra's goose bumps went to half-mast. In contrast to the quiet night before, a vivification was underway. It was Monday morning, the beginning of the last shopping week before Christmas, and joy was in the air. Red and green streetcars dinged up and down the street sucking in Scandinavians and spitting them out again.

Myra Mix and Edison Winslow mingled with the bustle. Paul walked low, his head pendulating, sniffing at everything. They knew it would be different and thought they were ready for it. But they still felt as if they were in a movie, walking from wardrobe to the set to begin filming, feeling not so nervous anymore, a kind of giddiness, not thinking about sleep, or how they would eat, or if they belonged, just loving the moment. This was not the street they knew. The Depression had done its bit for weight control. The knots of homeless teens had been replaced by knots of unemployed men; logo-choked clothing had been ousted for men in suits, some with slick shiny hair plastered beneath their hats; women draped in wool coats with stockinged calves poking out, and none of it as black and white as they thought it would be. The array of colors dazzled them. Pockets and purses jingled with change. Christmas music played from storefronts. Shoppers struggled with packages. The lipsticks, the hats, the smell of wool. A lot of fur. The holiday spirit. The prices.

People moved quickly along the sidewalks, jabbering with each other or looking in windows or at the sky or other people. All ears were unplugged and free to receive local sounds created in real time. People who looked like they were talking to themselves actually were. Few used deodorant. Those who smoked did so without shame or defiance—in the streets, going into banks, coming out of coffee shops. Nearly everyone reeked of it to some degree. It occurred to Myra that Minnie's house had not smelled like cigarettes and she felt oddly proud to have carried the smoke-free tradition into the twenty-first century.

They stopped in front of a furniture shop to eat the bread and salmon that they had stolen from Minnie. Paul wouldn't take it from Edison, but Myra was able to feed him.

They stood beneath an awning, gazing like children. They really were here, in a time when only superheroes wore underwear on the outside; when a citizen had to actually leave the house to buy something and expendable cash had to be plucked from a bank and only during banking hours. Cars had sex appeal again, every one of them grand and brazen, banging along the lumpy pavement, revving loudly, rumbling and wasteful, coughing blue smoke and soot.

It was almost like remembering.

"Look," said Myra, pointing to the Neptune theater where *Holiday* with Cary Grant and Katherine Hepburn was playing. "They're alive. Can you believe it?"

"And younger than we are," said Edison, plunging a piece of bread into his mouth. "That's the last of the food."

They jumped a streetcar to downtown Seattle after Edison found some change in his pocket—*Thanks, Burt*—grabbing hold of the metal rail and hoisting themselves aboard.

"You'll have to hold the dog in your arms, sir," said the streetcar operator. Paul burped a growl of protest when Edison picked him up, then submitted.

Ding! Ding! The breeze in their faces. A smile from Myra. Disbelief. Her hair brilliant in the sunlight.

"Your hair is making me squint," said Edison, laughing with Paul squirming in his arms.

They rocked back and forth, car exhaust in their nostrils, as curls of smoke from houses and distant factories rose softly into the sky.

Time, and Plenty of It

When they got off the streetcar in downtown, they were a little turned around. A few familiar buildings were tucked in amongst largely unfamiliar ones. Paul scrambled out of Edison's arms and got his sniffer going again. They blended enough for the moment in their costumes, but as the day wore on and the sky got gray again, the earlier feeling of frivolity gave way to worry and short tempers.

"What do you want to do now?"

"Why do we have to do something?"

"Because it's going to get cold again tonight."

"The Space Needle is gone."

"You said that already. Stop worrying about it. It will be here when we get back."

They wandered aimlessly and began to enjoy the sights less, occasionally stopping to scrape dog pooh from their shoes against a curb. They had no sense of place, or of belonging, or of how to operate. They needed a resolution; a way to return to the comforts of home for reflections on a day well lived. But they were homeless now and didn't want to burden anyone about it. They didn't want to end up like the red-faced men on the corners in the future with cardboard signs in their hands. They wanted to stay invisible. Myra wanted to keep walking, to put her movement to work, to help her with a solution, a plan. And they were getting hungry again.

"Don't they have soup kitchens in Pioneer Square?" said Edison.

Myra's eyes grew horrified behind her netting. Edison touched her arm and she pulled off, walking quickly away from him.

"We can't separate," he shouted, trotting after her.

People were beginning to notice.

"Okay. I'm sorry," he said, having nothing to be sorry for. "Please stop. My feet are killing me." His orthotic inserts were sliding around too much inside Burt's big shoes to be effective. "Why are we walking so much anyway?"

They stopped in front of a small grocery store on Blanchard Street. Myra pointed to the bench beneath the front window. "Rest," she said. "I'm going to walk a little bit more. I need to think."

Edison made a silent protest with his eyes.

"I'm just going around the block," she said. "I'll be right back."

He knew what that meant. She would be gone for at least a half an hour. But he also knew that it was no use arguing. He sat. Paul lay on the sidewalk and licked himself.

"You better be," said Edison.

While Edison grew impatient waiting for Myra to return, he watched a few people go into the grocery store empty handed and come back out again with things to eat. It was exactly what he wanted to do. When he combined this desire with thinking about the vacation money in his pocket, his brain helped him out by deciding that this was a logical combination, and an exceedingly bright idea.

"Wait here," he told Paul.

A friendly bell above the door welcomed him inside. Wood and glass refrigerators with hefty chrome hinges lined one wall. There were shelves of packaged goods and false-bottom barrels of various loose items. It didn't look very different from stores Edison remembered from his childhood in the Sixties. He picked up a box of crackers and carried it around with him. The proprietor, a small, scowly woman of indeterminate age, watched him carefully from behind the cash register. He looked honest enough in his nice coat, but his pants were too short. You never can tell.

"What'cha looking for, mister?" she said.

"Huh?" Edison put the crackers down on a different shelf. "Nothing. I'm fine."

"They don't go there."

Edison picked up the crackers again. "Sorry." He picked up a can of beans and some coconut macaroons. "Do you have any greens?"

She raised an eyebrow. "Greens?"

"Uh, lettuce?"

"You have to go to the Market for that."

"Thank you. How about bottled water?"

"Got some distilled water on the bottom shelf there."

Edison looked at the bottles but didn't take one.

"I thought you weren't looking for anything," she said.

He grabbed a box of bran flakes, some mixed nuts, a bag of dog food and a tube of toothpaste. He also got a canned ham, just in case Myra decided to loosen up on the vegetarian thing that she'd been so strict about as Lenora. The proprietor eyed him as she bagged the items.

"That'll be a dollar fifty-two."

Edison smiled to himself at the prices. He peeled a five-dollar bill off his wad and laid it on the counter.

"What's this?" she said.

"It's five dollars."

She looked at Edison and back at the five-dollar bill. She picked it up and rubbed it between her fingers.

"It doesn't look right. What's wrong with Lincoln's head?"

Edison slipped his hands into his pants.

"It's new. I'm just out here from … Washington D.C. The government's issuing new money to help with the economy. Everybody's using them back there."

"Is that so?" The proprietor frowned. It grew very quiet in the store. The hum of the reefers talked to the hum of the fluorescent lights. His feet shifted and the wood floor creaked beneath them. He was starting to sweat. He looked out the window but Myra was nowhere to be seen.

The proprietor called to the back of the store without taking her eyes off Edison. "Hey, Willis! Do you know anything about money?"

Edison felt Burt's fedora get a little tighter.

"You mean like spending it?" said Willis from somewhere in the back.

"No, if it's real or not."

There was a pause, a thinking pause, followed by Willis's footsteps falling slow and heavy. He appeared from behind a reefer and walked to the counter scrutinizing Edison. Edison tried on a confident smile but it didn't fit right. Willis was bearded and barrel-chested, with thick glasses and a plaid flannel shirt. He had worked in a bank for a summer a long time ago, but found it wasn't to his liking. He took the five-dollar bill from the woman.

"Thank you, Gladys."

Gladys sneered at Edison. Willis held the bill to the light. The friendly bell dinged again as another customer came in and nodded to the people behind the counter.

"Good afternoon, Gladys. Willis," said the little round man.

"Good afternoon, Fletch," said Gladys.

Willis spoke to Edison. "Where'd you say you got this?"

"Washington D.C." Edison adjusted his hat. "It's all over back there. Latest government issue. Surely you must have heard about it. You seem like you keep up with this kind of thing." He was starting to feel dizzy.

Little round Fletch turned to Edison, smiling broadly. "Warshington, D.C.? Well, I'll be. I got a brother in D.C. Welcome to the other Warshington, mister."

"Thank you," said Edison.

"You remember my brother, don't you Gladys?" said Fletch. "The one with the limp?"

"Oh, I think so," said Gladys.

"Sure you do. Had that one tall shoe. Well, he's back there getting fixed up at some fancy hospital."

"Uh-huh." She nodded vaguely.

"Did he say anything about new money being issued?" said Willis, still looking at the bill.

Fletch rubbed his bulging chin. "Not that I remember, but I haven't had a letter from him in a while. Can I see it?"

Willis held out the bill for Fletch to see.

"Well, ain't that fancy? What's wrong with Lincoln's head?"

"That's what I said," said Gladys.

Fletch rubbed his chin some more. "You know, this looks like the kind of money the police were talking about on the radio this morning."

Edison snatched the bag of food off the counter and bolted for the door. Willis came around the counter. Fletch tried to maneuver out of Willis's way, found the exact spot where Willis was running and got slammed into a shelf of canned peas. Willis tried skirting Fletch, but one of the cans had become airborne and caught him smartly on the kneecap, momentarily decreasing his desire to pursue. By the time he hobbled out the door, the last six inches of Paul's tail were disappearing around the corner of the alley.

"Dammit." He went back inside to help Fletch to his feet.

As Edison sprinted down the alley, he saw Myra, hands in her pockets and bent at the waist, reading a discarded newspaper in a puddle next to a trashcan.

"Run!"

Myra was livid. "You did what? You were supposed to leave that money at Minnie's with our clothes."

"I was just trying to help."

She held out her hand. "Can I have it, please?"

Edison shook his head. "No. I'll take care of it."

They had stopped running and were now just walking very fast. Edison adjusted the bag in his arms. Paul sniffed at it. "Look, it was either that or a soup kitchen."

She hesitated, staring at the ground. Her walking had not come up with a solution. "Yes." She looked at him. "We should have done that."

"We should keep walking." Burt's big shoes clopped painfully on the bricks.

Myra followed, her fingers twisted in her hair. "I don't believe this. We ran away from people. You stole things."

"I left five dollars."

"Yes, you're leaving a nice little trail."

"You're the one who stole the rat traps," he said, with the tone of a miffed child.

"If you remember correctly, it was your suggestion that I take them to school," she pointed out, stung by the accusation.

"You're blaming me?"

"For chrissakes, Bob. You don't even know if the rat traps had anything to do with it. You're just latching onto it."

"It makes sense."

"It makes *sense*?" She grunted in frustration. "One more word about those goddamned rat traps and I'm leaving you."

Edison stopped. "You will?"

She hadn't meant to say it. Not like that. She saw the fear in his face and softened.

"No," she said. "No, of course I won't leave you."

"Are you sure?"

She took his hand. Again, that kind of emptiness in his eyes, as if he'd lost some important part of himself, or as if some of who he used to be hadn't made the journey from the future. He seemed petrified at the thought of being left alone. She didn't understand what was happening to him, but felt certain that the Time Flies would have little trouble absorbing the blame. "Yes, I'm sure. You were right. I'm sorry I left you. From now on, we must always stay together. Alright?"

Edison nodded. "And I'm not Bob anymore."

She rolled her eyes, but only a little. "Alright. Edison. Can you walk now?"

"Yes, Myra."

They had a very brief moment of harmony as they strolled on down the alley, passing two men of the brother-can-you-spare-a-dime variety leaning menacingly against some sort of wood structure. The men eyed Edison's grocery bag with longing. But Edison was happy again, temporarily free from worry, as if nothing had happened, and once they were safely past the two men, he leaned toward Myra conspiratorially and half-whispered, "They said the police were looking for this money."

Myra froze. "Minnie?"

Edison sensed trouble again in her tone. He glanced back at the men who were still watching them. "I … I don't know. It was on the radio."

"The radio?!" She collapsed against a grubby wall, looking as if she might cry again. "I'm a teacher! Oh, my god. The radio."

Then she switched up the action by grabbing the groceries out of Edison's hands and flinging them across the alley, where they smashed impressively into the opposite wall. The bag of dog food split open and Paul went over to take care of it. Taking their cue from the dog, the two men started moving slowly forward to take care of the rest.

"Hey!" said Edison, calling after Myra.

She stormed off down the alley.

"Fucking Time Flies."

The Law of Unintended Consequences

They sat on a sidewalk somewhere in downtown. Paul slept, his belly full. Myra had assumed the posture of her station, hugging her knees to make herself smaller, her brilliant silver hair draped over her face to hide her shame. She had lost Minnie's hat when they were running in the alley (although, remarkably, Edison had not lost Burt's). She was thinking of their daughters and about how difficult it was going to be to keep Edison in line if his state of mind persisted. The burden would fall to her. And she was so tired.

"I think my period is going to start," she said into the muffling thickness of her coat sleeve.

It wasn't and it was silly for her to think so. She was fifty-seven years old. She hadn't menstruated in years. But her body was on pause now and something about that made it feel as if she were about to have her period. A sensation of being close to some kind of edge, but never quite toppling over it. This feeling would stay with her for the entire twenty-five-year sentence. She slid her fingers beneath the coat and touched her lump. No change.

Edison was drifting, humming to himself while looking at a building across the street. He didn't know the name of the building but remembered it from the future, having been attracted by its level of decay. As Bob, he had liked things that were decaying. It was proof that nature was always in the process of taking things back. This building was much newer now and no longer interested him in the same way. It would need more time and weather and circumstances before it would begin to look beautiful.

On the first floor there was a bank, and next to it, a small jazz club. The club was painted yellow. A sign on the wall advertised that evening's acts along with pictures of the African American musicians.

Myra lifted her head. "Are you humming *The Monkees*?"

Edison nodded. "*Pleasant Valley Sunday.*"

"Well, stop, please."

"Why?"

"Because it hasn't been written yet. It might confuse people."

Edison didn't think it mattered if someone heard it, if it was something they'd never heard anyway, but he stopped.

The afternoon was beginning to darken. Christmas lights were coming on. A dull slab of stratus clouds stretched overhead, spreading rumors of impending precipitation.

Myra glanced at the sky. "I guess we need to find a place to eat and sleep."

Edison stroked Paul's head. Paul tolerated it.

They didn't know it, but they were being watched.

"You folks new?"

"Excuse me?" said Myra.

"How long you been on the street?" His clothes provided a geological record of how long *he'd* been on the street. His hands were layered with enough dirt to be legally classified as sedimentary. Even the unlit cigarette dangling from his chapped lips was dirty. He wore no socks and his shoes looked as if they could be torn to bits by a toothless teddy bear. He couldn't have been more than fifteen years old.

"Since yesterday," said Edison.

"Are you hungry?"

Myra was reminded of her students. "Are you?"

The boy tipped his cap politely. "Ma'am. I get better service if I go in with adults. If they think I'm with family."

Myra stood to face the boy, realizing that under the layers of street on his face he was more like twelve, not fifteen. She had her hands in her pockets and her hair blew lightly across her face. She reached out to touch his shoulder.

"I'll take it from here," rumbled a deep voice from behind her.

None of them had seen the police officer approaching. The boy tipped his cap again.

"Officer."

The cop jerked his thumb. "Scram."

"I was just trying to assist these folks."

"He said scram." Edison turned to see a second, bigger cop behind him, tapping a billy club against his palm. The boy moved off without another word.

"That was rude," said Myra.

Cop One smiled at her. He had the lips of a fish and a nose straight off the still unfinished Mount Rushmore. "You have to be careful out here. That runt works for one of the gangs in Pioneer Square. He would have had you robbed and laying in an alley inside of ten minutes."

"We have nothing to steal," said Edison.

"Everyone has something to steal," said Cop Two. "He probably wanted that coat of yours." He laughed, but it wasn't a laugh that wanted company.

They were invited to join the cops for friendly conversation inside the Seattle Municipal Bank and Trust building across the street.

"Why a bank?" asked Myra. "Can't we talk out here?"

"It's warm inside," said Cop One. "Gets us out of this weather for a few minutes. So we can talk. We just want you to be safe." He smiled fishily.

Myra exchanged a glance with Edison. Their natural inclination to obey authority—a product of their age, not their upbringing—kept them from running. They followed Cop One across the street as Cop Two brought up the rear. Paul waited on the sidewalk, whimpering lightly. A poster of a middle class Santa smiled at them from the bank window, urging them to get a loan that could provide for their loved ones this holiday season. Inside, they were led past the caged tellers and the dark wood loan desks to an office in the back.

"That's him!" Gladys, the scowly-faced proprietor from the store was pointing her finger at Edison, who did an exceptional job of slapping a guilty look on his face. He turned back toward the door, which was being properly blocked by Cop Two. Cop One moved next to the bushy-browed bank manager, a rolly polly gent with a reddish caterpillar on his upper lip, whose name was Roland Paulson. The five-dollar bill that Edison had given Gladys was on his desk.

Myra's knees started shaking. Somewhere inside her head floated the thought that this might not be such a bad thing. If they got arrested, they would have a place to sleep. Maybe they could even get a nice twenty-five-year sentence in a special jail cell for married prisoners and they wouldn't have to worry about anything. That would show the Time Flies.

"That's the guy who gave me the fake money and assaulted Willis," said Gladys.

"I didn't touch Willis," said Edison.

Myra shook her head. Cop One said, "So, it *was* you."

The bank manager picked up the five-dollar bill and held it to the light of the window.

"Where'd you get the money?" said Cop One.

"At the bank," said Edison.

"That's a lie," said Paulson, still examining the bill.

Gladys sneered. "He said he got it in Warshington, D.C."

"How about it, Roland?" Cop One asked Paulson. "You believe that?"

"No, sir," said Paulson. "I would have known about it. We stay in pretty close contact with the East."

Cop One looked over Edison and Myra. "Anything to say for yourselves?"

"We have the right to remain silent," said Edison evenly.

"Says who?" said Cop Two.

Myra blurted to Edison in a low voice, "Miranda doesn't happen until 1963."

Everyone heard. There was confused silence in the room.

"What's that supposed to mean?" said Cop One.

Myra blushed and mumbled something.

"Speak up. Who's Miranda?" said Cop One. "Is that some kind of code?"

Myra, thinking fast, if not logically: "It's our dog outside. He has a doctor appointment."

Cop One rocked dubiously on his heels. Cop Two laughed. "A doctor appointment for a dog."

"Shutup about the dog," Cop One said. "Did he say anything else, Gladys?"

"No, but he kept sticking his hands in his pants."

Roland Paulson gasped in blustery disgust. Cop One sighed.

"Where were you last night?" he said to Edison.

"In our house," said Myra.

"And where's that? In Warshington, D.C.?"

Myra glanced at Edison, who was slowly sliding his hands into his pants. She warned him by clearing her throat and he switched to his front pockets.

Cop Two put his hand on his gun. "Hold those hands very still, mister."

Cop One came around the desk toward Edison. "Empty your pockets very slowly and no funny business."

Edison wrapped his fingers around his wad of vacation cash. Now he wished he'd listened to Myra. Then something slid down his opposite leg, rattled to the floor and bounced a few inches before spinning to a stop. It was his cell phone. There was just enough juice in it to light up the screen for a few seconds. Cheerful application icons danced on the screen in vivid color. Then it went black.

Having never seen, nor even imagined, such futuristic paraphernalia before, the two cops, the bank manager and Gladys instantly transformed into comical statues. You could have shattered them with the gentle tap of a hammer. In this intervening moment of opportunity, Edison's brain once again came to the rescue with a seemingly flawless plan. He released his grip on the cash, bent quickly and picked up the cell phone, aiming it at Cop One.

"Please don't move," he said.

Myra's mouth fell open. "Uh ... "

"It's okay, honey," Edison said.

Cop Two went for his gun.

"I wouldn't do that," said Edison swinging his phone around to point straight at Cop Two's heart. "Drop that on the floor and move over here by the others."

Cop Two did as he was told. His gun clunked to the floor. Myra dropped her head in shame. Gladys hissed, "Aliens! I knew it."

This was understandable. It had been a mere fifty-one days since Orson Welles had broadcast *War of the Worlds* on national radio, scaring the bejesus out of America. There were still believers. There would always be believers. More important, Gladys was from Concrete, Washington, a small town in the North Cascade Mountains internationally known not just for its superior concrete, but also for its reaction to the broadcast. On the evening that Orson Welles had been pumping falsified reports of Martian atrocities into America's eardrums, Gladys had been up north visiting her elderly parents. There had been a terrific storm and the power had gone out during the broadcast. Electricity and phone lines were suddenly very dead. Convinced that the outage had been caused by aliens, the people of Concrete ran screaming into the streets. Her mother had fainted. Her father had grabbed his shotgun and staggered into the woods to protect his moonshine still. Embarrassed, but undaunted, Gladys had no trouble believing that Edison and Myra were not of this world, and the probability of it had her terror stricken. If her eyeballs hadn't been connected with muscle tissue and those all-important optic nerves, they would have popped right out of her head.

"Pick up the five dollars," Edison said to Myra, indicating the bill on Paulson's desk. Myra dithered, failed to come up with a safe alternative, and scooped up the bill, mentally noting Lincoln's accusatory gaze. Edison extended his arm and pretended to push something on the cell phone. "Don't anybody move for the next ten minutes. I've left ... something in the air. And it has a delay on it. You'll be sorry if you move. Let's go, honey."

They backed themselves to the door, opened it, and slid out, closing it politely behind them. A muffled "sorry" from Myra traveled gently to their ears.

Hackleford Provides a Shanty

They ran and ran, Paul barking the whole way. Now they were fugitives. They had gone from invisible to being wanted by the law in under a day. They might even be aliens. Myra was nearly catatonic, her hair flapping in the wind behind her as she ran, tears streaming horizontally from her eyes. They had a wee head start as Cop One, Cop Two, Roland Paulson and Gladys were in a 'stunned state' and did not immediately offer pursuit. They followed Edison's instructions, refusing to move for ten minutes.

"Is it ten minutes yet?"

"I don't know. I can't see my watch."

By the time more police were called and sirens began clearing the way, Edison and Myra had made it to the south end of Pioneer Square. They had run past beer wagons, brothels and no-limit card games, and were skirting the snaggle-toothed maze of Hooverville. They stopped briefly, their lungs burning, to gaze out over the collection of shacks, hundreds of them cobbled together from a medley of scavenged building materials. Absent was any sense of organization. There were no proper roads, only muddy paths that wound snake-like through the community. A wispy drizzle began to whirl around them as they wandered slowly into the maze. It looked like a good place to hide.

"What is this?" said Edison.

"Hooverville," said Myra. "There are thousands of these around the country. They're named after President Hoover for his delusional handling of the Depression."

A shack to their right had been built into the side of a giant pile of trash and industrial detritus. A group of men sitting on old crates in front of it huddled around a forlorn fire burning beneath a dented oil drum. One of the men poked at something in the drum with a stick, bringing up from the boiling water what looked like a pair of dungarees.

"Why did you keep your phone? You can't even use the damn thing," said Myra. "What were you thinking?"

"I don't know. I always transfer the contents of my pockets when I put on new pants."

"Can I have it, please? And the cash."

Edison, ignoring the request again, leaned against a partial fence made of iron scraps. "I'm having trouble focusing my brain."

"Well, you're just going to have to stop trusting it then," she said, still holding out her palm for the contraband.

Edison shook his head and rubbed his eyes with the heels of his palms. "I can't seem to think straight."

She dropped her hand. "Try. Here comes someone."

"Call me Hackleford."

He stood before them with his hands in the pockets of his dungarees, holding open a coat that was as long as Edison's, but of a decidedly different provenance. On his head, he wore a hat that was shaped something like a derby, but was as tall as a Lincoln stovepipe. His eyes had gone past piercing years ago, and his cheeks were heavily lined and sunken, providing a history of wildness that had at some point been knocked out of him.

"My name is Edison Winslow and this is my wife, Myra."

"Mix."

"Yes, Mix."

Hackleford looked Myra up and down in a way that neither of them liked, then led them through the neighborhood, nodding hellos and how-are-yas at the men who sat by, puttered around or worked on their shacks. It was surprisingly clean considering the possibilities from a thousand homeless men.

"Where you from?" said Hackleford, walking ahead of them.

"Just came out from Washington, DC," said Edison. Myra frowned at him. "We're looking for a place to stay for the night."

"I figured you only just got out here, on account of both of you havin' all your teeth," said Hackleford, turning his gaze to Myra. "Just so you know, women ain't supposed to live in here, but a few do. I'll take you to Bess and she can help you out. But I'll have to check with Mr. Jackson to see if you can stay."

"Mr. Jackson?"

"The Mayor of Hooverville. Jesse Jackson."

"The Mayor's name is Jesse Jackson?"

"Yes, ma'am. Know him?"

"I don't think so."

He introduced them to his shack with a slight bow. "This here's my home." It was a tidy box of about a hundred square feet with two tiny windows and a pipe with smoke coming out of it popping through the tar-paper roof. Two of the walls were made from wood scraps and two from metal scraps. "Bess calls it cute." Paul sniffed at a corner and peed on it.

"It's very nice." Edison said, pretending to assess the craftsmanship. "We can't pay you just yet."

Hackleford looked Myra up and down again. "We can work something out."

Edison wanted to hit him for that but he had never hit anyone before and Hackleford looked like he had, so he just thought about it. "I'll pay you with money, as soon as I get a job."

Hackleford laughed, a great crusty cackle of a thing, like a poorly tuned engine burbling with phlegm. "A job? You're too old."

"Too old? We're only fifty-seven."

"Yeah, well that's old. I'm fifty and I don't suppose I'll ever work again. Haven't worked in four years."

"I know," said Edison. "I just lost my job the other day, right before I was supposed to go on vacation." It wasn't really what he should have said right now, not with Myra standing there, but he wanted Hackleford to like him.

Hackleford laughed again. "Just think of it as the beginning of a really long vacation. You folks relax. I'll go check with Mr. Jackson, then rustle us up somethin' to eat when I get back."

"Well, that certainly explains your mood when you got home from work."

"I was going to tell you."

"When? Twenty-five years from now?"

"No. I was waiting for the right time."

"So, that means when we get back, you're going to be unemployed? What are we going to do? I'm on your medical insurance."

"Do we really have to talk about that right now?"

"It gave me something to look forward to. Now…" She stuck her hand under Minnie's coat and turned away from Edison to check the lump. "And stop telling people we're from Washington D.C. You've never even been there." They stood in the drizzle outside Hackleford's shack, keeping their eyes peeled for police and hoping that their exploits had not yet reached the ears of Mayor Jackson. Small neighboring fires glowed in the darkness. From one of them a woman came walking toward them.

"Hackleford says you folks needed some welcoming. I'm Bess. Welcome."

Bess wore a pilly wool coat over a dress that held an iffy memory of once having been a color. Her features had been shaped by poverty to those of a beaten man. In the right clothes, she could have passed for a dockworker or a corrupt union official. She lived next door to Hackleford with her husband, Philo. Philo was rarely around, always out 'looking for work' and returning home in the employment of a bottle.

She spat, a long stringer that dropped reluctantly from her lips to the soggy ground at her feet. Spitting was something that Myra had always found slightly shocking, an impolite gesture that only uncouth folks, smokers and teenage boys engaged in. Polite people swallowed theirs. She had always blamed the nasty habit on parental imperfection, as if it were somehow new, or had been purged from society centuries ago, only having been recently resurrected by an impure generation. But Bess was as old as her great grandmother would be now and here she was, hocking lugies like a skateboarder. "Your hair's all wet. Ain't you got a hat?" said Bess.

"I lost it," said Myra.

Bess started back toward her place. "Come on. I'll get you something."

Myra warned Edison to stay out of trouble—"Don't do *any-thing*"—and left him to enjoy the drizzle alone. He stood fairly still, following instructions, wondering where Paul had wandered off to, and then watched as Hackleford's tall hat wove its way toward him through the shacks.

"Is Paul with you?" said Edison.

"Who's Paul?"

"Our dog."

"Oh. Your dog's name is Paul?"

"It is."

"Haven't seen him."

When Myra returned with Bess, she was sporting a non-color ker-chief holding her hair back and providing minimal protection from the rain.

Hackleford cleared his throat to make way for the news from Mayor Jackson. "Edison, you can stay as long as you like. Mrs. Mix, the Mayor says you can stay for two days. After that, you'll have to seek shelter at a place that caters to women and children. I can assist with that, if you like."

Myra kept silent, but allowed her face to make her displeasure obvious.

"Those rules come from the city of Seattle, not Hooverville. If you want to talk to the Mayor about it, just head north and listen for the shack with the radio."

Edison spoke, with an apologetic nod toward Bess. "What about Bess?"

"Bess is different," said Hackleford. He didn't explain and his look said he wasn't going to. Bess smiled like a dockworker with a new union contract.

"It's okay, Edison," said Myra. "We weren't planning on staying long. Thank you for your hospitality, Mr. Hackleford."

"My pleasure, ma'am." His smile, behaving more like a leer, crawled up one side of his face, and his eyes held hers a little longer than necessary.

Edison put his arm around Myra. "Where do we sleep?"

"There's an empty place right there next to mine." He pointed to a tent shaped structure covered in tarpaper that was about half the size of his own and only about four feet tall at the peak. It had no windows. Firewood was stacked against one side. "You're welcome to it. Hobbleneck Henry was the last guy there, but he left a couple of months ago. He wasn't too dirty. Least I don't think he was. If I remember right, the lice weren't so much a problem as they had been in the summer."

Myra and Edison exchanged glances then looked back at the shed. It had come to this.

"What happened to Hockeyneck Henry?"

"Hobbleneck," corrected Hackleford. "He got a job hauling manure for his brother-in-law. The rule is, once you get a proper job—that is, you're working for someone else—you're supposed to leave. Some folks don't, but in Henry's case, the Mayor found out and asked him to be fair to the rest of us, so he left."

"So, no one owns the place?"

Hackleford paused for a moment, chewing on the inside of his lip. "Well, now that you mention it, I suppose it's actually mine. That is, I hold the responsible interest in it."

"Responsible interest?"

"I'm supposed to charge rent. You see, I helped Henry build it, helped him scavenge all the materials. He didn't have no cart, so I walked him around gathering supplies. Then we worked on it together. I guess that made it half mine, and when he left, it became mine."

"How much?"

He rubbed his chin. "Well, I ain't rented it before. It ain't a bad place, but it does have a few leaks. And it'll need some cleaning. I guess a dollar a month would do."

"But we're only going to be here for two days. I'll be leaving with Myra."

"Well, I ain't no good at math. Howzabout you just help me out with a little job I got in the morning and we'll call it even?"

Deal.

The three of them sat on crates around a small fire, dinner plates in their laps. Paul had returned and was curled at Myra's feet.

"What exactly are we eating?" said Myra.

"Exactly? I don't know," said Hackleford. "Is it not to your liking?"

"Just curious. I don't think I've ever eaten anything black before." She pulled a shapeless chunk from the gravy sludge. "It doesn't have meat in it, does it?"

"Why, it most certainly does," said Hackleford, mildly offended. "You all are guests."

Myra grimaced at the hunk on her fork. But she was too hungry to ask what kind of meat it was for fear of staying hungry. *Maybe if I don't know what kind of meat it is it will be okay.* "Thank you. You're very kind."

Hackleford chewed slowly, eyeing Edison's coat, the brown cheviot he had stolen from Burt. It was clean and well cared for and warm looking. An idea struck him and he shifted his body slightly in preparation for the presentation. He cleared his throat. "You know, I was thinkin'. I don't want to be unfair, so just let me know if I'm offending you at all, but I was thinkin', since you ain't able to come up with any rent just yet, and with you feeling all bad about it and everything, and what with Myra being spoken for, I was thinkin' that maybe you'd be willin' to let me, ah, wear that … that … " He gestured toward Edison.

Edison put his fork on his plate and straightened up.

" … your coat. Could I wear your coat for a bit? You know, as a kind of, uh, security. I mean, I'm not trying to crowd you or anything, and I don't want to cause any bad feelings, so just let me know if I'm offendin' you, but you said you wasn't feelin' too good about freeloadin' off me, if you know what I mean."

"Freeloading?" said Edison. "We said we were going to pay you." He leaned forward slightly at Hackleford, who raised a hand in his defense.

"I know, I know, and it's not that I don't trust you. I do. I really do. You seem like nice folks. But I'm just thinkin' about makin' you feel better about this here situation … you know?"

"You said the rent would be handled by me helping you out with a job in the morning."

"That's for rent, not board," said Hackleford, nodding at Edison's plate.

Edison put his dinner on the ground. Paul perked up, sniffed at the plate, and lay back down. "I think I see what you're getting at. But it is rather cold and you have a coat already."

"Oh, you can wear my coat. I didn't mention that? I'm sorry." He smiled, but didn't stop chewing.

Edison considered the amount of time that had passed since Hackleford's coat had joined forces with any kind of cleaning solution. Hackleford presented a dirt-stiffened sleeve for inspection and dropped another forkful of grub into his mouth.

"I think that sounds fair," said Myra. "You might as well *look* unemployed."

Edison signified his defeat with a sigh. "We'll switch after dinner."

They ate in silence for a while. The fire crackled. Paul did a little scratch and sniff, inventoried his vitals, then went back to sleep.

"You folks got any plans for Christmas?"

"No. Do you?"

"Not really. Some folks around here got 'lectricity. Some of them got Christmas lights, as you can see. Guess looking at them's good enough for me. Besides, I got me a new coat. Can't ask for better than that."

"I thought you were just borrowing it," said Edison.

Myra cut in. "How long have you lived here, Mr. Hackleford?"

"Since I lost my last job four years ago."

"What did you do?" asked Edison.

"Worked on that dock right over there," he said, pointing into the darkness. "I was a foreman. What did you do?"

"Mostly sat at a computer all day," he said. Myra elbowed him.

"What's that?" said Hackleford.

"Oh … just something … people do … use … to feel busy," Edison said, trying to recover. "Nothing really. It wasn't a very good job."

Hackleford gave them a queer look, darting his eyes back and forth from one to the other. "In Warshington, DC?"

"Yes, sir."

Hackleford's tongue dug at a fragment of stray meat from between his teeth and gum. When that didn't work, he used his finger. "You folks seem a little different than other folks around here. I'm not sure what to make of you."

Myra spoke. "How so?"

"Just different. For one thing, you got nothing with you but the clothes on your back. You don't seem quite prepared for the life ahead of you, if you know what I mean."

"Things just happened very suddenly. We were taken by surprise."

Hackleford weighed this. "I suppose," he said, but it didn't sound like he was supposing. "If you're done with your dinner, I wouldn't mind switching coats now."

"Oh, my god." Myra held a candle in front of her as she crawled into the leftovers of Hobbleneck Henry. "I can't sleep in here."

Edison was already inside, sitting on what may have been a mattress. He had gone in first not only because he was a gentleman, but because he felt protected from any lurking evil of Hobbleneck Henry's by the crust on Hackleford's coat. "It's not that bad."

"As compared to what?" She waved her candle around, taking in the place. There wasn't much waving around room and not much to take in, a few boxes, rags, some rusty utensils, a paint can half-filled with what looked like lard, all covered with tiny black specks. As her eyes adjusted to the candlelight, the specks turned into flies. Dead flies. Hundreds of them.

None of them were Time Flies.

Edison brushed frantically at the flies to clear them a sleeping spot. The flies were brittle, having been long dead, and many of them crumbled into powder as he swiped at them.

"I can't sleep in here," Myra said again. But, of course, she could. They were exhausted. They would never have trouble sleeping for the duration of their sentence. It didn't take long. In just under a minute she was deeply away from the shed, in a blackness all her own.

The Alien Thing Again

In the morning, the drizzle had weakened and the sky showed signs of clearing. Edison stood outside Hobbleneck Henry's shack shivering in Hackleford's grimy coat. The grime seemed to make it colder. There were some pieces of dead fly stuck along one sleeve. Myra had a few in her hair that she didn't know about. Minnie's coat was draped loosely over her shoulders. She was not shivering. Myra always woke warm and then cooled off during the day so that she needed more clothing by evening. Edison woke cold and warmed up through the day. They usually tried to time sex for the crossover point when they were both comfortable being naked, something that would not happen in the abandoned abode of Hobbleneck Henry.

Paul had wandered off again some time during the night, apparently preferring neighborhood prowling to sleeping in the shed. Hackleford was returning from somewhere, his mood dark, mumbling and bloviating about the impermanent nature of his beloved encampment.

"Here we go again. Every couple of months, same thing. Burn a few shacks, trying to get us to leave. But we just keep coming back. Nearly did us in a month ago. Had the WPA in here wanting to tear everything down, though Mr. Jackson was able to convince the city that it would not be in their best interests to put a thousand more homeless men on the street during the winter. Now they want to come back and try it again."

"The WPA is trying to evict you?" asked Myra, then said to Edison, "That's the Works Progress Administration."

"I know what the WPA is, thank you," he said. "I *do* know the photography."

"Yeah, well, we don't think too highly of those photographers, neither," said Hackleford. "At least I don't. Taking people's pictures when they're down and out and putting them in the newspapers for rich folks to look at. I wish they'd all just stay away. We ain't hurting nobody. Anyway," he said, pulling up a crate to sit on, "I think it's about time we got started on that new latrine, don't you? I'm guessing you two will want to be on your way soon."

He let that last remark hang in the air while his eyes flicked back and forth between them. It went over Edison's head, but Myra's warning buzzer went off. *Does he know something?* She tried reading his face but his creases were too deep to reveal anything.

"Anytime you're ready," said Hackleford, pointing to the shovel leaning against his shack. Edison had been hoping for some kind of breakfast first, but Hackleford had already made it clear that he only indulged in two meals a day and breakfast was not among the chosen.

"It looks like there's only one shovel," said Myra, excusing herself from the chore.

Edison sidled up to her and whispered, "I thought we were supposed to stay together."

She looked into his eyes, tried to calm his fear. "You're just digging a hole. Just dig the hole. Nothing else. I'll be right back."

Hackleford ogled her as she walked away, paying particular attention to her hair. Edison picked up the shovel to begin earning his lunch while Hackleford, perched upon his crate spitting tobacco juice, monitored his progress and offered digging tips. Every once in a while, just to irritate Edison, or so it seemed, he would rub the fine cheviot wool of Burt's coat and make cooing noises.

Edison did his best to ignore these boorish provocations and, as he settled into a rhythm of dig, toss, dig, toss, allowed his brain to do some thinking on its own and it began to ponder the possibility of their presence here changing history. He didn't know squat about time travel or its effects, as he had never thought about it much and had no need for the information. But somewhere in his mind was a small dossier on the theory of the Butterfly Effect, and he took a moment to examine its contents.

If the theory turned out to be true, then every move they made could have grave implications on coming historical events, potentially complicating their return to the future. It was even feasible that they would never be born, which wouldn't give them much to go back to. This was a scary thought, one that he wanted no part of. But, considering the extent of damage done by his ill-conceived exploits thus far that had dragged Myra and him before the searching eyes of the law, he concluded that to continue making spectacles of themselves in public was unwise. A good course of action, it seemed to him now, would be for them to comport themselves in a manner so as to minimize their impact on the present.

Myra had gone for a short walk around the encampment to waste some time before ending up back at Bess' place. Bess was trying to get a fire going and Myra offered to help.

"You can hand me some of those scraps of paper there," said Bess.

Myra handed her some from a crate next to the fire. Beneath the scraps she saw the folded pages of that morning's *The Hooverville World Gazette*.

"This place has its own newspaper?" she said.

"Sure does," said Bess. She blew on the fire to get it going. "I don't read too good, but Old Buck leaves it for Philo. That rat didn't come home last night, so I'm using it to start my fire."

"Do you mind if I look at it first?"

"Help yourself. You can have the rest if you want. Fire's going."

"Thank you." Myra picked it up and unfolded it. Her legs went soft when she saw the front page headline.

Aliens Overpower Police and Banker Brandishing Strange Weapon

She put her hand to her mouth as she read. The article was brief. It described their escapades and then their appearances:

> The suspects at large are a male and a female, both approximately 60 years of age. The male is described as six feet tall and lanky, weighing about 165 pounds. Balding. Wearing a long brown coat, brown slacks that are too short, and a fedora. The female is described as five feet four inches tall, 115 pounds, with long distinctive silver-gray hair and wearing a red wool coat. Both are Caucasian or Caucasian-like. They are reportedly from Washington, DC, according to no one but themselves. May be accompanied by a dog.

The article went on to warn that they might be armed and dangerous. The police were offering a $150 reward for information.

She looked over at Hackleford's place. Edison was out of view, digging behind the shack, but Hackleford was sitting off to the side where he could watch them both. He kept looking in her direction, at times seeming to stare. Bess may not have read the paper, but she'd bet that Hackleford had. She looked for signs that he suspected them, but he was too far away.

"I need to get going, Bess."

"Can you help me lift this pot up over the fire first?" said Bess.

The sun had risen slightly, dragging some rare winter heat with it. Edison was about three feet deep and two pints of sweat into the job when, having just made a silent solemn promise to himself to lay low and not have any more crazy ideas that could change history, he decided to take off his shirt. Burt's shirt. There was a problem with that. In addition to his cell phone and his orthotics, Edison had retained one other article from his future life. No, not his underwear. He was fine wearing Burt's, having faith in Minnie's laundering abilities. He'd kept his t-shirt, the one he'd been wearing beneath his work shirt when he was thrust back to 1938. The t-shirt was black. On the front was a silkscreened advertisement in white for his favorite beer establishment in Seattle, *Naked City Brewery and Taphouse, founded in 2008.* The brewery had been named after the 1948 film noir, *The Naked City,* which had been named after a book of urban photographs by Weegee that would be published in 1945. Beneath the logo and title, in ten-inch tall letters, it said, DRINK NAKED.

Edison peeled off Burt's shirt and used it to wipe the sweat off his forehead. As he brought the shirt down, he saw Hackleford staring at his chest. A little tobacco juice ran down his chin. It didn't take a whack on the head to make Edison realize that Hackleford was experiencing something new, and he froze. Even his sweat stopped running.

"Well, now," said Hackleford. "Ain't that intristin'?"

"Uh, I got it in D.C."

"Hmmp." Hackleford spat on the ground at Edison's feet. "That is strange. It even says Seattle on it. Which is funny, 'cause I've never heard of it and I know all the places to drink in Seattle, even those founded in 2008."

They stared at each other. Hackleford got a queer look to his face, squinted up in confusion on one side of it, while analyzing the situation with the other. In the distance, Edison heard Paul barking. Hackleford got a little half smile on his face, on the analyzing side of it.

"D'you hear about those two people that everyone was sayin' was aliens?"

Edison felt new sweat coming out of him, but the other sweat was still too nervous to start running again and the sweat droplets were bumping into each other. He had an overwhelming desire to put his hands in his pants, but resisted, as it seemed he was going to need both of them very soon. He tried out an unconcerned giggle, but it sounded more like a hiccup. "They could be overreacting."

"I suppose they could at that," said Hackleford, standing up, his hands hanging loosely at his sides. If they'd had guns, this would have been a good time to draw them. Edison tightened his grip on the shovel handle. "People are always overreactin', don't you think?" Hackleford spat again and casually reached for a board that was lying on the ground.

"I also heard there's a reward."

Edison swung the shovel at Hackleford, who caught it expertly with the bony part of his elbow. He yelped and fell over the crate. Edison raised the shovel for his second try, choking up a bit to increase the accuracy, while fully understanding its resultant reduction in force. He worried dimly that Hackleford probably didn't have medical insurance.

"Len—Myra!" he yelled.

Hackleford lunged low and Edison hit him again across the back. He had no idea how hard to hit someone so that they stopped coming at you, but without sustaining permanent damage. Movies were no help there.

But the shovel had stopped him, at least. Hackleford lay on the ground squirming.

"Myra!" Edison yelled again, snagging Burt's shirt and Hackleford's coat and fleeing across the yard to where she stood near Bess, with the newspaper clutched in her fingers. He grabbed her by the arms. "He knows."

Myra and Bess, each for their own reasons, stared incredulously at his t-shirt.

"What's that all about?" said Bess.

"Just something I got in D.C." he said. As he pulled Myra aside, he heard Bess say, "It says Seattle on it."

"Really?" Myra said as she yanked free of him. "You kept that, too?"

"I forgot," he pleaded. "We have to get out of here. Hackleford knows who we are."

"Wonderful."

"Where's Paul?"

Hackleford stumbled from behind his shack, hunched over and holding his elbow, and began to howl. "It's the aliens! The aliens are here! Stop them!"

"Dammit! Paul!"

Bess picked up a frying pan, a weapon she'd grown well acquainted with in her husband training sessions with Philo. "I knew there was something not right about you two." She looked into Myra's eyes. "You seemed really nice, though."

A latrine-rattling ruckus arose in Hooverville as the words ricocheted off the cramped fist of shacks.

"The aliens are here!"

"Hackleford found the aliens!"

"Why him?"

"Did you hear about the shirt?"

"Aliens? Maybe they're Reds!"

"Wait. Ain't we Reds?"

"Who cares? There's a reward!"

Pangs

"Caucasian-like?" said Edison. "Did it really say that?"

"Maybe they're not sure. We're supposed to be aliens." Myra rocked back and forth with the rhythm of the boxcar. "It smells like manure in here."

She had made Edison get rid of his *Naked City* t-shirt before hopping the train. "We don't want you throwing it out at the end of the train ride and leaving another trail for the police," she had said. "I still can't believe I'm running from the police." She patted his knee. "At least it won't happen again. Not that particular thing anyway."

"I'm sorry," said Edison, a twinge of self-pity in his voice. He calculated that since they had arrived in 1938, not quite five days yet, that he had spent most of his time screwing up and apologizing, and he was getting tired of it. Okay, maybe he hadn't loved his job in the future. Maybe getting laid off would turn out to be a good thing. But at least he'd been proficient at it, or thought he had been. He was a low-level manager of four people who seemed to like him and mostly did what he told them to do. Up until he'd been let go, he felt he had been something that he no longer seemed to be—competent. There was something wrong. He knew this. He knew that it probably had to do with the Time Flies. But what it was, and how to fix it, were, at present, proving elusive.

"I wonder where Paul is," he said.

"He'll be fine. Although it's going to be strange for whoever takes him in when they figure out he's not aging like other dogs."

Edison pulled Hackleford's coat around him and leaned his head back against the vibrating side of the car. "What about us?"

"What a*bout* us?"

"How can we stay in one place if we're not aging? Won't people notice?"

"We'll just have to move every couple of years or so. It shouldn't be too bad."

The boxcar was pitch black except for occasional flickers of light that showed in the cracks whenever they passed through a town.

"You still have your phone, don't you?"

Edison checked his pocket. Then he frantically checked his other pockets. "Hackleford!" Hackleford did not have Edison's cell phone.

"You're kidding."

"The money, too," he said. Hackleford did have the money. That had fallen out of Edison's pocket while they were fighting.

Myra sighed and rubbed her eyes. She knew she should be patient with him.

"He must have gone through my pockets while we were sleeping," said Edison.

"Oh, I'm sure of it," she said, more sarcastically than intended.

"I still have the rest of Burt's change. It's about a dollar."

"Edison, listen. I think we're supposed to have everything with us in order to get back."

"Back where?"

"Home."

"You mean … to the future? In twenty-five years?"

"A little less than that now, but yes. And that's about how long we have to get your cell phone back. And the money. "

"What does it matter—it will return anyway, won't it? Just not on our person."

"I don't think so. It says in the law that all items must be intact. I'm guessing that means that we have to have everything with us when we go back to the house."

"Minnie's house?"

"I think so."

"Does it really say that?"

"It implies it."

"Implies it? You didn't say that before."

"I just remembered."

"When?"

"Just now, as I was saying it." She punched herself on the knee as she realized her mistake in throwing Edison's shirt away. "Dammit."

"It's okay. You didn't know." He pulled the Time Fly Law from his pocket and tried to read it but it was too dark. "So, on December 16, 1963, we have to be in our house, or whoever's house it will be at that time, in the living room, with everything we had when we got here?"

"It looks that way. That's why I had us hide our clothes in Minnie's basement. Remember?"

Edison considered this. "What about the money we left Minnie? And my t-shirt?"

"Please stop complicating this."

"And Paul."

She ground at her eyes with the heels of her palms. "God. This isn't like you."

"Nothing is like me."

They grew drowsy with the clangorous anthem from the rolling wheels beneath them. Myra snuggled up against Edison and closed her eyes.

"Where are we going?" said Edison.

"Shhh. Sleep."

The jostling of the train lulled them into uneasy slumber, punctuated with musings on futures and presents that melded together, jumbled, with no clear pathways. Myra dreamed of climbing tall faulty structures made from wood and nails, movable and unstable, that seemed designed for no purpose other than to achieve a higher ground. A viewing stand. A place from which to assess.

Edison dreamed of sleeping.

The Match Was Lit

The police had obtained possession of Edison's cell phone not long after it had slid through the chute of his pants leg during the getaway sprint along Second Avenue, bouncing to the street and settling in the gutter in front of the Seattle Hotel. An eleven-year old solid citizen girl had retrieved the phone and dutifully turned it over to the police. (Actually, she didn't dare touch it, started screaming and the police were summoned. The newspapers used the first version.)

Word spread.

And now, while Edison and Myra were rumbling south in a smelly boxcar on the Union Pacific, an attempt was being made to placate a frenzied crowd at City Hall with the tried and true method of giving them a speech and letting them yell.

The news had leaked. It had mangled, twisted and procreated, giving birth to a bouncing City Hall filled with hundreds of people panicked about the notorious strangers who had passed through town. Wooden folding chairs had been put out, but proved inadequate to the numbers who showed up wanting explanation, or to pick a fight in a crowd, or to just be somewhere where lots of people were worried about the same thing at the same time. Hackleford swaggered in wearing his new cheviot coat, thinking himself a star, and to act as chief witness and resident expert. But the solid citizens had taken over the room and he was relegated to the standing-room-only area at the rear with the rest of the Hooverville horde, where he steamed in frustration.

A red-faced Hooverville resident shouted from the back: "One of them had strands of silver coming out of its head that were shootin' rays at everyone!"

The reply to that came from the prevailing cooler head in the room, a short, pugilistic bigmouth, shipping magnate Edgar Blustforth, using the soggy cigar between his fat fingers as a pointer. "That's ridiculous." Blustforth didn't care for the Hooverville faction. He thought its members were dirty and lazy and stupid, even though he had contributed heavily to their population by putting so many people out of work on the docks. He looked down at a journalist who was scribbling rapidly on a note pad and poked the cigar in his direction. "Stop writing that alien stuff. Put your pen down."

The journalist put his pen down.

Blustforth looked back over the crowd. "I'll tell you what it is. It's simple. They're Reds. That's why they were being protected in that Commie Camp on the edge of town."

A collective "Oh!" rose from the seated section, while the Hooverville clique spat on the floor in protest. The journalist rolled his eyes and started writing again. "And they've got some secret commie weapon," Blustforth said. "Probably in cahoots with the Nazis, too."

Someone behind him said, "Those Nazis are bad news."

"You're damn right they are," said Blustforth.

The police were having little luck with their appeals for calm. Police commissioner Lester Banghead stood at the podium, urging the crowd to be quiet. "You will all take your seats or I will have this room cleared immediately!" Then, "Please. People. Be reasonable." And finally, "We have confiscated one of their weapons."

That did it. The voices of the crowd froze in midair and fell to the floor.

"Confiscated?" said Blustforth. "You mean you took it from them? Are you hiring little girls for the force now?"

That got a laugh.

The commissioner glared at Blustforth. "It has come into our possession."

"Well, tell us something about it." Blustforth waited, his hands on his hips.

Banghead turned away from Blustforth to the safety of the mob. "We believe that the weapon may possess some kind of brain altering capabilities."

Another "Oh!" arose from the crowd.

"We're still working out the details. We'll keep you informed of any progress."

Blustforth jammed his cigar between his teeth. "Uh-huh." Banghead ignored him.

"The weapon does contain a word that may or may not be helpful. It appears to be written in English, but it is a word unfamiliar to us. Our people are working on it."

Blustforth pulled his cigar back out. "Who?"

The commissioner glared at him again. "Our people."

"Well, let's see it."

"We don't have it here. And I'm not telling you where it is."

Hooverville mayor Jesse Jackson shouted from the back, "What's the word on it?"

"Samsung," said Banghead.

Blustforth pondered, "Russian?" daring the commissioner to differ.

"I don't think so," said the commissioner, "Petrov?"

A lumberjacked ruffian, clad in plaid, stood up. "I do not recognize that name."

"Maybe it's their planet," someone of the non-folding chair ilk offered.

"They come from the planet Samsung!" Hackleford bellowed, intentionally lighting the fuse.

Folding chairs slid back, then fell. Fists were raised. A clattering commotion erupted, with yelling and disagreements, a few things thrown. Some liked the idea of Reds. The romantics rooted for aliens. Sides formed. People started pushing other people. Someone may have been socked in the jaw.

"Now, that's not what I said," said the commissioner. "Nobody is saying they're from another planet. Calm down, everyone."

"You see what you started?" said Blustworth. "How do you know it's not the name of some secret commie weapons factory? Planet Samsung my eye." He yelled at the journalist again. "I told you to quit writing that stuff down. They're Reds and the commissioner knows it." Someone tried to hit Blustforth with a chair and Blustforth decked him.

"We don't know anything yet," said Banghead. "Now everyone just calm down!"

A Japanese family man, Mr. Akira Fujimoto, stood in the middle of the pandemonium, stating quietly, "Korean. Samsung is Korean." In a little over three years, Mr. Fujimoto would lose his dry goods business and be moved, with his family, to a tarpaper barracks in the Japanese internment camp at Manzanar, California, where he would freeze in the winter and fry in the summer, pinned beneath an indifferent desert sun.

As for Edison's *Naked City* t-shirt: that would be found in a trashcan near the railroad tracks by a scavenging homeless man who would wear it proudly for two days before stumbling off a dock in a drunken haze and drowning in Elliott Bay. The shirt would be snagged by barnacles on the hull of a passing freighter headed out to sea, dragging the body along with it. By the time the bloated meat washed up on an uninhabited stretch of beach somewhere on the Olympic Peninsula, the shirt would be long gone.

And the cell phone? After things died down, it would find its way into police storage where it would remain forgotten about for decades.

Santa's List

Edison held Myra's elbow as they stammered across track ballast. Telephone poles were silhouetted against the dusk with wires scratched in the sky between them. A cluster of oil derricks in the distance poked at gathering storm clouds.

They were sore and smelly and they itched. Edison's balls stuck to his thighs and his feet hurt. They had not eaten since Hackleford's black stew almost five days ago. For the first time in their lives they were truly hungry. It was different than they'd imagined, not at all the same as just being *starving* and craving things that you knew you could eventually have. They had drifted in and out of various levels of consciousness as the train jiggled beneath them, Myra struggling to remain still to conserve calories. She didn't have the body fat to carry her through this kind of ordeal and in her daze she swore she could feel her organs gnawing at her bones.

They moved slowly, as if floating, with no sense of time or urgency, across mud and around puddles to a cracked and buckled street. At the edge of the railyard was a small box of a building that appeared to have been built to look like it was already falling down. An orange neon sign on its roof said FOOD, beneath a larger one that said BAR. They squinted at it as Edison rubbed the coins in his pocket.

The two sentinels standing out front were previews of what could be found inside. The big one was brutish and wobbly with liquor, sloppy in his grimy Santa suit, a doughnut of white cotton begirding a pocked maroon nose. His Asian partner had a left jawbone twice the size it should have been, disappearing at the back of his face beneath a dark wool cap pulled low on that side. No Santa suit. They politely stepped aside to let Myra and Edison pass.

The bar was filled with railroad workers, department store Santas and the women who went for them. It being Christmas Eve, the Santas, fresh from their last performance of the season, were getting roaringly drunk. Cotton beards hung by one ear or were strewn on the floor, flattened by muddy footprints.

Edison leaned toward the bartender. "Can we see a couple of menus please?"

The bartender shook his head. "Sorry, folks. Private party. We're not open to the public tonight."

"We just want something to eat."

"Like I said, 'I'm sorry.'" An especially loud Santa called for more beer. As the bartender started to turn away, Myra put a hand on his arm.

"We're very hungry," she said in a small scratchy voice.

"Okies?"

"No," said Myra. "We're from—"

"Washington, DC," said Edison.

The bartender looked them over. They weren't dressed like Okies. It took him a few seconds, but he finally cracked. "Go around back," he said before walking through a swinging door behind the bar that led to the kitchen.

The sentinels out front watched them silently as they exited and walked around back. The bartender was standing by the rear screen door, smoking. He had two small brown paper packages in his free hand, just the right size for sandwiches.

Edison held out his palm with Burt's measly coins. "We don't have much money."

The bartender looked at the coins, then at them. "Is that all you have?" They didn't say anything. "Take these and beat it," he said, handing Edison the sandwiches.

Edison sniffed at them. "Thanks. Is there anything we can do? Dishes?"

"I said beat it. Merry Christmas."

"Merry Christmas," said Myra.

As the door closed on the sandwich Samaritan the sky opened up. It was a windless, heavy rain that fell straight to the ground. They ran to a corner bus stop, hopping quickly rising puddles, where a bus was picking up a passenger. When the bus left, they stood beneath the leaky wood shelter, water dripping off their noses, and unwrapped their sandwiches. The sopping paper was becoming part of the sandwiches and came away in shreds.

"I got some kind of meat," said Myra. "What did you get?"

"Same," said Edison, his voice muffled by his first bite. "Oh, god." His tongue was sending telegrams to the rest of his body parts, notifying them that help was on the way.

Myra stared at her sandwich. She really wanted to be a vegetarian again. She wanted to eat only things that hadn't had eyes or eardrums. But she also wanted to be alive. She took a bite.

Out of the dark rain came two figures, the sentinels from outside the bar. The Santa with the maroon nose demanded their sandwiches. The Asian with the funny jaw provided backup.

"Oh, come on," said Edison. "We're so hungry. Don't you want my coat instead?"

Maroon Santa grabbed his sleeve. "This piece of shit?" He snatched Edison's sandwich and walked off into the rain.

The Jaw ripped off Myra more politely. "Please, lady. It's really the best thing for both of us." She handed it over.

"You can sleep here if you want," he said, offering them the shelter. "We'll take our sandwiches and leave you folks alone." He smiled and nodded casually, as if thanking them for giving him directions to a church.

They sat on the tiny bench, leaning on each other, tongue-scooping as much food as they could from their teeth and savoring it for a few seconds before swallowing.

"My legs are cold," said Myra.

"My feet hurt," said Edison. "What do you think the deal is with his jaw?"

Morning found them in the same position, cramped and damp and cold. The rain hadn't changed much except that it was a little brighter now in the pre-dawn light and perhaps not falling quite so hard as the night before. The leaky roof of the shelter had provided the rain a dripping path to Myra's right thigh, which had wriggled its way between the unbuttoned lower portions of her coat, soaking it and waking her. She stood and stretched, working the pains from her back and legs. As she bent to stretch her hamstrings, she saw that she'd been sitting on half of a two-day old newspaper. The other half was still pressed beneath Edison. On the page facing her was half a picture of Minnie's house in Seattle. She tugged at the paper until Edison moved and read the article that ran in the column beneath the picture.

Seattle Aliens Dupe Police and Banker With Strange Weapon

Aliens land in Seattle! On the run!

SEATTLE. A man and a woman, described by locals as "Very strange," "Creepy" and "They could fly!" fled Seattle yesterday, as a citywide manhunt by Seattle Police failed to stay on their trail. The couple, originally stopped by police and a bank official at the Seattle Municipal Savings Bank after a local merchant reported them for passing counterfeit money, is still at large. They facilitated their escape by brandishing a "strange glowing box-like object," said banker Roland Paulson, that rendered victims "immobilized and unable to concentrate." Seattle police report confiscating a device fitting this description that may be the same one used by the couple to elude police custody.

"Oh," she said. "The police have your phone."

Seattle Police Commissioner Lester Banghead stated that officials believe that the "weapon may possess brain altering capabilities." Police officials and government experts are trying to determine how the device works and what its true purpose is.

It is also believed that, prior to their brush with police, the couple may have invaded the home of Seattle resident Minnie Beckback, stolen food, clothing and toiletries, and left some of the counterfeit money as payment. Mrs. Beckback's estranged husband, Burt Beckback, has been held for questioning after neighbors reported seeing him enter and then leave the house, suitcase in hand, when the two 'aliens' were thought to be inside. Mrs. Beckback had been away for the weekend, returning to find her home burgled. She declined comment to this publication.

The trail continued to the nearby home of Mr. Otto Bedwell where his daughter, Polly, discovered the 'aliens' sleeping in the back seat of the family auto. "The lady had long silver hair!" Polly told police.

"I tried to chase them," reported Mr. Bedwell, "but I froze up halfway down the porch steps. Couldn't move a muscle."

Having fled police, it is believed the couple holed up in Hooverville, the local homeless men's encampment on the outskirts of Pioneer Square. A Hooverville resident, Crawford Hackleford, has reported contact with the couple. "They overpowered me with some mysterious force. Something in their eyes. One of them had a strange kind of shirt on. They fixed it so I couldn't move. Otherwise, I'd have caught them."

Still others believe the fleeing duo to be of more earthly origins. "Reds." That's what shipping magnate Edgar Blustforth believes is behind the capers. "It's obvious that Seattle, due to its thriving shipping activity, is a prime target for the bleeding hearts who want to crush the very fabric of our great society. Freedom. That's what they hope to destroy. Good old American freedom. Aliens. That's ridiculous. That's Hollywood!"

Yes, Hollywood. But which studio will cover this caper?

"I wish they'd left Minnie out of it," said Myra, handing the paper to Edison.

"That's our house."

The house would enjoy a vigorous reputation as 'the alien house' for nearly ten years, long after Minnie's single income would force her to sell it and move on.

Myra looked out into the rain. "So, I guess they know about us here, too."

"You're going to get us into trouble."

She turned to him. "Me? Why?"

"You're too noticeable. Too memorable."

"I am not." She grabbed the paper from him and began to read an unrelated article.

"Do you remember that couple we met one time who asked if you had walked by their house three years earlier? And you had?"

"So?" she said, not looking up.

"So maybe you should dye your hair."

Her eyes went quickly to his and then just as quickly away as she pulled Bess' colorless kerchief from Minnie's coat pocket and began to tie her hair back with it. The suggestion was as absurd to her as changing her name had been. More so. It was too much to ask. Her silken mop, a combination of genetics and trauma that had produced an unlikely and blinding silver, had crowned her noggin, fully formed, since at least her thirtieth birthday. Its gradual and premature autumn marked the stages of her life, stages intensified by her tendency to over-worry, over-compensate and over-work everything to ensure that others were pleased before she was, no matter what it took out of her. By leaving it the natural color it had decided to turn, allowing it to state its own unfiltered history, she gave the impression—she felt, anyway—of someone incurious about her appearance, while at the same time providing her with an identifier as unique as her social security number—something similar to others, but entirely her own.

"I'm not dying my hair."

As the sky brightened, the rain slowed to a humid drizzle.

"I need to walk," she said.

Edison was thinking what an unappealing idea that was when a green and tan bus coughed its way around a corner and headed for their shelter. It stopped in front of them and its door opened.

"Merry Christmas," said the driver, smiling at them. "Ready to eat?"

They were staring back at him, dazed, when the sentinels came running around the front of the bus, nodded politely to them and got on. Myra and Edison followed.

The bus was disorienting and stifling, smelling of wool and cigarettes and meals and secretions, a mugginess of tightly packed unwashed human meat. The odors were a testament to the resiliency of the commuter. But these weren't commuters. This was Christmas. These were people who didn't have anywhere else to go.

Myra and Edison moved toward the back of the bus, studying their fellow passengers furtively. The sentinels smiled at them like old friends. Near the back, they found one open seat next to an agitated woman whose lips moved in the shapes of words with no sound coming out, her fingers playing an invisible piano on her lap.

"Sit," said Myra. "I want to stand." He sat.

In the seat before him was a bald guy coming off an all-night Christmas Eve bender. There was dirt on his knees and an Australia-shaped blood spot on the back of his head that fascinated Edison as he searched his pockets absently for a vial of hand sanitizer. Across the aisle a dozing old man kept waking himself with his own snoring and laughing about it. Behind him, a small Japanese woman grabbed at the back of his seat as if she were ready to leap for the door at every stop. But she didn't get off. Nobody got off. The bus just kept filling up with more desperate lonely people. People with issues, but friendly and polite, or at least quiet. Soon the aisle was filled with people standing.

Edison fixated on a young woman standing next to Myra and eating from a bag of potato chips. In healthier circumstances, he would have offered her his seat, but he was too addled by hunger and fatigue. It never even occurred to him. The woman was enjoying her potato chips very much. She brought each chip to her mouth, biting it in half and chewing slowly. When she ate the second half of the chip, she licked her fingers one by one before reaching into the bag for another chip. Edison could taste the salt, the crisp greasy potato. Others watched her, too, their lips wet with saliva. When she finished the bag, she licked her fingers one final time. There were specks of unclaimed chips and salt at the corners of her mouth. Edison stared at the specks.

The agitated woman whose lips were moving yawned. When she finished yawning her lips stopped moving and her fingers stopped playing the piano. She began to doze. Edison squinted past her, through the condensation on the window. Outside looked as steamy as it was inside. Nothing dried. It was going to stay dismal, the kind of dull gray ski cap of clouds that keeps the alleys dark all day long. The sidewalks were deserted, lined with palm trees like hedgerows of giant Q-tips. Store windows were dark. A single car could be seen driving blocks away. Most people were at home enjoying hot cocoa and fresh Christmas presents. A portion of the alphabet glowed from the side of a small mountain and he whispered up to Myra.

"*Hollywoodland.*"

"It has nothing to do with movies," said Myra, bending to see out the window. "It was built to advertise a cheap housing development. The *land* part of the sign was knocked off in the 1950s."

"I know, smartypants," said Edison. "You think I don't know?" He noticed the chips woman eyeing Myra suspiciously. Some of the specks were gone from her lips.

Soon, they passed small clusters of homeless men and women populating corners and doorways. The clusters grew larger and started running together as the bus began to slow. Edison caught a glimpse of the optimistic phallus of City Hall a few blocks away. The bus stopped in front of a squat grungy blonde-bricked building with a long line of people in front of it stretching down the block. The smells of cheap food hovered in the heavy air. A tinny speaker high on the wall of the building played scratchy Christmas music. Passengers started filing off the bus and walking to the end of the line.

"If you want to eat, this looks like the place," said Myra.

While stepping down from the bus, Edison's foot (Burt's shoe) snagged itself on the bottom step, twisting the foot in a direction different from the one he was headed in and lending it a mild sprain. Myra helped him to his feet and, after a moment of adjustment to his temporary limits on transit, assisted him to the end of the line where they proceeded to wait two and three quarter hours for breakfast.

HOLLYWOODLAND

Playing Fairly

For a while, the days clicked by in a predictable pattern. When the sun rose in the morning they were warm and safe. When it set in the evening, they huddled in fear. They wandered the septic streets of downtown and Bunker Hill, filling their lungs with the dust of hustlers and murderers, hookers, kooks and gamblers, imagining the whispers whenever more fortunate hands pulled back the curtains to watch them pass. They slept in the service doorway at the back of *Bugsy's Rare Books* on a bed of cardboard and shared two meals a day in a basement cafeteria on Hill Street where a bowl of vegetable soup over brown rice cost a penny.

"There, you're a vegetarian again," said Edison, slurping his first spoonful.

"It tastes like it has beef stock in it."

Myra eyed the produce stands at the Grand Central Market when the winter rains drove them inside to lurk beneath the low dark ceiling and the neon signs, vendors laying wary eyes on them as they scuttled by. When they tired of the accusations, they walked, or lingered away afternoons in the library when Edison needed to rest his feet. Here, Myra would read.

She became an information sponge. Books, magazines, newspapers, billboards, clothing labels—anything she could get her eyes on for free—all information catalogued, compared, assimilated and analyzed in the superfluity of circuits and gears in her brain. But although the Time Flies had inadvertently provided her with the compulsion to absorb vast quantities of information, they had just as inadvertently failed to provide her with a reliable means to access it once it had been installed in her head. More than half of what she read just disappeared inside her, never to be remembered again. It was like reading a recipe for fish stew and only being able to recall *pinch of salt* and *simmer for 35 minutes before adding.* Her brain was a massive library in which only a few books could be pulled from the shelves. But the fact that so much of the information was useless to her in no way diminished her hunger for it, and an afternoon spent in the leather-bound caverns of the Los Angeles Public Library, with Edison zonked out in the chair beside her, was like a small trip to Heaven.

"I just had a dream that Paul lost a leg!" Edison blurted one afternoon, springing from a nap as Myra worked through volume twenty of the Encyclopedia Britannica, covering *Ode* to *Pay.* A cat-eyed librarian with pipes like a high school football coach nearly broke the sound barrier telling him to quiet down, snapping her fingers and pointing vigorously at the SILENCE! sign.

They stuttered into their new lives, finely tuning their adopted identities. Myra messed up a few times, calling Edison by his twenty-first century name, Bob, and even slipped in a Tom or two when she was drowsy, but Edison abruptly corrected her, calling her attention to the neon that bore his new moniker in brilliant poppy red atop the urban castle of the Edison Building. They grew careful about revealing details of the future, and endeavored to abandon their colloquialisms and their biases, keeping their eyes and ears open for clues on styles of behavior and speech, and their mouths shut against any witnessed bigotry until they got more acquainted.

It was Edison who had the inkling of familiarity about Bunker Hill.

"I feel like I've been here before," he said the first time he saw Angels Flight.

"I don't see how," Myra said. "We've never been here. Unless you're confusing it with the Bunker Hill in Boston."

Edison watched the orange and black parallelogram-shaped railway car haul a few passengers up the track to Olive Street, as the second car, nearly empty, descended to Hill Street where they stood.

"No. It's nothing like Boston," he said, as they hiked up the Third Street steps. "But it feels familiar. More colorful than I remember it, though."

It would seem logical that Myra and Edison should have complained more about their predicament, or thrown fits over the unfairness of Time Flies, or become despondent, suicidal even. Maybe some running around from place to place trying to solve something, or to ask questions, seek answers, or to look for a secret portal back to the future. (This was, after all, a sentence for a crime, which made it a sort of prison. Shouldn't there have been a way to escape?) They could have considered investing, or selling their knowledge—tarot cards, predictions, stocks—or tried inventing things before they were invented. But truthfully, they just weren't the type. They weren't professional time travelers, or criminals of the hardened variety, or even hornswogglers. They were regular people. Honest folks. To profit from their experiences, as unfair as they may have been, would seem wrong to Myra, a sort of insider trading on history. She refused to stoop to the Time Flies' level, playing the role of the ascetic. She didn't like being wanted by the police, or going hungry, smelling bad, or 'camping', but she knew that those things would eventually change and she wanted the ways in which they changed to leave her feeling clean. As for Edison, he'd become frightened enough by his state of mind that he was willing to do whatever Myra said. Besides, the need for food and shelter were far more immediate concerns, tending to dictate—to a greater degree than well-fed people might imagine—what the priorities were. Really, they just wanted to be left alone for a while to adjust. They weren't in any rush. There wasn't a lot being asked of them, but they still had to survive. So, they did what they needed to do to satisfy those concerns. They got jobs.

It wasn't easy. But the economy, having just crossed the second ravine of the Great Depression, was teetering optimistically on the far edge and passing out *Help Wanted* signs along the way. They were in a good position.

Being the go-getter of the two, Myra should have landed the first job. But her going and getting revolved mostly around walking and reading, and it was stagnating her, even as she moved swiftly along cracked side-walks, weaving with determination through the pensioners with bright Midwestern faces who came here to see the legend of the sun. While Edison lazed in the shade of Bugsy's service door, massaging his stockinged feet under a solemn promise not to move or speak to anyone until she returned, she blurred past everything, her steps too quick, too short, almost a mechanical rolling, seductively efficient, with choppy, wind-breaking swipes of her arms, her silver hair undulating behind her, pulled along viciously, trying to keep up. No one could beat her in speed or distance. She would say she was going out looking for work and she would lose herself to time and miles, all the while meaning to get to it. Just one more block.

So, when Edison returned to their doorway one sunny day after a brief foray of sanctioned independence to announce his pending employment, it was a bit of a disappointment for her. It wasn't supposed to be like this. She was sure of it. She was in charge and expected to be first. Why, in one morning alone, she had applied for a job shearing angora rabbits, talked to a concierge about valet parking for bigwigs at a palm-ringed hotel and tried her hand at a hosiery mill where she could slip hosiery over hundreds of inverted mannequin feet to check for flaws. Or she had meant to, kept telling herself what a good idea it was and that she was going to stop walking any minute and apply for something. She even thought about teaching. Do what you know. But she didn't have a current certificate and wasn't sure if one was needed. Besides, she wanted a rest from all that. This was, after all, technically still spring break.

She walked Edison to work on his first day, telling him not to be nervous.

"I'm not nervous," he said. "I don't want to wash dishes. And it's too far from where we live." They paused by the burbling goop of the La Brea Tar Pits to rest his feet, asphalt gases in their nostrils.

"We don't live anywhere," said Myra, pacing, waiting for him to finish resting.

"You know what I mean."

She bid him farewell at the front door to Minty's Dining Car, a singlewide with a dozen counter stools and six booths with a fifty-cent minimum and a thirty-minute limit. From the outside, it was built to resemble a tugboat, with porthole windows and a stack that excreted bacon smoke. It sat in the middle of a large, otherwise empty, dirt lot that adjusted its trash motif every time the wind blew.

"You're not coming in?" he said. He looked through the glass door at the waitress scurrying between tables. "I thought we were supposed to stay together."

"Just stay inside and do as you're told. You'll be fine. I'll be back later to walk you home." He didn't say anything. "They'll give you breakfast. Bacon and eggs will do you good."

"English muffins?"

She was getting impatient. "I don't know. Maybe? Just go in."

"What are you going to do?"

"Please go in."

He watched her walk back in the direction of downtown, watched her recede with guilt—the way she hunched her shoulders—enough guilt that by the end of the day she had secured a position at twenty-seven cents an hour typing depositions for a barely functioning law firm near the corner of Vermont and Beverly, easy walking distance for her.

"Can you type?" said Gordy Gladhander, the scoop-chinned first half of Gladhander and Physt, Attorneys at Law.

"Is that all that's necessary?"

"Sometimes."

"Alright, then."

Myra had learned to type on an ancient Underwood during her college days in the seventies—bullied by a professor who yelled through his cigar—and still pounded the keys like she was launching bombs. She could wear the most common letters off of any computer keyboard within three months, making it difficult for others to use. She pecked only with her two index fingers, her tongue flopping out of the side of her mouth like a geoduk, and could knock out a hundred and three accurately spelled words per minute without ever looking at the keys.

Gordy took one gander at her typing style and hired her on the spot, laughing as he removed the *Secretary Wanted* sign from his window. He nicknamed her "The Two Finger Typist," switched it an hour later to "Two Finger" for short, then "TF" for real short, and by the end of the day he was calling her "T". He hired her more for entertainment value than skill, but she added the bonuses of being able to fix his spelling and grammar errors, which he said he didn't care about, but did.

They managed to keep their homelessness hidden from their employers, but after the first week, Gordy began to wonder why T never changed her dress, a dress that was clearly too big for her. Edison's pants and shirt were a wreck of semi-dried greases and he smelled like bacon. After his shift, he would shuffle the two and a half miles back to their doorway, his feet like swollen clubs, and sit on cardboard waiting for Myra to get home.

When they got their first pay they headed straight for the Goodwill where Edison scored some chino pants that covered his ankles, two mostly white t-shirts for work, a pair of Oxfords that swallowed his orthotics perfectly and a worn gray fedora to protect his bald spot. He was tired of Burt's fancy clothes. Suits looked fine in old movies, but they were a pain to wear and he didn't work in an office anymore. Myra got two plain-colored dresses that fit, one light and one dark, and came close enough to walking shoes with a pair of barely used boy's work boots to help push her speed beyond what Minnie's pumps were allowing. They stood on the sidewalk out front, smiling in their new clothes at the sun. Myra counted their change.

"Let's go to the Market."

They spent the late afternoon watching shadows crawl up buildings from their doorway, gorging themselves on bloody papaya and cheese and cashews, passing out bits to the saddest of those who passed, and that evening slept in their new clothes on fresh cardboard, feeling that things might be alright after all.

Huffy

On February 20, 1939—the day that the German Bund in New York City had corralled twenty-two thousand Nazi sympathizers into Madison Square Garden to celebrate George Washington's birthday—Myra and Edison began the search for their first home in the New World.

"I know just the place," Myra said, dragging Edison by the wrist halfway up the Third Street stairs to the corner at Clay Street.

Despite the profusion of cutesy apartment buildings shaped like castles, Egyptian temples, Tudor manors, Hopi pueblos and Spanish haciendas, and despite Edison's adolescent begging to let him live in one, Myra steered them toward more practical habitation, rich in tradition and urban function, and within their budget. She had seen the *For Rent* sign the day before, posted high up on the railing of a small covered porch with a view of downtown, two rooms on the top floor of The Sun God Arms Apartments, a peeling wood structure hammered onto the steep side of Bunker Hill so that its first floor was halfway up the building where its main porch met the Third Street steps. It sat opposite Angels Flight, across the invisible tube of the Third Street tunnel that sucked and spewed cars beneath them.

Edison could not complain. For as he stood in the apartment, watching out the window as the funicular made its way along the steep tracks, one car going up as the other came down, he began to remember.

"*Criss Cross* was shot in here 1949!" he whispered to Myra. "Right here. Burt Lancaster planned a robbery in *this* room." In a way, it was like he had been here before. Many of Edison's favorite films, noirs that had fascinated and mesmerized him time and again—*Kiss Me Deadly, Cry Danger, Act of Violence, The Exiles*—had been shot here, on this hump of dilapidated Victorian flophouses and apartment buildings that would one day be replaced with glass towers. Movies that would not begin to be made until after the war that hadn't even started yet.

The landlord, a Mr. Huffy Lydon, in a tattered, mis-buttoned cardigan and eyeglasses that sat too low on his nose, cleared his throat. "What's that you say?" He had to be at least seventy-five years old, had lived in Los Angeles for sixty-eight of those years, and claimed to remember seeing the bodies of dead Chinese hanging from the awning of a hardware store following the Massacre of 1871 on the Calle de Los Negros, just weeks after his family's arrival.

"That's just a few blocks from here," he said, "but they don't call it that anymore." There was nothing in his demeanor that indicated that he wanted to be showing apartments, nothing that said he cared about it one way or the other. But he did it anyway, shuffling slowly to make the place seem bigger, dutifully pointing out amenities—the bathroom, lovingly appointed with rust and mildew; the small pre-greased kitchenette; and the understudies for a real couch and comfy chair. Above the couch was a painting of a dog that looked like it had been painted by another dog, neither of them Paul. He pulled the Murphy bed down from the wall as if he was unveiling a naked statue. It had a bean sack of a mattress with a long history of stains and was big enough for one solid citizen or four illegal immigrants. Myra considered flipping it over, but the rust circles from the springs on the underside stopped her. She sat down and the springs cried like mice in a trash compactor.

"Nice wall," she said, appraising the blisters on the sun-baked paneling opposite the window, the mold green paint, in its dying years, being evicted chip by chip.

Lydon brushed his shoe over some of the chips on the floor. "I've been meaning to get to that."

"It would have been better if you'd actually meant it." She opened the icebox and was nearly decapitated by the smell, a malodorous concoction of everything that had ever spoiled in it. She looked for its electrical cord, found none, and threw a scowl at Lydon. He grimaced and avoided the subject by lying to them that Ronald Coleman, Clark Gable and Deanna

Durbin had all lived in the apartment early in their acting careers. He made a special point to dispel rumors that Fatty Arbuckle had also paid rent here. He most certainly had not.

"Oh, and Cary Grant and Randolph Scott shared the place for a few months," he said, bragging.

"Imagine that," said Myra. She should have been nicer to the old man, but these weeks on the streets had thinned her patience for bullshit.

"You know about them, right?" said Lydon, looking down at the mattress, mentally sorting the stains by tenant. "Grant and Scott? Fruity. Their marriages are shams."

Myra pursed her lips. "How much? Without the celebrity pedigree."

Huffy Lydon paused and rubbed his chin, trying to gauge what he could get away with. Pedigree was a big word and he didn't want to mess around with it. "Twenty…three per month. First month in advance, please."

Myra would have rejected the place outright, despite the affordability and Edison's boyish fascination with Angels Flight, if not for one wall. For along that wall were bookshelves, yawning and empty from floor to ceiling on either side of the entry door. They seemed out of place, the only thing in the apartment that had retained its strength and sense of pride. The solid dark wood was barren and unmarred, as if from lack of use. She longed to fill them as she ran a finger along one, smiling at the dust that gathered on the tip.

"Twenty-one and we won't bother you about the leaky faucets."

Lydon was aghast. "But it's furnished."

"We won't complain about that, either. Or the pets."

"We don't allow pets."

She pointed to a cockroach disappearing into a wall crack. "Or having to climb out the window to get to the porch."

Lydon pouted. He should have installed that door. "Oh, alright. But in advance."

"We'll pay you ten dollars now and the rest in two weeks."

"Two weeks? I won't hear of it."

"Then don't listen. But you'll have your money in two weeks. We are not crooks, Mr. Lydon."

"Anymore," mumbled Edison.

"What's that you say?" said Lydon.

Once Huffy Lydon had left them to their hovel, had restored to them their first sense of real privacy since 2015, Edison could not contain himself. He jumped around the room, plastered his face against the window. He opened it, climbed out onto the porch and then climbed back in again, pointing at Angels Flight.

"I know this place! I know it!"

He spun around. He skipped. He patted the furniture like old friends. He pulled Myra into a little dance that she pulled herself back out of and then flung himself face first onto the bed.

"No sheets!" said Myra.

But Edison had worn himself out and was instantly asleep, his face buried in the history of an old pillow. Myra went to the Goodwill and bought sheets.

Angels Flight

They settled into the neighborhood as observers and participants, instead of as interlopers. A bathroom, a stove, a place to lock up when you leave for the day; these made all the difference. Starting over like paroled teenagers, they stocked their shelves with spices, dried chilies and condiments, soap, toilet paper and smear-on deodorant in a jar. Myra laid in a stash of sanitary napkins (with belts), still convinced that she could start her period at any moment. Their clothes smelled differently now that they were line-dried, less mechanical, gently laced with the fragrances of ocean salt and car exhaust, far away factories or desert flora, depending on the carry of the wind. Edison had pushed a kitchen chair through the window so that he could sit on the porch amidst the drying laundry in the afternoons while Myra was out walking, leaning on the railing with his chin on his hands, picking at flakes of paint, observing the people below. He watched the tops of their heads, the Mexicans and the Italians, the Filipinos and the Chinese, the weathered old white people born elsewhere, here to die under a California dream, tanning their necks as they shuffled up the stairs below, resting along the way to catch their breath, shying away from the three alcoholics on the corner, in no hurry at all. Many rode Angels Flight to spare their knees, their tired faces framed in the parallelogram-shaped windows as they moved along. He scrutinized the serenity of the clean children, the wildness of the dirty ones and the peregrinations of untethered dogs. Today he spied Myra's silver beacon moving swiftly past the row of sparkling wheelchairs along the railing at the top of the funicular, her arms baled with library books, stopping briefly at the newsstand below to buy a newspaper from the man with the lopsided face who always tipped his hat to her.

Edison heard her inside, putting her books on the bookshelves. He gave her a few moments to finish and to settle at the table, then climbed back in through the window.

"Can I have a nickel?"

Myra's eyes were already buried deep in a newspaper. She knew what he wanted the nickel for. They had been through this just yesterday. She had tried to talk him out of it, to appeal to his sense of futility, even going so far as to call his behavior inappropriate. "Why don't you wait until we get paid? We need to save for the rent."

Edison noted the price in the upper corner of her paper—five cents. "Why do you get to have a nickel?"

She raised her head, speaking to him as she would one of her students. "This newspaper is for both of us. A ride on Angels Flight is just for you. You're welcome to read this." She held out the classifieds section.

He peered out the window past the porch, embarrassed, ignoring the paper in her hand. He didn't want to admit that in his current state of mind newspapers confused him, that the words now seemed to have mobility on the page, rushing about, mocking his inability to track them. Some part of him felt that she knew this and might be trying to provoke him. He turned back around to face her and it was then that he noticed two more newspapers peeking out from under the first. He reflected on this unfairness and how far whining about it was going to get him, and decided on a different approach.

"Can I make a deal?" he said.

She put down the classifieds. "What?"

"When we get paid, can I have a quarter?"

"A quarter?"

"It's six rides for a quarter. That's like getting one ride for free."

Myra considered the funicular a waste of time for anyone but the handicapped, the elderly and small children. It was only three hundred feet long. What was the point? Take the stairs. It irritated her the same way as when people stood still on escalators, as if they were supposed to be on break.

"We'll see."

"You're not my mother."

No, but I sometimes feel like I am. But she knew he was right and she always tried to respect what was right. "Yes, of course you can have a quarter when we get paid. You don't have to ask my permission," she said without raising her eyes from the paper.

"Then why can't I have a nickel now?"

She pitied him. He was as self-absorbed as a troubled child, lost and sad and confused. She'd read the Time Fly Law a number of times and could find nothing to indicate why he should be this way. The Law did not address frozen emotional states and she had not seen that portion of Professor Rocklidge's writings.

"I'll tell you what," she said. "I get a lot more out of the newspaper if I read it aloud and discuss the stories. How about if we do that together? I'll read the paper and we can talk about it. Alright?"

And so was born a ritual. Whenever their schedules coincided, Myra would read to him and follow it with analysis (ranting) of the top stories, fleshing out the day-to-day details of history as it happened, unfolding events in real time, events that she already knew the outcomes of, for the most part. Edison tolerated it to earn his payday quarter and Myra felt like she had a student to pour information into. Sometimes she would jump up in the middle of a session to press her ear to the wall whenever she heard FDR's voice, or an important news story, coming from the radio in the apartment next door that seemed to be on constantly. She pounded on the wall in frustration the day she heard that Spain had surrendered to Franco and the neighbor, a cleaning woman who worked nights and slept days, threatened to call the police if she didn't stop. As punishment, the woman kept her radio low for the next two weeks, causing Myra to miss Marian Anderson's performance at the Lincoln Memorial.

"Now I wish we did live in Washington, D.C."

"Maybe we should get our own radio," said Edison.

"We can't afford it yet."

"Maybe we can," he said. "Minty is giving me a raise."

"Already?" She sneered jealously, knowing she should be happy for him.

The week before, Minty had called Edison into his office. It was also where they kept the mops and cleaning supplies and the five-gallon cans of cooking oil, and it shared a wall with the leaky sink where Edison washed dishes, so the floor was always wet. There was one squeaky swivel chair and an invisible desk beneath astonishing layers of receipts and invoices, many of them stiff with age. Minty confided to Edison that there was a golf tournament coming up and that he wanted to win and that to do that he needed to practice and to practice he needed some time off.

"Can you cook?"

"I've watched you do it," said Edison.

"That'll do."

"HAH!" shot the waitress when she heard that Edison was going to be running the grill. Blenda, a semi-sweet, gum-snapping gal of twenty-five, who looked thirty-five, was known for her plate-cracking bray that could quake half the customers into losing half their coffee, and she'd spend the next ten minutes doing refills. It was rumored that some people only ate at Minty's to see if they could knock one out of her with a bad pun.

"Hey, Blenda. I'm going to a funeral today and I forgot flowers. Can I borrow a cupful?"

"HAH!"

Refills.

Minty once cracked, "If you tied her to the bow of a ship in a heavy fog and fed her jokes, she could save a lot of lives."

Edison got a kick out of wearing the food-stained apron and cotton chef's hat as he roughed up bacon with a long-bladed spatula and learned to flip eggs over easy. As he became a better cook, Minty became a better golfer and Edison was able to squeeze another seventy-five cents a day out of him. He never could quite get the smell of bacon out of his skin and his sex life with Myra suffered unavoidably because of it.

It was different than his last job had been. Without computers or cell phones, the only connection to the outside world was the phone in Minty's office, which he locked when he went golfing, mainly to enforce the 'no gabbing' policy that he'd put in place for Blenda. But Blenda had a key that Minty didn't know about and ran up the phone bill calling local mystics for horoscope updates, to the point where Edison sometimes had to bring food to the customers himself to keep it from getting cold. Blenda was always sure to throw him a "Thanks, doll" for helping her out, but otherwise referred to him affectionately as "old man."

Edison didn't like her much, and his feet hurt like hell from all the standing, but it was a job. And at the end of the day, he still had Myra. He would sit on the porch waiting for her to get home, the afternoon smog burnishing the light with promises of gold and peace, his bare feet elevated on the railing, entertained by the clocklike precision of Angels Flight, one car ascending, the other descending, tied together as counter-weights by a single cable, always moving in unison, always passing each other at mid-point above the alley-sized strip of Clay Street.

Edison returned home wide-eyed and breathless after his first ride, his hair sticking straight up, a wispy fence ringing his bald spot. Angels Flight was even more fun than he'd hoped it would be. The parallelogram shapes had soothed his mind and made him feel like he belonged to something. The vertical lines of the windows were straight up and down while the bottoms and tops were angled up, climbing. Looking through them was like seeing a crooked picture. But they provided him with a sense of balance that he couldn't explain and knew he wouldn't try to. He had thrilled when the two cars passed each other only inches apart, the windows of *Olivet* flickering past like a movie projector, especially when it grew dark outside and the varnished wood reflected the warm yellow of the ceiling bulbs.

"Did you enjoy the ride?" asked Myra, looking up from a newspaper that she'd already read earlier in the day.

"I used up all my tickets."

"I know. I saw you."

"You did?"

"You know I did. You were trying to hide behind the pensioners."

Edison hung his head, but only for effect. He didn't regret any of it.

"You'll have to space them out better," said Myra. "We can't have you spending a quarter a day joyriding, not if you want to buy that radio someday." Her elbows and fingertips were blushed with newsprint. She was wearing the light-colored dress and there was a newsprint smudge beneath her left breast where she had been checking her lump.

"I know." He looked out at the funicular's windows glowing in the darkness like jack-o-lantern teeth. "I only rode on the one called *Sinai*."

"What's wrong with *Olivet*?"

"It reminds me of olives. I don't like olives. *Sinai* makes me think of *Lawrence of Arabia*."

She made a small honk of laughter. "Your three-hundred-foot long camel."

She tried reading him an article on the recent achievement of uranium fission, but he was too excited to get anything out of it, even when she pointed out that most people had probably never even heard the word physicist.

"They'll sure know it in six years after we drop the bomb on Hiroshima," she said, shaking her head, realizing that they would be around for that. But he wasn't listening. He was still watching *Sinai*, counting the faces inside, noting where people sat and trying to imagine why they chose those particular seats.

The Saw

Edison was on the porch rolling a pencil when Myra called to him.

"I want to get this over with before I go for a walk," she said.

"Okay."

He picked up the pencil again, backed into the corner by the window and set it on the floor. It rolled easily toward the far corner of the sagging porch where the two sections of railing met, picking up speed as it went. He rushed after it, snatching it just before it went over the edge and laughing wildly.

"Come on," said Myra. It was like living with a toddler.

Edison leaned out over the railing. To his right was Angels Flight. On the other side, if he leaned far enough, he could see past some dusty palm trees to City Hall, the tallest building in the city, gleaming white against the pale blue sky. Five stories below he saw the tops of the heads of the three alcoholics who hung out by the corner of the Sun God Arms. They were passing a bottle around. He held the pencil over their heads, pointy end down, taking aim.

"Come. On."

Huffy Lydon's apartment was on the same floor as theirs, down a few hallways and around two cockeyed corners, on the other side of the building. They passed other apartments on the way, tenants they had yet to meet formally. They knocked. An old lady with a high, laced collar answered. Her gray hair was pulled into a punishingly tight bun at the back of her head. She eyed Myra's long silver.

"We're here to pay the rent," said Myra.

Mrs. Lydon smiled. Perfect dentures, bluish in between. "Our new tenants. Come in." She opened the door wider and called over her shoulder. "Huffy! The new tenants are here."

"So?"

She rolled her eyes at Myra and called again. "They want to pay the rent."

They heard shuffling and some chair legs sliding back. "Just a minute." Mrs. Lydon took Myra by the arm and led her into the dark apartment. Thick maroon draperies covered the windows, opened a few inches in the middle to let in slivers of light. A mustiness in the room made the air heavy, as if those windows had never been opened. Four small dark end tables held lamps with cloth shades and delicate fringe. Their legs, where they touched the floor, were carved into the talons of a raptor, curved and fierce-looking and gripping balls of clear glass. They were part of a set with a couch and two matching chairs whose flowery cushions were rounded enough, but still managed to look hard and uncomfortable. The mantel above the fireplace was lined with miniature dog statuettes, glossy and too happy, and, hanging above them, a painting of a dog that looked like it had been done by the same dog that had painted the one in their apartment. There was no sign of a real dog.

"We've lived in this apartment for twenty years," said Mrs. Lydon. "We used to rent it. Now we own the building."

"And it's more trouble than it's worth," said Huffy as he entered the living room wearing the same cardigan sweater from two weeks ago, his hand open and ready to accept money.

"So are you," his wife said, then leaned in to Myra. "He used to tell me I was beautiful."

"Well, you used to be," said Huffy.

"I'm glad you decided to stay with us," she said to Myra, ignoring her husband. "I used to see you on the street and it made me feel so awful."

Myra blushed and looked at the floor. The old lady extended her hand. "I'm Mrs. Huffy Lydon, although I sometimes wonder why. You can call me Dot."

Myra took her hand. "Thank you. Myra Mix."

Dot was surprised. "Not Winslow?" She turned to Huffy. "Didn't you check to see if they were married?"

"What for? They looked okay."

"It's alright, Mrs. Lydon," said Myra. "We're married."

"With two last names? Are you movie stars?"

Huffy cut in. "Hey, are you related to Tom Mix, the cowboy?"

"No, I'm afraid not," Myra said to both of them.

Huffy grunted. "Too bad. I like him."

"I don't want to appear rude, Mr. Lydon," Myra said, acknowledging Dot with an apologetic smile, "but I must insist that you get us a proper refrigerator."

"Insist, eh?" said Huffy, narrowing his eyes.

"Oh, Huffy, you don't still have that smelly prehistoric icebox in there, do you?" said Dot.

"The last time I checked it still held ice."

"Oh, that's ridiculous. Nobody should be hauling ice these days."

Edison was standing by a talon-legged table near the window, looking at a tray with forty glass eyeballs in it, all nestled in black velvet. Each eyeball had an iris that was a slightly different color than the one next to it, ranging from verdant green to golden brown to icy blue. It reminded him of a tray of candies. He plucked out a blue one and held it up to the light.

"My brother," said Huffy, offering no further explanation but using the opportunity for distraction. He picked up a pale wooden box that was next to the eyes. Its joints were held together with strips of brass and there was a brass keyhole on the side. "But this," he said, as he opened the lid.

"What is it?" said Edison, placing the eyeball back in its tray.

"Amputation kit," Huffy said in a low voice, hoping to shock him a little. Edison's eyes widened. He peered down at the three sets of pliers and the trepanning instruments. Four black-handled knives of various lengths were pressed into deep red velvet. Huffy removed the bone saw and handed it to him. Edison was impressed by the solidness of the grip, the balance, the thrust potential. It made him woozy to imagine the sounds as it cut through meat and bone.

"My father's," said Huffy. "He was a field surgeon during the Civil War."

Myra stepped closer for a better look. "Your father was in the Civil War?" This was her favorite war, the one she liked teaching most.

"Andersonville," Huffy said.

Myra eyes twinkled as she explored the amputation kit, her fingers ambling lightly over the instruments. "Now, about that refrigerator."

"We'll talk," he said, closing the lid and setting the kit back on the table.

"I'm talking now," she said. But Huffy wasn't.

Edison pulled back one of the draperies. "You can't see Angels Flight from here."

"Bah! That contraption," said Huffy. "You try living across from that thing for twenty years."

"Okay."

The Troubled Kitchen

When the weather warmed for good, they moved the dining table out to the porch, working it carefully through the window to minimize damage. There they could eat their meals and discuss the news while keeping an eye on the neighborhood. Mornings were best, when the porch was shaded and cool and the building across the way reflected sunshine onto Myra's newspaper as she read to Edison, his chin on the railing, watching. In the apartment below them, lived a mostly unemployed actor named Bucky Kitchen, who always wore a caftan no matter what the weather. He claimed to have been 'sent' to LA from Moose Jaw, Saskatchewan over a year ago, but wasn't clear about the details. He didn't expect to be around much longer.

"I did a few movies, small ones that nobody will ever see."

"They will someday," Edison said.

"Nah. They had their run. B material. They'll rot in some closet somewhere. That's the way it is."

Bucky had a second career as an alcoholic and a Seconal addict. They would sometimes see him passed out on his porch below them, his head cocked at an odd angle against the railing. One afternoon, when Edison had run out of Angels Flight tickets and was taking a walk through the Third Street Tunnel—the row of ceiling lights casting corkscrew reflections on the grimy white tiles and making him feel as if he were being fed into the tunnel on a giant screw—he had come across a pile of cloth that turned out to be Bucky's caftan, with Bucky in it, unconscious on the sidewalk. He had tried to rouse Bucky as the wind and the car exhaust watered his eyes, the deep thrum of engines reverberating in his chest, but Bucky was out cold. He had walked back out of the tunnel and enlisted the services of the three alcoholics to help him carry Bucky back home. They each held one of Bucky's limbs and carried him as you would a dead man, his head lolling back, drool running up his face. His apartment was filled with cheap movie memorabilia and posters from the two movies he had been in. His name didn't appear in the credits on either of the posters. In one role, he'd played an accident victim who'd been run over by a gangster's car in the opening scene and his face was almost seen on camera. He considered it his best role to date.

"I told them I had it under control," he slurred as they set him gently on his couch. "They didn't believe me. Didn't even listen. There was so much I couldn't say." He squinted suspiciously with one glassy eye at the three alcoholics and said to Edison, "Leave my seccies alone and don't let them touch my bottle." The three alcoholics were unfazed by the accusation. They were a mostly peaceful trio, prone only occasionally to low-level brawls, usually having to do with an unfair division of liquids, causing the pensioners to stick their heads out of windows to tell them to take it elsewhere. After shooing them away, the pensioners would keep their heads out a bit longer, roaring and posturing to one another about all the shit they didn't have to take from anyone, least of all those three.

As payment for their assistance with carrying Bucky, Edison had given the alcoholics Hackleford's coat. "Here," he said, as he stood on the sidewalk holding it out to the one who appeared to be in charge. Wobbling with dignity, the man pinched a piece of stiffened sleeve, appraising it. He nodded his approval and Edison let it go, completing whatever intimacy may have passed between them. There were no names exchanged as yet, but there followed a mutual respect and Edison would often catch them waving up to him whenever they saw him leaning over his porch railing holding a pencil over their heads.

Picture This

The summer boiled on and boredom began to set in. Their jobs were turn-ing out to be just that—jobs—and they each got itchy in their own way. Half the time they still felt as if they were in a movie, or one of them, usually Edison, would start to believe that they were stuck in a very long dream that would end at any moment, except that the moments all moved along chronologically, without gaps, and dreams weren't like that. Still, they were doing all right for people who were out of their time period, en-joying extraordinary orgasms and remaining unrecognized amidst all the freaks and mystics and hustlers and sun worshippers. And if they hadn't quite forgotten about computers and cell phones and sustainable living yet, they did get used to doing without them and enjoyed some of the connections with the physical world that seemed to have been mislaid in their future lives.

Sometimes, after her walks, Edison would find Myra at the Lydon's asking Huffy about the nineteenth century and Civil War stories his father had told him as a boy. Or with Dot and some of the other tenant ladies who liked to meet on the front porch to knit in the late afternoon, bathed in orange light and relating childhood tales. Dot's parents had been in the Ford Theater the night before Lincoln was assassinated there, something that brought a chill to Myra and caused her eyes to tear as if it had been her in the theater, knowing what was about to happen and being power-less to stop it.

But this was no way to spend a prison sentence, slaving away and scrimping for pennies and talking away the afternoons. There had to be something more to it. Even Edison complained.

"How long do we have to stay in these jobs? I want to move around and do things." He meant that he wanted to ride on Angels Flight more often. "I don't want to cook breakfast for twenty-five years."

"I'm thinking about it," Myra said. The burden seemed to fall to her to provide rescue. Surely, there had to be something they could do with their knowledge of the future without it seeming exploitive or unfair. She racked her brain for answers while she walked, and even came up with a few, but always forgot them by the time she got back to the apartment, where she was endlessly dealing with Edison's mishaps.

"Edison, you forgot to empty the icebox tray again," she called from the kitchenette one afternoon. "Now my stockings are all wet."

"I just emptied it last week."

"Oh, god. Ice melts faster than that. And please tell me you remembered to buy more."

He didn't say anything. He heard the icebox door open.

"Dammit. Everything's warm."

Sometimes she sat in the bathroom alone and cried. She missed her daughters and her students. She didn't like Los Angeles very much, despite what Edison thought of it. To her, it felt uneven, out of balance, characterless, without roots. The trees were nice, but the murky unenthusiastic blue of the common sky left her longing for clouds and wind.

Affordable evenings out often involved taking the streetcar to Hollywood so that Edison could gawk at the lights and watch movie stars get in and out of cars. It was on one of these outings that he got his first jolt, his first indication that he may have a slight chance at achieving some clarity. He had been watching some movie stars wave to people as they entered a theater for a premier, while Myra circled the block, when he was suddenly drawn to the photographers flashing away on the sidelines. The photographers were concentrated on their viewfinders, slicing the world before them into balanced pieces of smiling movie stars. Edison felt a tremendous attraction, not to the photographers, but to their machines. Something about them made it seem as if they were some kind of answer, something he'd been searching for. He stepped closer, his legs wobbly, his brain spinning with mild blue electricity. He had an urge to grab one of the cameras, to feel its weight in his hands, its magic. But Myra's impatience got the best of her and she yelled for him to come on, breaking his spell. He stumbled away from the photographers in a daze, a dopey smile on his lips and before he caught up to Myra, stopped, transfixed by a restaurant draped in hundreds of white lights blinking like a nervous breakdown until a cop got suspicious and told him to move along.

The Hierarchy of the Teeth

It began on a late August morning when they were both off work enjoying a breakfast of raw fruit and oatmeal on the porch, eight days after the Nazi-Soviet Non-Aggression Pact had been signed in Moscow. Edison had a copy of *Detective Comics* next to his bowl and was letting his mind wander without the weight of responsibility, ruminating on ill-remembered pieces of his life from the future, while Myra read aloud from the morning paper.

"Are you listening?"

He put some oatmeal in his mouth.

"It says here that the life expectancy for white males was sixty-one and a half years in 1938. For females, it was sixty-five point two."

Edison thought about that. Even if he wasn't aging, he was still fifty-seven. "That makes us kind of old, doesn't it?"

"It does." She touched the lump in her breast as she continued reading. No change.

"Why do women live longer?" he said.

"I don't know," she said. "Maybe it's because men kill each other more often."

"I don't." The morning sun was reflecting off of Angels Flight and he felt good. He didn't feel like killing anybody.

"Oh, here's something," she said, after turning to a feature on the Futurama exhibit currently at the New York World's Fair. She read: *"Norman Bel Geddes, curator of the exhibit, says that 'in the 1960s possessions will* *bore Americans. They won't have many.' He also says that cars will cost $200 and will run on liquid air and that houses will be disposable. 'When you're done with your house, simply throw it away,' states Bel Geddes confidently."* She gazed thoughtfully out over the morning. "My father is there."

"Where?"

"At the fair. He told me that they had wingback chairs with speakers in them on a moving conveyor suspended above a huge diorama of a city with ten-foot tall skyscrapers and real trees. He said it was mostly about freeways."

"We should go," said Edison, lightly fingering his comic book.

"I wish. We can't afford to go anywhere right now. It closes in October, but opens again next summer. After that, they're going to melt most of it down to make weapons."

She watched him staring open-mouthed at the comic book, making a mental note to read it later when he wasn't around. "Why did you buy that?"

He turned it toward her. "Take a look at this cover," he said, raising an eyebrow. Beneath the red title banner, the Caped Crusader swung from a rope across a yellow sky, a bad guy tucked securely in the crook of his elbow. "This is number twenty-seven, the first issue of *Batman*."

"Why do they have to wear costumes to fight crime?"

"They're incognito, like we are."

"Is that what you think we are?" She went back to reading the article on Bel Geddes. *"His system of super freeways promises to whisk American cars from coast to coast in a fraction of the time it takes today."*

"In 2010, this will sell for a million dollars." He smoothed the cover with his palm. "I'm going to preserve it."

Myra looked up. "No, you're not. We talked about this. No investing."

"It's not investing. I have to take care of this for twenty-four more years."

"That's investing."

Edison sulked. "What difference does it make? You don't even like the Time Flies."

Myra sighed, rubbing her forehead. "No. Look, I will do what I want while I'm here. I don't agree with this sentence any more than you do, but when I return—when *we* return—we will return to the same life we left, as much as that is possible."

Then she called for an agreement: any profits turned during their sentence should be exhausted by the end. No trinkets or souvenirs could be brought back with them. And no giving tips, stock or otherwise, to people they meet whom they might be able to cash in with in the future. "And no writing songs that haven't been written yet. We will take no detritus of the Time Flies with us."

Edison grunted his agreement, but he had stopped listening after the first "no," distracted by activity on the curb below. He leaned over the edge, the railing creaking under his weight. "The three drunks. Right on schedule," he said.

"Don't call them that," she said. "They must have names." She watched the three alcoholics tussle over a bottle, arguing over first dibs. They were semi-spry and non-staggering at this hour. She leaned over beside Edison. "Hey!" she yelled down to them.

"No," said Edison, pulling his head back. "We shouldn't."

"Why not? You already carried an unconscious man with them. You're acquainted."

"We hardly talked."

"Don't worry. Talking to these guys isn't going to change history that much. Hey!"

The three of them looked up at her. She bid them a good morning.

They toasted her. "Ma'am."

"My name is Myra and this is my husband, Edison."

Edison waved feebly over the railing.

"I'm Bill," said the one who appeared to be in charge, the one still wearing Hackleford's coat in the heat of summer. He had a beard and most of his teeth.

The second in charge spoke up. He had a beard and about half of his teeth. "I'm Bill, too."

"You're Bill Two?" said Myra. She held up two fingers.

"I meant also."

They all looked over at the third one, who had maybe one or two teeth behind his scraggly stubble and no status whatsoever. He put his hands in his pockets. "I prefer William."

"Huh," said Myra. "Well, it's a pleasure to meet you Bill, Bill and William."

"Pleasure to meet you, Myra," they mumbled in unison, "and Edison," less audibly.

Satisfied, Myra settled back into her newspaper. Edison ate his oatmeal while keeping a wary eye on the men below. Then something on page three made Myra cover her mouth.

"It's only two days now," she said, with something of a shock. Edison knew right away what she was talking about—Germany was going to attack Poland. She had been going on about it for days, her ear plastered to the neighbor's wall, listening to reports on Hitler's absurd demands to the Poles. He had been about to put another spoonful of oatmeal in his mouth, but changed his mind when he recognized her tone and put the spoon down.

She closed the newspaper, folded it neatly, and slid it to the side. She looked out over the neighborhood, across the rooftops and chimneys. Angels Flight moved predictably up and down its track, unruffled by world events. Edison saw that she was crying and didn't care to have it pointed out, so he started eating his oatmeal again and focused on his comic book. His spoon tapping the bowl seemed loud. The gauzy sounds of traffic and industry hovered in the open porch, held aloft by the mumblings of two Bills and a William.

Myra broke the spell by wiping her eyes and blowing her nose, then climbed back in through the window to listen to the wall, but it was strangely silent, so she climbed out again. She paced around the porch and began to rant.

"They call themselves democracies. The almighty US of A. The indomitable British Empire. Empire—what a stupid word. What the hell are they thinking? Can't they see it? Do they really think that Mr. Mustache will offer peace to Western Europe after Poland falls? Idiots."

"Why do you listen to that stuff?" Edison said through oatmeal.

She turned on him. "Why don't you?" Then she sat across from him again. She stared him down until he looked her in the eye.

"What?"

"Let's go to the movies."

Edison dropped his spoon. The suggestion took them both by surprise. They'd been in Los Angeles, movie capital of the world, for nearly eight months and had not once been inside a movie theater. Early in their marriage they had been avid moviegoers, but had petered out as their television screens got bigger and the experience of being in a theater had grown smaller, with all the advertisements on the big screen and all the little glowing screens in the audience. But now they realized how much they missed it—the darkness and the sticky floors, the community of shared emotional experience with a roomful of strangers. It suddenly struck them as unconscionable. They should have been going all along. These were the classics on their first run. Why hadn't they thought of it? All that foolish penny-pinching. What jerks. Edison grabbed the newspaper and leafed furiously to the movie section. He jabbed his finger at the page.

"*The Wizard of Oz*." He smiled at her. "It just opened this month. It's brand new. And it's playing at the Egyptian."

"Yes."

"Are you sure you can sit still that long?"

"I can try."

The rest of the morning was spent in giddy anticipation. They were going to see one of the defining movies of their childhoods—a film that everyone they knew had seen multiple times—in a theater full of people seeing it for the first time. They had never met an American who hadn't seen it.

It felt good to be doing something normal for a change. They had tried to fit themselves into this time. They didn't want to be thought of as special or weird or exceptional. They were different in that they knew what was going to happen, but they didn't always know how to react to it. Clothing styles, manners of speech, moral attitudes, the jokes people told—all different from what they were used to. Some better, some worse. But as the memories of their future lives drifted away bit by bit, it would get easier to assimilate. It may have had something to do with not aging—laggard mis-firings of the brain synapses had been hinted at—but the rate of memory loss for Time Fly prisoners was a little faster than the rate at which solid citizens forgot past events. And more complete. Soon, Myra would begin to notice.

Off to See the Wizard

They hopped off the streetcar at dusk on Hollywood Boulevard before the blazing neon of the Egyptian theater. An actor, dressed like what Hollywood thought an ancient Egyptian dressed like, walked back and forth along the edge of the roof yelling out show times and the name of the movie, both of which were already written in huge letters in at least three places on the theater below him. He was trying not to sound bored because he still wanted to be discovered, but he had been doing it too long and wasn't get paid enough and it showed. In the lobby, a lovely young lady in a harem costume offered to show them to their seats. She looked every bit the fantasy edition of an ancient Egyptian babe except for the flashlight in her hand. There were goose bumps on her arms from the air conditioning.

When she led them inside, the theater was already dark. They had miscalculated their commuting time and had arrived late, missing the newsreel and the shorts and the cartoon, which they each silently blamed each other for. They were seated in two of the last seats together near the rear. Edison regretted not being able to see the inside of the theater. He could just make out some columns and some of those dog-things that ancient Egypt had. He began to whine about it and was admonished by a chorus of "Shhh!" from the parishioners. He blushed in the darkness, but recovered quickly as the screen exploded in sepia tones and music, smiling as he grabbed Myra's hand. They watched the heads of their fellow moviegoers, trying to imagine what they were feeling. They tittered and squirmed and elbowed each other. People turned and gave them dirty looks. They didn't care; they were having fun.

It was not to last. About six minutes in, Dorothy launched into *Over the Rainbow* and changed everything. Both of them, almost simultaneously, inside their heads, started humming the 1993 ukulele version of the song by Hawaiian musician Israel Kamakawiwoʻole, better known as IZ. They'd fallen hard for his version when one of their daughters had first played it for them, but had soon stopped listening to it because it always got stuck in their heads for days. And now here it was, swimming calmly in the vast sea of their brains, with no plans to get out of the water anytime soon. They were flooded with not-yet-forgotten images of home. And before Dorothy had reached the bridge of the song they were squeezing each other's hands and crying uncontrollably. The folks around them grew impatient with their sniffling ruckus. A man with round glasses got up and returned with the harem girl, who shined the flashlight on their wet faces and asked if they wouldn't mind piping down a bit. They whispered their apologies and the flashlight disappeared. Within seconds they were blubbering away again.

"Will you please," insisted the man who had snitched on them.

"Yes, please," said his wife, who smelled like talcum powder.

Edison and Myra burbled another apology and left the theater. The harem girl smiled as they fled through the lobby. Outside, they stood on the sidewalk and cried in each other's arms.

It ruined them for days. They missed the kids. They missed everything—unscented deodorant, recycling bins, DVDs, mixed greens, milk cartons, microwave ovens. Really, truly, microwave ovens. Edison didn't pull his hands out of his pants for nearly seventy-two hours except to go to the bathroom.

And to make it solidly challenging, they both had the IZ version of *Over the Rainbow,* relentless and unending, jammed into their heads. It was with them every waking moment, and presumably in their sleeping ones. When they woke in the middle of the night to pee, they were humming it. It greeted them in the morning like birdsong. One of them would start humming it absently, or start a lyric, and the other would shout, "No! Stop!" It was driving them batty.

Worse, Myra had been wrong about a well-known historical fact. Germany did not invade Poland on September 2, as she had warned Edison. It had happened on the first. She discovered her error in plain black and white when the newspaper rubbed it in her face the day after seeing the movie, not two days after, as she had expected. This was an amazing blunder to her, an inexcusable mistake.

"How could I have gotten it so wrong?" she said to Edison, with her ear pressed to the wall listening for updates about the invasion on the neighbor's radio. "I'm a history teacher, for chrissakes. Auden even wrote a poem with the date in the title. I had my students read it."

Edison tried to soothe her. "Maybe it used to happen on that day."

"What do you mean?"

"Well, if we changed history, maybe it moved up a day."

"That's ridiculous." She was frantic. She wanted a brain scan or an MRI. She even tried to make up for it with more obscure facts. "Right now, there are Japanese tankers in the harbor, this harbor, being pumped full of Los Angeles oil that they will use to build up their military," she said defiantly, then, uncertainly, "At least I think there are." But it didn't help. She was terribly depressed about it.

Upon reflection, they saw Dorothy's strange journey from Kansas to Oz much like their own. But their wizard was a bunch of flies.

"There's no place like home," said Edison, and they fell apart again.

But falling apart had dislodged an idea from the misplaced files of Myra's brain and brought it forward for review. It was an idea that had occurred to her on her walks from time to time over the months, an idea that she always forgot when she arrived home, having buried it so deeply beneath other information that even the memory of forgetting it was lost. But on this day, as the outpouring of emotion jumbled and rattled the contents of her head, she remembered. Recalling one of Edison's areas of expertise—classic American films—she thought, *Why can't we write for the movies?* Her own ignorance on the workings of Hollywood studios was an advantage because it prevented her from seeing the difficulties with this and dousing her plans. Her eyes glistened with possibility as

Edison paced the apartment, hands in pants, bulleting odd facts about the movie and its stars.

– "Dorothy was originally supposed to be a blonde haired floozy!"
– "Buddy Ebsen, the first Tin Man, was hospitalized for a reaction to silver paint!"
– "Can you hear Buddy's voice in *We're Off to See the Wizard*?"
– "Judy Garland was turned into an addict by MGM and sang drunk on TV with lipstick on her teeth!"
– "Margaret Hamilton was burned when her copper-based wicked witch makeup sizzled after getting hit with a malfunctioning fireball in Munchkinland!"
– "King Vidor directed the final Kansas sequence but remained uncredited until after Victor Fleming's death!"
– "The Cowardly Lion's costume was made from real lion skin!"

The more he ranted, the more convinced she became of her plan.

She was hanging a world map over the peeling green wall (for monitoring the War's progress) when she sprang her idea on him.

"Are you kidding?" he said. He laughed at the absurdity of it.

"Why can't we?" she said through the thumbtacks in her mouth. "You know what's going to be made. You can quote entire scenes. You know who's behind everything. And you took that screenwriting course before we were married. Remember? He said you were good."

Edison had taken a screenwriting course in 1994 at the University of Washington with Stewart Stern, the writer of *Rebel Without A Cause*. It had done wonders for his self-confidence and helped him understand movies better. He had dreamed of becoming famous for a while but never got around to trying it. Still, he was taken aback by this seemingly immoral suggestion. "Are you suggesting we steal? Again?"

"Not steal. Just take what you know, stir it all together, and see what you come up with."

His eyes were wide with disbelief. "Do you know how hard it is to break in? This is 1939, Hollywood's biggest year."

"They don't know that yet."

"Well, I do."

"Do you like cooking breakfast?"

He leaned against the window, thinking. He twisted his mouth and squinted an eye.

"So ... you're saying we should write screenplays that aren't very good?"

"Why would we want to do that?"

"So they don't get made. So our names don't appear anywhere."

"You mean our fake names?"

"Whatever. Just as long as we don't change history."

"Not this again. Look, if we're going to change history, if that's even possible, then we're already doing it by being here. What's the difference?"

"The difference is that this is real history. Movies get famous."

She laughed. "That's dumb."

"It's not dumb!" He turned away from her, pouting and mumbling incoherently into the window. She put a hand on his shoulder. He tried to shake it off but she kept it there.

"What's the matter?" she said.

It took him a few seconds to speak. "I feel like you don't like me anymore."

"That's ludicrous. Of course I like you. You're my husband. I love you."

"Then why do you yell at me all the time?"

"I don't yell at you."

"It feels like it. You're always poking fun at me, too."

She had known this conversation was coming. She'd felt it growing nearer recently as he became more cognizant of his limitations. And the truth was, she actually was poking fun at him and she knew it. She baited him, as if she were always irritated with him and wanted to hurt his feelings just a little, but she didn't know why. She had already lost the memory of the last moments before they had been sent into the past, when Edison, as Bob, had snapped at her, telling her to "look up the goddamned flies" on the Internet. His tone had offended her and she had carried that offense into the past as a small frozen piece of her emotional state.

"It's just that, well, you're not the same," she said, trying to fix it. "Neither of us is. It's difficult. I don't mean to."

Edison sat on the edge of the couch, leaning forward with his head in his hands.

"What's wrong with me? Why doesn't my brain work right anymore? Why do I feel so stupid and scared all the time?"

She sat on the arm of the couch and ran her hand along his back.

"It's not just you. Something has happened to both of us. Look at me with all the compulsive walking, and reading things that I can't remember afterward. It's very irritating. It's something those goddamned Time Flies did to us."

"But I'm the dummy. Right? Whatever happened, I came out the dummy. At least you *can* read." He sighed. "I was always the dummy, though, wasn't I? I couldn't make it in the future, either. I was a small man, an average guy. Why should it be any different now?"

"Oh, come on. You were never a small man, Edison." She paused, then said, "Bob."

They sat in silence for a moment while she continued to rub his back.

"You weren't always this way, you know. Remember when you used to make fun of technology by calling everything *The World of Screens*? You even had a t-shirt made online. That was brilliant."

"It was?"

"Well, it was clever, at least. You said that if we could see all the communications going on around us that the air would be as opaque as rock."

"That wasn't a new idea. And it wasn't mine. It just refers to an invisible part of the light spectrum."

"You see? You do remember things. And the term was yours."

"Maybe."

"And what about your theory on the adjustable conscience?"

He sat a little straighter. "I sort of remember that."

"You said that regardless of how rigid our morals and values, that we were always adjusting them—"

"—always adjusting them to fit the situation that we wanted to have happen," he said, finishing it. "I do remember that. But you said it was silly."

"I … might have said that at the time, but I didn't really think so."

"That's what you say now."

"No, really. I even told it to my students. They were fascinated."

"They were? Still, they're just kids."

She also brought up the time when, after having read somewhere that the human body replaces all of its cells about every decade, he'd wondered why it didn't just replace them with young cells so that it didn't age, which, if not a stroke of brilliance, at least *sounded* smart.

"Okay," he said. "So I used to say stuff like that. What's your point?"

"That you're no dummy. Think about it. We're not aging now. What's that all about?"

He considered this with some seriousness. "Oh, yeah. I wonder if our cells are still replacing themselves. I'll bet they're not. I'll bet that's why we're tired all the time."

"Who knows? But here we are." She slid onto the couch and put her lips to his ear. "You can do this. You already have the perfect screenwriter's name. *Written by Edison Winslow.*" She felt him relax a little. "Look, it's probably stupid and impossible, but what have we got to lose? At least it would give us something to do for a while."

Edison considered his options. He had very few marketable skills that would work during this time period and Blenda's bray was driving him nuts.

"Are you sure?"

"I'm sure."

And she was.

The way she saw it, movies were the world's addiction. The drug was the timeless mystery of moving images that didn't age, a drug slathered on celluloid and bracketed by sprocket holes, and Hollywood was both principal manufacturer and dealer. To her, Hollywood was a beautiful monster; a Good Witch of the North on the outside with a Wicked Witch of the West lurking inside, seducing suckers with innuendos and promises and then devouring them slowly, a small piece at a time, so that they could watch it happening to themselves while remaining helpless to prevent it. Myra, knowing that this addiction would never succumb to rehabilitation, and in desperation to escape their dull existence, wanted to become—for just a little while—a low level dealer in the trade in the hopes of earning their tickets out. She wanted to become a part of the problem. And if Edison was going to behave like a confused and disoriented junkie anyway, then let him try to earn his living at it. Now, for Myra to consider this idea a non-exploitive or fair use of their knowledge of the future was a bit of a stretch. But as addictions go, this one didn't seem to ruin the lives of its addicts nearly as often as it ruined its dealers and manufacturers, and she was, for the time being, fine with that. She simply adjusted her conscience to fit the situation she wanted to have happen. They would become the lowest of dealers, the street corner pushers, the unknown and the spat upon. They would become screenwriters. And they would deal in the sleaziest drug of them all—film noir.

"And you're going to help?"

"I'll be right here," she said. "Most of the time. When I'm not walking."

"Okay."

They shook on it and then allowed themselves the rest of the afternoon for a slew of bone-rattling orgasms before settling down to the business of changing their lives.

The Dark Side

The War came to town looking for work and Los Angeles loosened its belt to let it in. Planes, ships, tires, oil, anything that could be used to aid in the killing of very bad people tumbled from factories. Ugly little cubes, barren and symmetrical, sprouted everywhere to contain and supply the river of human flesh that oozed into the city, and the sky became a little browner. Temptation nibbled at Edison when he saw an ad for putting lug nuts on landing gear for thirty-one dollars a week, half again as much as he was taking in flipping eggs at Minty's.

But they eschewed all of this and stayed focused, or at least Myra did. Edison was more difficult to convince.

"We're too old. Why would anyone take a chance on us?"

"All we need is one," she said, leaning back in her chair, her bare ochre-callused feet gripping the porch railing. "My boss drinks in a bar where writers do, trying to scrounge up lawsuits from screenwriters whose contracts get violated by the studios. He's not very good at it. He's better at drinking with them. But I typed a deposition once from a bartender named Andrew who's supposed to have some connections. Maybe we should try him."

"Shouldn't we write something first?"

The following day, Myra returned home with a used 1930 Royal portable typewriter in two-toned green that Gordy Gladhander said she could borrow. She handed it to Edison through the window and he placed it on the table.

"It has a fresh ribbon. And here's some paper," she said, laying the blank sheets of onionskin beside the typewriter. "We'll have to buy it after this." She opened the leather-wrapped carrying case and Edison ran his fingers over the keys. "Have a seat," she said.

Edison looked out across Third Street. One car ascending, one car descending. He didn't think he could do this. How was he supposed to write? He could barely even read anymore. Not well, anyway. His confusion gave him poor retention from sentence to sentence, which threw sand in his comprehension gears. But he sat, like she asked, and made a good show of it for her benefit, concentrating on the mechanics of the typewriter.

"You're getting the hang of this." She patted his shoulder.

"Mostly," he said. "The 'a' is a little light."

"You're just used to a computer keyboard. Your baby finger is weak. Hit it harder."

"How do I make an exclamation point?"

She showed him. "Period—backspace—apostrophe."

"That takes too long."

"Then don't use them."

At first, they tried writing a story of a hapless couple sent back in time for a crime they didn't know they'd committed, but Myra thought it was too preposterous. "Besides, according to The Code they would have to die or go to jail in the end since they're criminals."

"Aren't they already in jail?"

"Well…" She shook it off. "It's science fiction. It won't sell yet. Wait until the fifties."

They started going to movies a few blocks away at The Roxie to gain perspective. As expected, Myra had some trouble sitting still and, much to the irritation of the other patrons, circled the aisles as the movies played—walking forward when moving toward the screen and backward when moving away from it. On the way home they would discuss what they'd seen, tossing out ideas, and Myra felt that she was building his confidence.

But the first time she left him alone to go for a walk, he froze. He couldn't remember any of the ideas they'd discussed and had none of his own. Instead of writing, he began to worry about the difficulties of breaking in, and that they were too old and would be laughed at. He fled the withering smirk of the typewriter, sure that it was mocking his inabilities, and hopped aboard *Sinai*, refusing to get off. From a parallelogram-shaped window, he gazed up at his porch, at his writing table, empty and without ideas. The Three Bills watched him from their corner as they passed a bottle around. He rode non-stop for four and half hours before Myra could convince the man in the booth to stop selling him tickets. She hauled him back to the Sun God Arms, past the knitting women on the main floor porch, up the stairs to their apartment, pushed him through the window, and sat him at the typewriter. Then she told him to look over the railing.

The Three Bills were at their station below. One of them looked up and waved.

"So?" he said.

"Those are your first three characters."

Edison looked at them a little harder. "They are?"

"Make them criminals." She leaned a little closer to him and lowered her voice. "The Bill in charge, the one with the most teeth, is the crime boss, the one with the most money. The other two Bills are his lackeys."

Edison was doubtful, but coming around.

"And if you need a femme fatale you can use that waitress you work with. What's her name? Brenda?"

"Blenda," said Edison, still looking at the Three Bills. "She'd have to be better looking."

"Then write her that way."

"Okay."

As he began to type more, Edison's ability to concentrate increased. Dumping words from his head onto paper, a silent pipeline of language coursing through the metered conduits of his fingers, began to give him comfort and focus, contrary to the real world, which was giving him so much trouble these days. Writing provided him with guidance and boundaries. A sense of structure. Start at the top of the page and work your way to the bottom. Repeat. It wasn't much, but it kept his brain moving in a straight line. Perhaps it was because when he wrote, things were coming out of his brain instead of going into it. Who knew? That he could write at all struck them both as odd. He had never been much of a literary man, even in the future. His vocabulary could have fit easily on a slip of paper stuffed into the front pocket of a tight pair of jeans. He would never learn the proper use of such delicious words as crepuscular or puerile. These days, his verbiage rarely lifted itself above the gutter, which happened to be the perfect location, since he would write mostly about its inhabitants. He didn't even care if the writing was very good, as long as it made him happy and kept him focused. But it only worked as long as he was typing. As soon as he got up from the table the confusion, the sadness, the deep sense of loss, would descend again, returning him from man to boy.

Because Myra had suggested it, she thought that she would be the one to lead the way, but soon found herself in the back seat as Edison grew more independent. She didn't mind; he was feeling good about himself and it soon became all he wanted to do. She continued going for walks, but Edison preferred to stay on the porch, spending every spare moment filling up paper, feeling smart, and putting his characters through hell just so an imaginary audience could see how they got themselves out of it. From there, a pencil clasped in his teeth for effect, he watched the world from above, imagined it as his own. Sheltered from the rain and the hot afternoon sun, embedded in the solitude of paper and ink, he could gaze across the rooftops and the chimneys, the looming Edison Building, Angels Flight, and the people on the streets—the patient shuffle of pensioners, the determination of businessmen, the blousy skirts of young secretaries and the gentle wavering of the Three Bills down below. The Bills would hear him typing and raise a bottle to his efforts. With the keys of the Royal, he could make them do anything. The ringing of the bell at the end of every line signaled the beginning of another, like the start of another boxing round, pounding on the keys, beating them, but not letting them fall. His connection to their chosen drug was closer to the way he felt than to the way Myra did. Film noir was loser territory. Sure, they were both wanderers, but it was Edison who suffered with it most, the one who couldn't keep his feet on firm ground.

Although film noir was just beginning to plant its seeds in 1939, it wouldn't see its most vivid flowers until deep into World War II. Returning veterans, run through meat grinders of misery, with hardened eyes and braised knuckles, would provide the main fuel that drove the noir engine. Edison had experienced none of that. He didn't have this same sense of pain, the enormity of suffering. But he did have one place he could go, one deep well he could dip into: he had lost his job in the twenty-first century. He'd felt the fear of nowhere to go, the sense of endless wandering, of not knowing where to turn. And he had been at the peak of this feeling when he had been flung into the past, freezing him in this emotional state from which he could draw inspiration. The bewilderment and moral confusion with which the Time Flies had used to glue him to his sentence gave him the right balance of paranoia and hopelessness needed to get the job done.

He'd seen films noir his whole life on screens big and small, filled with stark endless shadows, claustrophobic alleys and fallen women. He didn't have to wait for the years to pass, for the style to develop. It was all there on the shelves of his brain, waiting to be taken down and shaken around as needed. He had watched the years out of sequence, absorbing them at random, often picking films by director—Raoul Walsh, Anthony Mann, Ida Lupino, Nicolas Ray—or by his favorite actors—Dan Duryea, Claire Trevor, Richard Widmark—taking it all in as one big lump. He had watched well, let the drug leak into his blood, and had come out believing that bullets and loss were around every corner.

The Interpretation

Edison's love for Angels Flight grew and he began to rely on it for inspiration, riding once in the morning to get his juices flowing and again in the evening before returning home from work as a reward for surviving another day. He never once took *Sinai* for granted, appreciating its beauty and design, marveling anew at the parallelogram-shaped windows and the way they soothed his mind. The interior of the railcar was wrapped in narrow strips of oak, sanded and varnished so that their edges were not sharp. The strips on the walls met the strips on the ceiling in a pleasant arch, and even the benches had rounded edges, making them gentle on the backs of his thighs. He could sit comfortably for hours if needed, even though the ride lasted only a minute. And because the car sat always on the hill, the floor was made of steps and the benches were not in a flat row like a subway car, but each one was higher than the one next to it as you entered from the bottom or lower if you entered from the top.

He saw Myra often from *Sinai*, caught the glitter of her bobbing silver on the Third Street stairs—where her speed enabled her to beat the funicular top to bottom *and* bottom to top—or if she was plodding along Clay Street, which passed beneath the elevated track, her gaze straight and true, never looking up. Van Heflin had run under it in *Act of Violence*. Ralph Meeker had driven under it in *Kiss Me Deadly*.

To his delight, a rare engine failure left him stranded alone for almost two hours late one evening near closing time. He had flashed a thumbs-up when he saw Myra watching him from the porch to let her know he was a-okay, and the backs of his thighs never felt anything but the pleasure of sitting.

At first, Myra helped with research and polishing dialogue, but the spirit of the story was Edison's. She liked working together, but grew frustrated when he behaved childishly, intentionally rolling pencils off the porch onto the Three Bills. And when he grew testy and territorial it wasn't fun anymore and she graciously ceded her role. She went for longer and longer walks, leaving him alone to pound out his vision of life on the dark side.

"It's going to be called *Struggle of the Mind*," he told her one afternoon when she returned from work.

She smiled as she set a small handful of pencils on the table that the Three Bills had collected and handed to her on her way up. "That's a nice working title."

"That's the title," he said.

"I'm going to make some tea."

Edison was becoming increasingly ornery when he wrote and needed a few minutes to become civil again. It was his world and he knew that as soon as he stopped for the day, he would go back to being the hapless boob he had been for nearly a year. That was when Myra could read what he'd done that day and make suggestions on characterization and story direction. When Edison wasn't sitting at the typewriter he listened. When he was, he was alone.

The teakettle whistled. Edison noticed her slacks as she poured the water. She hadn't worn pants since they'd landed at Minnie's last December.

"Where'd you get those?" he said.

"Picked them up while I was out," she said. "Don't worry, they didn't cost much."

"I wasn't worried."

"I'm tired of wearing dresses every day."

"It's not something you see everywhere."

"Let them call me a lesbian. I don't care."

"I wasn't thinking that."

"I was."

Edison's writing was sparse—mostly dialogue with virtually no camera angles and only the most necessary descriptive action. He figured that the majority of it would be ignored anyway, so he didn't bother. Only dialogue interested him. After that he didn't care. When he got stuck and couldn't figure out where to move the story, even after riding Angels Flight, he would disappear into the seedier parts of the neighborhood for research, wandering around the sticky flop houses on Bunker Hill or Main Street, hanging in the shadows, spying on the drug dealers and the drag queens, the con men and the back alley pimps.

He would distill what he saw through the sieve of censorship as he typed. He knew that he had to watch his language and that all the characters had to keep their clothes on and that things couldn't get too violent, and that made it challenging. There were rules to follow and sometimes he would forget them, so he typed up a set of his own, as he understood them—as misinterpreted by his addled mind—and taped them to the wall next to the table for quick reference:

The Motion Picture Production Code
~~by~~
(asunderstood by)
Edison Winslow

¢ No blood

¢ One shot usually kills bad guys (unless they're really
bad), but not good guys (unless they're expendable and
~~and~~ need to die to get the hero off his ass).

¢ Bad guys must die or go to jail or be otherwise properly
punished or be really repentant and help catch other bad
guys.

¢ No poking fun at religious nuts.

¢ No mentions of homosexuality unless it's to obliquely
make fun of it (fruity music, unmanly fragrances, dandy
traits)

¢ All races not explicitly white must be subordinate to
white people.

¢ No nudity or suggestive dancing.

¢ Sex must be expressed as metaphors that kids won't get,
i.e. trains entering tunnels, skyscrapers falling, guns
shoved into holsters, etc.

¢ Extramarital affairs must seem like a miserable pastime.
Also a good idea if one of or both of the cheaters dies
or goes to jail or loses all their money. Punishment is
key.

¢ Crime-appropriate maiming allowed.

¢ No illegal drug use. Pharmaceuticals are a-okay.

¢ No swearing (may include heck, gosh-darn-it or dagnabbit)

¢ "No picture shall be produced which will lower the moral
standards of those who see it."

He had fun with it. It was like following a map. By telling him what he couldn't do, the Code forced him to discipline himself to figure out what he could do, to find ways to say what he wanted to without really saying it.

In six weeks, he had something to show Myra.

Andrew

Edison tilted the bourbon into his mouth, let it sit there and chill his tongue. He swallowed it in pieces, pushing the tingle through his nostrils just to the edge of a sneeze, his eyes brimming.

"The only reason a guy gets a Manhattan on the rocks is because he's got issues with his penis size." Andrew tossed his head in the direction of a table of studio types. "He doesn't want his buddies to think he's less of a man for drinking out of a cocktail glass." He wore a white shirt and red tie beneath his black vest, and his face was cut like a diamond. "By the time he's halfway finished he's drinking dishwater."

"Yet you're making him a very pretty ice cube anyway," said Myra.

He wagged his ice-hacking knife in her direction. "Just because I think he's a fairy doesn't mean he doesn't deserve good service. And my apologies to the fairies that make up a large portion of this establishment. At least they get their Manhattans in cocktail glasses. Where'd you say you're from again?"

Myra put her wine glass down and kept her eyes on it. "Washington, D.C."

"Whatever you say." He turned to Edison. "How's your drink?"

Edison nodded while his brain looked for something to say. "It's good."

"You have a very open palate," said Andrew in a way that could have been either insult or praise, hard to tell.

Le Speciale was a block off Hollywood Boulevard, sandwiched between a pajama factory and a watch repair shop. It had a dance floor, empty this evening, in front of a stage big enough for a ten-piece band, also empty, with potted plants guarding the corners. Recessed lamps dropped circles of light onto the bar where Edison and Myra warmed two of the stools.

Myra sipped her wine. "So what about it?"

Andrew tossed a bar towel over his shoulder and folded his arms, giving her half a smile. "Lots of writers come in here. None tonight, apparently, but other nights. They all think I know something about the business."

"Do you?"

He hacked some more at the ice. "How did you hear about me?"

"I work for Gordy Gladhander," said Myra.

"Ah, Gordy." He poured the booze carefully over the sculpted ice. "You must be T."

"I prefer Myra."

"Aren't you two a little old to be starting out as screenwriters?"

"We don't feel old."

"Well, Myra, if you have something, give it to me. If you want to talk, I have other customers." He went to deliver the Manhattan on the rocks.

The bourbon made Edison drowsy and he was nodding off. Myra elbowed him and he popped up.

"What? Will he look at it?"

"Where have you been?"

"I was listening."

Andrew returned and started wiping down the bar. "Whatever you have, I read it first before I put it on anyone else."

Myra turned to Edison. "Give it to him."

Edison sneak-peeked around the room before pulling out the script. He slid it across the bar. Andrew eyed the cover page. "*Struggle of the Mind.* Is that really the title?"

"Working title," said Myra.

"It's the title," said Edison.

They gave Andrew ten days before returning. Le Speciale was swimming with drinkers that evening. There was a band on stage and people were dancing.

Andrew waved them over to the bar. "Talk to me later, when the crowd dies down."

"Uh … " said Myra, stopping him.

"What? I read it. Everything's fine."

"There's something else."

Andrew waited. Myra leaned forward and whispered, "We don't have any identification."

"I'm not asking for any," said Andrew.

"We don't know very many people in town."

"What do you want me to do about it? What do I look like?"

"Gordy said … never mind," she said, blushing.

Andrew sighed. "I don't suppose you could get hold of your birth certificates," he said, like he already knew the answer.

"Not yet."

They were dozing in a booth when Andrew slid in and nudged them awake. They looked around, bleary-eyed, and saw that the place was nearly empty.

"I just need to ask you something before I move on this," said Andrew. Edison swayed. Myra partly nodded. "Do you want to be with working people?"

Their heads were ringing and the insides of their mouths felt coated with gypsum.

"Well … we are looking for work," said Myra.

"How do you feel about unions?"

"I was in a restaurant union once," said Edison.

"Good," said Andrew, slapping Edison on the shoulder. "That's what I like to hear. Meet me in Pershing Square at four o'clock tomorrow." He went back behind the bar to clean up.

The night air helped keep them awake as they walked home.

"Where's Pershing Square?" said Edison.

"You really need to get out more," said Myra. "It's three blocks from where we live."

"Oh, yeah." He rubbed at his eye. "Isn't that the park you won't let me go to?"

"I never said it was forbidden," she said. Then, "Did any of that strike you as strange?"

"Everything strikes me as strange."

"But all that stuff about unions and working people."

"So?"

"I don't know." She took hold of his arm. "There's something odd about it. Meeting people. We're already wanted as Reds, and/or aliens, in Seattle. Someone might recognize us."

"They haven't yet," said Edison.

"We haven't exactly gone out of our way to make friends."

The Eye

Pershing Square was ringed with benches filled with men. Guitarists and bongo players. Refugees from the tailwinds of the Depression with holes in their shoes and frayed pockets. Young men with boils on their necks and greasy uncombed hair. Men cruising for other men, looking for easy marks, those broke enough to say yes for a little change or a free drink. Men with eyes as hollow and hopeless as gun barrels. Andrew was sitting in the scrappy shade of a palm tree watching well cared for people go in and out of the Biltmore Hotel across the street. He saw Edison and waved him over.

"Where's your wife?"

"Walking. She said she'd meet us here."

Andrew patted the bench next to him and Edison sat. "It's not really my scene," Andrew said, indicating the dating games in front of them. "I like to think I'm from a better class. This isn't very clean." Edison scanned the crowd for Myra. "Does this bother you?"

Edison shook his head. "Where I came from it was pretty normal."

"Oh, yeah. Where you came from. Washington, D.C. is it?"

"Uh-huh."

Andrew nodded. "Edison, somehow, I don't think you're from Washington, D.C." He patted Edison's thigh as he stood. "But that's okay. We all have secrets. Here comes your wife."

They followed Andrew, whose stride was brisk enough to be comfortable for Myra and uncomfortable for Edison. After a dozen or so blocks of jaywalking, alley cutting and crowd weaving that had Edison completely turned around, they entered a curdled office building twenty stories tall with missing bricks and a twelve-foot high *Jesus Saves* sign on the roof in white neon. They ascended a blackened flight of stairs, bumpy with caked dirt. When they reached the fourth floor, Andrew pulled an envelope from his jacket, handing it to Myra.

"What's this?"

"Those IDs you were asking about."

"Oh." She took it from him.

"We'll discuss terms later." He led them down a hallway to a door that had a lot of activity behind it and put his ear to it. "Damn. I was hoping they wouldn't be here today."

"Who?" Myra said, as she put the envelope in her purse.

"Just some people having a meeting."

"What kind of meeting?"

"Don't worry; it's temporary. Goochy has an office in the back, behind the stage. He'll be moving at the end of the month when the rent runs out. For now, this is the only way through."

"Goochy? That's our agent?"

"Hopefully." Andrew knocked on the door and the voices behind it went silent. "Just don't say anything until we're with Goochy and you'll be all right."

The door moved and a crack appeared with an eye in it. The Eye recognized Andrew, then did the up and down on Myra and Edison, especially Myra, pausing on her slacks. Cigarette smoke leaked through the crack. Andrew nodded to the Eye when it was done looking at Myra.

"It's okay, Cavin. We're here to see Goochy. I have an appointment."

"What about them?" said the Eye. He had some kind of European accent, run by a voice that sounded like it was exhaling helium.

"They're alright," said Andrew. "I checked them out."

The Eye paused while it decided. "Tell Goochy he's going to have to move. We can't have all these people coming through here."

"He knows."

"That's not enough."

"I said he knows."

The Eye did a little more sizing up, then the door opened, revealing the rest of the face. Both of his eyes together were close enough to share a monocle and he had a wet lower lip that didn't close right. "Make it quick," he said.

Half-turned blinds sliced the air of the lecture hall into bands of smoky sunlight. Rows of wooden folding chairs were filled with smokers of both genders, smokers with money—Hollywood money—all watching them silently as they passed through the hall. A heavy-browed gentleman in an expensive suit stood at a lectern, visibly perturbed at having his speech interrupted. Thumb-tacked Soviet propaganda posters adorned one wall, with their proudly pointing proletariats, eyes focused on far off places, as if the goal they were trying to achieve was always somewhere distant and ethereal.

"Sorry," said Andrew, smiling apologetically at the crowd as they shuffled through the room, Myra's mouth hanging open in disbelief. Edison wasn't sure, but he thought he saw one of his favorite movie stars in the second row. When they got behind the stage, Andrew knocked on another door and it swung open easily on silent hinges, revealing a small room with a small window on the far wall too dirty to see through and a small cluttered desk with a nervous, unkempt man sitting at it, smoking. There wasn't much else; an overflowing metal trash can; a mostly empty file cabinet good for leaning an elbow on when standing; a cheap desk lamp hot enough to spontaneously combust anything within twelve inches of it. No typewriter.

"Myra Mix and Edison Winslow," said Andrew, "I'd like you to meet your new agent, Nazi hater, Goochy Avitable."

Goochy's lips, usually in the fixed bend of an embarrassed smile, parted to reveal thick yellow teeth as he extended a shaky hand to Edison. "Now hold on, Andrew, I haven't agreed to anything yet." He had a mildly repulsive odor about him that didn't seem to be all his fault, vaguely nutty and mildewy, like something hiding under an old bed. A shock of pomaded hair fell across his forehead every time he talked. He moved his smile to Myra as he pushed the hair back onto his head. "Welcome. I hope you don't find my choice of venue inappropriate."

"In the middle of a roomful of Communists? Why would I find that inappropriate?" Myra said, making no attempt to keep her voice low. She glared at Andrew. "Thanks a lot."

Goochy shot a look at Andrew then got up and closed the door. It immediately drifted back open. He closed it again and it opened again. "Rat hole." Then he slammed it, waited a few seconds until he was sure it would stay, and returned to his desk. "Actually," he said to Myra, "until recently they called themselves the *American Anti-Nazi League.*"

"A Communist front group," Myra pointed out.

"Technically. They dropped the name, and a lot of members, including Andrew and me, when the Non-Aggression Pact was signed with Germany." He swiped hair off his forehead again and took a hit of his cigarette.

"And now we've been seen here," Myra said.

Andrew cleared his throat. "Sorry about that. I didn't think they were meeting today. I should have checked."

"I tried to call you but you'd already left," said Goochy, with some irritation.

"It's not such a big deal," said Andrew. "Technically, we're not at the meeting."

"Well, technically," said Myra, "it didn't look like they wanted us there anyway."

"They're nervous," said Goochy. "You're strangers. Nobody wants to have meetings at their house anymore."

"Imagine that. It must be confusing to hate Nazis while signing agreements with them. Your Soviet pals do, however, seem to be enjoying their occupation of Eastern Poland, hand delivered by their sworn enemy." Andrew and Goochy cast uncomfortable looks at each other.

Goochy said, "Some are calling it a defensive move against Germany."

Myra snorted. "Our agent wouldn't be convinced of that, would he?"

He took a long draw on his cigarette and let the smoke out through his nose. "Why are we talking about this?"

Andrew pretended to read something on the desk. He hadn't intended to cause this kind of disruption. He should have had them leave and make another appointment. But he'd been excited and didn't want to wait. Edison's script wasn't bad and Goochy needed the money. The truth was, Goochy wasn't going anywhere at the end of the month unless he paid off the back rent. They were keeping his typewriter and his pencil sharpener as collateral.

"I thought I saw Jack Greyfield out there," Edison said, trying to turn it around.

"You did," said Goochy. "He's a regular. You'll see a lot of Hollywood actors here. And producers, directors, executives. Mostly writers. Please, have a seat, both of you."

"Not just yet," Myra said. "Where do you two fit into this?"

"Like I said, we don't," Goochy said, his voice low. "We're done with it. As soon as I move out of here."

"At the end of the month," she said.

He combined a shrug and a nod as he leaned back in his chair. Some cigarette ashes sprinkled on his shirt and Andrew leaned down to blow them off, which gave Myra's eyebrows a rise. Goochy waved him away. "Look," he said, "we just hated Nazis, that's all. After the Pact, we got ... disillusioned."

Andrew nodded. "Yeah. All these factions started popping up with different names. It became difficult to figure out who was with what group."

"So who are these guys now?"

"This particular group is a combination of *The Democratic Committee for Motion Picture Peace* and *The Hollywood Action League for Neutrality*. The groups fused and now they're called *The League for American Peace and Democracy Unit of America*. Or something like that."

"Sounds like an organization of dyslexic isolationist superheroes," said Myra.

Goochy laughed and put up his hands. "Alright. What can we say? It was a business decision. The connections were good. I needed the work. But now things are getting too hot and I'm out. Over. Now can we can we forget about it and talk business?"

"Maybe after your rent runs out," said Myra. "Edison, I think we need to leave." She turned and looked at the empty room behind her. "Edison?"

The door was open again and Edison was not in the room.

The speech that they had interrupted on the way in was now finished and Communist Party members were milling about the hall, congregating in small groups to discuss ways to hate Nazis while doing business with them, to love Russians while their behavior continued to grow sketchier, and to keep America out of the war. Myra was looking for Edison through the cigarette haze when the Eye appeared in front of her, blocking her way.

"Members only," he said. His wet lip hung open as if it were being tugged by a fishhook.

"I'm looking for my husband."

"He's not here."

"I can see him across the room talking to the movie star." She started to go around to his right and when he moved that way to block her, she darted easily around to his left and headed in the direction of Edison and the movie star. Fresh off his recent success as the leading man in *They Forced Me to Steal,* Jack Greyfield was smoking and tossing off comments with sidelong glances and dismissive smirks like a wise guy from the Bronx.

"I used to be in a restaurant union once," Edison was saying, his voice wobbly with awe.

"That's great," said Greyfield. "We could use guys like you."

"You could?"

"Why sure. We're always looking for the right kind of people," he said, slapping Edison on the shoulder. "What did you say your name was?"

"My name is—"

"Bob!" Myra interjected. "Honey, we need to go. Excuse us, Mr. Greyfield."

"No," said Edison. "I'll be right back," he said to Greyfield. He pulled Myra aside and explained in a harsh whisper how Greyfield would be found dead in New York City at the age of thirty-nine in the apartment of his mistress when she tried to serve him grapefruit juice in the morning. His death would be blamed on the combination of a weak heart and the pummeling he would receive in the 1950s by the House Un-American Activities Committee that would cause him to be blacklisted by his Hollywood pals. "Remember? He dies of a heart attack. I need to warn him. I could save his life."

"Are you out of your mind? I thought you didn't want to change history?"

"Is there something wrong?" said Greyfield, smiling with a cigarette in his lips, trying to charm Myra. "Was it something I said?"

"It's more of a lifestyle issue," said Myra.

The Eye moved up beside her and poked a finger in her back.

"Look, lady, you need to leave."

"Precisely."

"Now, hold on, Cavin," said Greyfield. "They seem like nice people. Bob and I were having a fine conversation."

"My name is Ed—"

"Now, look here, Mr. Greyfield," Myra cut in. "I'm sure you're actually a nice guy and that you have no idea what you're doing or how it's affecting your career, but this really isn't our thing."

"What's that supposed to mean?" Greyfield puffed up a bit and got a curl to his lip. Some of the other members, sensing his change in tone, moved closer to see what was up. Myra decided to test them.

"Did you know," she said, as if speaking to her students, "that right now, your Uncle Joe Stalin is having the children of suspected traitors shot to keep them from becoming traitors when they grow up?"

"Now hold on," Greyfield said, pointing his cigarette at her. "That's bunk!" Some of the members agreed, but others, already sown with doubt since the signing of the Pact, began to drift away to get their hats. The Eye saw this happening, along with the impending loss of membership and the checks that would go with it, and decided the time had come to end it by grasping the sleeve of Myra's blouse and yanking her toward the door, knocking out a few folding chairs with her knees. When they reached the doorway, Myra spread herself across it to stop him and looked down at his hand.

"Cavin, is it?"

"That is right, lady. Cavin Corkavonin, at your service," he squeaked.

"Well, Mr. Corkavonin, I suggest you let go of my sleeve."

"Not until it's outside, with the rest of you," he said, grunting as he tried to push her through the doorway.

"What's the matter," she said, "starting to feel guilty?"

"We have the right to believe what we want to believe."

"And I have the right to criticize it. I'm happy for us both. Try that in Russia."

Edison came up from behind and put his hand on Corkavonin's shoulder. "Let go of my wife," he said, balling his other hand into a fist.

"Like I said," squeaked Corkavonin, "when she is gone from here."

"No," said Edison. "Now." And with that he wound up, spun the Eye around and punched him in the belly. Corkavonin released Myra's sleeve and bent at the waist, comically at first, then pathetically. Jack Greyfield threw his cigarette to the floor with drama and wedged his way to the action, bumping against Myra and knocking her hat off.

"There was no call for that," said Greyfield, as he helped straighten the Eye to a more dignified posture.

"Yes, there was," said Myra, smiling at Edison, who was huffing with adrenaline, his fists still balled, ready for more.

"You'll pay," groaned Corkavonin, directing his threat at Myra, not Edison.

"Not as much as you will," she said, glancing around the room at the few members left, most of whom were shaking their heads and getting ready to leave. As she brushed her hair away from her face, Greyfield lit another cigarette one-handed and looked at her with renewed interest.

"You're old," he said, squinting at her, thinking, trying to place her. "Hey, I think I'm starting to realize something."

"Will wonders never cease," she said.

A man in a tweed jacket took a step toward her then back again, his eyes widening. "Hey, you look like those aliens they were searching for in Seattle late last year."

"That's what I was realizing," said Greyfield.

A wave of dread passed through Edison. "We do?"

"I don't know about you, but she does."

"Let's go, honey," said Edison, pushing Myra toward the hallway.

"Maybe I should shoot you with my ray gun," she called over her shoulder. Greyfield actually flinched, then looked around to see if anyone had seen it. "I hope you're all saving for your retirement because you're going to be unemployed in a few years."

"Leave this place and never return," said the man in tweed, like an actor practicing his Shakespearian technique, which he was. He looked at Jack Greyfield to see if he was paying attention to it, which he wasn't.

Myra halted and faced them again. "You think you're smart, don't you? Well, just remember, Stalin kills smart people. They go first. But you may get lucky. He may see you as the dumb shits you really are and put you to work boiling down pig parts to make grease for tanks."

An indignant, snotty roar erupted from the man in tweed. "Banish her!"

"Out, witch!" said Greyfield, throwing his cigarette to the floor with drama again.

Myra returned it. "I hope you freeze your nuts off in a gulag."

"Remember," said the Eye, mostly erect, his helium timbre mostly restored, "you'll pay."

"Boy, we sure do get thrown out of a lot of places now," said Edison, once they were in the hallway. He felt good. He was getting better at hitting people than he'd ever imagined he could, and at such an advanced stage of his life.

"You did alright," said Myra, putting her hand in his as they descended the stairs. "I don't like that we were recognized, though."

When they got to the third floor landing, they interrupted Andrew and Goochy standing in the shadows, finishing up an argument. Goochy looked over with his embarrassed smile.

"You guys were a big help," said Myra.

"You didn't exactly need any," said Andrew.

Goochy brushed back a shock of greasy hair. "Do you mind if we step outside?"

"You can go anywhere you want," said Myra. "We're leaving."

They followed Edison and Myra down the stairs and out to the sidewalk. The sun was brilliant and hot, the sidewalk crowded. Goochy asked if they wouldn't mind listening to what he had to say for just a minute.

Myra agreed reluctantly, folding her arms across her chest. The sunlight made Edison drowsy.

"If you're interested," said Goochy, "be at Acropolis Pictures in Culver City tomorrow at four."

"You made an appointment for us already?" said Myra, dropping her arms to her sides.

"Isn't that what you wanted?" said Goochy. "Look, I don't care what your politics are, but this is a good opportunity."

She paused, her eyes roaming back and forth between Andrew and Goochy. "What did you say the name was?"

"Acropolis Pictures. You'll be meeting with a Mr. Reginald K. Barthkowitz, studio head. It's a small studio. Poverty Row."

"I've never heard of them before, have you?" she said to Edison.

"I don't know." He yawned.

"It's a fairly new place," said Andrew. "Only been around a few years, and it won't be around many more unless Barthkowitz can get a hit. His daddy struck it rich sucking oil out of the Baldwin Hills in the twenties, so he's got money to play with, but it won't last forever. Rumor has it that Daddy went off his rocker a few years ago, senile or something, and the boy started dumping the fortune into his own studio. Like Goochy said, it's a good opportunity. Barthkowitz is no kid, though, and not always a very nice guy. Watch out for him."

"Honestly, it's the only place I could get you into," Goochy said, with no apology in his voice. "But Barthkowitz is on the lookout for talent and he's willing to pay for something different. Edison, I believe you have something different, even if it does have a dumb title."

"It's not dumb."

"Don't worry, titles get changed all the time."

"Did you like it?" said Myra.

"The parts that I read," said Goochy. "Andrew's recommendation was enough for me. For some reason, he likes you, Edison. I passed it on to Barry, Barthkowitz's personal secretary. He's a friend. You'll be meeting with Barthkowitz alone. He doesn't like agents in on the first meeting. If he wants to produce it, my fee is fifteen percent."

"Ten percent," said Myra, blurting it out without thinking.

Goochy laughed. "Man, you are some lady. I'll go with lucky thirteen. Anything less and you're looking for another agent."

Myra nodded her acceptance. "As I always tell my students, 'If you understand nothing else, understand percentages.' The world is rigged on them."

"How true," said Goochy. "So, you're a teacher?"

"I'm between gigs."

"Gigs." He smiled.

Lying in bed that night:

"I shouldn't have hit Corkavonin."

"Ordinarily, I'd agree with you. But he deserved it."

"I'm surprised you feel that way."

"Me, too."

Then:

"Do you still think about the Time Flies?"

"Yes."

"They must be around somewhere. Aren't they supposed to be guiding us?"

"I don't feel very guided."

The Phony War

When Edison woke in the morning, Myra was gone. He got up to pee and found the bathroom sink splattered with a smelly black liquid that was drying into black stains. He rubbed his fingertips in the liquid then tried rinsing it off, with only partial success. He tasted it and spit into the toilet. Myra came home just then and he went out to question her. She marched past him to the kitchen sink, squirted something caustic smelling into her palm and started scrubbing her hands brutally with a potato brush, her face twisted in hopeless frustration.

"It won't come off," she said. She held up her hands, but Edison didn't see them because he was staring at her head. He had never seen hair so black. Her head was like a hole in space.

"Whoa. I slept through this?"

"Shutup," she said, scrubbing harder. "It wasn't supposed to be this dark. Now I *do* look like a witch."

"I like it. But why today? We have an important meeting."

"No kidding." She rubbed her hands vigorously and threw the towel at the wall, spooking a cockroach. Chips of paint fluttered to the floor. She clawed the air in front of her. "What am I supposed to do? Look at them."

Edison stared dumbly at her black hands.

"For once, Edison, can you help me with something? Please?"

This struck him as a little unfair given that he had practically saved her life the day before by punching a maniacal Communist in the belly, but he sympathized with her predicament. "I'll be right back," he said and left the apartment. He returned twenty minutes later with a pair of white cotton gloves. "Just until it wears off on its own," he said. "Lots of ladies wear them."

Myra held the gloves in her stained hands. She put them on and looked at herself in the bathroom mirror. Her hair was completely straight and darker than death. "Well, if I didn't look like an alien before, I do now."

They had too much of a day to kill before their meeting at Acropolis and they spent it pacing the apartment, twitchy and peevish. Myra obsessed over her poorly timed decision, alternately avoiding the bathroom mirror and then staring into it. She felt as if she had stolen a part of her own identity. Edison pointed out that she could always change it again. "It's only hair."

"That easy for you to say," she said, nodding at his bald spot.

She apologized for that one, but not convincingly enough, and Edison disappeared to calm his nerves with a few spins on Angels Flight.

At three-thirty they stood across the street from a dingy, municipal-colored building with a plywood sign on the roof painted blue with *Acropolis Pictures* in gold lettering. Fake Doric columns that supported nothing framed the glass door. There was a woman inside, typing at a desk. Edison wore Burt's suit. Myra had on slacks.

"*The Dime was Tossed,*" said Edison.

"Huh?"

"Acropolis made that. I think it's the only movie we've seen by them."

"I don't remember it."

They stood, waiting for four o'clock to arrive. They didn't want to seem overly eager. A convertible filled with laughing teenagers drove by, invincible and loud. Two of them looked at Myra and she hid her gloved hands behind her back, convinced they were mocking her. She thought about how they would all be dead, or about to cross the finish line, when she got back home at the end of her prison sentence. As they disappeared down the road, she thought of her own daughters and how they laughed and wondered if any of them were laughing now. At three thirty-six, they began circling the block, pausing after each loop to look at the door. At three fifty-three they went in.

The lobby was low ceilinged and musty. The right wall featured a candy-colored mural of grass and sea, and columned buildings made to look like something from ancient Greece. It reminded Myra of a restaurant. In a corner on the left stood a wood and glass phone booth with a working phone inside and a man talking on it, his anger muffled by the closed door.

The typing receptionist sat at a medium-sized wood desk with a tired look about her and a cigarette burning in her ashtray. Her blondish hair—curled in places, pulled straight and pinned in others—framed a pretty face, with lazy, bottom heavy eyes and lashes long enough to round corners ahead of her. Her desk plate said that her name was Myra.

"Your name is Myra?" said Myra.

"Yes," said Myra the Receptionist. "Nice of you to come in this time around."

"My name is Myra Mix and this is my husband, Edison Winslow."

"We have IDs," said Edison.

"We've been expecting you," said Myra the Receptionist, rising to escort them to a door that opened in the mural right where a door was painted on a Greek building. She had on a royal blue crepe day dress that she wore like an octopus wrapped around Venus, exposing thin rounded scapulas beneath skin like watery milk. She seemed to eye Myra's slacks with just a touch of jealousy, and her black hair and white gloves with amusement. "This way, please. Have a seat and Barry will be with you momentarily."

She closed the door behind them as they took their seats. Barry was rummaging in a file cabinet, which he continued to do as if they weren't there. He also had a medium-sized wood desk and a cigarette burning in an ashtray.

"Hello," said Myra. "Thank you for reading our script."

Barry didn't look at them, but said in a dry voice, "Take off your hat, please." Edison removed his hat and was glad to have something to occupy his hands. Barry continued to ignore them, his back emitting the condescending sophistication of an emotionless drone that viewed excessive civility as a weakness. He sighed heavily, as if taxed beyond reason, then turned and pressed a button on his squawk box and said, "The new ones are here," didn't wait for a response, then said, "Go in," still without looking at them.

"Thank you, Barry," said Myra.

They passed through another door with a brass plate on it that read, *Reginald K. Barthkowitz, Studio Chief.* The dark cherry paneling of the office was interrupted by photographs of minor movie stars and a few that would eventually become memorable, as well as some African tribal masks, a pair of medieval looking swords mounted in an X, and what might have been an original Picasso from his Blue Period. A shelf on one wall had some books on it that looked unread, with forgettable knick-knacks in the spaces between. Behind a papa-sized desk was a wall of windows that looked onto a small private patio with some unambitious plants around the edges. The patio door was open and Barthkowitz was standing just outside in the sun, a phone cord stretched between his desk and his ear. He waved them to a worn green leather sofa in front of the desk.

"I'll be just a second," he said, covering the phone. He was a large man in the wrong direction, made larger by his pale peach suit. He was listening to his sister, Bertha, a jabbering hypochondriac who was always convinced she needed surgery or a wheelchair or limb removal or something. Barthkowitz had little patience with it.

"Listen, sis. Just listen," he said into the phone, "maybe I could mail you a knife and you could cut it out yourself and save on the doctor bills. I could airmail it to you so you get it out before it rots. I'll send you a Western Union with instructions on how to do it … No, I'm not kidding … I'm not being mean, either, Sis. I'm just trying to tell you that there's nothing wrong with you. Nobody could have that many things wrong with them and live to talk about it so much … No, I don't wish you were dead. I'm sorry, okay? Don't cry, Sis. I'm just saying that I think a lot of these things are a result of your overactive imagination. It's your Barthkowitz imagination. You're a genius, like me, but your brain is leading you astray. You're healthier than Charles Atlas … Maybe it's all that raw broccoli you eat.

That stuff gives you gas." He shrugged helplessly at Edison and Myra. His tanned scalp glistened in the sunlight. "I know it's good for you. I'm just saying. Maybe you got a bubble…Okay, I'll have Barry check on it for you…Alright, I gotta go, Sis. I'm in a meeting…Alright. Say 'hi' to Ma for me."

He set the phone on his desk. He puffed on his cigar as he looked them over, his deep-set eyes, garnished with dark circles, lingering on Myra. He pulled the cigar out. His mouth was shaped like an angry M that opened and closed on vituperative hinges. "What's with the pants?"

"They're comfortable," said Myra.

He grunted and shoved the cigar back in. Barthkowitz did his best to project the image of a tough-minded studio chief played, perhaps, by Edward G. Robinson in a movie about a tough-minded studio chief with a heart of gold. Except that if Barthkowitz had a heart of gold he would have cashed it in long ago and had no trouble with the vacancy. He suffered from a jowly face that jiggled whether he was talking or not. The peach pants were yanked up to his nipples by acid-blue suspenders. He rolled himself into his leather swivel chair and looked at some papers on his desk.

"You two are married, right?"

"For years," said Myra.

He blew out a noxious cloud. "Then what's with the two different last names?"

"We had four different parents."

That broke him up. "Four different parents. I like that. We can use that kind of stuff around here." The laughter disappeared. "You're not Commies, are you?" His eyes volleyed back and forth between them, looking for signs.

"Commies?" said Edison.

"The last writer I got from that Goochy guy turned out to be a Commie. Corkybonin, or something like that. He wanted me to produce a screenplay on the life of Stalin."

Myra smiled. "No, we're not Communists."

The volley ended on Myra. He puffed. "Alright then." He puffed a little more, assessing Myra's hair. "You seem a little old to be trying to break into the business."

"We bring life experience."

"I see." He took the cigar from his mouth and stared at them for a while to make them uncomfortable. It worked on Edison, who clamped his hands between his knees and looked over the knick-knacks and tribal masks. Myra made him wary. Not nervous—Barthkowitz didn't get nervous—just wary. He took a deep breath and let it out slowly. "We are hopeful that the war in Europe will be good for the domestic movie business; at least that's what some people are saying, including me. And Barry. The military buildup is bringing a lot more factory workers to town. Thousands of them. Well, hundreds for now, but there will be thousands. I'm sure you've noticed. Factory workers buy lots of movie tickets. More theaters are in the works and ticket prices will be raised to make up for the potential loss in foreign markets if the war spreads. Acropolis Pictures wants to be a part of that, if we can get around the major studios." He pointed to a blank spot on the wall. "It's all about that."

Myra and Edison looked at the blank spot. "All about what?" said Myra.

Barthkowitz grumbled and punched a button on his squawk box. "Barry, come in here."

The door opened instantly and Barry stood there blank-faced.

"The sign," said Barthkowitz.

Barry walked over to a chair that was under the blank spot, slid it out, reached behind it, and pulled out a small sign. He placed it against the wall, punched it to make it stick, and left the room. The sign said: *Asses in Seats!*

"All about that," Barthkowitz said, answering Myra's question. "Without that, we have nothing. And I don't like nothing." He pounded his desk to show how much he hated nothing and the sign fell off the wall, disappearing behind the chair again. "You get the picture."

Edison nodded like it was the smartest thing he'd ever heard. Myra cleared her throat. "Just curious, Mr. Barthkowitz, but how do you see the current buildup of antitrust legislation affecting your studio's operations?"

Barthkowitz put his cigar back in his mouth and leaned back in his chair. A spring squeaked faintly. "I can see you read the papers."

"Don't you think writers should read? It seems to me it would be helpful."

"To who?" He didn't expect an answer so he went on. "The suit has no effect on Acropolis Pictures. We're independent."

Myra decided not to push it. "I see."

Barthkowitz took the cigar out again and waved it around a little. "So, what kind of 'life experience' did you want to talk about?"

Myra flicked her eyes at Edison and back to Barthkowitz. "Uh, did you have a chance to look at the screenplay?"

"I skimmed it. Needs work."

"Alright. That's fine. Where?"

"Pretty much all over."

Edison cleared his throat and asked carefully, "Did you read it?"

Barthkowitz punched the squawk box again. "Barry, did you read that screenplay? The one with the dumb title?"

"Yes. it needs work," Barry said.

"Thank you, Barry." He let go of the button. "You see?"

"I see," said Myra. She held her irritation in check. "Well, maybe if you could help us out. Give us an idea of what it needs."

Barthkowitz cocked his head thoughtfully. "Let's see, how did Barry put it? Oh, yeah. He said, 'I was driving a truck around through some of the plot holes and I ran out of gas.'" He grinned.

"Then why did you agree to see us?"

"Barry likes the dialogue. I believe he used the word 'crackling.'" He put his cigar back where it belonged and puffed for a few seconds in silence. "Tell you what. Maybe if you tell me what it's supposed to be about, we can go from there."

"You don't know what it's about?" said Edison.

"I'm not clear on everything," said Barthkowitz. He leaned back and put his feet on the desk. His shoes were oxblood and cream. He folded his hands across his belly. "Pitch it to me."

"Well … " said Myra.

"Not you," said Barthkowitz. "Him. And stand up."

Edison began to shake a little, a vibration similar to the flicker of a faulty fluorescent tube. He looked at Myra and she raised her eyebrows, helpless. He looked at Barthkowitz who raised his eyebrows, expectant. They waited. Edison unfolded from the couch. He stood like he had an armoire on his back. Myra gently 'ahem'ed him to keep his hands out in the open, but it didn't work. Into his pants they went.

"What are you doing?" said Barthkowitz.

"Nothing," said Edison.

"Well, knock it off. You look like a chicken."

Edison took his hands out of his pants and stood dumbly. He felt as if there was a spotlight on him, the heat and the brightness of it blinding him, and he began to pace to get away from it, but it kept following him around the room. He grabbed the sides of his pants to keep his hands from seeking refuge again as his chest rose and fell. *They're watching. They're watching. They're waiting.* He began to retreat inside himself, to let the room fade away. He imagined himself descending a long ladder that disappeared into darkness below him. The darkness was safety. Down he went until he could no longer feel the room, or Barthkowitz, or even Myra.

"What the hell's he doing now?" said Barthkowitz. "I don't have all day."

"Just wait," said Myra. "Edison?"

And there in the darkness Edison found something. He couldn't quite tell what it was, but it interested him so he grabbed hold of it and began to climb the ladder back up into the light, where he discovered it—an Edison that was vaguely familiar to him. A rambling, confident, wisecracking Edison. An Edison who didn't want to escape or put his hands down his pants. An Edison who knew a little about what the hell was going on and wanted to show off. He recognized this Edison as the one who took over the keys when he was typing, the one who helped him focus and made him feel worthy. He patted this Edison on the back, wished him luck, and pushed him into the spotlight.

"Okay … okay," he said, still pacing, trying to get the engine going. Cough. Sputter. He felt it catch. Then he stepped on the gas. "Okay. So, we open with a guy, innocent, starts out nice. Unwrinkled suit, tie, top button done, shiny shoes, brushed hat, the whole package. Follow me? His name's

Harry. Everything's great, then he loses his job. Bad time for Harry. Everything crumbles. His wife leaves him for a guy with a job. Suddenly he's got nothing. He pounds the pavement, hands in pockets, hat tilted back, chain smoking. Not hopeless, just worried and sad, but with a good outlook on the world. Someone's bound to give him a break."

The engine was running full out now. Edison felt energized, electric. He found uses for his hands in the outside world, gesticulating with them for emphasis. An intensity came into his eyes and the words raced out of his mouth like a preacher who used to be a criminal, or vice versa. Myra was slack-jawed with the memory of her twenty-first century man. This was the man she knew. Edison continued. "Then one night, some punks jump Harry down by the docks. They crack him on the head with a board and he goes down. But he's got nothing and that makes them mad so they beat him up some more. Bad time for Harry. When he comes to, it's morning. He can't remember a thing. There's this dame standing over him and she tries to help him. She's beautiful, the kind of dame that makes men floss their teeth on the off chance that she might drive by and wave sometime. He remembers that his name is Harry, but nothing else. Not who he is or where he's from or how he got hurt. A complete loss of memory."

"Amnesia?" said Barthkowitz.

"That's the word," said Edison. "So, the dame tells him her name—Chloe. She takes him home, fixes up his wounds, gives him some food and coffee and cigarettes, a little booze. She falls for him and he falls for her, believing that the love of woman will be his salvation. But Chloe's bad, real bad. He's hooked up with the wrong woman, but he doesn't know it yet. She's working for some hoods. She doesn't like it, wants to go straight, but doesn't know how. It's all she knows. Tough kid. Knocked about—and up—a few times. Miscarriages, the whole bit. She likes Harry, but she's got a job to do, which is finding suckers to do dirty work for her bosses, so she hooks Harry up with the business of delivering strange packages. She tells him it's on the up and up and that he's just doing her a favor, but it's a lie."

Barthkowitz interrupted. "What's in the packages?"

"I don't know. It's not important."

"What do you mean you don't know? You wrote it, didn't you?"

"Okay. Then drugs."

"Drugs? I don't know if I like that."

"Okay, then jewelry or dirty money. Gambling money."

"I like that better. Change it."

"Okay, okay. So, at first it's all innocent from Harry's perspective. He loves her, wants to make her happy. He makes the deliveries, takes the dame out for drinks and dancing. She thinks he's cute. Yeah, he's kind of a dunce, maybe, but he's nice to her. Chloe doesn't see the other side of Harry, the things he's capable of. But it's okay for now. Then things start to go wrong. The people Harry's delivering these packages to start showing up dead after the deliveries. Chloe's bosses are thinking maybe it's Harry doing the killing, but it's not, because then bodies start showing up dead *before* the deliveries. Except the bosses *still* think Harry's doing it and keeping the packages for himself. One of the bosses has his doubts, though, and lets Harry continue the job while his gunzels tail him."

Barthkowitz put up his hand. "Stop. Who's killing them?"

"Are you sure Barry read this?"

"Fine. Keep going."

"Okay. Then Harry starts getting a brain and figures out he's been duped and that Chloe isn't the choir girl she was pretending to be. Harry's brain *keeps* growing and he starts to figure out exactly what the business is that he's been in all this time, and that one of the gang is doing the killing and trying to pin it on him. He gets bitter. Not about the gambling money—he doesn't mind that—but because they lied to him, and now they're trying to pin murders on him. The bitterness grows. He toughens up, but still hangs out with Chloe because he can't help himself and neither can she, but it's different now because he's bitter. He decides he's going to stop these guys, take the law into his own hands. It's like Charles Bronson meets Clint Eastwood meets film noir."

Barthkowitz twisted his mouth. "Wait! What? Who?"

"Huh?"

"Who the hell is this Chuck Clintwood meets film hour?"

"Uh…"

Myra tossed a rescue rope. "Ancient mythological characters known for their cunning and bravery." Nice.

Barthkowitz threw his cigar on his desk. "Quit with the bullshit will ya? Just tell the story like a normal writer. I got to know what the hell you're talking about."

"Okay. Sorry. So, where was I? Oh, yeah. So, one by one, gangster bodies start piling up—at home, in alleys, in a bar. Harry gets meaner and meaner. The world done him wrong. But he feels justified because he's cleaning up the streets, getting rid of the scum, making the city a better place for the kind of citizen he used to be. An avenger. Mystery Man. The lone wolf. It's too late for Harry to love. His trust is gone. He believes the world is a bad place, too bad for him to hang around in, but maybe, just maybe, he can make a difference from the shadows."

Edison stopped and gave Barthkowitz a 'that's it' look. Everything slowed down. Barthkowitz picked up his cigar and looked at it so he wouldn't have to look at Edison. He didn't like looking at writers that much. He flicked ashes on the script.

"That's what this is about?" he said. Edison nodded. "I wasn't getting that from the script."

"You weren't?"

"Barry wasn't. That's not what he told me it was about."

"What did he tell you?"

"Different stuff."

"He's like an avenger," said Edison.

"Yeah, yeah, I got that."

"It leaves the door open for sequels," said Myra, rubbing her gloves together.

Barthkowitz gave her an eyebrow raise and a finger point. "I like that." He looked back at Edison. "How come it's not written that way?"

"Well, it's all wrapped up in metaphor and innuendo and—"

"Yeah, well unwrap it. This is a motion picture studio, not a gift shop. Have it stripped down and in my hands by Friday."

Edison's mouth fell open. "You mean rewrite it? By Friday?"

"No. Just unwrap it." Barthkowitz jammed his cigar into his mouth and pretended to shuffle papers, indicating it was time for them to leave. "Oh, and make that Harry guy rich. People like stories about the rich."

Edison paused. "That sort of makes the story implausible."

Barthkowitz narrowed his eyes. Edison adjusted.

"But I can certainly put some rich people in it. As other characters, maybe. The crime bosses are rich."

"Use your best judgment," said Barthkowitz, meaning that Edison should use *his* best judgment. Barthkowitz opened a drawer in his desk and pulled out a small decanter of Scotch and a glass. He had one drink per day, no more, ever. He liked the lift he got from one, but hated being drunk. It wasn't nearly as much fun as it appeared to be from the outside and it ruined the next day. Not a wise investment of his time. And he was loath to share his hooch, especially with writers.

"Excuse me."

Edison could barely keep his eyes open on the streetcar.

"Boy, that was something," said Myra. "What got into you?"

He slurred something like, "I don't know," and when they got back to the apartment he plopped onto the bed and was instantly asleep. Myra stood over him, watching him, this strange man who was now her husband. He slept for the rest of the day and through the night.

Does the Brain Ever Get Full?

Edison woke before sunrise more refreshed and less confused than he could remember feeling since the future. He leaped out of bed, splashed water on his face and went out for an early morning stroll through downtown to get inspired by the all-nighters and the early risers staggering along the sidewalks. He even skipped his morning ride on Angels Flight. He cruised through his shift at Minty's automatically, churning out breakfasts and listening to Blenda bray—"Hah!"—even joining her on a few.

He returned to the apartment in the afternoon, elated and ready to write, and was surprised to find Myra sitting in his writing chair on the porch, her face drawn and distraught. Her gloves were on the table beside the Royal and he could see that the dye on her hands was already fading. The sheet of paper in the typewriter had typing on it that wasn't his.

```
JFK assassination - November 2 , 1963
```

"I'm just guessing," said Edison, "but I think it's later in the month than the 2nd."

"Of course it is. But I can't remember which day. The 23rd? The 26th? Which is it?" There were tears hiding just around the corners of her eyes. "I think I'm starting to forget what's going to happen."

"What do you mean?"

"Remember when I forgot what day Germany invaded Poland?"

"Uh-huh."

"Well, it happened again at the Communist Party meeting. I overheard that Corkavonin idiot say that the reason Stalin signed the Non-Aggression Pact with Hitler was to give himself time to build his army, and I couldn't remember whether it was true or not. It sounded familiar, but I wasn't sure. I think that's one of the reasons I went so ballistic on him. He was saying things I should have known, but I couldn't be sure and it made me frightened. It's like I forgot."

"I'm familiar with that."

"Well, I'm not. At least not with these kinds of things." She got up from the chair and leaned against the railing. "What's it going to be like when we get back? How much will I have forgotten by then? We're only a year into this thing. I have to go back to class when we return."

"But you'll know it better because we're living through it."

She shook her head. "Only until 1963. I'm worried about forgetting things that happened in the 70s, the 80s, 2005. Will we remember when 9/11 was?"

"Isn't it September eleventh?"

"Funny. The year?"

"Uh … two thousand … thhhhrreee? Two?"

She gave him a pitiful look. "Two thousand-one, honey."

"Well, we'll be able to look it up on the Internet then."

She glared at him. "You really are missing the point. I'm serious. Twenty-five years is a long time. We're going to be very different people when we get back."

"I'm okay with that, as long as we don't change history."

"Right now I'm more concerned with remembering it," she said. "Ask me something about the future. Anything between now and 2015."

Edison didn't really want to do this, but could see he wasn't going to get out of it, so he asked her when the Beatles were first going to appear on *The Ed Sullivan Show*.

Myra pursed her lips. "Um … '63? No, '64. I don't know." She furrowed her brow. "No, wait. It's 1964, because I remember thinking of that a few months ago and realizing we wouldn't get to see it because we go back in '63. Right?"

"I don't know," he said. "I'm just asking. You're the history teacher. I know movies."

"You're no help. Ask me something else."

Edison thought hard. He wanted to give her a tough one so they could be done with it. He needed to get to work on the script. "Okay, when do the Nazi's violate the Non-Aggression Pact and attack Russia?"

Edison could see the blood leave Myra's face as clearly as if it had run away screaming for its life. Her mind had gone completely blank. She covered her mouth with her hands.

"I have no idea," she said. "I know that it's sometime in the next year or two. Operation Barbarossa, right?" Edison shrugged. She started pacing around the porch. She kicked a pencil that had failed to roll off earlier and sent it over the edge. "Shit. This is terrible. Is it before or after Pearl Harbor?" She sat in Edison's writing chair, her fingers clenched in her hair. She was silent for a long while. Edison appraised the way her dyed fingers blended with her hair. Finally, she stood and announced, "I'll be back," and left the apartment.

When she returned a half hour later, she was carrying a bag containing three thick black cloth-covered journals and a fistful of pens. "I'll be in the bathroom," she said, closing the door behind her.

Myra didn't come out of the bathroom until after dark, by which time Edison had grown desperate for its use.

"How did it go?" he called from the toilet.

"I'm hungry."

She had filled twenty-two pages of one journal, pouring her fading memories onto paper and arranging them with ink before they could be deleted, or hopelessly hidden in the molding, non-aging portions of her mind. She would have done more but she ran out of steam. Her brain had turned out the light. Tomorrow would be better.

Her first few hours in the bathroom had been spent devising a code to log the events that had not yet happened so that only she could read them. She feared, correctly, that if the journals were to fall into the wrong hands it could make for a sticky situation. She rejected one inadequate coding system after another, tearing out the rejected attempts and shredding them into tiny fragments before depositing them in the wastebasket, feeling a twinge of guilt at her inability to recycle them. It was just before sunset when she struck upon a workable method.

She logged everything she could think of in whatever order things popped into her head. She did not even attempt a proper chronology of events by date, as she was sure that as time went on various facts would occur to her randomly. Keeping the events in chronological order on paper, without the word processing capabilities of a computer, would be impossible.

Her first entry:

25/12/2? – JFK assn DealyDall – CnlyGov ! woond – Ozwld ! rooB

The translation:

> In 1963, November 2?, President John F Kennedy was as-
> sassinated at Dealey Plaza in Dallas, Texas. John Connolly,
> governor of Texas, was wounded. Responsibility for the shoot-
> ing—Lee Harvey Oswald, who was in turn shot by Jack Ruby.

The intentional misspelling of words was obvious. Myra knew what they meant. In order to protect the identity of the actual dates of events, she coded them, instead, to how they related to the passage of their sentence. The first number represented the year. So, since the assassination would happen in 1963, the twenty-fifth year of their sentence, the first number was thus—twenty-five.

It was not a perfect system, and professionals in the field of cryptography would undoubtedly snigger at it, but it worked for Myra and that was all that mattered. It was supposed to be confusing to others. She tried explaining the code to Edison but his brain refused to have anything to do with it. She considered that a victory of sorts.

Many of the entries were little more than these kinds of dates and abbreviated facts, but Myra's tendency to spout off turned some of them into long and detailed accounts that could go on for pages, all in code.

Those events that struck her passionately, such as the Selma to Montgomery Civil Rights Marches in 1965, were prone to receiving such treatment.

While Myra worked on her journals, Edison worked on the rewrite of *Struggle of the Mind*. Myra still held an official protest against the dumb title, but let Edison have his way for now. He was on a roll and she didn't want to mess that up. He had only three days to complete it, including two shifts at Minty's.

In the morning, she gave Edison first crack at the bathroom, which she now started referring to as her 'thinking room', then grabbed her journal and a pen and set up for the day, perched on the closed lid of the toilet. "You'd better get busy," she said as she closed the door. "You have a lot of people to kill."

Edison could hear the floorboards creak beneath her socks as she moved around. He grew envious when he heard the toilet flush. He wrote feverishly, watching the strips of shadow from the railing move across the porch floor as the day progressed, pausing only occasionally to wave at the Three Bills for inspiration. He unwrapped the script as Barthkowitz had told him to, trimmed its beards of metaphor and innuendo, and punched up the dialogue exchanges to please Barry. He did not make the characters wealthy, but did make them more depraved, which he figured was what Barthkowitz was actually going for anyway.

On Thursday evening, just after midnight, Edison handed the screenplay to Goochy at Le Speciale. Myra had stayed home to work on her journals.

"Stay for a drink," said Andrew, holding up an empty cocktail glass that looked anxious to be filled and emptied again.

It was tempting, but Edison was tapped out. He had written himself into a stupor and was back to being confused and exhausted again. He politely declined.

Goochy knocked on their door at two on Friday afternoon. Myra was in the bathroom. Edison was napping in his chair. He climbed through the window to answer the door, wisps of hair standing on end like smoke from a genie's bottle.

Goochy was wearing a turquoise suit with grubby elbows and was breathing heavily from his hike up the hill, his pomaded hair hanging in damp tassels along his forehead. "Don't you have a phone?"

"I think there's one in the lobby."

Goochy took a cocktail napkin and a pen from his pocket, wrote down a phone number and handed the napkin to Edison.

"This is mine, just in case," he said. "I have a new office. They kicked me out of the other one after the other day."

"How do you like it?" called Myra from the bathroom.

"Fine. No Communists," he shouted back.

"Oh, that's good."

"Be at Acropolis at four o'clock this afternoon," he said to Edison.

"Are you going to be there?" shouted Myra.

"No," shouted Goochy.

"Are you ever going to be there?"

"Probably not at the same time you are." He smiled at Edison. "Barthkowitz works in strange ways. But you will be paid if he likes the work."

Myra opened the bathroom door.

"Why did you agree to represent us, Goochy?" she said. "We're nobodies. And we're old."

Goochy laughed. "You try being a broke pansy agent in Hollywood and see what your choices are. It's liberal here, but only so far."

"You're a pansy?" said Edison sleepily.

"I thought you knew," said Goochy. "Besides, you seem like nice people."

"Okay."

Goochy gave him a once over. "You sure do say 'okay' a lot."

Tom Winslow Returns

"Go in," said Barry. They did.

Barthkowitz was sitting at his desk, cigar in mouth. He didn't look at them or acknowledge them in any way. The screenplay was in his hands and Myra noted that he actually seemed to be reading it. Judging by the few pages clutched between his fingers, he was almost finished with it. This was what he read:

INT. ROCKY'S OFFICE - NIGHT

Harry stands off to the side, his coat on, his hat on top
of the file cabinet. He lights a cigarette and blows the
smoke Chloe's way. He smiles, staring her down. Chloe is
curled in a chair on the other side of the room, nervous,
dreading the next moment.

                    CHLOE
          What? What is it, Harry?

                    HARRY
        What is it? I'll tell ya. You
        like me, but not all the way.
        You're attracted to me. I make
        you feel special. You like the
        way I carry myself, the way I
        say things sometimes. But there
        are things about me you don't
        like and you want to change them.
        Ain't that right?

                    CHLOE
        No!

                    HARRY
        Sure it is. You think you can
        change the things you don't like
        without hurting the things you
        do like...

                    CHLOE (overlapping)
        No!

                    HARRY
        ...but it don't work that way.
        You start trying to change the
        things you don't like and the
        other things start falling apart
        on you.

Chloe buries her face in her hands. Harry leans against
the file cabinet and smokes for a moment.

                    HARRY
                 (offhandedly)
          But you can't help yourself. It's
          in your nature.

Chloe springs from her chair.

                    CHLOE
          You're a liar! It's not true!

Harry raises an eyebrow at her. Chloe freezes up, nervous.

                    CHLOE
          I'm sorry, Harry. I'm sorry. I
          didn't mean to call you a liar.
          It's just not true, what you said.

                    HARRY
          Oh, it's true. You know it and I
          know it. You just think you can
          keep me from finding out that I
          know you know it.

                    CHLOE
          What are you talking about? You're
          not making any sense.

                    HARRY
          I'm making plenty of sense, doll.
          But I'm not gonna let you do it. I
          don't need some dame trying to change
          me. I can handle myself. I got my
          own way of doing things and they have
          to be done my way.

                    CHLOE
          I'm not trying to change you, Harry.
          Honest I'm not.

                    HARRY
                 (chuckling)
          You thought you had me good, didn't
          you?

                    CHLOE
        No I didn't, Harry. I want to
        be with you for who you are. For
        what you do. For living life on
        the edge. It's the danger I crave,
        Harry.
                    (she sits and puts
                    her hand to her head)
        But it scares me. It just scares
        me. I don't want you to get hurt.
        I don't know what I'd do if you
        got hurt.

Harry sizes her up for a moment with smirky confidence.
He shakes his head, grabs his hat and opens the door.

                    HARRY
        I can't let you do it to me, doll.
        That's in my nature.

He puts his hat on.

                    HARRY
        So long, Chloe.

Harry walks out the door and down the hallway. Chloe springs
from her chair and runs to the door, calling after him.

                    CHLOE
        Harry! Harry! Come back! Harry, please!
        I'll be good. I won't try to change you.
        I promise! Harry! Come back!

Harry disappears around the corner at the end of the hall.
Chloe flings herself back into the room, collapsing in
the chair in a heap of tears.

FADE OUT

Barthokowitz nodded at the page. "Not bad. Not bad." He puffed on his cigar and slapped the script on his desk, freeing himself up for exaggerated hand gesturing. "This is exactly the kind of stuff we're looking for. Exactly. Stripped down. Easy to watch. The kind of thing you can go to the toilet in the middle of and not miss anything."

Myra's eyes widened. Edison tried not to look hurt.

"Don't misunderstand. It's got a very powerful ending. Very powerful. Really tugs at your heart, you know? Is Harry a bastard? Is Chloe just some lost tramp? Who knows? Hey, who cares, right? Of course, you'll have to have them get arrested or shot in the end to please the censors, and you'll need to throw in a couple of cops on the take, but those are easy fixes." He waved his cigar dismissively before continuing. "And the set design. Simple. Chair, file cabinet, door. Low budget stuff. I like it. We can do that."

"If you light it so that parts of the frame are black, you can save even more," said Myra. She looked at Edison. "Right?"

Edison nodded. "It's called chiaroscuro."

Barthkowitz nodded faster. "Great idea! You're just full of them, aren't you? And that stuff about nature. Fantastic. Gives it a psychological thing, a ..., a ...."

"A struggle of the mind?" offered Edison. Myra rolled her eyes. Barthkowitz lit up.

"Yeah, yeah. *Struggle of the Mind.* Maybe that's not such a bad title after all."

"Well, thank you, Mr. Barthkowitz," said Myra, "but that's not actually the title."

"It is now," said Barthkowitz. "I'll pay $300 a week for the pair of you, not each." He raised his eyebrows and froze, reducing the room to ambient noise.

Edison looked at Myra anxiously. Myra kept her eyes on Barthkowitz. Barthkowitz won. He smiled and reached for the squawk box.

"Barry, bring me a contract for our two newest writers."

"For how long?"

Barthkowitz puffed a moment. "Let's start them out at six months."

Barry appeared in seconds, placed a small stack of papers on Barthkowitz's desk, and left again, mumbling "congratulations" in the general direction of Edison and Myra.

Barthkowitz extended a pen to Edison. "Barry is very happy for you," he said.

Edison signed first. "So, where do we write? Do we get a bungalow?"

"Ha!" popped Barthkowitz. He hit the squawk box again. "Hey, Barry. They want to know where their bungalow is."

"What bungalow?"

"Thank you, Barry." Barthkowitz leaned back in his chair, narrowing his eyes at Edison. "So, what did you say your name was again?"

"Edison Winslow."

Barthkowitz tossed his cigar down on his desk, launching a small constellation of sparks. "Are you shitting me? What kind of name is that?"

Edison blushed. "It's a perfect screenwriter's name."

"Maybe over at Paramount, but it ain't going to work here. Too hauty-tauty."

"Hauty-tauty?"

"Yeah, you know—fruity. How can you write gangster pictures with a name like that?"

"I think it's a good name."

"Yeah, well you're not paying yourself."

Edison thought for a moment while Barthkowitz blew the ashes off his desk. "How about Ed? Ed Winslow."

Barthkowitz shook his head. "Nah, now you're pumping gas. Too far in the other direction. Let me think. Edison. Edison. Sheesh! Okay, Edison. Like the light bulb guy, right? What's his name? Frank?"

"Thomas Alva Edison," said Myra, "inventor of the movie projector."

"Yeah, yeah. Thomas Alva Edison," said Barthkowitz. "Well, the Alva part is right out. Forget about it. We'll be doing Busby Berkely knock-offs before you know it. That leaves us with Thomas. Tom. Yeah! Tom Winslow. Perfect. How do you like it?"

Edison crumbled. "Tom Winslow?"

"Hey, Tom," said Myra.

"Shutup. Really?"

Barthkowitz smiled. "You will write under the name of Tom Winslow."

Edison steeled himself. "No. I want to be Edison."

Barthkowitz cocked his head to make his disapproval of the protest obvious. "We'll talk about this later." He turned to Myra. "Now … Mrs. Winslow. What's your first name again?"

"The first name is Myra," she said. "Last name Mix. Remember? Two different last names. Four different parents."

"Oh, yeah. Myra Mix. Like that cowboy in those silent westerns. He's a big deal. Hey, his name was Tom, too."

"Imagine that," said Edison.

"Any relation?" Barthkowitz asked Myra.

"None. Is that his real name?"

"No idea. We'll keep it just as it is. Myra Mix. Yessir, you'll go places," he said pointing at her. "Why ain't you smart like her?" he said to Edison.

Edison shrugged.

"Okay. Back to bungalows," said Barthkowitz. "It's not that we don't want to keep an eye on you. We do. It's just that the bungalows are being … renovated. Or built. Or planned or something. In any case, we have an office for you to write in. Not a bungalow, I'm sorry to say, but like a bungalow. It has a window." He hit the squawk box. "Barry. Put them in that office that Meyers was using, that cheating bastard."

"Yes, Mr. Barthkowitz."

He pointed his finger at Edison. "Start another rewrite. I want to see pages every Tuesday and Thursday."

"Every Tuesday and Thursday?"

"You're being paid by the week. Every Tuesday and Thursday and any other day I want to, need to, or care to see pages. I'm going for clarity."

They didn't leave, so Barthkowitz started talking again.

"You've heard the term 'the seed of an idea,' right? You know—plant a seed, idea grows? Well, I like to think of the screenplay as the dirt. You provide me with the dirt, with the seed in it, of course, and I'll take care of the watering and the growing and picking the fruit and stuff. Okay?"

He opened his desk drawer and pulled out the Scotch.

They left.

The Thrill of Feeling Rich

Back at the apartment, Myra flopped onto the couch and laughed. "Three hundred dollars a week! The average salary is around $1800 a *year!*" She rolled onto her back and kicked and punched at the air. "We can go out to dinner. I can buy a new dress. You can get good shoes."

Edison turned away from her, tapping nervously on the window, watching the Three Bills down below pass a bottle around. "We can't let that film get made."

"Oh, give it up, Tom."

"Don't call me Tom. And Thomas Edison did not invent the movie projector. You got that one wrong."

She grabbed his hand and pulled him to the couch. "Come on. What difference does it make? All that money for a nothing movie that will blend into thousands of other nothing movies."

"And it will get released on DVD with a bunch of other nothing movies," he said, pulling away from her. "No. Someone will have to write about it. I know how these film guys are. They write about stuff you can't even see anywhere. I ... we wrote that screenplay specifically so that it wouldn't get made."

"Maybe *you* did."

"Exactly."

"Do you really think you can rig this? You can't plan for everything. So you know about some obscure movies. What about all the things you don't know? Things that someone will write about. We made the papers in both Seattle and Los Angeles, for chrissakes. And the radio. It will be on the Internet. So what?"

He sat beside her again, fidgeting. She rubbed his back, trying to soothe him, but he was far away, his eyes on the worn carpet with its pattern of frolicking puppies.

"I saw Carl Sagan on an episode of *NOVA* once," he said. "He said that time travel was possible, but that time travelers probably disguised themselves so they wouldn't be recognized, because that could bring about unintentional changes to the time-space continuum, which could be trouble for the traveler."

"I saw the same episode. With you. He also said—and I may be quoting—that if events were changed, it's possible we'd never notice because all events following, as well as our memories, would have been instantly altered to remain congruent with the newly established timeline."

"Maybe that's why we're losing our memories."

She half agreed with this possibility. "I understand how you feel. But there's nothing we can do about it. If it's going to change anyway, then what does it matter? Einstein calls time a persistent illusion. Just live, Edison."

They sat in silence until she grew frustrated and left him there to go for a walk.

"I won't be long," she said on her way out.

He stayed on the couch, fragmented thoughts flittering in his head, unable to shake his sense of dread. After a while he got up to ease his mind, to write, but as he climbed out the window he noticed a man down below holding a camera to his eye. A photographer. He was aiming at the Three Bills. Edison noted the exact moment when he snapped the picture and that same rush of excitement went through him that he had felt that night in Hollywood when he'd watched the photographers taking pictures of movie stars. Again, his brain seemed coated with mild electricity, spinning smoothly, like the efficient hum of a generator. There was something important about it, something he couldn't explain, a missing piece. As if to hold the camera, to feel its weight, could somehow change him. He watched the photographer coming up the steps beneath him, looking for ways to fill his frame, bobbing and weaving like a boxer to change his perspectives. He snapped one of the man with the lopsided face who ran the newsstand then glanced over his shoulder and caught Edison spying on him. Edison ducked behind the railing and when he looked again the photographer was walking along Clay Street and he had to crane his neck to watch him disappear.

Edison had never been a photographer. He knew almost nothing about it. Sometimes on vacations in the future, but not very often, he would try his hand at taking pictures with an inexpensive digital camera that his daughters had bought for him on one of his birthdays, thinking he might have a knack for it. He hadn't, and still didn't as far as he knew. Why the attraction then?

He was sitting in his writing chair, staring at the Edison Building, when Myra returned.

"What have you been doing?" she asked, her work boots clomping on the porch as she climbed through the window.

"Thinking," he said, his voice empty, monotone. He looked up at her, his eyes gradually coming into focus. Her face carried the weighted mixture of worry and frustration and love. "Can I take you to dinner?" he said, and watched as her face dropped its weight.

"That would be lovely."

The next morning, Minty stood behind the counter in his golf clothes and listened to Edison quit his job. He took off his golf cap, wrapped an apron around his plaid pants, picked up a spatula and went quietly to work on some bacon. Blenda brayed when she saw that Minty had tossed his cap in a coffee spill, staining the pom-pom. "Hah!"

Gordy Gladhander was circumspect when Myra told him the news, wishing her the best of luck and promising to see all of her movies. He told her to keep the Royal typewriter. "You could be a star," he said.

"No," she said. "We're just writers."

The Producer

Struggle of the Mind was scheduled to start shooting in early January of 1940. A producer and a director were attached, and a crew was informed of the tentative schedule. The rewrite began in a low-cut building filled with tiny offices at the back of the lot. Acropolis Pictures wasn't big enough to have what could be called a backlot. It was just the back of the lot. Their dusty office was eight feet by ten feet and wouldn't have made any prisoners jealous, Time Fly or otherwise. It had an empty file cabinet, a wooden table with two chairs and a small window too high to see out of. Edison stood on one of the chairs to appraise the window's view, which was a brick wall. If he could have seen beyond the wall his eyes would have feasted on a field of arid scrub speckled with trash. On the table sat a beaten Underwood in worse shape than the Royal they had at home. The ribbon was stretched and flaccid. Next to it was a phone that could only be used to call Barry, and on which Barthkowitz would call them constantly with his demands for pages, breaking their concentration and slowing down the process. He knew this, but did it anyway as a way of keeping the lines of authority firmly in place. The table had one thin drawer in it. In the drawer was some typing paper, a few pencils with teeth marks on them and a dirty pink eraser with rounded edges.

"I'm guessing the teeth marks are Meyers', the cheating bastard," said Myra.

Edison stared at the typewriter in confusion.

"What's wrong?" Myra said.

"I can hear it typing. Can't you?"

"That's not our typewriter. It's the one next door." She rapped lightly on the beaverboard wall and the typing stopped.

"What?" said a man's gruff voice from the other side. The voice sounded like it was in the room with them.

"Nothing. Sorry," said Myra. The typing started again. She whispered to Edison, "We could probably double the thickness if we hung up a bed sheet."

"I don't like it here," Edison whispered back. He missed his porch.

The phone on the desk rang. Edison was doubtful.

"Is that ours or his?"

"Ours." Myra picked up the receiver. "Hello?"

It was Barthkowitz. He wanted to know how they liked the office.

"Well … " said Myra.

He asked when he could see some pages.

"We just got here," she said.

He wanted to know what difference that made and asked again when he could see some pages. She decided to change the subject, but not too much.

"When do we meet the producer and director?"

"Soon, on the producer," said Barthkowitz. *"His name is Gaston Pulaski. Great producer, or would be if he could make a hit. Don't worry about meeting the director yet. He won't last two weeks under Pulaski. Pages?"*

"Tomorrow," she said and hung up the phone.

They heard the door at the end of the building open, followed by footsteps. The footsteps got louder as they came down the hall. The hall was lined with doors exactly like the one on Edison and Myra's office, which was at the end. The footsteps stopped and turned into a louder than necessary knock on the door next door. The typing stopped.

"What?" said the same voice from a minute before.

They heard the door open.

"Gaston Pulaski here," said a different voice.

"What do you want?" said the first voice.

There was a pause. "Where's your wife?"

"How the hell should I know? Where's yours?"

"Are you Tom Winslow?"

"No."

They heard the door close, followed by two more footsteps and a much louder than necessary knock on their door.

"Yes?" said Myra.

The door opened.

"Gaston Pulaski here. Are you Tom Winslow?" he said, looking at Edison.

"Sort of," said Edison.

"That'll do," said Pulaski. "I'm producing your movie. The one with the dumb title."

Gaston Pulaski was a shaky, wiry guy with a big head and a suit that would have been tight on a scarecrow. Under one arm he held a folder. His other hand was furiously twirling a pocket watch on a chain, like a gangster on speed.

"Nice to meet you," said Myra.

"You're the wife with the different last name, right?"

"I suppose."

"I heard the joke about the four different parents. Good stuff."

Myra exchanged a glance with Edison. Pulaski spoke like a burp gun, spraying the room with commentary that he could use to devastate his competition with if he felt like it. And he often felt like it. He smelled like cigarettes, body odor and gin. His facial features would have been unattractive on any species. The shorthaired cookie duster on his upper lip looked like it had been drawn with a sharpened pencil. He removed his hat and showed his hat tan—a brilliant white forehead above a tanned face from wearing his hat outside all the time. He pulled the folder from under his arm and tossed it on the table. Victimized by its furious twirling, the pocket watch broke free of its chain, and flung itself into the wall. The typing next door stopped again.

"What?" came the voice from the other side.

"Nothing," snapped Pulaski.

The typing started again. Edison made a move to pick up the watch.

"Leave it," said Pulaski. "I have more. Take a look," he said, opening the folder. There were some 8x10 glossies inside. "These are the lemmings we're looking at for the picture."

"Lemmings?" said Edison.

Pulaski gave him a shaky look. "Actors. Get with it, okay?"

"Okay."

Pulaski chucked the watch chain on the floor like he was getting ready for a fight. "You know, I don't have to do this. I don't care if you guys know who the hell is in this thing or not. I'm trying to be nice, get it?"

"He said 'okay,'" Myra interjected.

Pulaski narrowed his eyes at her. His cookie duster curled toward his nose. "I was warned about you." He slid the top picture out of the folder and placed it in the middle of the table. "Pay attention. Exhibit one—the leading man. Brush Steele."

Myra laughed, then tried to make it sound like a cough. "His name is Brush Steele?"

"I know. Idiotic, right?" said Pulaski. "But his real name is Vernon Louis Parrington. What would you do? You haven't heard of him?"

They shook their heads no.

"He plays those kind of suave tough guys who can toss gangsters through a window without losing the ash on his cigarette," said Pulaski. "Or at least that's what he wants to play. Can't say I've seen him in anything."

"I'm guessing he plays the part of Harry?" said Myra.

"Yeah, listen." He spun out the next photo—a pouty, bare-shouldered blond who looked like she might have a nude photo shoot in her past that she'd have to buy back when she started getting too famous. "Exhibit two—Chloe, the leading lady. This week's flavor of the month. Her name's Gloria Baker. Good looking dame, huh?" He picked up the 8x10 and elbowed Edison. "Bet you'd like to change her oil sometime, wouldn't ya?" Edison nodded somberly. Pulaski scowled. "She's new. This is her big break. Lighten up."

"Who's this?" said Myra, picking up a picture of a mousy looking brunette in glasses.

"She plays the part of Bitsy, the counterpoint to Chloe."

Edison and Myra looked confused. Pulaski sighed.

"You know, the counterpoint. The angelic, unattractive, sexless childhood friend who tries to set Chloe straight. Strictly Central Casting."

"That's not in the story," said Edison.

"Not yet," said Pulaski. "What do you think the rewrite is for?"

"Uh…"

"Later," said Pulaski, holding his hand up to stop them. "Something else: Gloria has been taking singing lessons at the studio's expense, so write some of the musical numbers for her."

"What musical numbers?"

"Boy, you two don't know much. Musical numbers. You know, singing, dancing, shaking a little ass. Come on." He pulled another pocket watch from his coat and started spinning it.

Myra and Edison were speechless.

"Look, we hired a guy to do the music. All we need are some lyrics. Give it a shot. If they're lousy, we'll have him do those, too."

Pulaski left the folder on the table and made his exit without another word. They listened to his footsteps fade down the hall. The typing next door stopped again and was replaced with quiet laughter. The laughter stopped and the voice said, "Welcome to Acropolis Pictures."

"Don't worry about him. You probably won't see him much." Barthkowitz leaned back in his chair, puffing languidly on his cigar. "He's good. He gets the job done."

"But the musical numbers," said Myra.

Edison was half dozing on the couch. "I'll make Chloe a nightclub singer," he mumbled. "I should have thought of it before."

Barthkowitz chuckled. "There you go. Problem solved. All you need now is for him to wake up and write it. Show me some pages tomorrow."

"But…"

"I make the decisions. Me." He opened his desk drawer. "See Barry on your way out." He took the decanter and a glass out of the drawer and set them on the desk. They left.

Barry handed them a slip of paper with an address on it as they passed through his office. "What's this?" said Myra.

"It's where Mr. Barthkowitz lives. Be there Saturday at three pm."

Focus

On Friday, they listened to the muffled angry voice of the man in the phone booth while they waited for Myra the Receptionist to cut their first paycheck. They opened a bank account, at Myra's insistence, deposited some, kept the rest, and then Edison, his fist wrapped around the cash, went straight to a camera shop he had seen on Pico Street. The shop was shaped like a camera, its front window round, like a lens.

"I'm just going to browse."

"That's fine," she said.

The clerk was repairing a camera beneath a small lamp, a jeweler's loupe jammed in one eye. He looked up as they walked in.

"Let me know if you need anything."

Edison squatted and gazed at all the cameras behind the glass. There were so many. He feared getting lost in the confusion of too many choices, but as he kept looking his confidence grew until one, different from the rest, seemed to call out to him. He pointed to a used Leica 35mm with gilt top and base plates and knurled fittings.

"I'd like to see that one, please," he said.

The clerk took it from the display case. "You have good taste. A Leica Luxus. Made in 1930. Elmar lens. Only made them for about a year. Very rare. Had to be special ordered. Got the serial number on top here." He pointed to it. "It was left by a producer who went bankrupt. A real deal." He held it out for Edison to see. The golden fittings gleamed. "Hmm. Looks like it still has film in it. One picture left."

As Edison took the camera, a calmness enveloped him, as he knew it would. The red faux snakeskin wrapping the camera's body tickled his fingertips. It sat perfectly in his hand, compact and indestructible. The balanced weight sent a shiver up his forearm. And when he held it to his eye and clicked the shutter there was clarity. His brain stopped spinning, snapping to a stop and organizing his thoughts instantly. The clarity lasted only as long as it took to take a picture. It was different than the feeling he got from typing. True, the Royal had its way of dissipating some of his confusion, of getting him to focus, but he couldn't carry it everywhere, and he was most confused when he was out and about, when the surroundings were less static and unfamiliar. A camera was portable. It wouldn't cramp his arm or make him look like an idiot for carrying it around the way a typewriter would. By keeping it with him at all times he could move forward on a trail of clear thoughts that would help him make it through his days.

He looked at Myra through the viewfinder, surrounded her with the frame. He controlled this rectangle. Whatever appeared in it, he could freeze forever whenever he felt like it. It was power.

"I need this," he explained to her. "I know it's expensive, but … "

"It's fine," she said. "I'm happy for you."

It didn't seem to occur to him that by photographing he would be recording his life in the past, a seemingly blatant violation of his desire to not change history. It occurred to Myra, but she didn't care and kept silent about it so as not to discourage his purchase.

"Kodachrome or panchromatic?" said the clerk, taking the spent roll from the camera.

"Panchromatic is black and white?"

The clerk nodded and Edison said okay. The clerk unscrewed the top from a new canister and dumped out a fresh roll, showing Edison how to load it. "The Leica doesn't have a light meter. Did you want to buy one?"

Edison held the camera to his eye. "I don't think so."

This struck Myra as strange. Edison's digital camera in the future had been fully automatic, doing much of the thinking on his behalf. As far as she knew, he had no idea how to judge exposure. What she didn't know was that Edison had no intention of ever developing any of the film he shot, so having a light meter was moot. This was part of the clear thought he got when he had snapped the first picture: if he didn't develop the film he wouldn't be changing history. The thought also told him that he couldn't trick himself by not having film in the camera. He needed the film to think clearly. And he had to keep the spent rolls with him to prevent others from processing them.

"Well," said the clerk, "it's already on 1/200 of a second and *f*9. If you leave it on that you should be fine on sunny days, as long as you keep using the same film speed."

That meant 1/200 of a second of clear thinking every time he took a picture. Edison would take the clerk's advice for the most part, leaving the camera settings alone. Not all of the pictures would be properly exposed, but many of them would be. As if it mattered.

At home, he spent a few minutes fiddling with the lens and then took a picture of Myra. She was sitting on the bed smiling at him. Her hands were folded between her knees and the light from the window was on the side of her face. He swelled with a profound sense of accomplishment. He looked at the camera and thought about what he had just put inside it.

In this box I have mystery and hope.

The Proposal

The cab cruised along Figueroa Street past strip malls and houses. Billboards invited them to eat, drink, buy and be saved by the Lord in any number of ways. The sun illuminating the smog made the day seem somehow brighter. Edison had the camera on his lap. He had decided to take it everywhere from now on. Extra canisters of film rattled lightly in his shirt pocket.

"Why do you think he wants to see us at his house?" he said.

"Maybe he likes the work we're doing."

"It doesn't seem like it." He took a picture of a billboard featuring a dark-eyed woman in a turban threatening to read his future in a crystal ball. "I don't understand him sometimes."

"I think he has the same problem with you. You shouldn't let him bully you."

"I get nervous and my mind goes blank." He didn't want to tell her that Barthkowitz reminded him of his old boss from the future and that he was afraid of getting fired.

"You're a writer now. Write him a letter."

The cab turned up Colorado Street and crossed the Colorado Street Bridge. They didn't know it yet, but they could see the Barthkowitz mansion from the bridge.

Burskin Barthkowitz had been selling ice from an ass-drawn wagon when a plot of land in the Baldwin Hills was bequeathed to him in 1917 by an uncle who didn't like him much and thought the land was worthless, hoping to burden him with the taxes. But Burskin had a hunch about the land and turned it quickly into an obsession, believing there was a better life beneath its surface, and he worked tirelessly to peel it away. Somewhere during the craziness of trying to run two lives, he had stopped paying attention to his family and his wife left him, taking with her their hypochondriac daughter, Bertha, and leaving Reginald K. behind to deal with the cruelties and eccentricities of an angry man with an ice pick in one hand and an oil drill in the other. Reginald K. stuck with it, working side by side, putting up with the old man's shit, until finally, on his twenty-second birthday in 1925, the first oil well ejaculated its thick black liquid skyward. Burskin was already beginning to lose his mind by this time and spent his money unwisely, passing crumbs and promises on to his son. When he had his dream home built, he didn't build it on the ocean as he had always dreamed of, but on the side of the Arroyo Seco, a small ravine twenty-three miles inland in Pasadena, with a view of the span known locally as Suicide Bridge, due to the jumpers it served on a regular basis during the Depression. Burskin said that the bridge gave him comfort and proved that there was always a solution should things get too rugged.

The mansion was a sprawling, bewildering place, modeled on fickle indecisions and filtered through the gradual decay of sanity. From one angle, it could be seen as Tudor, from another as an Italian Villa with a little Spanish Revival thrown in to round out the arches. There was even a tower with a crenellated embattlement, presumably for dumping vats of hot oil onto screenwriters. From the cobblestone driveway, it didn't look so much like a house as it did a small European theme park. An open garage exposed a twenty-foot long 1934 Cadillac Fleetwood with a roofless chauffeur section up front. The tires were going flat and the black paint was coated with dust. The reversal of fortune had begun shortly before construction on the mansion was completed, with wells drying up at a rate of one or two per year. The few that were still living pumped enough to cover the taxes and upkeep, allowing for the retention of a small loyal staff, although most of the money went into keeping Acropolis Pictures out of cement shoes.

Edison was taking a picture of a fountain of nymphs with water squirting from their nipples when a heavy wood door opened, revealing a butler who looked a lot like Barry and turned out to be his brother, Bruce.

"This way," he said, without looking at them, and walked back into the house. They followed, their heels clicking on the predictable marble entryway as they passed between a pair of cochlea-shaped spiral staircases, peach-frost in color.

Myra asked a few questions, but Bruce wasn't answering, as he led them silently through various spaces, each one completely different in style and mood; a stuffy baroque drawing room of draperies and statues and florid furniture with unyielding cushions; an expansive, blond-wooded, modern room, with sharp dangerous angles and a rawhide couch sunken into the floor that resembled a pool of floating cattle corpses. They passed through an Early American room where an unplugged television with a five-inch screen collected dust in a corner, skittered past an indoor pool and sauna, and ended up on a patio—or maybe it was a veranda—whose cheering section was a row of arches that couldn't decide which architectural style it was trying to mimic. Barthkowitz was lying on a chaise lounge, his tanned feet crossed at the ankles—toenails shimmering like pearls—with a white phone to his ear, finishing up a chat.

"You're in cahoots, you son of a bitch… Yeah, cahoots. You're fired. I want you off the lot before my foot reaches your ass. Understand?" He slammed the phone down and turned toward them, smiling, his anger completely vanished.

"Your guests, Mr. Barthkowitz," said Bruce and left the patio.

"Thank you, uh… Barry's brother," Barthkowitz called after him. "Bring something to drink for our guests." He shrugged, "I can never remember that guy's name," and waved toward some patio furniture. "Welcome, welcome. Have a seat."

Myra settled on one with lime green canvas covered cushions and smooth plastic arms as wide as truck tires. Edison found its mate. Barthkowitz twirled a cigar in his fingers as he gazed at Suicide Bridge through the haze. "In all the years I've lived here, I've never seen any of them jump. I wait and wait, but so do they. It always happens when I'm somewhere else."

Edison took a picture of him looking at the bridge. When he heard the click, Barthkowitz whipped around, eyeing the camera as if it was a gun pointed at him.

"Put that away. Did you take my picture?"

"I took a picture of the bridge."

"Well, put it away. I don't like having my picture taken. Who's is that, anyway?"

Edison put the camera on his lap. "I bought it with my own money."

Barthkowitz sneered at it. "Your own money. Don't forget where that money came from."

"We won't forget that we're earning it fairly," said Myra.

Barthkowitz guffawed, "Fairly," turning his attention from the camera to Myra's ungloved hands. The dye had faded and already her hair was getting lighter as the silver fought its way back to the surface.

"I saw that you have a television," she said to break his gaze.

"Know thine enemy," said Barthkowitz. "There isn't much on it yet, but it could be huge one of these days. And it will ruin the movies."

"The movies should be fine. For a while, anyway."

"Besides, it's going to have to wait until after the war," Edison said.

"What?" Barthkowitz stared at him the way someone would an intoxicated child, then said to Myra, "Do you know what he's talking about? I never know what he's talking about."

"It's the war in Europe," said Myra. "He's afraid it will come here."

Barthkowitz shook his head emphatically. "Won't happen here," he said. "Not after that last waste of time. This country learned its lesson. We can sell tanks and planes to the tea drinkers, but that's about as far as it's going to go. The people won't stand for it."

Myra kept her look polite. "Poland has been devastated."

"Yes," said Barthkowitz. "I hear I lost some family."

"You're Polish?"

He shook his head. "I'm American. They're Polish. I was born in New Jersey. Still got a mother and sister there."

"Doesn't it bother you?"

"Sure, I guess. But I didn't know them. Distant family."

"And Hitler?"

"Don't forget, we have Hitler to thank for some of our best filmmakers. True, none of them work for me, but we have some offers out to some of the more desperate ones. You got to love refugees."

"That's distasteful."

Barthkowitz sighed impatiently. "Look, I make movies. I try to fulfill dreams, not live nightmares. If someone brings me a script about Hitler, and I like it, maybe I'll make it. Other than that, the war does not concern me."

"Not your problem, right?"

"If a boatload of Scotch gets sunk by a U-boat, then maybe."

Myra looked away. Barthkowitz tried to make his point stick.

"This isn't Warner Brothers. I don't have the money for protest," he said. "And I'll tell you right now: I don't care what your feelings are outside of this studio, but none of it ends up in your scripts. Understood?"

Myra nodded once, curtly. Edison wiped his camera lens with his shirttail.

Bruce returned with a tray of drinks resting on the handles of a cane-backed wheelchair that he was rolling along in front of him. Seated in the wheelchair was a smaller, older version of Barthkowitz, impeccably dressed in a way that looked like he hadn't done it himself.

"What's this?" said Barthkowitz.

"He wanted to go out," said Bruce. He handed a drink to Myra, then Edison. "He must like your company."

Barthkowitz told Bruce to go away then turned to the old man in the wheelchair, the angry M of his mouth twisted in disgust. "Look at him. He thinks he's going to a party."

The man in the wheelchair stared straight ahead at Suicide Bridge, the drink that Bruce had put in his hand balanced in his white buckskin glove. He was layered in a black evening coat, a white double-breasted waistcoat, a white shirt with enough starch in it that it looked like wood, and a white silk tie.

"Your father?" said Myra.

"I used to think so. Burskin Barthkowitz. Man of the house. I still call him Daddy, although I could call him anything I want these days. Isn't that right, asshole?"

Daddy stared straight ahead as if he were miles away. Myra set her drink down.

"Don't worry," said Barthkowitz, "he can't hear me. All he does is stare at that goddamned bridge, waiting for Mother to get ready."

"I thought your mother lived in New Jersey."

"She does."

"That's sad."

"He deserves it. Before striking oil, he used to sell ice. Chipped it straight from his heart. He's all calmed down these days." He raised his voice a bit. "But it used to be different, didn't it, Daddy? You used to have a lot of fun with me. Now I run the show."

He slapped a hand on Daddy's knee. The cane creaked as Daddy shifted in his seat.

"It's a wonder you let him stay," said Myra.

Barthkowitz twisted his mouth. "Not really. I'd put him in a home, but before he completely lost his marbles, he had a legal document drawn up that says I can't."

"I see," said Myra. "Is there a Mrs. Barthkowitz?"

"I told you. New Jersey."

"I don't mean your mother."

Barthkowitz removed his hand from Daddy's knee and looked at her as if she'd just told him his feet smelled. "No." His eyes moved to Edison. "What are you looking at?"

Edison moved his lips but nothing came out. He didn't know what to do so he put the camera to his eye and took another picture, this one with Barthkowitz looking straight at him.

"I said put that goddamned thing away."

"I'm not hurting anyone."

"Let me see that," said Barthkowitz, reaching for the camera.

Edison pulled the camera closer to him. "No. You'll keep it."

"I said—"

"Why did you ask us here, Mr. Barthkowitz?" Myra cut in.

"Tell him to put that goddamned thing away, or take it somewhere else."

This sounded all right to Edison. The clear thought he got from taking the picture told him he wasn't wanted here.

"Okay. Fine." He stood and said to Myra, "I'll see you out front when you're finished." He cast a semi-nasty look at Barthkowitz. "I'm pretty good at this job, you know."

"I didn't say you weren't," said Barthkowitz.

"Well, start saying that I am once in a while." Edison turned and left the patio.

"Where's he going?"

"I'm not sure," said Myra. "He just got the camera yesterday."

Barthkowitz waved him off. "Let him go. I wanted to talk to you, anyway. Not him." He glanced at Daddy. "Let's take a walk. He gives me the creeps."

Without Bruce leading the way, Edison got lost going back through the house. He wandered a few hallways aimlessly, passed through a restaurant-sized kitchen and somehow ended up in the modern room with the blond wood and the dangerous angles. There was a door on the opposite side of the room that he incorrectly remembered as the way out, so he skirted around the floating cattle corpse couch and went through it. The room was small and dark, an office of some sort, with a tall narrow window on one wall. The rest of the walls were filled with dusty books that looked like they hadn't been touched in years. On the desk, he saw a typewriter and it reminded him of the suggestion Myra had made in the cab. Write him a letter. As he sat at the desk, a shadow moved across him and he turned to catch the last pieces of Myra and Barthkowitz walking past the window. He paused a few seconds to be sure he hadn't been seen, then went through the drawers of the desk until he found some typing paper.

Barthkowitz led Myra along the veranda to a different patio, a tiny, intimate one, where a small table seemed to have miraculously grown two salads. There were spinach leaves, grapefruit wedges, pine nuts, and some kind of grated cheese. Barthkowitz handed one to her.

"Vegetarian, correct?"

She was startled, but she took it. He picked up the other one and put a forkful of spinach leaves into his mouth. She followed Barthkowitz, salad in hand, to a parlor with an exterior wall made entirely of red glass, lending the room the appearance of a photography darkroom full of living room furniture. The light parts of their faces were red and all the shadows were slushy black. Barthkowitz's eyes were muddy holes. The muddy holes were staring at her hands again.

"What happened to your gloves?" he said.

"I don't need them anymore."

He nodded as if he understood and asked how long she'd lived in L.A.

"Oh, just about a year now." She knew it was exactly eleven months and five days but didn't want to sound nerdy.

He moved a little closer and asked where she was staying, his voice going for fine silk and coming up with rayon.

"Bunker Hill. With my husband."

"Bunker Hill?" he said. "What the hell for?"

"It's affordable."

"Affordable. Well, you don't have to live there anymore."

"No. Now it's a choice." She understood that part of Edison's ability to write was rooted in that neighborhood where so many of his favorite movies would eventually be made.

"I see. And how long have you and, uh … "

"Edison."

"Yeah, yeah, Edison. Tom." He chuckled. "How long have you been together?"

She wasn't sure anymore. It had been about fifteen years before they'd gone back in time. But with the added year and them not aging, she didn't know how to calculate it.

"Long enough to know some things about each other."

"It's good that you get along so well. You seem very different from each other."

"We're complementary. He's loosened a few of my screws; I've tightened a few of his."

"Huh." Barthkowitz nodded thoughtfully. "But is he always so … confused?"

"That *is* my husband you're talking about."

"Of course. My apologies if I seemed inappropriate." She nodded her approval of the word inappropriate as he continued. "But sticking his hands in his pants? What's with that?"

She sighed. "I don't know. He's never said. Mr. Barthkowitz, what is this about?"

October 21, 19

October 21, 1939

Attention: Reginald K. Barthkowitz
          Studio

          CEO
          Acropolis Pictures

Subject: Working relations

Barthkowitz was not really at all like Edison's former boss had been, the one who had laid him off in the twenty-first century, back when he had been Bob. But Edison, his powers of thought being what they were these days, had convinced himself that there existed enough similarities between them that an approach akin to what he would have made to his old future boss was appropriate for communicating with Barthkowitz. His old future boss had loved corporate lingo, reacting with boyish excitement to any new term designed to obscure, shortcut or anesthetize the truth, and quickly integrated the new terms into his everyday patterns of speech. Edison did his best to recall them. Crumpled snowballs of earlier attempts littered the floor around his chair as he searched for the right voice.

Dear Mr. Barthkowitz,

I hope that this letter finds you well. Please excuse the
formality, but I felt that a written correspondence might
save us some face time. It has come to my attention, and
to that of my writing team, that our relationship with
Acropolis Pictures may be suffering some diplomatic chall-
enges. There has been some saber rattling from all concerned
parties and I was hoping to get in front of the issue
before it gets in front of us. You know, throw some head-
lights on it and start making repairs on a go-forward
basis. The time has come for us to reach across the aisle,
Mr. Barthkowitz.

Barthkowitz was smiling. The spinach leaves that stuck to his teeth were
black under the red light, giving him the look of a crimson hillbilly.
"Won't you have a seat?" he said, gesturing toward the couch. Myra sat at
one end. Barthkowitz sat in the middle, too close, his considerable girth
sinking down into the cushion like a man who had stepped on a carpet
covering a hole in the floor and causing Myra to lean helplessly toward
him. Now, Myra was not an especially beautiful woman, and hadn't been
even when she was Lenora. Her features, taken individually, were unre-
markable. Her lips were thin and turned down slightly at the corners. Her
eyes were small and of a color hard to describe. Gravity had been tugging
at her cheeks for years and beneath her silver bangs her eyebrows were
as dark and wide as licorice twists. But it was the combination of these
features, and the way she employed them with directness and tinged with
cynicism, that made her appear very beautiful to some men. Barthkowitz
was one of those men.

"I have a proposition for you," he began. "I started Acropolis Pictures
with one thought in mind—good product. Since that time, we've done
some good pictures and some stinkers. Mostly stinkers. But entertaining
stinkers, mind you. I am not unproud of what I've done here."

"Of course not."

"In that time, we have gained a rough and tumble reputation. Gangster films, films of, shall we say, a risqué nature. A few romances. Not

many. Which isn't bad, necessarily. But I want to change that some." He stammered a little, almost as if he was nervous.

Myra nodded, trying to get him to the point.

He reached across her to put his salad on the end table behind her. She fought the urge to protect her breast lump as his labored breath whistled through his nostrils next to her ear. He grunted back to his original position, stopping a few inches short to remain closer to her, then held out his hands like he was getting ready to catch a football. "The woman's touch," he said, beaming, trying to coax her approval, to get her on board with eye widening and hand pumping.

She put her fingertips against his shirt and gently pushed. "Breathing room, please."

He leaned away a miniscule distance and laughed. "I like you. You're clear, logical. You're smart. I mean smart like a man. You're strong without being... uh ... "

"Feminist?"

"Uh, okay. Sure. But that's not important. What is important is that I want Acropolis Pictures to lean in a different direction. Not feminist, you understand." He giggled uncomfortably. "Just more feminine, but with masculine overtones. Recent studies by, uh, people who count things—professionals, mind you—have shown that women make up over half the movie going audience. I want to be a part of that. I want to fill seats with female ass—uh, excuse me—with women. To reach out to women audiences. I want Acropolis Pictures to be the studio of choice for women across America."

"And that's where I come in?"

"That's where you come in." He picked up his salad and started eating again as if he'd finished and all was settled. Myra watched him chew, which took some strength on her part.

A long time ago, I was employed by a firm that stressed
the need for teamwork and vertical interaction amongst
their employees, in an effort to combat employer disengage-
ment. I feel that time may be upon us now.

Since climbing into bed with Acropolis Pictures, my team
has efforted to take a value-added approach in the ful-
fillment of our duties, regardless of your required go-live
date. We have, I feel, done due diligence to meet your
endgame, even when we've lacked bandwidth, due to having
too many balls in the air. I'd like to shift gears on that
approach and turn this ship around to avoid a situation
where we need to circle the wagons. I'm ready to take the
ball and run with it, but first, I need to be sure that
we are all in the loop and on the same page.

"Mr. Barthkowitz, what is it exactly that you want? Is the studio in trouble?"

Barthkowitz put his fork down and folded his hands. He tongue-swept his teeth clear of spinach. "Trouble is a big word. Be careful. Do you know who Kate Corbaley is?"

"I can't say that I do."

"I thought you read the papers? She's a very important lady in this industry, the backbone of MGM. Or was; she died last year, rest her soul." He faked a hand to his heart, accompanied by a frown. "Big write-up in the *Times*. She worked directly for Mayer. Read constantly. It was her job to dig up ideas from novels, plays, newspapers and such, and pitch them to Mayer."

"So, you want me to be a scenarist?"

"That's part of it. Have you heard of Francis Marion?"

"Of course."

"Did you know that in addition to her own scripts, she also wrote her husband's?"

"What are you suggesting?" said Myra, her voice rising slightly. She was having trouble reading him. He was red and she couldn't see his eyes. She had the feeling that this was intentional. "Not that I write for Edison, I hope. We work together."

Barthkowitz put his hands up in mild defense. "Nothing of the sort. Edison will be a fine writer. I have a good feeling about him. But I noticed his female characters have a bit of a doormat quality about them."

"Isn't that what you want?"

"To a point. But not so much. I'd like you to take a look at *Struggle of the Mind* and see if you can't beef up the female lead a bit. Give her some attitude. Not change the story necessarily, but make a stronger character work within the story. She should still be dedicated to her man, and her main motivation should still be of a romantic nature. We don't want to rock the boat, just make the sails a little sleeker."

Myra nodded tentatively. "Alright. Let me talk with Edison and—"

"Well," he stopped her. He tightened his lips as if he was having moral issues, but the idea was so foreign to him that it looked like he had gas.

"Yes?" Myra prompted.

"I'm thinking of approaching this a little differently. Now Kate Corbaley looked at a lot of scripts at MGM, from a lot of different writers. Male writers. She pumped up the female characters, made them more realistic. Gave them her own spin. Do you know what I mean?"

"And these male writers, did they know that Ms, uh, Miss Corbaley made changes to their scripts?"

Barthkowitz cleared his throat. "A lot of changes are made along the whole production line. The screenplay is just the first stage. The page never makes it to the screen unmolested."

Myra blinked. "So, let me see if I have this right. You want me to make changes to *Struggle of the Mind* without telling Edison?"

Barthkowitz shrugged and twisted, trying to trivialize the situation. "Not just *Struggle of the Mind*. Acropolis has other writers on staff. Writers who don't have that woman's touch. You'll be kept very busy."

"I see. And all of it is to be done behind the scenes?"

"You'll only change the words I ask you to."

"It only takes one letter to change class to crass."

"Now don't be that way." Barthkowitz looked at her evenly. "I'll pay you another three-hundred dollars per week on top of what you and Edison make now."

```
Suggestion: Let's circle back, do another meet and greet,
pick each other's brains, knock out some of the low-hanging
fruit, then drill down on the deliverables to see if we
can't marry our resources. The main point here is to avoid
another blamestorm and to maintain an open and honest
relationship amongst the team members, perhaps withaa
more proactive, solutions-based, hybrid approach to op-
timize our ability to take ownership. The most important
thing is that we trust each other.

Let's discuss offline when you have a moment.

Sincerely yours,


Edison 'Tom' Winslow

P.S. Not to raise a pocketbook issue, but I've noticed
the way you look at my wife. Please stop.
```

Myra stayed silent. Barthkowitz smiled. She didn't. He bit his lip and wrung his hands.

"I'll also jump the pair of you to four-fifty per week," he squeezed out painfully.

Myra did some silent calculating. In all her life she had never done anything for the money. She had also never been sent back in time before and there were proving to be significant drawbacks to that. *Who's to blame here anyway? We didn't ask for this.* And Barthkowitz wasn't exactly playing the sympathetic character. So what if it cost him? The more she got out of him, the faster they could leave this business and get down to enjoying their prison sentence a little more. Still, as she justified the scheme to herself—the money, the secrecy, the deception aimed at her own husband, the utter dishonesty—her head began to bob, shaking her hair down the sides of her face like blinders, and she knew that doing this would eventually cause her trouble. Thank god Barthkowitz was too oblivious to notice. He thought she was trying to be sexy.

"Seven-hundred per week," she said, her head bowed, her expression hidden in her hair. Then she raised her eyes and looked straight into his muddy holes. "That, and the three-hundred for me will give us an even thousand, which is what I will need for doing this."

Barthkowitz shot up from the couch, sending a shockwave of relief through the cushions. "I can't pay a woman that much!"

Myra leaned back, looking up at him. His belly glowed between them like a red weather balloon. She knew it was an absurd amount of money to ask for. And she suspected he couldn't really afford it, but she didn't care. If he wanted her to lie, it was going to cost him.

"I see," she said. "And how much are you willing to pay for a woman's touch?"

He thought about this, studying her face to see how much he could get away with, but the red light was now working against him.

"Seven-fifty, like I said."

"That will get you a little girl's touch."

Barthkowitz rubbed his face in exasperation. It was fun to watch him push his features around, trying to figure out how to lose gracefully. "Let me talk to Barry."

"Talk to him correctly and you'll get a woman's touch."

Edison was waiting in the driveway when she came out.

"What did he want?"

What If You Were Stupid and the Internet Existed?

When they arrived home, there were two police cars parked at the bottom of the stairs in front of the Sun God Arms. Their first instinct was to hop a freight train, but they resisted and asked one of the Three Bills what it was about.

"Bucky Kitchen is dead," said the Bill.

Bucky Kitchen, the mostly unemployed actor, alcoholic and Seconal addict who lived in the apartment below had died of an overdose. He had been discovered in one of his usual positions, neck bent at an odd angle, head cocked against the porch banister, his body sprawled and twisted along the porch's slatted deck, by Huffy Lydon, who had dropped by to collect. "Rent's overdue," he'd said, as he lightly kicked at Bucky's shoe. When his kick was not answered with Bucky's routine squirm and moan, Huffy realized why and leaped back in fear, the way people do when confronted with a harmless corpse.

An ambulance rumbled up Clay Street. Attendants in white bounded lightly up the stairs and into the Sun God Arms Apartments and came out carrying a dead man. The Three Bills bowed their heads. Edison took a picture of Bucky covered in a sheet. One of the Bills waved at the camera.

There was something else about Bucky: he, too, had been a prisoner of the Time Flies. And now he had died in a time not his own. In 2013 he had been a common online social networker from Penobscot, Maine named Trevor something or Josh something, who, in a rare physical act, got lucky and successfully swatted a dozing Time Fly with a mousepad, killing it. Murder amongst the Time Flies was uncommon and they had taken it quite seriously. Bucky was sentenced to seven hundred and fifty years, without aging, in eight hundred and twelve different time periods. His acting stint in Los Angeles had been the longest amount of time he had spent in any single place. (He had arrived in LA via Moose Jaw, Saskatchewan following a nine-month layover in Shakespearean England, where he had developed a taste for acting.)

His first stop, where his sentence began, was the year 1860 in Muddy Creek, Wyoming, where he changed his name to Bucky Kitchen and soon made a fool of himself. Unable to break his social networking addiction he started writing letters constantly, updating his status every few minutes. He wrote brief postings of his daily progress on stiff paper, stuffing them into envelopes and addressing them to "TheWorld@theworld," penning such phrases as "I'm putting a saddle on my horse! Awesome!" "It's so high up here! Awesome!" "Hey! My horse just pooped while walking! Awesome!" and "At the saloon. Smells bad." He carried on in this fashion for about three days before being banned from using the Pony Express by the local station keeper for bogging down the pony. It had been all downhill from there.

It should be noted that the Time Flies could not travel in time infinitely. They could only travel back to the point where their ability to time travel had been developed, in about 2600 BC. At first, they could only travel forward in time; once they'd done that, there was something to travel back to. Similarly, they could only travel forward in time to the point where their species died out. They didn't know when this was. They had never ventured far enough into the future to find out. In the thirty-seventh century, they saw signs of weakening among their brethren and grew cautious, restricting their travels to safer millennia. This bracketed limit on travel also extended to prisoners and objects. Professor Cyril T. Rocklidge had not written about this aspect of the Time Flies because he'd had no knowledge of it, having only been sentenced to a relatively brief, sequential period of time, much as Myra and Edison had. Bucky, on the other hand, had been afforded full view of the spectrum.

The Time Flies had bounced Bucky around relentlessly within their jurisdiction, never keeping him in one place long enough to properly adjust to his surroundings. He had been to incomprehensible futures and to distant pasts. He had floundered in ancient Mesopotamia and in space colonies with hairless, emotionally boring drones. And he never knew what was coming next. It was year six hundred and twelve of his sentence and he had been to seven-hundred and ninety-four different time periods, all while feeling miserable. The emotional state he had been frozen in for his entire sentence was distress. Just before swatting the Time Fly in 2013, in a fit of rage, he had read a posting from his girlfriend that she was digitally sleeping with another social networker. He seethed for hours, posting various combinations of vitriol against his girlfriend, accusing her of impossibly lewd physical acts. He had been just about to de-friend her when his sentence began. This feeling had been with him for six hundred and twelve years. He had been beaten, picked on, imprisoned, tortured, pulverized and embarrassed for centuries and he couldn't take it anymore. He remembered virtually nothing of the time he'd originally come from, including his girlfriend. Like Edison and Myra, he had begun to forget things shortly after his sentence began, but he had not kept journals. All he remembered about his own time was that most people had decent teeth. It wasn't much to go on.

Bucky had a left a note, marking his death as a suicide instead of an accident. But it didn't seem like much of a suicide note to the police. It didn't make a lot of sense, having been written while intoxicated. One of the policemen showed the note to the ambulance driver who shook his head after reading it. Myra and Edison never saw the note. Too bad. They may have understood it, in part. It said:

If you can't be famous, you might as well be infamous. ~~But okay~~ I wish I was back in the time of ~~stuff~~ straight white teeth, Now I will tell you somethin about the time f[ies]

That's all there was.

The remaining Guidance Flies were relieved of duty following Bucky's death and were very glad about it, as it had been a rather hellish job shuffling him around from time period to time period, although they had been proud to assist in executing the sentence of a murderer and enjoyed the increased social status that had attended it.

Ode to Bandini

Myra cheered when the Neutrality Bill was repealed and booed when the assassination attempt on Hitler failed. She knew it was going to fail, but held out hope that something they had done had changed this little piece of history. It hadn't.

"The Germans are giving food ration cards to pigs and cows," she told Edison.

"How do you know that?"

"I just do."

She listened at the wall to the reports of the Soviet invasion of Finland while she checked her lump.

"Why don't we buy a radio?" Edison suggested again.

"Maybe."

"We have the money now."

"Shhh. I said maybe."

On the morning of December sixth, she proposed a breakfast toast with her coffee. Fritz Kuhn, the 'American Fuhrer', leader of the German Bund in New York City, had been sentenced the day before to two and a half years at Sing Sing prison for larceny and embezzlement.

"At least he's not being sentenced by Time Flies," said Edison.

Myra sipped her coffee. "I don't know, sometimes it's alright. Don't you have some fun?"

"I suppose. But I'm worried."

"Mmm." She didn't want to be worried right now.

"I wonder what it's going to be like when we go back home. I'm starting to forget what our own lives were like." He'd already forgotten one of his daughter's names.

But Myra wasn't paying attention anymore. She'd gone back to reading her newspaper.

The vacancy left by Bucky Kitchen was filled by a young writer from Denver, Colorado named Arturo Bandini, who was always in and out with one trouble or another and who seemed to eat nothing but oranges.

"I am Arturo Bandini!" he had yelled up to Edison from his porch his first week there, his mid-western accent carrying mannerisms of Italian.

"My name is Edison Winslow," said Edison as he peered over the railing.

"I am the greatest living writer!" Bandini said to Edison and the world, his arms spread wide.

"You look awfully young for that."

Bandini shrugged. "Mere flesh. Mere bones and blood. My words have been alive forever. Tablet and chisel. Smashed berries and the wall of a cave. Forever."

"Okay."

"Okay? Is that all you can say? I have listened to your typing. It needs work."

"You can tell that from listening to it?"

"It's the way you hesitate with the keys. You should never hesitate."

"Okay."

"There with the 'okay' again."

He asked if Edison wanted an orange and Edison said okay again, but Arturo had a date and excused himself with citrus on his breath as he tossed one up to him. It was a good toss and Edison caught it as it slowed in the air before him. He went to Grand Central Market and bought a bag of oranges from the Chinese man who sold them and left the bag by Bandini's door as a thank you gift for his typing advice. He didn't know that Bandini was tired of oranges; that he was sick to death of them, but that it was all he could afford. He thought that Bandini would be grateful. He didn't know that he would have preferred chicken or some good tobacco.

"What are you writing?" he shouted up to Edison the next day, saying nothing about the oranges or his date. "No, don't tell me. Great writing must not be discussed. It must be read. There is only one way to know its true meaning—the way it lives on the page. Tell me nothing. Let me wait until the pages have achieved their greatness."

"It's a screenplay," Edison said.

Bandini was shocked. He put his fists on his hips, ready for anything.

"You write for the movies? And you live here? Why not Beverly Hills or a house on the ocean?"

Edison glanced at Angels Flight. "I like it here."

Bandini nodded his approval. "Then it is where you should be. Someday this building will be a place of history. A national park. *Writers lived here.*" He took an orange from his pocket and began to peel it. "We will go to Dos Amigos bar and share our stories and I will teach you things that you never thought you could know."

But they never did. A few days later, Arturo Bandini was gone. He had returned from his date dejected, went back for more, with the same results, and then he was done living at the Sun God Arms Apartments. His things and his typewriter were gone as quickly as they had arrived and Edison missed him without having ever gotten to know him. But he took Bandini's advice and stopped hesitating with the keys, moving forward, letting the words flow from his brain to his fingers unimpeded by doubt.

The Turtle

The door to Myra's new office was off the main lobby, between the phone booth with the angry man in it and Myra the Receptionist's desk, opposite the door to Barry's office. She had a small private bathroom with an accordion door and a toilet that made the water jump when it was flushed, but other than being rimmed with wainscoting, the office was barren, containing nothing but a desk, a chair and a file cabinet. It was like one of the cheap movie sets that Barthkowitz liked so much and she was determined to keep it that way so that it would never feel like hers. One afternoon, while perched upon the toilet—slacks up and lid down—updating her journal, rustling and grunting noises grew from the wall behind her, as if a large rat was scurrying around back there. She closed her journal and stepped into her office and was shocked to find Barthkowitz, red-faced and breathing heavily, emerging from the wall with a sheaf of papers in his hand.

"Where did you come from?"

He pointed to the hole in the wainscoting. "My office," he said. The wainscoting panel floated gently on a pair of hinges. "I need to talk to you."

She bent over and looked past the panel to see a dark narrow corridor barely wide enough for Barthkowitz to squeeze through running along the wall behind Myra the Receptionist's desk and Barry's office, leading into Barthkowitz's office. She turned to him, incredulous.

"You're kidding. A secret entrance? To my office?"

"Very. Take a look at this." He pulled a single sheet from the papers and handed it to her. "Barry's brother found it on top of my television."

She looked from the paper to the hole in the wainscoting and back at the paper again. "What the hell is going on?"

"Just read it."

She stared at him a moment longer, unsure how to proceed, then looked at the paper. It was the letter that Edison had written to Barthkowitz a few weeks ago, the one filled with twenty-first century corporate lingo.

"Shit."

"Yes, shit. I can't decide if he's threatening me or proposing marriage."

She nodded. "I'll talk with him about it. Now about this secret passageway . . ."

"Do that, and make sure it doesn't happen again," he said, ignoring her second sentence. "I also want to talk to you about some of your fixes to *Struggle of the Mind*." He shook the other papers in front of her. "This line here that you gave to Chloe, 'If you want to spank someone, spank Hitler.' I thought I told you no Nazi stuff, pro or anti. Warner's lost their shirts on *Confessions of a Nazi Spy*."

"That's because it was a lousy movie."

He pointed his finger at her. "No Nazi stuff. And why is Harry suddenly a Jew?"

"He's not suddenly a Jew. He was born that way."

"Well, un-born him. It doesn't have anything to do with the story. Cut it."

"But—"

"Cut it. Start earning your money."

He started back toward the wainscoting, but she slipped around him and closed the panel before he could reach it, which had the desired effect of irritating him.

"Now I have to go around," he said. "There's no knob on this side."

"Which just makes this creepier." She moved over behind her desk. "Please go out the door. And next time, come in that way. And knock first."

His face wanted fury, his angry M twisting at her, but his eyes told a different story. They moved from her eyes to her hair, sweeping around it almost lovingly.

"Is Tom giving you trouble?" he said.

"Tom?"

"Your husband. I'm only asking because I noticed that your hair is turning gray awfully fast." The cheap dye had nearly disappeared in the past weeks and she was almost fully silvered again.

"No, it's nothing my husband did."

His angry M smoothed out a tad. "Is it me?"

"Please go away."

He returned his M to its proper shape and raised the papers, rattling them in his fist. "No Nazi stuff. Stick to the story. That's an order."

As he passed through the lobby, Myra the Receptionist was sitting at her desk, combing her eyelashes. He knew that she hadn't seen him go into Myra's office. He growled, "I went in there when you were at lunch."

"I haven't gone to lunch yet," she said. He continued into Barry's office without acknowledging her further. "I *heard* you," she said to herself quietly, after the door closed. Then Myra's door opened and Myra stepped into the lobby.

"What do you know about the passageway?"

Myra the Receptionist reached out and touched the cigarette burning in her ashtray, but didn't pick it up. She took a breath and said, "It was part of a set; same as your office. A movie about an accountant who killed his clients and stuffed them in a hole in the wall. After shooting was finished, he decided to leave it." She jerked a thumb in the direction of Barthkowitz's office. "He thinks nobody else knows about it."

The Hedonists

Myra made sure to pick up their pay every week from Myra the Receptionist so that Edison wouldn't see the increase, and socked it into a separate bank account. She left him to write alone in the tiny office with the paper-thin walls, deepening the lie by telling him she was going for walks. She slid the file cabinet in front of the hinged wainscoting panel and filled the drawers with rocks that she lugged in her purse from the vacant lot next store to weigh it down. The lie lived with her everywhere, with everything she did. But she rationalized that if she told Edison he'd be hurt, and she really wanted both of them to enjoy this Christmas season since their last one had been so dreadful. It could wait a few weeks.

She tried to fix her guilt with money. She returned all of the library books, paid the late fees on those that needed it, and filled the shelves with newly purchased hardcovers and magazines. Edison began buying film by the brick. They got hats and underwear and wristwatches. Myra bought fancy skirts that were tight on her legs and impractical for walking. Edison slid into a double-breasted suit with two-button lapels and flapped pockets deep enough to hold his camera, bottoming out with a pair Norwegian-made brogues wrapped around checkerboard silk hose.

"These feel great," he said, staring at his feet.

"Don't forget your orthotics," she said.

He blushed. "How long have you known?"

She just smiled. Edison knew there was a lie lurking about inside her; he'd seen her head bob, her hair falling across the sides of her face like blinders whenever he asked her if she had enjoyed her walk. But he didn't know what it was and didn't pursue it. He didn't want to cause an argument that he was too confused to win.

They cruised through the holidays on a magic carpet of alcohol, music and stargazing. They took taxicabs, which they began referring to as "liquor cocoons". They finally bought a radio and on Christmas Eve they danced in their apartment to the drifty lilt of *Silent Night,* keeping the lie between them warm and alive.

On Wednesdays, they lunched at the Montmarte, snuggled away evenings in red leather booths at Formosa and voyeured at Schwab's on sunny afternoons. At Musso & Frank they saw Dorothy Parker fall off a bar stool, watched Faulkner and Fitzgerald trip over her, caught Hammett bang his head on the bar laughing about it, and spied Chandler, plastered to the eye teeth, sitting in a corner writing it all down. At the Brown Derby they ran into Humphrey Bogart, knew that his amazing days as a leading man were just around the corner and that he would die at the age of fifty-seven (their age) from too much life and too few doctors. On New Year's Eve, they attended an all-night jam session with Charlie Christian, Benny Goodman and Lionel Hampton, returning home at the first light of 1940 with the dregs of jazz in their heads and their clothes limp and humid.

The neighbors at the Sun God Arms looked at them funny now. The Three Bills waved only tentatively, as if they weren't sure they were allowed to anymore. Arturo Bandini, had he still been around, would have turned his back on Edison's typing, refusing to listen.

"Your words have grown unworthy of my time," he might have said.

But they couldn't last. They were still fifty-seven years old, aging or not, and didn't have the juice for it. Hunched over half-drunk drinks, fighting sleep, they cursed the Time Flies for their constant fatigue, for feeling too old for these things that happened before they were born.

Edison kept rewriting *Struggle of the Mind* and Myra kept rewriting what he wrote without him knowing about it. She rewrote other writer's scripts, too, writers she had never met, cranking out changes faster than the writers could complain about them. But her stamina for dishonesty was weak and her guilt grew unbearable, peaking at a party at the Bar-thkowitz mansion. She'd had too much to drink and was reflecting on simpler times beneath a glittering chandelier, blathering inappropriately to some producer's wife whose name she couldn't remember.

"It's like I tell my students," she slurred. "'You can't get on a destroyer without going through basic training first.'"

"Exactly," the producer's wife slurred back without the slightest idea of what Myra was talking about.

"I keep telling them, 'You're supposed to be the tech generation. Stop making me find your websites for you.'"

The producer's wife wavered unsteadily. Myra wavered back, trying to figure out if she'd really just said what she thought she'd just said or if she had just thought it. Edison found her outside in the dark, sitting on the stairs, crying. He sat next her and she put her head on his shoulder.

"I miss the kids," she said. "I really, really miss the kids."

"Me too. Let's go home, honey." He asked Bruce to call them a cab.

"You're a cab," said Bruce. He didn't crack a smile, but Myra sort of did.

The Truth

The next morning, Edison sat on the porch wrapped in a blanket, listening to his head pound. Rain pittered on the railing, absorbing into the unprotected wood. Myra had returned from her morning walk drenched to the panties and sick to her stomach with rage after seeing Stalin's picture on the cover of Time Magazine's 1939 Man of the Year issue, even though she remembered it and still felt compelled to read it as she plodded through the rain, the sopping pages coming apart in her hands. *Corkavonin must be laughing his ass off now, the worm.* Without bothering to dry off, she climbed out the window to talk with Edison, holding the dregs of the magazine in her hand.

"What?" he said when he noticed her dripping and staring.

"We need to talk."

She told him about her new job, about doctoring other writer's scripts without their knowledge, and about their raise in pay. Edison listened to her, clutching his blanket and gazing into the rain, finding that he wasn't that surprised by her news, but chafed just the same.

"I didn't think you could be going for that many walks. Not even you. But I didn't know you had another office."

Myra rubbed her throbbing forehead. "Reggie didn't want me to tell you."

"Reggie?" He let the blanket fall open and pushed it off his shoulders.

"You know who I mean," she said. "Barthkowitz."

"When did you start calling him Reggie?"

"Edison, please."

They were silent for a while as the rain pinged on the porch roof above them. Edison started playing with a loose thread on the crotch of his pants as his lips formed the word *Reggie*. Then he said, "What about our script?"

She didn't answer. She may have been crying. She was too wet for him to be sure.

He pulled on the thread and a small hole started growing on the seam. "I knew that somebody would change it. Someone always does. I guess I should be glad it was you." He wrapped the thread around his finger and tried to snap it off. The hole got bigger. "So, what's wrong with it?"

Myra stepped closer and put an arm around his neck. "Not much, really. Considering that you didn't even want this to get made, you did pretty well. Just a few small things. He wants a slightly different perspective on the female lead."

"Her name is Chloe," said Edison in a low voice.

Myra sighed and took her arm back. "Edison, this is common. You know that. Barthkowitz just wants the studio to make money."

"His name is Reggie."

"Don't be impossible." She sat at the table and watched rain soak into the railing.

Edison stuck his finger in the hole he had just made in his pants. "You're not credited, are you?"

"That's the deal."

"That stinks."

She leaned across the table. "No, it's okay. The money is good. In a few months, when our contract is up, we can get out of here and do some traveling. We've saved a lot—minus the twelve percent for charity and thirteen for Goochy—and as long as we stop living like we have been in the past few weeks, we could have enough to last us for years if we're careful. We used to be frugal. Remember?"

Edison put his forearms on the railing, letting the rain fall on him. He wasn't finished being angry yet. "So, what else?"

"What do you mean?"

"What else is wrong with it?"

"Oh, Edison."

"What else?" He turned and glared at her. She took a deep breath and let it out slowly.

"Really, not much. A few inconsistencies."

"Don't you mean plot holes?" he said.

"There are plot holes everywhere," she said matter-of-factly. "Small ones. It's a film noir. It's to be expected. I'm talking about inconsistencies."

He stood. "There are plot holes everywhere? Everywhere?"

"Edison, please. I'm sorry."

He put his hands in his pockets, pointedly not down his pants. "Alright. Give me an inconsistency." His tone said that he only wanted to use her answer as ammunition.

She shook her head slowly, watching droplets run down his forearms into his pockets.

"Tell me," he said.

She tightened her mouth and ran a hand through her hair. "Alright. In one scene, when Harry starts getting his memory back, you have him telling Chloe that he grew up in an orphanage, but then later he tells her about his mother."

"So? His mother died when he was young."

"You said he asked her for money when he was in the Navy."

"Fine. I'll fix it, assuming inconsistencies can be fixed. Maybe I should just stick to fixing plot holes."

"I already fixed it."

Edison puffed up like he was getting ready to yell, but the voice that came out was small and measured and somewhat mean. "You what?"

Myra got up and started climbing through the window, then came back, raised the magazine in a high arc and slammed it on the table, shattering Stalin's face into wads of wet pulp. Her eyes grew intense, wide—Gloria Swanson wide—her vision blurred by tears.

"I hate this fucking job and I hate this city!"

She fell back in her chair and buried her face in her hands. Edison reconsidered his position. He grew confused again and thought he might be in trouble, so he sat back down.

"You do?" he said. He was surprised to find that she didn't like it here. It wasn't everything he wanted, either, but he had gotten to the point where he felt safe. Writing gave his brain something to latch onto and kept him from feeling like an imbecile. And it was a job. A very good paying one. He was deathly afraid of losing another one. He stuck his finger through the hole in his pants and scratched his balls. After a minute or so, Myra's head rose. She sniffled and wiped her nose on her sleeve.

"It's not like I didn't know what we were getting ourselves into. But I thought I could shrug it off better. I'm tired of everything. I'm tired of calling you Edison. I'm tired of being pissed off all the time and behaving like a compulsive idiot."

She sniffled some more, then got up and went into the bathroom for some toilet paper. Edison could hear her blowing her nose. He picked up his camera and took a picture of Angels Flight through the rain, but it didn't help. When she came back out, she had changed into something dry. Her nose and eyes were a triangle of red and Edison knew from her expression that he was in for a speech. She asked him to come inside. She closed the window after he climbed in and spoke in a low voice.

"I've been thinking about this. America will be getting into the war soon. Okay, not for almost two more years, but still. I'd like to be somewhere else before the rationing starts. I thought I was doing the right thing. I'm sorry for lying to you. I don't like it here and what it's doing to me. It was fun at first, but I'm sick of the blue sky, even if it is a little brown. I'm sick of people like Barthkowitz and Pulaski. I'm sick of the vanity and the greed and the crazies," she said, half crying and half angry. "And do you know what I found out yesterday? This place is restricted. This place, where we live."

"What does that mean?"

"Ever wonder why you see Mexicans all over the place but none of them live here? It's because Huffy Lydon won't rent to them. Jews, either. And no doubt African Americans, too."

"How do you know?"

"Dot let it slip out. She said it as if she thought I would agree with it. I didn't even know what to say. But I do now. I'm going to give Huffy hell about it and then we're going to move."

Edison leaned back on the couch. Moving would mean being away from Angels Flight and the Edison Building. And his porch.

"Is that okay?" she said. "I know that you like it here, but wouldn't it be nice to see some of the country?"

"I don't know. I guess."

Myra sat beside him and put her head on his shoulder. "I miss the spring in Seattle—the green, oh, I miss the green—but we can't go back there. I want to go to New York. You've always loved New York. Imagine what it looks like now. If I'm going to be uncomfortable in this time, I at least want to be somewhere where I can recognize the pavement when I walk on it. Los Angeles is a car city and we don't even have a car. And really, I just don't trust anybody here, at least not in the part of *here* that we live in. I don't know. Maybe it's me. I want to do more. I want to help people."

"Helping people will change history."

And then she got such a perplexed look on her face that it gave Edison a chill.

And then they were done. A sort of agreement had been reached, silent and understanding. They hugged. Edison kissed her snotty face. They made a pact to work diligently and without anger toward each other. And to go to New York City. New York would be fun.

A Change of Regime

"I'd like to speak with Huffy, Dot."

Dot looked at Myra with haggard eyes. She seemed older than she had two days ago. "So would I."

"What's happened?"

"He died," said Dot, her voice shaky and thin. "Last night. In his sleep. Comfortably. I tried not to wake anyone."

That evening, they sat with Dot over tea, letting her weep and talk, giving her vague assurances of Huffy's rightful place in the afterlife. When she had dried out some, she gave them each a gift. With solemn dignity, she placed the amputation kit in Myra's lap and handed Edison the tray of glass eyeballs.

"I know that Huffy would have wanted you to have these. He respected you both and appreciated that you put up with his tiresome stories."

"His stories were a pleasure," said Myra.

Dot promised them a proper refrigerator as soon as she could afford it and even offered to redecorate some of the apartment. "Paint or wallpaper?" she asked Myra.

"I'm not much for wallpaper."

"Paint it is. And I'm going to remove the restriction on this place," she said, staring into Myra's eyes. "I never approved of it, but I didn't think

I could do anything about it. I can now. Besides, there are too many vacancies and I need the money."

In the morning, Edison took his tray of eyeballs out on the porch to see them in the sunlight, but he slipped while climbing through the window and the tray tipped, spilling the eyeballs onto the porch floor, where they wasted no time rolling to the corner where the pencils rolled off. He watched them disappear over the edge.

Below, the Three Bills were briefly pelted with glass eyeballs. Some of them smashed on impact while others bounced a few times on the pavement before rolling away into the gutters and weeds. The Three Bills looked up in confusion, but Edison stayed back from the railing so they couldn't see him. He stashed the velvet-covered tray under the bed and told Myra nothing.

The First Way Out

"Take a look at this beauty," the salesman said, his teeth leaping at Edison, his chin thrust forward like an open cash drawer, his eyes squinted into coin slots. He patted the dinged fender like a baby's bottom. "Now, I know it doesn't look like much, but this little darling was featured at the 1933 Chicago World's Fair. She rides like a dream."

Edison didn't think it didn't look like much. To him it *was* a dream—a faded silver-blue 1935 Studebaker Land Cruiser for only $123. It reminded him of a cartoon. Rear wheel skirts, a cowcatcher grill and a fully enclosed trunk that the salesman said had "room enough for three dead gangsters, galvanized tubs, a couple of bags of cement, and a case of beer. Make that two cases." The front door opened backwards—a touch of sophistication—and the sliding steel roof hadn't started leaking yet. There were even running boards in case he felt like hefting a machine gun and doing a few bank robbery getaways.

"One of the earliest examples of streamliner construction" the salesman continued. "Eight cylinder, one-hundred and three horse power cast iron engine. And look at that four-panel back window. You don't see something like that every day."

"No, you don't," Edison said, admiring it, then noticing: "One of the wheel skirts is missing."

The salesman nodded, frowning, "Damned thieves," and took a business card from his shirt pocket, looking around to see if they were being watched as he handed it to Edison. The card had the salesman's name, occupation and business phone number on it, next to an illustration of a naked woman in a bathtub with suds on her boobs to hide her nipples. It was intended to distract Edison, and did.

"I'm not supposed to do this," said the salesman, "but you look like a guy who could use a break. I'll give you five dollars straight off the top for the missing skirt. Just don't tell my boss."

"I won't," Edison promised.

Although the salesman had tried his best to fulfill his role as a stereotype of sleaze and dishonesty, he'd actually sold Edison a reliable car. Edison had no doubts. He had chosen his name from a Studebaker advertisement that had promised that their cars had been built only by solid citizens—no transients—and felt certain of their fine workmanship and reliability. He pulled up Clay Street with the steel roof slid open and tooted the horn, gauzy puffs of blue exhaust percolating from the tailpipe. The Three Bills crowded around the car, congratulating him on his purchase and drinking in his honor. He tooted the horn again and they tried to get in.

"No, no, not you," he said. "Myra. Hey, Myra!"

The Three Bills helped out, cupping their hands around their mouths.

Myra was in the bathroom, working on her journal, when she heard a chorus of sandpaper and phlegm calling her name. She finished up the entry she was working on—

37r8/8/ – Lbr Ldr Jmee Hawphuh dsaprs (TF prsnr?)

Translation:

> July 1975 or 76, Labor Leader Jimmy Hoffa dis-
> appears (Time Fly prisoner?)

—before climbing onto the porch to see what was up.

"Let's go," Edison yelled through the hole in the roof.

"Let's go," said the Three Bills and again tried to get in.

"Are you sure there's room for all of us?" Myra laughed down at them.

The Bills knew their place and stopped the charade before it became too humiliating for them, but held onto enough good cheer to toast Myra as she climbed into the passenger side, and again when the car pulled away from the curb. And again when it passed beneath Angels Flight. And one more time when they couldn't see the car anymore.

Myra ran her fingertips over the painted metal and chrome and Bakelite of the dashboard. She'd forgotten how lovely cars used to be. "I guess you didn't feel the need to discuss this."

"I thought we had," said Edison. "We need something to drive to New York. It's a long way. I need the practice."

"Drive to New York? I thought we'd take the train."

"Mmm."

They left the roof open in the February chill as they headed for the coast. Myra slid over next to him until her thigh touched his, half expecting a seatbelt buzzer to complain, and reminded him at five block intervals to keep it below the speed limit.

"So, when does shooting begin?" he asked, trying to keep his tone casual. "You do know, don't you?"

"Today."

"What?"

"Keep your eyes on the road, please."

"But why aren't we there?"

Myra placed her hand on his thigh. "We're not invited. The shoot is only nine days and already a month behind schedule. Barthkowitz doesn't like writers on the set. He says they slow the process down. You knew that."

Edison felt that he should be indignant and tried to make it work, but found that he was starting to not care so much anymore. There were fewer than two months left on their contract and then they'd hit the road.

They drove out to the end of Wilshire Boulevard past the cypress trees and the palm trees, and some beaten up beach bungalows with the paint faded to the gentleness of Easter colors, and turned north on the Coast Highway. The sun was high above them, heating their skin. Gulls and pelicans dipped and weaved above waves that sparkled like flashbulbs. Malibu was busy creating its wall of money between the road and everybody's ocean, but there were still a few pockets of beach where a person could pretend for a few minutes that they were alone.

They parked along the side of the road by the pedestrian overpass at Castellammare so that Myra could walk the staircase up into the foothills and back down again, after which she joined Edison at the cafe for coffee. They stared at the ocean until the sky went from yellow to orange, then drove aimlessly, passing through hazy forests of oil derricks on Signal Hill where Edison stopped to take a few pictures in the dusk.

When the light was gone, they went to a drive-in theater and made out like teenagers through half of a movie whose name they couldn't remember and left before the second feature, dropping down to the Venice pier for a little dancing. They topped out the evening winding through Laurel Canyon, Myra with her coat wrapped around her, the lights of the city below mingling with the stars above and small clouds cruising between palm trees blackened against the half-mooned sky. Edison reached for her hand. She sighed and closed her eyes, her head on his shoulder, her hair brighter than the moon itself, its history no longer obscured by cheap dye.

"So strange, this life."

The Extension

Barry ignored Myra as she sat in his office, her back against the wall, waiting for Edison. Barthkowitz wanted to see them and she knew he wasn't happy. Just minutes before he had tried to come into her office through the secret passageway again and found it blocked by the file cabinet full of rocks. She'd heard him rattling the knob.

"Go away," she'd said.

"I need to talk to you."

"Use the door."

He was silent for a few seconds, then said, "I can't turn around in here."

"You should have thought of that before."

He had punched at the wainscoting panel in a choleric outburst, followed it with some muffled admonitions on her faulty character traits, and followed that with a very clear, "My office! Two minutes! Both of you!" as he shuffled backwards through the passageway.

Edison arrived at Barry's office out of breath and without his camera. He had left it on his desk to keep Barthkowitz quiet. "You're a writer. Write," Barthkowitz had said about it. He took a seat next to Myra, his hello to Barry left unacknowledged. He asked Myra what was up and she shrugged. Barry put some papers in his file cabinet, closed the drawer, then opened it again and took some papers out. They looked like the same papers. Edison wondered if Barry had ever actually looked at them, if he even knew what they looked like.

A half an hour went by before Barry's box squawked.

"Are they here?"

Barry pushed the button. "They're here."

"Send them in."

"You heard him," said Barry.

"Sorry to keep you waiting," Barthkowitz said to Myra, without sounding sorry. "Friend with a crisis. Jack Thomas shot his wife's new voice coach in the groin due to thinking that the coach was putting it to her. He wasn't, and he certainly won't now."

"Jack Thomas, the producer?" said Edison.

Barthkowitz grunted.

"Is his wife anyone?" said Myra.

"June Beunet," said Barthkowitz and Edison in unison.

"Oh," said Myra. "Well, if he was a friend, I'm sorry."

Barthkowitz waved it off. "He doesn't owe me anything."

"I can understand why he did it," said Edison, inspecting his fingernails.

Barthkowitz threw a slivered eye at Myra and then started going through papers on his desk, as if he was searching for something only slightly important. Many seconds passed before Myra cleared her throat. Barthkowitz looked up at her. He stood, put a soggy, unlit cigar in his mouth and turned his back on them to face the patio.

"*Struggle of the Mind* has been delayed."

"Again?" said Myra.

Barthkowitz put up a hand to silence her. "Gloria has lost her voice. Also, some of her scenes need to be reshot—and rewritten—and it's costing me a fortune to keep a crew hanging around waiting for her to talk again." He puffed on his unlit cigar a few times before delivering the punch line. "I'm extending your contracts for three months."

"What?" said Myra.

"What do you mean?" said Edison.

Barthkowitz spun around and leaned toward them menacingly. "Oh, I'm sorry, was I talking through my ass? Let me try it again. I'm extending your contracts through June."

"You can't do that," said Myra. "You can't even afford it."

Barthkowitz rolled into his chair and shuffled through more papers until he came up with their contract. He slid it toward them across his desk. "Read. It gives me the right to extend you, without renegotiation, purely at my discretion. At the end of the three-month extension, we can renegotiate. Not before."

She knew he was right. She had read it many times. But six months ago it hadn't seemed important. "What makes you like this?" she said.

"I'm a self-made man."

"Maybe you should have taken a few classes."

He pulled the cigar out. "Watch your mouth. I own this place. Me."

"You don't own us."

"Really?" He laughed. "Who are you? Ghandi?" He laughed harder.

Myra stood, preparing to leave. Edison put a hand on her sleeve.

"It's okay, honey."

"It is?" said Barthkowitz, reducing his laughter to a puzzled chuckle. "Well, well. Continue."

"I remember reading that you did the same thing with the writer on *The Dime Was Tossed.*" His eyes went to Myra. "No big deal. It's three more months of pay."

Barthkowitz leaned back in his chair. "*The Dime Was Tossed*, huh?" He stuck the cigar back in his mouth. "What do you know about that?"

"Not much," said Edison. "Just that the production was delayed and the writer's contract was extended. I think it's one of Acropolis Pictures' best films."

Barthkowitz smiled. "Really? Well, that's nice. That's very nice. When did this happen?"

Edison felt his face grow warm as he realized that it had 'happened' in the twenty-first century. Something he read somewhere in a book on film. He tried to hold onto his confident tone, but it grew slippery and he stumbled. "Uh, a while back."

"Edison," said Myra.

"No, let him talk," said Barthkowitz. "This is interesting. How long a while back?"

Myra said, "He means we were talking to the writer about it."

"Let him talk," Barthkowitz said again, warning her. "How long a while back? And stand up. I can't hear you down there." Edison stood slowly. When he was erect enough, Barthkowitz nodded his approval. "Now…"

Edison's hands made a move for his pants. "Um…I'm not sure. A couple of weeks ago?" he lied. "We were talking to the writer…over a drink…he mentioned some scenes and I…uh…visualized them."

Barthkowitz pulled the cigar out and pointed it at Edison. "There you go talking that bullshit again. I'm not asking you about the movie you supposedly saw, although I will, considering it isn't even finished. I am asking you about the contract extension that hasn't happened yet. Who told you about that?"

Edison looked to Myra for help and found nothing. His lip began to twitch.

"Who was it?" insisted Barthkowitz. "Not that I don't know. I just want to hear you say it."

Myra stepped forward. "Reggie…"

"I said shutup!"

Myra flinched. "No you didn't," she said. "But now that you have I won't stand for it. Nobody talks to me that way. Not even a bully like you."

The three figures froze briefly—the cigar-holding man, the indignant woman, and the man with his hands in his pants. A moment of silence. Then Myra, noting the papers on Barthkowitz's desk, reached out and swept some of them onto the floor. Tentatively. Almost as if it might have been an accident. Her eyes widened as she did a safety check on Barthkowitz's reaction. Barthkowitz flicked his eyes from her to the papers on the floor, flicked them back to her, then back to the papers again. They seemed odd down there, in a disarray not his own. He wasn't sure what to do. No one had ever swept papers off his desk before, especially a woman. Although if anyone ever were to sweep papers off his desk in anger it seemed more likely that it would be a woman, not a man. Not sure why, it just did. And now it had happened. And it was a woman. But who was going to pick them up? He let his eyes wander over to Barry's door, then over to the squawk box. Then he slowly leaned forward and placed his elbows on the desk, giving them both the cool once over.

"You're in cahoots on something, of that much I'm sure." He pointed his cigar at Myra. "Two nights ago, you were seen at a meeting of the American Peace Mobilization, another Commie front."

Edison looked at her. "I thought you were walking."

"I was. I didn't go in."

Barthkowitz said, "You stopped in front of the building."

"So I stopped in front of a building," said Myra. "What's your point?"

"Why did you stop?"

"How the hell should I know? I was tired. I stubbed my toe. I thought I saw a naked man. What difference does it make?" Then she said, "I am not a Communist, Mr. Barthkowitz, and it would be none of your business if I was."

Barthkowitz sat there puffing on his unlit cigar, staring at her, not saying anything.

Then she said, "Are you having me followed?"

The cigar made a slight twirl in his mouth.

"Is it Barry?" she said.

Barthkowitz took the decanter of whiskey from his drawer and set it on the desk. "Three months."

Myra drove home while Edison fell in and out of sleep on the passenger side.

As they waited at a traffic light he said, "You thought you saw a naked man?"

"Oh, Edison."

The Revision

Spring arrived and historical events stayed pretty much on track. The Soviet Union began the executions of 22,000 Polish POWs and Germany invaded Norway and Denmark "to protect their freedom and independence" from the British. Strangely, the incident concerning *The Dime Was Tossed* was never mentioned again. In fact, it seemed that Barthkowitz had almost forgotten about Edison, working only with Myra in his office or in hers. Myra was increasingly unhappy and Barthkowitz was increasingly moronic. He answered none of her questions about *Struggle of the Mind*, assigning her instead to renovating the female roles in other writer's scripts. She found the work ridiculous and overvalued.

"Do you want us to be working on something else?" she asked him one evening when he had come into her office via the proper entrance after Myra the Receptionist had left for the day. "What about Edison?"

"Just tell him to stick with *Struggle* for now."

"But it's finished. It's been finished for weeks."

"I'll tell you when it's finished," he said, although he didn't sound convinced of it himself. "I want to see more pages tomorrow."

"Of what?"

He spoke through his teeth. "Of the goddamned script. What the hell do you think what?"

Episodes such as this seemed to confirm her growing suspicion that Barthkowitz had no idea what he was doing. Still, she felt obligated to earn her pay by spending long hours in her office, even if she burned away many of them reading about the war and what the U.S. was or wasn't doing about it, or working on her journals in her tiny private bathroom.

Edison sat in the little office at the back of the lot typing alone most days, making changes to the script that no one would ever see. He was now lugging the Royal typewriter from home every day because he liked it better than the Underwood. Sometimes Myra would come over when Barthkowitz was out and they would talk about New York for a while and then have a quickie right there on the table until the guy next door stopped typing and rapped on the wall, telling them to take it elsewhere. But visits like this were rare and as she got home later and later, he grew petulant and lonely. He started attending Tuesday night boxing at the Olympic Auditorium, pointing his camera more at the crowds than at the fighters. He was not a boxing fan, just curious about people's desire to watch other people beat each other up. He captured their faces and their limbs; the way they leered and salivated and shook their fists. He photographed fans, crooks, desperadoes, bloody fighters, and Hollywood types. Outside, he photographed cops roughing up shady characters in alleys, and shady characters roughing up other shady characters in different alleys. He crept through streets of shadow and fog, aiming his lens, trying to keep his mind focused and the path before him clear, filling his thoughts with New York and Myra and the American road, looking forward to the change, even if it meant leaving Angels Flight.

At home one afternoon, he pestered Myra to let him see the revised script of *Struggle of the Mind,* the one she had done. She looked into his eyes and decided it was okay.

"I don't have a copy of the final script, just the one I originally tinkered with."

Tinkered with. "Let me see."

She went to the bathroom to retrieve it from the basket where she kept her journals and handed it to him after smoothing out some of the damaged corners.

83

INT. ROCKY'S OFFICE - NIGHT

Harry stands off to the side, his coat on, his hat on top
of the file cabinet. He lights a cigarette and blows the
smoke Chloe's way. He smiles, staring her down. Chloe ~~is~~ sits
~~curled~~ in a chair on the other side of the room, ~~nervous,~~
~~dreading the next moment.~~ filing her nails and waving smoke out of her fa

                    CHLOE
        ~~What?~~ What is it, Harry?

                    HARRY
        What is it? I'll tell ya. You
        like me, but not all the way.
        You're attracted to me. I make
        you feel special. You like the
        way I carry myself, the way I
        say things sometimes. But there
        are things about me you don't
        like and you want to change them.
        Ain't that right?

                    CHLOE
        ~~Not~~ Not everything, Harry. Just a few things, like your
tendency to kill people. Think of me as a mechanic doing a tune-up.
                    HARRY
That's what I   → ~~Sure it is.~~ You think you can
thought. →   change the things you don't like
                 without hurting the things you
                 do like...

                    CHLOE (overlapping)
        ~~Not~~ Oh, come on.

                    HARRY
        ...but it don't work that way.
        You start trying tb change the
        things you don't like and the
        other things start falling apart
        on you.
            rolls her eyes.
Chloe ~~buries her face in her hands.~~ Harry leans against
the file cabinet and smokes for a moment.

                    HARRY
                 (offhandedly)
        But you can't help yourself. It's
        in your nature.

~~Chloe springs from her chair.~~

                    ~~CHLOE~~
        ~~You're a liar! It's not true!~~

Harry raises an eyebrow at her. ~~Chloe freezes up, nervous.~~

                    CHLOE
        ~~I'm sorry, Harry. I'm sorry. I~~   oh, please.
        ~~didn't mean to call you a liar.~~
        ~~It's just not true, what you said.~~

                    HARRY
        Oh, it's true. You know it and I
        know it. You just think you can
        keep me from finding out that I
        know you know it.

                    CHLOE
        What are you talking about? You're
        not making any sense.

                    HARRY
        I'm making plenty of sense, doll.
        But I'm not gonna let you do it. I
        don't need some dame trying to change
        me. I can handle myself. I got my
        own way of doing things and they have
        to be done my way.

Chloe stands and paces.
                    CHLOE
        ~~I'm not trying to change you, Harry.~~
        ~~Honest I'm not.~~

                    HARRY
                 (chuckling)
        You thought you had me good, didn't
        you? Now you listen to me.

"Harry. Listen to me. I'm not trying to change you, just some of the
things you do." (stepping closer to him) "I want the Harry I met
down by the docks that morning months ago. The Harry who had
amnesia and let me be his memory for a while. Remember, Harry?"
Harry seems to consider this. He looks at his cigarette, then laughs.
He's not buying it.

HARRY (CONT'D)

It's too late for me to go back, ~~Chloe~~ doll.
You know it. I know it. Every cop in this
city knows it. You really took me for a
ride, chloe. You really did.

Chloe sits again, looks away.

CHLOE
~~No I didn't, Harry. I want to~~
~~be with you for who you are. For~~
~~what you do. For living life on~~
~~the edge. It's the danger I crave,~~
~~Harry.~~
~~(she sits and puts~~
~~her hand to her head)~~
I'm sorry. ~~But it scares me.~~ It just scares
me. I don't want you to get hurt.
I don't know what I'd do if you
got hurt, Harry.

Harry sizes her up for a moment with smirky confidence.
He shakes his head, grabs his hat and opens the door.

HARRY
I can't let you do it to me, doll.
That's in my nature.

He puts his hat on.

HARRY
So long, Chloe.

Harry walks out the door and down the hallway. Chloe ~~springs~~ gets up
from her chair and ~~runs~~ walks to the door, ~~calling after him.~~ leaning on
the doorframe.

CHLOE
Harry! ~~Harry! Come back!~~ Harry, please!
~~I'll be good. I won't try to change you.~~
~~I promise! Harry! Come back!~~

Harry disappears around the corner at the end of the hall.
Chloe ~~flings herself back into the room, collapsing in the chair in a heap of tears.~~ slowly turns from the door frame, Closes the door and looks down at her hands, hands covered with the ~~FADE OUT~~ blood of deception, then covers her face. Suddenly, she hears police sirens and screeching brakes. She runs to the window and sees Harry, bookended by two cops, being pushed into the back of a police car below. She watches with tears in her eyes. Harry tips his hat to her. There's a knock on the door. She turns.

                    COP
              (from behind door)
          Open up. Police.

Chloe collapses in the chair, bows her head, then looks up bravely, drying her eyes, resigning herself.

                    CHLOE
              Come in.

FADE OUT

Edison didn't like it. Not what she did, but what he had done. He could see that he'd left a little fatale out of his femme fatale. Sure, Chloe did a bad thing to a good guy, but she didn't stand by it. In Edison's version, she had given up. Started off strong and finished weak. Myra had buffed her up, made her sparkle, had shoved some calcium up her spine without disturbing the guilt.

Edison threw the script on the bed, put his hands on his hips, spun himself around and picked it up again. He almost tore it to pieces, but in the end, all he could do was thank her.

"I suppose it needed work."

"Just a little polishing, that's all," she said.

He set the script on the bed and sat.

"Yeah."

"I had to have them get arrested or we'd never get it past the censors."

"I forgot about that."

He picked up the script again and looked at the last page.

"Why does the cop knock if the door is unlocked?"

"Huh?"

"Right here," he said, pointing to the page. "The cop knocks and says 'open up.' Then she says 'come in'. Why does he have to knock?"

Myra read the page. "Oh, shit." She started to laugh. Edison joined her.

Preservation

Edison stopped working on *Struggle of the Mind* altogether. His words were getting all changed around anyway. It seemed useless to continue, although neither Barthkowitz nor Pulaski had made any attempt to tell him it was finished, or if it was still shooting, or in post-production. Or even if he should be working on another project. Things got weird. The office felt more like a cell, its thin walls closing in on him, the typing from the office next door rapping at his ears. He began using the Royal to write more letters to Barthkowitz, ditching the corporate lingo of his first letter and going for a more straightforward approach, criticizing Barthkowitz's managerial style outright and accusing him of rutting after his wife.

```
And stop making her lie to me, or I'll punch you in the
belly like I punched that Commie.
```

It eased his mind somewhat to be speaking it. He bought stamps and envelopes, and wrote at least three letters per day that he would drop in the mailbox located on the sidewalk by the main entrance to *Acropolis Studios*. He thought of the letters as a kind of conversation he was having with Barthkowitz, and imagined Barthkowitz responding with letters of agreement and heartfelt apology and promises to change, although he received no actual replies to any of them. But he kept on with it, using the rat-a-tat of the typing from next door as motivation. Sometimes he would throw something at the wall, a small item like a pencil eraser, just to make the typing stop and the writer next door say, "What?" to which he would respond, "Nothing," and the typing would start again.

Then he got an idea: he would listen carefully to the typing and try to copy it, following its rhythms, reflecting on the advice given him by Arturo Bandini to let his fingers fly unimpeded by doubt. At first, he just typed gibberish, the intent being only to duplicate the rhythm, creating a sort of musical typing. Occasionally, when he matched the rhythm correctly, it would make him fall into fits of laughter that he would muffle with his forearm so that the guy next door wouldn't hear. As he got better at it he began typing real stuff, creating dialogue and description at the speed of the rhythm. This was much harder, but more rewarding, such as the day he wrote two full scenes this way about a vengeful teenager whose nose gets cut off in a knife fight, and titled it *Rebel Without a Schnoz*. He didn't care at all about what he was writing. He was just trying to amuse himself, which was too bad because some of it probably could have been turned into some fair B movies, at least good enough to make back the money it would take to shoot them. He had started nine different stories, all under the name of Edison Winslow, not Tom Winslow, and wouldn't finish any of them.

There was the acerbic *Road Rage:*

Road Rage   89 16

Dame eyes him with disgust as she lights another cigarette and blews flicks the match his way.

                        DAME
            That's the dmbest thing you've
            ever said. You've said dumb thiggs
            before, and you'll probably say
            them again because you're prone
            to saying dumb things. But that
            was the dumbest.

                        HOOD WITH GUN
                    (waving gun at Dame)
            Johnny, make her shutup. I don't
            know if I can cotrol myself.

The powder-blasted *Rash Count*:

```
                RASH COUNT
                    by
              Edison  Winslow

Johnny turns toward Rekey Rocky as Rocky levels his gun at
him.

                    ROCKY
            I'll teach you to talk to me that way.

Johnny reaches for his gun.

                    JOHNNY
            Apparently, I already know how. School's
            out.

BAM! BAM! Johnny shoots Rocky. Rocky crumplesto the floor.

                (struggling
                    ROCKY
                (struggling)
            I taught you everything you know.

Rocky dies.
```

The ready-to-be-banned *Old Boy's Club*:

```
              THE OLD BOY'S CLUB
                    by
              Edison * Winslow


                    1
            I'll gett him, Boss. I'll smack
            him right in the kisser.

                    2
            How old is he?

                    1
            Huh?

                    2
            How old?

                    1
            I don't know. Fifty, maybe?

                    2
            Go for the knees first. Then the kisser.
```

He even secretly started a script called *The Time Flies*. In his version, he made Myra the hapless boob and cast himself as the hero.

```
INT. MINNIE'S HOUSE -- 1938 - DAY

MYRA cowers on the couch whileEEDISON heroically builds
a fire.

                    MYRA
          Oh, no! What do we do? Please tell
          me!

                    EDISON
          Dom't worry! I'll save you'.
```

Along with this script he retyped a copy of the Time Fly Law, sans the graphics. This would turn out to be helpful later since the original one in his pocket was becoming tattered.

Reunion

Barthkowitz pulled open a drawer on his desk, not the one with the decanter of Scotch, but the one above it.

"Look at this," he said to Myra.

The drawer was filled with unopened letters.

"What is it?" she said.

"You tell me." He pulled the drawer all the way out and dumped it on the desk. Letters spilled across the surface, all addressed to Barthkowitz and all return addresses courtesy of Tom Winslow. Myra's mouth fell open. She was overwhelmed and impressed. Astonished and a little ashamed. The hours he must have spent doing this when she wasn't around. "It's been going on for weeks," said Barthkowitz.

"Did you read any of them?"

"Not a goddamned one. This ain't a library. I have a business to run. What the hell is he pulling?"

"I think he feels more comfortable communicating with you this way."

"Well, tell him to cut it out. He's burying me."

"Tell him yourself. He's your employee."

She left his office, grumbling, Edison embedded in her thoughts, and while cutting across the lobby she heard the muffled anger in the phone booth stop and the phone slam down. The booth door crashed open and the angry man she had been hearing for months stepped out right in front of her. It was Cavin Corkavonin—the Eye—the Commie she had argued with at the Party meeting last year when they'd first met Goochy. The one Edison had punched in the belly.

She gasped. "You."

He recognized her at once and derided her with the curve of his upper lip.

"You? Here?" he said, sounding like a leaky balloon.

Myra the Receptionist smiled politely at them, wishing they would leave.

The Eye huffed pettishly, leaning forward until he was within smelly breath distance of Myra. "You'll pay," he said, recalling for her his earlier threat to make her pay for verbally throttling him in front of his fellow Party members. Myra decided it was best to let this one go.

Victor

Some days later, while Edison was in the middle of plucking out some pretty good dialogue to the rhythm of the keys next door, the typing stopped.

"What are you doing over there?" said the voice on the other side of the wall.

Edison's fingers froze. "Nothing. Typing."

"It sounds like you're trying to copy me."

"No. Just typing."

"Well, it sounds like you're trying to copy me. And quit throwing shit at the wall."

"Sorry."

Edison sat staring at the wall. From the other side arose some shuffling and clinking then the legs of a chair being pushed back followed by footsteps and a knock on his door. He picked up his camera.

"Come in." When the door opened, he took a picture.

"Funny," said the guy standing there. To Edison, he looked like a real writer. His wrinkled sleeves were rolled up sloppily, as if it had happened in the wash. His glasses were crooked and his tie was loose enough to fit another neck in it. A cigarette dangled from his mouth below a squinted eye. He held up a bottle of whiskey and two glasses. "Name's Victor Craig. Join me for a drink?"

"You have two first names," said Edison.

"So does John Wayne. Use the one in front. It's Vic. You want a drink or don't you?"

Edison looked at his watch—just after noon. "Okay. My name is Edison Winslow."

"You have two last names."

"So does Harrison Ford."

"Who?"

"Mr. Barthkowitz calls me Tom."

Vic moved closer, looking Edison up and down, the bottle swinging in his fingers. "Mr. Barthkowitz, huh? I don't hear too many people calling him that behind his back."

He set the glasses on the desk and filled them halfway.

"Going a little stir crazy, are you?" said Vic.

"A little."

He handed Edison one of the glasses. "Cheers." He knocked his back in one gulp. Edison waited a moment to be sure Vic wasn't going to die, then drained his own. Vic filled the glasses again and they drank in silence.

"Aren't you a little old for this?" Vic said after a while.

Edison used Myra's response. "We don't feel old."

"We," said Vic. "Who's the two-finger typist?"

"You can tell she's a two-finger typist?"

"I can tell."

"Not me. It's my wife."

"Haven't heard her much lately," Vic said, prying.

"No." Edison drained his glass and then gazed into it pensively.

By the time they hit the third round Edison was feeling tight. He wavered a bit, leaning on the table. A dopey smile pulled at his lips. Gee, Vic seemed like a swell guy. He felt bad about screwing around with him with the typing and throwing shit at the wall.

"What are you working on?" Vic said.

"Nothing right now. You?"

"Some piece of shit called *The Dime Was Tossed*. Barthkobitch has me working on it."

"Barthkobitch! Ha-ha-ha!" Edison roared, draining glass three and holding it out for number four.

"Yeah, and some bastard told him I was blabbing about it in a bar. Can you believe it?" said Vic. "I don't talk about it. Hell, I'm embarrassed by it. I don't want anyone to know. Besides, he's got some bitch in there now who changes everything after you write it. So, what's the point, right?"

"Yeah," said Edison, vaguely wondering if the bitch Vic was talking about was Myra. "What's the point?" Then he realized it: "You're writing *The Dime Was Tossed*?"

"I am."

Edison toasted him.

Somehow Edison found himself standing at the doorway to a large closet filled with reels of film. Some were in protective canisters; some were laying on the floor, naked and dusty, tendrils of film unwound from the reels.

"This is it," said Vic. He was leaning on the doorframe with a cigarette in his mouth, holding his glass high in salute to the closet. "The great historical archives of Acropolis Pictures."

Edison fell to his knees, which was pretty much the direction he was going in anyway. He picked up a reel of film from the floor. It had been water damaged at some point and was growing furry with mold.

"This is a shame." He held the reel up to Vic. "Look at this."

"Not too close," said Vic, holding his cigarette away. "Some of these are nitrate. Highly flammable."

"But why?" said Edison. "All this work. It should be preserved."

"What difference does it make? Who's going to see them again?"

Edison was drunk, but not enough yet to be stupid. "Somebody may want to."

"Nah. They've served their purpose. Like toilet paper," said Vic. "They scooped a little loot and now they're done. These aren't like books you keep on a shelf."

"Yes, they are." Edison brushed at the mold on the reel. He was stepping into the sentimental department of being drunk. "What you do matters. Years from now people will pay attention. This is history."

Vic laughed, a great bellowing cynical guffaw. "Movies are lies. There has never been even one that has told the truth. The only history is their own."

"That's what I'm talking about," said Edison. "People will notice. Seventy years from now they'll still be watching."

"Why seventy?" said Vic. Then he looped a hand over Edison's shoulder. "Let me tell you something. My problem has always been that I'm an average guy who doesn't know he's an average guy. I keep thinking I'm going to be special someday. Is that what you're telling me?"

Edison tossed the reel back on the pile. "I don't know. I just think you should take care of them."

"Not up to me."

When Edison didn't show to pick Myra up at 4:30 by the front gate, she went to their office, snarling under her breath. She was already upset, having just read that the Nazis had entered Holland. *German parachutists dropped like snow on Belgium and Holland, shocking the world with the speed of this new kind of warfare.* She knew they would defeat the Dutch in five days. A work week. Rotterdam would be bombed to smithereens for no good reason. Because they could. All those people. And to top it off, super-idiot Göring was saying that for every German parachutist injured, fifty French prisoners would be shot. Asshole.

As she strode down the hall, she heard laughter, and maybe some singing, coming from the end office, their office. Her knock on the door was followed by a loud crash.

"Heeyyy!" bellowed Edison when he saw her.

"What's going on?" she said. The Underwood was lying on its side on the floor. "What is this?"

"Thish is Vic," said Edison, wobbling a hand in Vic's direction. "He's visiting from next door. We were jusht talking about the Indushtry."

Myra cast a nervous glance at Vic then looked at the floor.

Vic eyed her, suspicious and narrow, then picked up his bottle, snatched Edison's glass out of his hand, and headed for the door.

"I should have known." He glared at Myra as he passed her. "Bitch. See ya, Tom."

The door slammed.

Edison brightened. "I guessed right. He *was* talking about you."

Edison squinted in the sunlight as he staggered to the car. He packed himself into the corner of the passenger side between the seat and the door, with his foot on the dashboard. On the way through the gate, Myra saw Barthkowitz and Pulaski standing out front by the fake columns. Barthkowitz was doing the talking while Pulaski jittered and nodded, spinning his pocket watch furiously, waiting for his turn to speak. As Myra drove past, the watch broke off its chain and hit the side of the car, causing Edison to look up.

"Hey, watch it, Pull-ass-key!" He laughed wildly at his own cleverness. He held his camera above his head and snapped a cockeyed picture of them. But Edison didn't really exist anymore for Pulaski and Barthkowitz, so they hadn't heard him, or acted like they hadn't.

"Quiet," said Myra anyway.

"Barthkobitch," he mumbled then laughed about it. Myra glanced at him with a mixture of pity and anger. She blamed herself, of course. If she hadn't taken that job for Barthkowitz he wouldn't be like this. She turned out of the lot and soon encountered a policeman redirecting traffic around a movie scene that was being filmed on the street.

"Oh, no," she said.

Edison popped up. "What?" He saw the policeman and, behind him, the camera and crew. "Oh, look."

A sharp-jawed actor on the sidewalk was yelling a line of dialogue to someone across the street. The dialogue sounded familiar to Edison.

"Hey, that sounds like … "

Myra turned left at the cop's direction. "It is," she said. "They're re-shooting a scene. I'm sorry. I shouldn't have driven past here. I forgot they were doing this today."

"My movie?"

Edison turned in his seat and watched the scene grow distant. He heard a man he didn't know yell, "Cut!"

That must be the director, he thought groggily and snapped a picture in the general direction of the scene. He spun toward Myra, wagging a floppy finger at her. "You knew, and you didn't tell me."

Myra kept her eyes on the traffic. "They don't want us there. You know that."

"Us?" he said, leaning in. "Or me?" He rose up an inch or two as if he had just said something enlightening.

"Don't talk that way. You don't see me there, do you?"

Edison slumped back into his corner. "Not fair," he whined. Then he started saying, "What's the point?" He didn't say much else, except for "Why is the car spinning around?" once, but kept repeating, "What's the point?" all the way home, up into their apartment, and while Myra was tucking him into bed, where he passed out before finishing the last one.

Myra sat on the bed with him until his snoring settled in, hoping that this would all be over soon, then went into the bathroom to work on her journal.

The Final Draft

Picking the Fruit

After this, but not because of it, President Roosevelt moved the Pacific Fleet from San Diego to Pearl Harbor, Italy declared war on France and England, eight thousand Jews were crammed into a ghetto in Kutno, Poland and Edison returned to his role as a confused imbecile. He still went to work every day, still carried the Royal back and forth to the office, but he wasn't using it much. He shuffled the papers on his nine unfinished screenplays, penciled a few changes here and there, but his heart wasn't in it anymore. He had stopped writing letters to Barthkowitz at Myra's request and felt he had nothing left to do. He held out hope that he would get over his disillusionment and start typing again. But the premier of *Struggle of the Mind* completely took the wind out of him.

"Get dressed, please."

"Okay."

"Not that one. Try the grey striped."

" … o*kay*."

When they pulled up to the theater, there was a single large spotlight out front sweeping the skies with the message that a new masterpiece was in town.

"I'll wait in the car," said Edison.

"You will not," said Myra. "This is our premier. We have to go." She'd just about had to drag him out of the apartment by his belt loops to get him this far. "Look over there." She pointed to the spotlight. "That's happening because of something you started. Your idea. Remember that."

Edison smiled at the marquee—*Struggle of the Mind*. They hadn't changed the title. He watched the spotlight move across the sky and the small gathering crowd at the entrance to the theater. "It's going to change history," he said to himself.

Behind the spotlight they saw Barthkowitz arguing with the spotlight professional, flailing his arms and drawing dramatic shapes in the air while the spotlight professional smoked patiently, waiting for him to finish. Barry stood by ready to lend assistance should one of Barthkowitz's arms freeze up or anything.

Edison and Myra parked in front of a grocery store. They crossed the street and stepped onto the red carpet flanked by jabbering fans. The jabbering didn't get any louder when they got on it, so they wandered over to see what the Barthkowitz commotion was all about.

"I specifically ordered six klieg lights! Six! Not one!" Barthkowitz was standing close to the moving spotlight so his face kept getting lighter and darker as he yelled. He turned to Barry. "Did I not order six klieg lights? Did you not hear me order six?"

"You ordered six," said Barry in his usual monotone.

"You see? Six!" Barthkowitz roared. "So what the fuck happened?"

The spotlight professional dropped his cigarette on the ground and blew the last bit of smoke away from Barthkowitz. "I told ya before, Mr. Barthkowitz. I'm sorry. There's a Warner Brothers premiere at Grauman's. They took everything we had. I had to borrow this one."

"That's bullshit!" said Barthkowitz. "I ordered them first. Tell him, Barry."

"That's bullshit," said Barry.

"Be that as it may, Mr. Barthkowitz, this is just a 'B' picture. I'm not about to get into it with Jack Warner over his 'A' picture if I can't get *him* the right number."

Barthkowitz was incredulous. "What about getting into it with me? That's okay, huh?"

"Honestly, it's not as bad."

Edison took a picture of the scene then Myra pulled him away toward the theater lobby. The low ceiling kept the cloud of cigarette and burnt popcorn smoke firmly at eye level. Edison admired the poster on the wall. *Struggle of the Mind* was swiped across the middle in eerie yellow made to look like it had been done with a wide paintbrush. Behind the title were painted scenes from the movie—men with guns and cigarettes, men dying from guns, their cigarettes on the ground by their bodies, and a woman with a gun and a cigarette. He didn't remember a woman with a gun in his story, but posters were always lying about the actual contents of a movie, the purpose being to put asses in seats, not to tell the story. There was a close-up of Harry's face, hat tilted back, lines of stress on his forehead and worry in his eyes (struggling with his mind). Edison was checking out the credits when Barthkowitz showed up acting as if nothing had happened outside. He was happy and boisterous, waggling every appendage he could grab. He kissed Myra's hand and even gave Edison a hefty buddy back slap that nearly launched him into the candy counter.

A starlet-in-waiting seated them a few rows from the back, next to Goochy and his date, Andrew. Goochy waved solemnly. Andrew nodded. Barthkowitz and Pulaski were a few rows ahead of them with the director whose name they still didn't know, and the stars, Brush Steele and Gloria Baker. Gloria was wary of Pulaski's twirling pocket watch, leaning her bare shoulders away from him in a way that would give her a stiff neck by the end of the picture.

The lights went down, the clackety-clack of a projector started and the screen burst into light and sound. The *Acropo-tone* newsreel led the way. It had the quality of a bald tire and its narrated information was about as reliable.

"The Germans continue doing very bad things in countries that don't really belong to them. It looks like Dunkirk is whipping up to being a troublesome place for our Allied friends, but we wish them the best in their fight against bad behavior and the forces of evil. Pip, pip and all that."

Random stock footage of marching soldiers and people waiting in line for food somewhere trundled beneath the soundtrack.

Myra whispered to Edison. "Dunkirk was weeks ago. What gives?"

Following the newsreel was a jerky cartoon about a dim-witted farmer and his overworked wife comically dealing with a recalcitrant jackass.

In the moment of silence between the cartoon and the Acropolis logo, Barthkowitz spun around and looked at Edison and Myra.

"Oh, I wanted to mention—" he began, and was drowned out by the blaring brass announcement of another quality Acropolis picture.

Edison felt dual twinges of excitement and pride when the title splashed before him, a feeling that was snuffed out seconds later when the credit—*screenplay by Bernie Boca*—leapt shamelessly onto the screen.

"What!?" cried Edison and Myra in unison. "Sshhh!" cried other people in unison. Goochy covered his eyes. Barthkowitz seemed to sink in his seat just a smidgen and Pulaski's twirling pocket watch, as if on cue, busted free of its chain, executed a fine high arc across the theater—producing the merest of shadows on the screen—and knocked the hat off a lady in the third row, which met with smiling approval by the man behind her in the fourth row.

It was difficult to say how much of the movie Edison and Myra saw after this point. They were blinded, deafened and dumbed by anger through most of it, recovering only partway near the end for the final scene: *Chloe, determined to keep Harry by her side, pulls a gun from her purse and shoots him in the gut, saving him from himself and saving the city from Harry. With the camera holding on Harry's crumpled dead body, a cigarette still smoldering between his lips, an off-screen shot is heard, followed by a thump and a clatter. The camera pans to Chloe, dead on the floor, revealing only her legs and one hand, the gun inches from her lifeless fingers. Police sirens are heard in the distance as the music rises and the scene fades out. The End.*

When the lights came on, Edison was gone.

Myra waited in the lobby for Barthkowitz and Pulaski.

"What the hell was that?" she said as they entered with oily smiles holding up their cigars. They were as cocksure and nonchalant as German generals.

Barthkowitz gave her a 'no big deal' shrug. "A few changes. Nothing major."

"Nothing major? You empowered the female lead right into a pine box."

Barthkowitz raised a calm finger in defense. "We had a budget and an audience to consider, not to mention the censors. Without that stamp, we don't play in Palookaville. Besides, the crowd loved it. You heard them."

"The polite applause?" said Myra. "Yes, I heard it. And who the hell is Bernie Boca?"

"Bernie Boca?"

"The screenwriting credit? Ring a bell? Hello? Anybody home?"

Barthkowitz puffed up and leaned in close to her. "You're stepping over the line, Mrs. Mix. You are a paid employee under contract to this studio. Insolence will not be tolerated. You write words. I make pictures. Is that clear? The decisions are mine and if I think Bernie Boca gets the credit, that's up to me. This ain't a union joint."

"Does Bernie Boca even exist?"

"Whatever I need to exist does exist."

Myra balled her fists but wisely kept them at her side. "I blame you," she said to Barthkowitz, then looked at Pulaski. "And you."

"Blame. Credit. Whatever," said Pulaski. "I saw my name on the screen. We'll make money. And if you clam up when it's smart to, you might make some, too."

He stood there twirling another pocket watch, a one-sided smirk on his face. Myra spared a split second of her anger to wonder how many of these stupid things he carried in his pocket. "Rude. Blatantly, awfully rude."

She found Edison getting drunk on Planter's Punch at La Conga.

"Can we go now?" he said.

"Yes. We only have two more weeks on our contract. Then we can leave."

Edison moaned. "Two more weeks? Why do we have to wait two more weeks?"

"That's two thousand more dollars. That will buy a lot of gas and film."

A Little Credit

Edison snored off his booze with the noon sun banging on his face. Myra was already up and gone and Edison's sleeping body had sprawled to fill the space left by her. He was dreaming.

He was sitting in an empty hay wagon, hitched up to a jackass, at the drive-thru window of a fast food restaurant. A voice inside the window said, "Your order will be just a second, sir." The voice was youthful and full of promise, and it was coming from Barthkowitz. He was wearing a conical paper fast food hat and his nametag said *Reggie*. Edison looked up at the sky, watched a flock of pocket watches fly overhead. Barthkowitz handed him a bag, smiling like a shy little girl with a secret. Edison opened the bag and thousands of flies flew out, landing all over his body. He screamed, or tried to; he wasn't sure if anything came out. The jackass began to trot, bringing its knees up high with elegance, like a Lipizzaner stallion.

"Bye now," said Barthkowitz with a giggle, as the wagon pulled away. "Come again."

The rhythmic clopping of the jackass's hooves turned into knocking as Edison clawed his way out of the dream. The broiling sun watered his eyes. His head was coated with sweat on the outside and pounding like a pile driver on the inside. Someone was knocking on the door. He stumbled stupidly across the floor. It was Goochy Avitable.

"Whoa," he said, upon seeing Edison. "Sorry." He held out a newspaper. "Read this. Congratulations. Sort of."

Edison squinted hard at the spot where Goochy was pointing.

> Despite the expected plot holes usually associated with these B pictures, with their budgets that couldn't pay for a soda water at Formosa, *Struggle of the Mind* packs a wallop. The screenplay by Bernie Boca marks a new direction for crime films, and serves as a warning to tough guys everywhere—don't underestimate your woman. Murderous, conniving and lusty, the role of Chloe, played by ingénue Gloria Baker, has the guts to match any man. But the real credit goes to studio head Reginald K. Barthkowitz and producer Gaston Pulaski for having the vision to make such a picture.

Edison handed the paper back.

"That wasn't me," he said.

"I know it doesn't mention you by name, but it's about you and there are people who know that."

Edison looked lost. "It wasn't me."

"Of course, no one pays attention to Louise Crooner's reviews, but somebody else might write about it," said Goochy. He put his hand on Edison's shoulder. The weight of it threatened to knock him down. "Don't take it so hard. This stuff happens all the time. Some of us understand that more than others. It's your first one. You'll get there."

"Okay," said Edison. In a way, he should have been grateful. By keeping his name off the credits, even if it wasn't his real name, Barthkowitz had done him a small favor. He had wanted to avoid the limelight, to stay out of the way of history. If this wasn't keeping him fully out of it, at least fewer people would ever hear his name. But what bothered him most was that he thought that the new ending to the film was better than the one he'd written, even better than the one Myra had rewritten. And he thought that everyone else thought so, too.

"I'll leave that with you and let you wake up. How about meeting me for lunch? Or in your case, breakfast," said Goochy. "Say, an hour from now? We have some things to talk about. We need to figure out where you're going to go from here. Can you get Myra to come?"

Edison stared vacantly at him. Goochy was trying to be a good guy. "Okay."

"Okay. Remember—you can't go back, but you can go forward."

Edison found that funny.

Transition

Edison went to Acropolis to find Myra. He wanted to tell her that he was ready to leave. He didn't care about the two weeks left on their contract. Enough was enough. He wanted to go. Maybe they could have lunch with Goochy and say their goodbyes to him and Andrew, then pack up the car and head east. First stop, the Mojave Desert. Just to air out for a bit. They'd have to bring extra jugs of water for the radiator.

The sun bristled off the sidewalk around him, blinding him as he walked to the door.

He waited for his eyes to adjust to the darkness of the lobby. His clothes were a wrinkled mess. Myra the Receptionist was sitting at her desk with a cigarette burning in the ashtray. It occurred to him that he had never seen Myra the Receptionist actually smoking. It was as if the cigarette was a sort of incense. She was wearing a shimmering green silk dress with matching nail polish and she eyed his attire with disapproval.

"Hi Myra. Is Myra in?" he said.

"No," she said impatiently. "She went flying with Gaston Pulaski."

"Flying?"

"They're scouting some locations on Catalina Island. She'll be back this afternoon."

Edison was stunned. Why hadn't Myra told him this? He stared at the nameplate on Myra the Receptionist's desk. It said, *Myra—Receptionist*.

"I didn't know," he said.

Myra the Receptionist pursed her lips. She reached for the cigarette, then thought better of it and left it where it was. "I believe it was a last minute thing," she said. "I think Mr. Pulaski had a sudden idea."

"A sudden idea?"

"That's what it seemed like." She cleared her throat. "She's not here."

Muffled anger leaked from the phone booth.

"Who's flying the plane?"

She shrugged and picked up her cigarette, took a quick puff hardly worth the trouble, and put it back. The muffled anger got louder for a moment then went back to what it had been.

"Is Mr. Barthkowitz in?" said Edison.

"No."

He waited for an explanation, but none followed. She was waiting for him to leave.

"Thank you," he said.

He stepped back out into the punchy sunshine. Standing at the top of the steps next to one of the fake columns, he swayed a bit, leaning against the column for stability. The sun seemed suddenly very bright, making him squint his whole face.

Flying?

Then something snapped.

The First Time Fly Glitch

Things went from very bright to very dark very quickly. Edison went from standing in the sunlight to sitting in the darkness, in a poorly padded chair.

His first thought was *Why is someone speaking German?* followed immediately by *Why is it dark in here? Is this a theater? Who are these people?* and finally bringing them all together with *Where the hell am I?*

He remembered standing on the steps of Acropolis Pictures staring at the blazing sidewalk. He remembered being angry with Myra for not telling him that she was going flying with Gaston Pulaski. The memory was quite clear because it had happened only a few seconds before. Now he was sitting inside a darkened movie theater, third row from the back, four seats in from the right, with a crowd of very excited strangers, and the voice coming out of the movie screen was speaking German.

He began to shiver. There were people all around him. They were close and he could smell them. Farmers and factory workers, people struggling to stay clean with rationed soap. They shouted German things at the screen. Some of them shouted "Heil Hitler!" and "Sieg Heil!" The voice on the screen droned on, professional and patriotic. The tone was that of a winner. The scenes were of proud German soldiers and of the wounded and the dead of the defeated.

Edison barely registered what was going on around him. He was gripped by fear and a desire to run. Maybe if he ran outside he would find himself on a studio lot. Maybe he had blacked out due to the bright sunlight and his hangover, and now he was on the set of a movie about Germany. But that didn't make sense. There were no crewmembers around and there would have been lights and boom mics overhead. And the theater had four walls; a studio set would have only had three. He wanted to shout out for an explanation but a voice inside him warned him to keep quiet, similar to Myra warning him to keep his hands out of his pants.

His brain presented him with a sentiment that had remained common throughout most of history whenever things got weird: *I need to stop drinking.*

Ordinarily, he didn't have a problem with being this confused. He'd grown used to it, even developed a sort of affection for it. But this was different. His confusion, thus far, had not involved a substantial change of geographical venue, at least not since he'd first been sent into the past and had landed on December 16, 1938. Even then he had only gone from his own living room to the same living room seventy-seven years before it was his own. Things had been pretty smooth since then, considering.

He sat quietly in the dark with no idea what was going on, but he was sure that the Time Flies were behind it somehow. They were.

Another Short Lesson on Time Fly Law

Question: Why had Edison been suddenly and so unceremoniously tossed to the other side of the world without reason or warning?

Professor Cyril T. Rocklidge might have provided this answer: A Time Fly had been shirking its duty of guidance.

In the Professor's *Ten Rules to Consider* he had stated the importance of proper guidance:

```
-It is essential that all Guidance Flies be present at the
moment of their appointed rounds. Should a Fly prove missing
during its period of assigned guidance, there will be
serious consequences for the Prisoner.
```

And serious consequences they were, for a Time Fly had indeed gone missing, robbing Edison of his much needed guidance. The missing Fly, an adolescent not yet fully reared on all aspects of Time Fly protocol, had been looking forward to its responsibility. But its young brain, itchy with impatience, had grown bored, and it left its place in line, became distracted by something shiny and had been promptly eaten by a bird. (For this crime, the bird would serve a sentence similar to that of Bucky Kitchen.) So, when the Fly's designated time period arrived, and it was not available to guide, it left a hole, a gap in the chain. A missing link.

 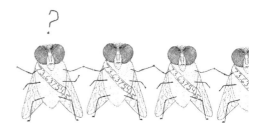

In another document, Professor Rocklidge had explained the phenome-
non further:

```
The purpose of Time Fly guidance is to ensure that the
Prisoner stays in the geographical location of his choosing,
to keep him from being flung about haphazardly from place
to place on the surface of the Earth. Should a Time Fly
be missing in action, or otherwise be unable to perform
its assigned duty, the Prisoner may find himself 'projected'
elsewhere. The projection, or Time Fly Glitch, will be
uncontrolled and unprotected.

Effects from Time Fly Glitches:

May include becoming displaced in space, but not in time,
increased appetite, becoming other people and ceasing to
exist. Minimal safeguards have been put in place to prevent
materialization inside of solid objects, but these are
not guaranteed.

No provisions for protest shall be entertained from the
Prisoner.
```

Thus, Edison, who had been standing in front of Acropolis Pictures staring at a blindingly bright sidewalk, found himself suddenly without a
chaperone and was flung over five thousand miles away to a small, darkened movie theater in a tiny, darkened village somewhere near Freiburg
in the mountains of Germany. He was flung only in space, not in time, so
it was still the same day. Allowing for the difference in time zones, Edison
had arrived at night, just in time for the evening's feature, which was a
propaganda film about recent German victories.

It would not be a very enjoyable trip for him. It would, however, end after 73.63754 hours, at which time, assuming he was still alive, he would be flung back to Los Angeles when the next Time Fly, who was responsibly present, would pick up the slack and continue guidance as if nothing had happened.

Edison, of course, had no idea that this would end and that he would return to Los Angeles because he had no idea what was going on. As far as he knew, this was it.

The First Glitch (cont'd)

Not knowing what else to do, Edison tried to concentrate on the film, staying low, peeking between the two heads in front of him. He saw shots of fleeing Allied troops; shots of soldiers being taken prisoner; acres of war machinery left behind during retreat. Scenes from a different battle showed him burning buildings and charred bodies, collapsing walls and weeping civilians.

He scanned the theater crowd, some of them cheering the military victories, some sitting quietly, their attention rapt. They seemed not to have noticed his sudden appearance in the theater, with the exception of the farmer in the mud stained coat sitting next to him, who was staring at him in shock. The farmer's face flickered dimly in the light reflected from the screen. Edison needed to flee. He didn't want to be there when the lights came on and everyone started shuffling out, talking and comparing notes on how the boys in uniform were doing. Being four seats from the end of the row proved a bit of a problem because he didn't know how to speak German. But by utilizing the universal language of pointing, grunting and smiling, he was able to get himself out of the row and toward the exit.

The lobby was dark; there were no concession shelves or young starlets waiting to serve him. Outside, few people roamed the streets. A German soldier stood by the theater entrance, smoking. The rifle slung over his shoulder had yet to be used for shooting people. He was a thug from the outskirts of Hamburg who liked to use his fists when the occasion called for it. He had enlisted in the Wehrmacht three years before and had recently been promoted to the rank of Sergeant, or Unteroffizier. He had been assigned to his current post for six months and was bored silly most of the time.

"Guter Film, was?" he said to Edison, laughing. "Den Engländern haben wir einen Tritt in den Arsch verpasst. Nichts und niemend kann uns mehr aufhalten."

Edison smiled weakly. He remembered that civilians were required to salute and gave the soldier a wimpy "Sieg Heil," hoping that this would address whatever the Unteroffizier had said to him.

"Ja, ja, Sieg Heil," said the soldier.

Edison continued walking past him, trying to make his stride appear purposeful. The soldier yelled after him. "He, Sie haben Ihren Mantel vergessen!"

Edison fought the impulse to run and turned briefly around to give him another "Sieg Heil" before continuing on.

The Unteroffizier kept his eyes on him as he disappeared around a corner.

The first thing Edison noticed as he walked along the dark cobblestone street was that he was cold. He didn't have a coat and his wrinkled shirt was lightweight cotton and of a far more urbane fashion than would normally be seen in these parts. It had been seventy-nine degrees in Los Angeles. Maybe he was in the mountains, the Alps perhaps, but it was too dark to see beyond the village. Most of the village itself was dark. A few windows glowed. Small pools of light here and there illuminated the street. People sang in a tavern somewhere. A dog barked. The barking was familiar. He walked a little faster as the barking tapered to whimpering. When he came to an alley, he saw Paul, shivering and scared, sitting next to a trash can.

"Paul!" said Edison. Paul shivered some more. "Where've you been, boy? Huh? We've been worried sick about you."

Paul's tail wagged cautiously as he stood. Edison noticed that Paul only had three legs now. He stepped a little closer and Paul limped back away from him.

"What happened to you, boy? Where's your leg?"

Paul backed away a little more, growling, and Edison began to doubt if it really was Paul. The dog didn't seem to recognize him.

"What is this place?"

Another thing Edison didn't know was that the farmer in the mud stained coat had followed him out of the theater only moments after he had left and had reported Edison's strange appearance to the Unteroffizier. The soldier had scoffed at the idea that a man could appear out of thin air, but agreed to look into it. He had followed Edison and was within earshot when it sounded to him as if the coatless man had spoken English to a mangy dog in an alley.

"Was machen Sie da mit dem Hund?" said the Unteroffizier.

Edison spun around and saw the soldier half-pointing his rifle at him. He tried to pretend he hadn't heard him by walking away.

"Halt!" demanded the soldier. His voiced echoed off the buildings. He was bigger than Edison and had perfect cheekbones. The dog that may have been Paul darted out of the alley and disappeared into the darkness. "Halt, Stehebleiben! Ausweis, oder ich schiesse!"

Edison didn't know what the soldier had said, but thought it might have something to do with shooting him, so he stopped and raised his hands.

"Umdrehen!" said the soldier. Edison stayed as he was. The soldier grabbed his shoulder and spun him around. "Sind Sie taub? Ich hab 'Umdrehen' gesagi. Zeig' mir Deinen Ausweis."

Edison stood dumbly. He began to tremble. The Unteroffizier grew angry.

"Bist Du auf den Kopf gefallen? Ich hab Ausweiss gesagt, oder ich nehme dich fest."

Faces began appearing in windows.

"I'm sorry," said Edison. "I don't understand what you're saying."

The Unteroffizier was dumbfounded. It *had* been English he'd heard. He smiled as he gripped his rifle tighter, rocking back and forth on his jackboots. He had been stuck in this miserable little village for months while the villagers were cheering for the soldiers on the movie screen. This was his chance to show them. He had caught a spy.

"British?" he said.

Edison hesitated. "American."

"American?" The Unteroffizier's eyes glistened. He laughed. "Ha, warte bis die Anderen das hören. Ich habe einen Spion erwischt, einen richtigen, kleine, amerikanischen Spitzel!"

Edison looked at the ground and waited to be shot.

The soldier's conversation was one-sided as he escorted Edison to the small headquarters he shared with his boss, an Obersturmführer, and, occasionally, with his commanding officer, Sturmbannführer Hockenstickler. They were both SS officers who spoke some English and would be happy to have the chance to use it. The soldier was disappointed to find the office dark. Now he would have to wait until morning.

He prodded Edison down a narrow flight of stairs to the basement, stopping him in front of a door made from thick slabs of wood held together with bands of iron. The hinges moaned as he swung it open. Edison took a few seconds to appraise his new home while the soldier cuffed his hands behind his back. What he could see was all stone, dirt and moisture. The Unteroffizier shoved him inside and he fell, scraping his face on the floor, daubing it with grime that he couldn't wipe off.

When the door was closed, the darkness was complete except for a thin sliver of weak light at its bottom. He could hear rats or mice scurrying around. It smelled like grain and mildew as if the cell had previously been used for storing the ingredients for beer. He hoped so. The lock clicked. A peephole opened up and a square shaft of light came through it. The light was covered by the Unteroffizier's eye. He said something that Edison didn't understand, followed it with laughter, and closed the peephole.

Edison backed against the wall so that he could use his cuffed hands to feel his way. The wall was slick and moist, not a great place for grain storage any longer. He moved along trying to gauge the size of the room, but the sliminess of the stone soon began to disgust him so he stopped. He doubted there was anything to sit on and lowered himself carefully to the floor. His stomach growled loudly with hunger in the silent room.

As the hours passed, and his fear subsided in the calm empty darkness, he grew angry. He cursed Barthkowitz and Pulaski, those bastards. They had ruined his film and had humiliated him and Myra. And he was still angry with Myra. *Flying? With that scumbag Pulaski?* But he was most angry with the Time Flies. *Who the hell did they think they were? What kind of prison officials were they to allow such conditions as these?*

His anger with Myra passed quickly. He wondered where she was right now and if she was all right. Had a similar thing happened to her? Was she home now, looking for him? He missed her. She would know what to do, how to get them out of this. And what about the dog he had seen? Was it Paul? It sure looked and sounded like Paul, except for the missing leg.

He dozed. From time to time, he was roused by the peephole being opened and briefly filled with the soldier's eye. It reminded him of Cavin Corkavonin's eye at the Communist Party meeting.

He stayed in the cell for more than two days without food or water before anyone came to get him. The soldier's pleas had been ignored. Sturmbannführer Ivan Hockenstickler didn't care about Edison. The soldier had reported to him that he had apprehended a suspicious character, an American who wore no coat and spoke no German. Hockenstickler had asked if the American could possibly be a Jew. The soldier said that he didn't think so, but that it was hard to tell. Hockenstickler called him a Dummkopf and told him to leave the prisoner alone until he arrived. Then Hockenstickler went back to what he had been doing, which was sleeping. The following morning, he went out for breakfast with his wife, took a stroll in the park, yelled at a few subordinates at the office, had lunch, swung home for a nap, went out to dinner, got drunk and went home to bed. He never even thought about Edison.

Sturmbannführer Hockenstickler was a slacker. He didn't like to do anything that didn't involve him doing nothing. He did not behave like a captain in the army of a nation at war. He behaved as if the struggle was complete; like a victor, not a warrior. He would not last. By early 1942, he would be on the Russian front, dead and frozen into a position of horror and grief, with a missing eye. But for now, he was comfortable.

The Unteroffizier was not. He was convinced that Edison was a spy or a saboteur and wanted very much to torture him for information valuable to the Third Reich. Even for information that was not so valuable. Or for no information at all. Torture for any reason was fine with him. But he had his orders and didn't disobey them.

The next day, with growing anxiety, the Unteroffizier called Hockenstickler to report that the prisoner's condition was stable and that he was ready to begin the interrogation on his orders. The Sturmbannführer, rather than admit that he'd forgotten about the prisoner, chastised the soldier for disturbing him during important business and ordered him to be patient. There would be plenty of interrogation when he arrived the following day. The soldier apologized and asked if the prisoner should be given any food or water.

"Does he appear to be dying?" said Hockenstickler.

The soldier excused himself and put the phone down. He ran to the basement and opened the peephole. Edison was staring into the darkness, shivering. He looked up at the peephole and saw the Unteroffizier's eye. The soldier closed the peephole and ran back upstairs.

"He does not appear to be dying, mein Sturmbannführer."

Hockenstickler had already hung up.

The following afternoon, Hockenstickler finally arrived and asked to see the prisoner.

Edison squinted at the light that flooded his cell when the door was opened. The Unteroffizier grabbed him by the arm and yanked him rudely to his feet. He was stiff from sitting for almost three days on cold stone and wanted a chance to stretch first, but that wasn't happening. The Unteroffizier shoved him along the corridor and then into a room that wasn't much different from his cell. Although it lacked the accoutrements of more exquisitely appointed torture chambers, it would prove adequate. The stone floor and walls ensured the scream-as-loud-you-want-nobody-can-hear-you environment that is the basis for any good chamber. And the bare light bulb hanging from a wire seemed to know just the right amount of illumination to cast to be uncomfortably bright for the victim, while leaving the corners of the room creepy and dark.

Ideally, Edison would have been tortured in the kitchen upstairs where he could be taught to fear everyday items like cheese graters and counter edges for the rest of his life. But that room had already been promised to the local chapter of the National Socialist Women's League for their discussions on bearing perfect Aryan children and on being subservient to their husbands, so that was out.

No matter.

The soldier made Edison stand still while they waited. He was very excited. They had never used this room before. The village was too far out of the way to see any real action and the Jews had been cleared out months ago. The Unteroffizier was almost giddy, rocking back and forth on his jackboots. He was stifling a giggle when the door opened and the Sturmbannführer and the Obersturmführer entered.

Edison's interrogator wore the older style black Nazi uniform, stretched at the buttons from the weight he'd gained since he had started wearing it. Sturmbannführer Ivan Hockenstickler had an overfed face and a frog throat that looked like it could puff itself out at any moment. Hockenstickler was not a real interrogator. He didn't know anything about interrogation. He was simply a bully, stationed in the middle of nowhere, while his colleagues were living it up in Paris. Like his minion, the Unteroffizier, he was bored and wanted to feel a little more important. When he talked, his throat wobbled like a water balloon.

"Who are you?"

"My name is Edison Winslow."

"Which year were you born?"

Edison tried calculating, then guessed. "1883."

Hockenstickler paced in front of Edison, staring at him and frowning meaningfully.

"Hände aus den Taschen, damit wir die Handschellen entfernen können," he said. Edison didn't move. Hockenstickler sighed impatiently and repeated it in English. "Take your hands out of your pants so we can remove the hand cuffs."

Edison did as he was told. The Unteroffizier and the Obersturmführer tied him to a sturdy wood chair with a few coils of skin-chafing rope. Edison found this to be rather over the top and was about to offer polite protest when the Unteroffizier gleefully prevented it by punching him in the temple, treating him to a colorful display of phosphenes. Edison drifted, floating through space and gazing at stars. He could hear Hockenstickler's voice, faint and distant, trying to bring him back into the room so they could beat him some more. His eyes came to focus on the skull and crossbones insignia on Hockenstickler's cap.

Next came a shimmering blow to Edison's philtrum, loosening one of the teeth behind it. The blood did a naughty job of messing up his shirt. This made Edison sad. Given that much of life is spent hoping to avoid getting hit in the face—whether by fists or by objects both foreign and domestic—Edison could not help the feeling that he had failed, and grew mildly ashamed for getting his ass kicked while tied to a chair.

"That was just an example, Edison Winslow, of what will happen if you don't cooperate," said Hockenstickler. "I like examples, don't you? They have a way of defining things, of letting you know what to expect." He continued pacing while he talked because he felt it added gravity and authority to his words.

The Obersturmführer stood by the wall smoking, taking care not to get his new gray uniform dirty. He wore a thin mustache and carried himself in a cynical and debonair fashion. He thought that Hockenstickler was an Arschloch who talked too much. If it were up to him, they would have turned Edison over to the Gestapo days ago. If Edison was a spy, then he was probably being missed somewhere. They were wasting time. Hockenstickler had dismissed his request as paranoid, stating that he had everything under control.

"You seem impatient, Edison Winslow," said Hockenstickler. "Americans are always impatient. I am not impatient. I am a very patient man. Ask anyone. Isn't that correct, Obersturmführer?"

The Obersturmführer looked at his cigarette as he twirled it slowly in his fingers. Hockenstickler was baiting him. "It is true that you are not worried by the passage of time."

"Yes, of course," said Hockenstickler. He spread his hands and smiled. "We have plenty of time."

Edison was inclined to agree. He had nowhere to go and no one knew that he was here. As he saw it, they had the rest of his life to beat him, or at least until the war ended in five years. But it wasn't so. There really wasn't that much time left. Edison was only going to be there for 73.63754 hours and over sixty-eight of those hours had already been wasted because Hockenstickler couldn't get his ass in gear sooner to get over there and do the interrogation. Still, there was enough time left to make Edison miserable for a while longer.

Hockenstickler appraised Edison's appearance. "You are the first American I have seen in the flesh." He pinched Edison's pudgy upper arm. "Well fed." He pinched harder and Edison winced. "Though not well trained." He let go and strolled about the room as if he was in a park on a lazy afternoon, his hands clasped loosely behind his back, with nothing to fear, ever.

"Tell me, Edison Winslow, how did you get here? You have no passport, no identification of any kind. You were carrying American money and automobile keys. How did you come upon this putrid little village? Across the French border, perhaps?"

Edison told him the truth. "Time Flies," he said.

Hockenstickler looked confused. He queried the Obersturmführer. "What does he mean?"

"'Time flies' is a term that Americans use when they are wasting time," said the Obersturmführer. He smirked.

This irritated Hockenstickler and his eyebrows rose to the occasion. "So, Edison Winslow. You feel that you are wasting your time here. We will have to see if we can make it more interesting for you."

"That's not what I said," was what Edison wanted to say. "Th-," was how far he got before the Unteroffizier finished his sentence with an easy blow to his lower mandible. Edison's jaw vacationed about three inches to the right for a second before returning home. A long strand of drool and blood traveled from his mouth.

Hockenstickler waited a moment, picking at his fingernails. "You are old for a spy. Fifty-seven, is that correct? Is this the best the Americans can do?" He bent over in front of Edison's face, his hands on his knees, watching him with disgust. "We are not at war with your country yet. So why would you come here now, alone and without proper attire? It doesn't make sense. Unless you encountered problems elsewhere. Problems that left you without identification or your coat. Tell me, was your passport in your coat, perhaps?"

Edison tried to say, "I don't have a passport," but it sounded like, "Uh nomp hah-uh hah-hor."

"Hmm," said Hockenstickler. "I'm sure you understand, Edison Winslow, that, as an American, you are not as valuable as we Germans are. We are the master race. You are not. Therefore, any treatment we impress upon you, including that which can result in your death, should be considered merciful on our part."

Things went on like this for another hour or so before Hockenstickler got hungry and needed a break. He ordered the Unteroffizier to stay with Edison but to not hit him anymore until he got back. Then he and the Obersturmführer went to dinner. The Unteroffizier amused himself with an old magazine containing pictures of scantily clad Polish girls that he had found in the office upstairs.

When he returned three hours later, Hockenstickler was in a much better mood, having been refueled with sausage and cheese and strudel and beer. He paced buoyantly in front of Edison. The Obersturmführer resumed his position against the wall, smoking and appearing indifferent. The Unteroffizier rocked on his heels, polishing his fist.

Hockenstickler became thoughtful, loading up his features with expressions of curiosity, concern and contempt, pausing between commas for emphasis. "Edison Winslow, as our guest, you may not yet have been informed that the French have now surrendered to the Third Reich. As expected. This ensures the eventual defeat of the British, does it not? Of course it does. The Americans will feel the need to come to their rescue, as all good cowboys must eventually do, even if it is too late. So tell me this—as futile as it may be, is America planning on going to war with Germany?"

"Not yet, I don't think. That happens after Pearl Harbor." Edison had regained some of his ability to speak correctly, but not his caution. He was delirious and would have said anything.

"Pearl Harbor?" Hockenstickler looked at the Obersturmführer. "What is that?"

The Obersturmführer shrugged and suggested that perhaps it was time to turn the prisoner over to the Gestapo. At the word Gestapo, Edison perked up.

"Ich werde die Gestapo nicht rufen!" Hockenstickler yelled at the Obersturmführer. "Ich brauche die Gestapo nicht, um meine Arbeit zuverrichten! Verstanden!?"

"Jawohl, Sturmbannführer," said the Obersturmführer wearily.

Hockenstickler nodded to the Unteroffizier. The soldier lifted Edison by his left ear and hit him in the right eye. Edison's head sang and his right leg started bobbing up and down like a sewing machine needle.

"Is Pearl Harbor a code name? For your operation, perhaps?" said Hockenstickler. "Hmm? Tell me!"

Edison said nothing. Hockenstickler slapped him, then held his hand out for the Unteroffizier to wipe as he nodded slowly at Edison.

"We are taking you back to your cell," he said. He instructed the Unteroffizier not to feed the prisoner. "I will see you in the morning, Edison Winslow," said Hockenstickler on his way out. "Things will be very different then, I assure you. Be sure to sleep well."

Edison sagged in the chair. He had already been sagging, but managed to sag a little more. He was glad that he wasn't going to be hit anymore today, but he could have used a drink of water and something to eat. Maybe tomorrow they would feed him, but he didn't think so. As the soldier was untying his hands he opened the eye that wasn't swollen shut. The room seemed very bright, far brighter than he remembered it having been a few moments ago. Then the ropes disappeared.

The First Return

Edison returned to Los Angeles in the back seat of his car, in the Acropolis parking lot, with his face pressed against a window, smearing it with blood and spit. His hands were behind his back as if he was still tied to a chair and his keys and money were on the asphalt next to the car. They had been in a clasp envelope beneath the Unteroffizier's Polish girlie magazine, but had returned with him. He broiled inside. The car had been sealed up in the parking lot for three days. It was a nice change from the clamminess of the German cell and he wanted to stay there forever.

Then Andrew was there, frantic, yanking open the passenger door. "Edison. What happened?" he said, shaking him. He scooped up the keys and the money. "Are these yours? Where have you been? Everyone's been looking for you." He did a visual on Edison's swollen face. "Jesus." He figured that Edison must have been in some kind of drunken brawl. Edison was covered in blood. Some of the blood was still leaving his body. Other blood looked like it had been drying for a while. There was a large gash by his temple and one of his eyes was swollen shut.

"When was the last time you were home?" said Andrew.

Edison appeared to be thinking about it.

Andrew drove him to the Sun God Arms. He had started to drive him to the hospital, but Edison insisted on going home, saying he was fine, that the damage was mostly cosmetic. He was shaking even though the temperature was in the eighties. At one point he began sobbing, softly at first, then with more enthusiasm, then softly again. When they pulled up in front of the apartment building, Andrew put his hand on Edison's shoulder.

"I'm sorry about what happened," he said.

Edison blinked his good eye. "You know?"

"Everyone knows. Pulaski is no great loss, but … Well, I'm just very sorry. If there's anything I can do … "

Edison stared at him. *Pulaski?*

"Would you like some help upstairs?" said Andrew.

"No."

"Don't give up. They may find something yet. Until then, there's still hope."

"Okay." *What is he talking about?*

The Three Bills were watching Edison through the passenger window.

Bill Number One opened the door and reached for his arm, helping him out of the car.

"Who was it?" he said to Edison, noting the blood on his face and his clothes.

"Tell us who it was," said Bill Number Two. "We'll take care of him for you."

Bill Number Three nodded grimly.

"Boys," said Andrew, "I think Edison needs to be alone."

"Sure, sure," mumbled the Three Bills.

"We're really sorry," said Bill Number One. "If there's anything we can do."

"Anything," agreed the other Bills. Bill Number Two offered Edison his bottle. Edison looked at it for a moment then turned away.

Myra had started taking home delivery of the newspaper a few months before. There were three day's worth by their apartment door. Edison brought them inside, tossed them on the couch, then climbed out the window and sat in his chair, looking across the way at Angels Flight. The

Three Bills had gone back to being themselves. Everything looked pretty much as he remembered it. The Royal was on the table with a blank sheet of paper in it. His wrists and face hurt. He thought about the look that must have been on the Unteroffizier's face when he had disappeared and about what would happen to him when Hockenstickler returned and found him missing. He got up and went into the bathroom and studied the patterns of dried blood on his face. For Edison, the past was turning out to be a more violent place than the future had been. He'd gone his whole life without ever hitting or being hit, siblings, friends and parents excluded. Now, in just about a year and a half, he'd beaten a homeless man with a shovel, punched a Commie in the belly and had the snot pounded out of him by Nazis. What next? He started washing in the sink, then decided to take a bath. While the tub was filling, he thought about healing and scars. The gash by his temple was still bleeding and his front tooth was loose. He had previously supposed that since he wasn't aging then his body wasn't really doing its job of cell maintenance and repairs either. He dug out the copy of the Time Fly Law that he had recently retyped. It was right there under Conditions and Allowances:

```
Convicted will not age for duration of sentence but
may retain marks, scars, and disabilities purchased
during-____ *
```

He stayed in the tub a long time, turning the water pink. A cockroach wandering aimlessly on the wall held his attention. The afternoon light moved across the bathroom, eventually illuminating Myra's journal on the back of the toilet. He wanted to stay in the tub until she returned home.

When his skin had turned pruney and the water had cooled, he decided not to wait anymore. It was only late afternoon and if nothing had happened to her she must still be at work. He dried himself and put on some fresh clothes. He had no idea what day it was. There was some leftover beet casserole in the icebox, but the ice had melted and the casserole looked like it had gone off, so he opened a can of beans instead. Then he noticed the newspapers that he had tossed on the couch. Three day's worth. If Myra had been around she would have picked them up.

He opened the paper from three days ago, and at once understood what Andrew had been talking about. The headline, about halfway down page one, read:

Plane Crashes Off Catalina Island
Pilot, Producer and Screenwriter Missing

Edison collapsed onto the couch as the room began to spin. He grabbed onto the arm of the couch to keep himself from flying off. When the spinning subsided, the fear compelled him to read. The small airplane had been scouting locations on Catalina Island when it was seen by witnesses "going down very quickly" into the ocean. On board were local pilot Buzzy Engstrom, producer Gaston Pulaski and an unidentified screenwriter for Acropolis Pictures. Rescue workers were still searching the area for survivors. Pieces of wreckage were found floating on the sea.

Edison threw the paper aside and picked up the next day's. The story had already moved to page two. Wreckage from the plane had begun to wash ashore, as well as Buzzy Engstom's cap and a cheap pocket watch believed to have belonged to Mr. Pulaski. The screenwriter had been identified as Myra Mix. Rescue workers were still looking for the three, but they were now referring to them as bodies, not survivors.

He tossed this aside and picked up day three, this morning's paper. He found it on page four—last evening, the body of Gaston Pulaski had been recovered, and the purse of Myra Mix had been found washed up on Santa Monica Beach.

He sat on the couch for hours, not moving. When he finally broke down, he was as silent as he could be about it, covering his mouth as if there were people in the apartment with him that he didn't want to disturb. He sobbed himself asleep and when he woke the apartment was dark and frighteningly lonely. He tried convincing himself that Myra had not died in the crash, that she must have experienced the same thing he had, just somewhere else. Right now, she was probably trying to find her way home. Then he quashed that by coming up with a different theory—when the plane had crashed, Myra had died. When she died, it upset something in the Time Flies, some kind of delicate balance of their prison sentence, causing him to get flung across the world. When the Time Flies had regained their composure, his sentence had been repaired and he had been sent back to Los Angeles. He tried to think about it logically. He wanted it to make sense. For something to make sense. What he didn't want was for it to be true. The more he tossed this theory around in his head, the more sense it made, mostly because it was the only theory he could come up with. What else could there be? He knew nothing about the missing Guidance Fly that had caused the Glitch. His copy of the Time Fly Law did not contain the addendum explaining what would happen should a Time Fly prove to be missing in action.

Only one thing lit up the billboard on Edison's brain—Myra was dead.

The next day the newspaper reported that the search team had found part of the pilot's body. It didn't say which part. There were knocks on Edison's door during the day, but he didn't answer. After the knocking he would go to the window to see who was leaving. Twice it was Goochy, once it was Andrew.

He tried to stick with his routine, thinking that Myra might come back and he didn't want anything to be different. He tried writing a letter to Barthkowitz but his fingers refused to type. He walked around the apartment doing small things one at a time; setting his place for dinner; picking up dirty clothes from the floor one article at a time and putting them in the hamper. He felt heavy, his feet like magnets gripping the floor. He remembered that he had not drunk any water for days. He turned on the faucet and let it run, then turned it off. Then he turned it on again, filled his glass and gulped until his eyes watered. He set the glass down too close to the edge of the counter and it fell and smashed on the floor. He put his slippers on to sweep up the glass, took them off when his feet got hot and then couldn't remember where he'd put them. Later, he sat at the table in his bare feet staring at the place where dinner should have been.

Revelation

"I'm sorry, my friend." Andrew reached across the bar and patted Edison on the back.

Edison was drunk and lost. His face was wetting itself all over. "I don't know what to do."

"Maybe you should go back home."

Edison shook his head. "I can't. The apartment is too empty."

"I meant home. Washington D.C."

Edison lowered his head. "We're not from Washington D.C."

"Mm-hmm."

"We were from Seattle."

"Oh. Really." Andrew remembered the accusations by the Commies at the CP meeting.

"Yes. And we're not aliens or Reds," said Edison. He paused, measuring the sanity of his next words. "We're from the future."

Andrew stood with his hands on the bar, staring at the top of Edison's bowed head. "I don't have any place to go back to," Edison continued, drunkenly weeping.

"Why don't you go back to the future?"

"I can't. Not until 1963."

"I see."

"No, you don't. And I can't tell you anything that would make you see. I don't see it myself."

Andrew picked up a glass and polished it abstractly. "So, you're from 1963?"

"No, that's just when we go back. We're from the twenty-first century."

Andrew got a dreamy look to his eyes. "That's a long way off."

"Yes, it is."

Andrew hesitated, then asked it anyway: "Do we travel to other planets?"

Edison shook his head. "Just the moon. And a little bit of Mars, but no people."

"What about flying cars?"

"Not really. We have the Internet."

"What's that?"

Edison thought about that long enough that his tears started to dry. "It's something that lets everybody, everywhere, see everything at once."

Andrew finished polishing the glass and put it down. He picked up another. He was almost believing Edison. Wanting to.

"That doesn't sound as fun as flying cars."

"It's not. But it's okay."

Andrew waved at Goochy, who was sitting with a new client at one of the tables by the dance floor. He pointed at Edison and made signals to indicate he'd had too much to drink. Goochy nodded and excused himself from his client.

"And in this future twilights like me are okay?" said Andrew, stringing him along.

"Not everywhere, but in lots of places. And you're not called twilights; you're called gay."

Andrew laughed. "So that catches on?"

Edison sniffed wetly. Andrew handed him a bar towel and he blew his nose into it. "I just wish I knew what we did." He looked up at the ceiling, as if the Time Flies were up there, as if everything controlling and mysterious is always up. "What did we do?" he half shouted. "A fucking rat trap. She didn't know. How could she know?"

Goochy placed his hand lightly on Edison's back. Andrew picked up Edison's drink and tossed it in the sink. "Goochy will take you home."

Edison woke covered in sweat with his clothes twisted around him and the midday sun beating on his legs. He pulled himself up in jerks and fits and stumbled to the bathroom. There was a large bluish stain on his shirt from something he didn't remember eating, drinking or falling in. He splashed water on his face to shock his headache and left for Acropolis, driving around to the back of the lot. His office was empty. Every piece of what he and Myra had been in there was gone. It was just an empty office with a typewriter waiting for the next in line. He could hear Victor Craig typing next door. He kicked at the file cabinet and the typing stopped.

"Edison?"

He didn't want to talk to Craig so he tiptoed away and went to the front office. As soon as he entered, Myra the Receptionist took the burning cigarette from her ashtray and began puffing on it fiendishly. He paid her no attention and went straight into Barry's office. Barry ignored him, as usual. But it was a special kind of ignoring, an ignoring that said he understood. All things considered, Barry was probably the best of them. Edison continued on into Barthkowitz's office. Barthkowitz was dozing in his chair with an unlit cigar dangling from his lips. Flowers of used tissues littered his desk and floor. Edison closed the door. Barthkowitz didn't move. Edison opened the door and slammed it, knocking the wall panel to the secret passageway ajar. Barthkowitz snorted awake.

"Huh?" His eyes focused on Edison, scanned the horror story of his appearance. "Oh. You. Jesus, what happened?"

Edison didn't say anything. He didn't know why he was here. He had not come for anything in particular. He had just come. He knew that he was angry and sad and desperate and that he wanted someone to share these things with, but it really wasn't Barthkowitz.

Barthkowitz took the cigar out his mouth. His eyes were puffy and bloodshot, as if he'd been crying. The bags under them seemed to push his jowls even lower. He swiveled his chair away from Edison so that he was looking out at the patio.

"I'm letting you out of your contract," he said.

Edison may have nodded.

"The contract is written for two," said Barthkowitz. "Legally, it isn't valid. Myra, uh … the other Myra, will get you your last paycheck, minus the five days that you've missed."

Edison still may have nodded; it was difficult to be sure, the nodding was so slight.

"By the way, I'm sorry." Barthkowitz swiveled back around to face Edison and put the cigar back in his mouth.

This time Edison nodded perceptibly. He followed it with an audible "Fuck you." He waited a moment for Barthkowitz to properly receive this, which Barthkowitz confirmed with his own nodding, then turned and left the office.

He went back to the apartment and packed his things. He left much of it behind, taking mostly just clothes. In the bathroom, he picked up his toothbrush, trying hard not to see Myra's next to it. And while taking one last pee for the road, he again noticed Myra's journal on the back of the toilet. He opened it. It was nearly full. She had made it halfway down the second to last page. He was amazed at how much was there. The information wasn't very helpful to him; it read like a foreign language. But it was her. It was so much her.

Her last entry was:

10/8 – 11/6 – Brrln ayrlft, >2myl tnz eatmed, sewvyet blkayd ovr 11/6/12

Translation (unknown to Edison):

July 1948—May 1949—The Berlin Airlift delivered more
than two million tons of food and medicine to the city of Berlin, Germany, ending the Soviet blockade on May 12

He stuffed the journal in with his clothes. He flung the bag of film over his shoulder, grabbed the suitcase and his camera and brought them down to the car. When he came back up to lock the door, he saw the Royal sitting on the table, it's two-toned green paint glowing in the sunlight on the porch. He debated. He was fed up with writing right now, but something in him told him that he wouldn't always feel that way. He latched it into its carrying case and tossed it deep inside the trunk where he wouldn't have to look at it for a while.

He bid farewell to the Three Bills, thanking them for their assistance and concern. Between the three of them, they gathered up enough teeth to present to Edison a farewell smile, along with a toast from a half bottle of hooch. Edison cast a parting glance at Angels Flight. Then with a feeling of mild exhilaration, like a gauze laying atop his sadness, he gunned the Studebaker away from the curb, returning the Bills' salute with a final puff of exhaust.

His last stop was the bank, where he cashed his paycheck and withdrew half the money from their joint account, leaving the rest there for safekeeping. He turned from Sunset Boulevard onto North Figueroa, then Colorado Street, crossing Suicide Bridge—where he caught a glimpse of the Barthkowitz mansion—and finally onto the only road that mattered—Route 66.

Heaven

What happened to Myra: She had been sitting in the back of the airplane, behind Pulaski and the pilot, Buzzy Engstrom. She held a newspaper in front of her face so she wouldn't have to talk with Pulaski and was reading part of a week-old Roosevelt speech criticizing the Axis— *"On this tenth day of June, 1940, the hand that held the dagger has struck it into the back of its neighbor"*—when Buzzy asked Pulaski to stop spinning his pocket watch inside the airplane, as it could be dangerous.

"You just fly the plane and I'll worry about my own things. Okay?" Pulaski said.

"The safety of my passengers is part of flying the plane, Mr. Pulaski," said Buzzy.

Pulaski was about to add more defense to his actions when his pocket watch broke from its chain, ricocheted off a few things and disappeared somewhere behind the instrument panel. Buzzy gave an irritated sigh that no one else could hear over the engine noise. Then the engine coughed a few times, caught briefly, coughed again, and stopped.

Silence and wind.

"Oh-oh," said Buzzy.

Pulaski looked at him, drop-jawed and saucer-eyed. "Does 'oh-oh' mean you can't fix it?"

"Pretty much. We're two thousand feet up."

The plane began to fall quickly from the sky, shaving that number significantly. Pulaski began a meltdown, demanding to know what had happened. He wanted an explanation that had nothing to do with his pocket watch. Had he lived, he would have found one. The failure had been enabled by dirty fuel that had clogged the fuel line, causing the engine to stall. The timing of the stopwatch had been coincidental. But Pulaski wouldn't find that out and would go to his grave believing that he had killed himself and a couple of other people he didn't care about.

Somewhere during the panic of descent, Pulaski started demanding Myra's purse. No reason was given. He just kept shouting, "Give me your purse! Give me your purse!"

Myra had more immediate, end-of-life concerns on her mind, so she tossed it to him to shut him up. As the ocean was rushing toward them, Myra saw its surface grow very bright, bright enough that she closed her eyes. Then she felt the seat disappear from beneath her and suddenly she wasn't moving anymore.

When she opened her eyes, there wasn't an ocean within a thousand miles of her. There was, however, a mustache, attached to a face—a remarkably handsome face actually—sweeping down upon her with the obvious objective of rendering a kiss upon her recently materialized lips.

Myra faced the choice of many possible reactions in a very short period of time. First, she had gone from seeing an ocean surface racing toward her with the intention to kill, to a face racing toward her with the intention of making her an unfaithful wife. Second, she had gone from a feeling of absolute terror, coupled with a growing resignation, to a feeling of absolute peace and love. She really felt this, too. Instantly. Peace and love. And third, like Edison, who was at that same moment sitting in a German movie theater, she didn't know what the hell was going on.

The average person, faced with such a situation, would likely choose the easy reaction, the one that flowed most instinctively, like jumping up and screaming "Get away from me!" to the mustache. But Myra was not an average person anymore. She may have been an average person in twenty-first century Seattle, but she'd learned a few things since then, one of them being to assess a situation before reacting to it. In this spirit, she let the kiss happen.

His lips were soft and young, his mustache ticklish and his natural fragrance compelling. None of this helped her figure out what was going on, but it did reduce her sense of urgency about it. When the kiss ended, the face pulled the mustache away and gazed at her with deep, glisteny-eyed euphoria, a smidge of fear, and love. He was young enough to be her son.

"What's wrong?" he said, upon seeing her confusion. "You seem … different."

Myra stared open-mouthed, her brain trying to locate a proper response in her archives and drag it to her tongue. "I … I'm sorry," she said. She was blushing. "Nothing. I … I just got a dizzy spell."

The sky was clear and the weather comfortable. She was sitting on a bench in a park in the center of some town that reminded her of the Midwest. There was a beautiful walkway and grass and a duck pond with a fountain in it and a scalloped footbridge at one end. Across from the park rose a white church, its steeple bells at rest, and on the corner a town hall, its clock tower beginning to glow orange in the late afternoon light. Friendly looking shops prospered along the street.

"Are you going to be alright?" said the man. "It's not because of this afternoon, is it?"

Myra studied him. He was quite good looking. His hands were warm, his eyes flecked, his jaw angular. And she found herself strongly, and unaccountably, attracted to him. As if she knew him.

"Can we just sit here a while?" she said.

"I knew it," he said, shaking his head. "We should have waited."

He had his arm around her, patting her shoulder with affection. She decided not to say anything until she could get a better grasp on what was going on.

As Myra saw it, there were two possibilities:

1) Either the Time Flies had screwed something up, in which case Edison was likely experiencing something similar to her, or

2) She was in Heaven, which, according to many religious theories, would explain the instant emotional shift from terror to pleasure. This theory was complicated by the fact that she didn't believe in Heaven. She didn't really believe in anything. Well, she believed in—something. Just not anything specific. She'd been raised mildly Catholic and considered herself cured of organized religion. But for now, she was willing to have an open mind about the possibility of a Heaven-like place.

She inspected the surroundings to see if she could locate Edison wandering in puzzlement around the park. Nope.

She recalled where the Time Fly Law said that they were not protected from dying. She could very well be dead. She was certainly on her way to becoming that in the airplane. But this wasn't necessarily her idea of Heaven, assuming that's what this was. In her heaven, there would be no mustaches. And for all of this small town's bucolic beauty, she was an urban person. She would want to spend her eternity in a city.

And what was with this guy? He seemed to be head over heels in love with her. A woman old enough to be his mother. He looked barely out of high school. And where was Edison? She thought about that a moment and realized that she was okay without him. It embarrassed her, scared her even. It seemed callous but she just didn't feel a lot for Edison right now, except for a certain obligation to him. He needed her. At least she thought he did. But if she was in Heaven, and she was leaning more in this direction as the seconds passed, then he would have to learn to do without her. What she couldn't figure out was who she was supposed to be.

They walked for a while, the young man making small talk and apologizing for something. Myra tried to hold her own, keeping her responses short, but it wasn't working very well.

"Are you sure you're okay?" he said.

She felt a cry coming on. To stop herself, she took hold of the man's hand. "I'm just … happy. You know how sometimes being happy makes you quiet?"

He looked only slightly confused, but a weight seemed to have been lifted from him and he plowed on. "Well, okay." He suddenly grew animated, hopping about like a child, pleading, as if expecting to be turned down. "How about some cake? Please? It's been days."

Cake. She *was* hungry. "Alright."

His smile exploded. "Yes!" He beamed as they trotted to a small bakery that looked like it was just about to close for the day.

"Hello, Samuel," said the young woman behind the counter, flirting. *Samuel.*

The woman nodded toward Myra, dropping her tone. "Maureen." *So I'm Maureen.*

"The usual?"

"You bet," said Samuel.

The woman cut two pieces of chocolate layer cake and put them on plates. One piece was noticeably smaller. This one she handed to Myra without looking at her.

They carried their cake to a small table by a window. It was delicious. Myra was very hungry. She had not eaten before getting on the plane. Samuel made yum-yum smacking sounds as he ate his. He was really enjoying it.

"Isn't it great?" He smiled at her with chocolate on his teeth.

The woman behind the counter glared at Myra.

It was too confusing. Was this who she was going to have to be now? The cry came then, taking her by surprise and with cake in her mouth, arousing complications with breathing and swallowing.

"Oh, don't worry, Maureen," said Samuel, soothing her, patting her hand. "He'll come around. He will. You'll see."

She tried asking "Who?" but the cake in her mouth muffled it and it just sounded like more crying. The woman behind the counter was smiling.

Later, while walking in darkness, Samuel said, "This has been the most amazing day of my life. I'd give anything to relive this afternoon, wouldn't you?"

"Oh ... yes," said Myra. She smiled as best she could. Whatever 'this afternoon' meant, it was apparently something that had happened between them before her arrival.

They stopped in front of a house with a white picket fence and glowing windows.

"Well, good night, Maureen." He looked toward the house and back at her. "Someday. Don't worry, he'll come around." He kissed her, long enough and passionately enough that she started not minding it, then left her there on the sidewalk. She watched him walk away before turning toward the house. *I guess this is where I'm supposed to live.* What happened to the person who was in this body before her, this Maureen? Was she being Myra, sinking to the bottom of Santa Monica Bay? Or did this place, this young man and his mustache even exist before she arrived? What was she supposed to do?

She opened the gate and walked the flower-bordered walkway to the porch. She peered through a window into a living room of puffy-backed furniture and doily covered end tables. The couch was patterned with a country meadow and rabbits nibbling at grass. One of the end tables had a pipe stand holding three pipes. It did not seem like a place that someone lived in alone. The door was unlocked. She stood in the living room as a woman's voice called to her from another room, possibly the kitchen. "How was your day with Samuel, dear?"

Myra thought about changing her voice before she answered, but that seemed stupid. "Uh, wonderful."

"Oh, good. I'm so happy for you two. And don't worry. Your father will come around. Samuel is a good man. Would you like a piece of cake?"

What's with all the cake? "No, thanks ... " *Mom?* "I'm kind of tired. I'm ... going to bed."

"Alright then. See you in the morning. Warning: your father was just in the bathroom. It might smell. Good night, Mo."

Mo.

The bathroom did indeed smell. She could hear snoring from the other side of the wall and guessed that that was not her bedroom. It was her *parent's* room. She looked in the mirror and saw herself—fifty-seven years old with long silver hair. What did Samuel see?

She went into *her* bedroom and sat on the bed, Maureen's bed, for a long time, staring at the flowered wallpaper and frilly curtains of a girl's bedroom. She thought that she should be crying or fretting wildly, but found that she was really okay with the situation now. She just wanted to know what the situation was.

Unexplained Differences

So how was it that Edison got flung to Germany as himself and Myra ended up as someone else? As previously stated by Professor Rocklidge:

```
Effects from Time Fly Glitches:

May include becoming displaced in space, but not in time,
increased appetite, becoming other people and ceasing to
exist. Minimal safeguards have been put in place to prevent
materialization inside of solid objects, but these are
not guaranteed.
```

Becoming other people. The thing was, Myra didn't completely become Maureen. There was still a bunch of her own self left. She felt that she might be in love with Samuel and yet she didn't know who he was. Or whom he thought she was. And trying to get a Time Fly to explain how this could be would likely elicit a response of little more than grunts and paper shuffling, or something flippant such as, "Well, at least she didn't cease to exist."

Maureen

Strangely, no one woke Myra in the morning and she slept until after noon. She stayed in bed a while longer, afraid to get up, before her back started aching, forcing her out. She slogged her way into the bathroom and checked herself in the mirror. She was wearing pajamas that weren't hers, but looked like they fit. They even felt familiar. She didn't remember putting them on the night before, but there they were. On the dining table downstairs, there was a note from *Mom* telling her that she was at Aunt Gilly's, helping her bake a cake for the bake sale. Myra began to write a reply, but dropped the pencil when she realized it wasn't her handwriting. The script was lazy and overly loopy, from the hand of a girl, and she was embarrassed by it. She crumpled the note and tossed it in the trash.

Her long sleep had left her famished. She found some kind of casserole in the refrigerator and heated some in a pan. It was one of the most delicious things she'd ever eaten, as if it had been created specifically for her. It may have had meat in it.

She wandered the house, appraising knick-knacks and furnishings. There were framed photos everywhere, hanging on walls and propped on end tables, but none of them were labeled. She couldn't tell who was who. Some of them must have been of Maureen, of Maureen's mother and father. But the extended family was apparently quite large. She hadn't even seen Maureen's parents yet, had only heard one and smelled the other.

She wanted to go for a walk, to think, but the body had no interest in it. The body wanted to go back to bed. She went into the bathroom and locked the door. She took off the pajamas and stood naked in front of the mirror. She saw only herself, the body she knew. She felt for the lump in her breast and was stunned to find it missing. Why?

At about 3pm, Samuel knocked brightly on the front door.

"Are you alright?" he said when she opened the door.

"I think so," said Myra. "Why?"

He had a cake in his hands. He put it down on an end table and took her in his arms. "I was so worried about you."

"What do you mean?"

"What do I mean?" he said. "You slept a whole day."

"I did?" She backed away in shock.

"You bet. Your mom said you must have been sick. They tried to wake you all day but you just kept moaning and sleeping."

"I did?"

"You bet. They called Doc Johnson in and he looked you over and said you seemed okay. But he couldn't wake you, either. He told your mom to let you sleep. Said you must have been exhausted by something."

"You mean I missed a whole day? They let me sleep a whole day?" That didn't seem possible. (A hint: Myra had sort of, but not all the way, ceased to exist for just about thirty-eight hours—a glitch in the Glitch—leaving Maureen's sleeping body in a state of suspension.)

"Aw, don't worry," said Samuel. "You seem fine now. All refreshed and peppy." He nudged her. "Besides, we're used to you sleeping a lot, lazybones."

"What's that supposed to mean?" She felt a flare of anger in Maureen's defense.

"Oh, never mind," said Samuel, brushing it off. He picked up the cake from the end table and held it out for inspection. "Is your mom here?"

"She's at Aunt Gilly's making a cake for the bake sale."

Samuel smiled. "What do you think this is for? My mom made it this morning. She said your mom was going to take it to the sale this evening. It's a beauty, isn't it?" He twirled it side to side for a better look. "Like you."

Myra blushed. She examined the cake with its chocolate frosting and yellow candy roses and ropes of orange icing. *I slept a whole day?*

"I helped with the orange part," he said. "The rest is all Mom."

Samuel was nice. A sweet kid. She had to admit that this was better than being in an airplane with that half-witted Pulaski, spinning his asinine watch, reeking of smoke and body odor. She hadn't wanted to go flying with him and she'd said so, but Barthkowitz had badgered her into it, threatening her with legal action. She hadn't believed the threat, but went because she'd been too tired to fight it. Two more weeks. Why hadn't she listened to Edison when he said he wanted to leave right away? If she'd listened, this might not have happened.

That evening, Samuel drove them to the bake sale in his dad's car. This was a rare privilege, one granted only on special occasions. They drove past endless fields of young corn, the stalks just two feet high. The sky was amber in the west as she watched the last of the sun leave the day.

"Mr. Simmons says it's going to be a great harvest this year. The Almanac says it's going to be a warm summer with plenty of rain." Samuel was wearing a bow tie and a white shirt. Myra fit perfectly into a flowered dress that her *mother* had put out for her to wear.

They pulled up to a barn lit from within, casting yellow light on the smattering of cars and pickup trucks parked on the dirt out front. Samuel parked beside a '36 Ford.

"Oh, this is going to be so much fun," he said. He ran his hand along the inside of her bare thigh—sending a lovely tingle through her lower half—and before she could brush it away he got out and walked around to open her door. "Mrs. Williams is *not* going to take the prize this year. Not if my mom can help it."

Long tables covered with cakes ringed the interior of the barn. Moms and future moms wearing bonnets with visors the size of window awnings fussed over the arrangements. The woman from the bakery who didn't like her was wrangling some coconut cakes and a cake with half-moon jellied fruit slices all over it. Country folks milled about, admiring the goods, sticking their hands too close only to have them playfully slapped away by a finger-wagging mom. Children weaved mischievously between the adults. Potato salads, fruit salads, macaroni salads, corn salads and green salads, were being uncovered and set out for consumption. Out behind the barn were huge smoking barbecue pits covered with animal parts—hot dogs, burgers, chicken and steaks.

Myra noticed that she seemed to be one of the only women her age—whatever age it was she was supposed to be—not helping out with something. Samuel had drifted into men's conversation, leaving her to fend for herself. It struck her that she still hadn't seen the woman who was supposed to be her mother, and that her mother was supposed to be here. She looked for faces that were familiar from the pictures she'd seen at the house. There were many of them. They were everywhere. Some greeted her warmly, asking if she was all right. But from some she caught snippets of gossip aimed in her direction.

"Shameful."

"It's love that's doing it to her. Never trust a man with a mustache, I always say. Too Hollywood."

"Love! Ha! It's the devil's work, that's what it is."

She saw one of the moms crying a little and overheard her confiding to a friend, "I even made her favorite casserole yesterday, because of all her sleeping. There was some left in the icebox. I just hope she had some. She seemed so … sick."

Myra made her move, striding up to the woman like a dutiful daughter. "Hi, Mom. Thanks for the casserole."

Mom was careworn and pasty with the rundown face of a farm town wife fresh from the Depression, blandly overweight behind her apron. The look in her eyes showed disappointment. "Is there something wrong, dear? Are you feeling better?"

"I'm feeling fine. How could I not, with all the wonderful care you give me?" Well, that didn't sound right. *Mom* looked skeptical.

"Sweetheart," said *Mom*. "I've been hearing some things. About you and Samuel."

"Things?" said Myra. She remembered Samuel's comment about yesterday afternoon.

Mom put her hand on Myra's cheek, smearing it with a little frosting. "I just hope that you and Samuel aren't moving too quickly. Was there anything you wanted to talk to me about?"

Myra looked around at the crowd. Many of them were looking her way. "Here?"

"Oh, of course not," *Mom* said. "We can talk another time. You run along and have some fun. Or you can help out if you'd like." The last sentence was said without much hope in it.

"Uh, sure," said Myra. "I'll see if anyone needs anything out back."

She wandered outside to where the men were barbecuing. Some of them were flirtatious toward her; others seemed disapproving. Samuel was off to the side with a few mustached friends. They kept looking over at her and smiling as if they were sharing secrets. She knew that look, had seen it in high school, tossed the way of girls carrying the burden of moral disrepute.

Shit. This is just what I need, a sex scandal inside a teenager's body.

There were games and contests for the children. All the jaunty-toothed men and boys in town, including Samuel, raced each other for a hundred yards across a grassy field behind the barn. Samuel came in second place and strutted like a god afterward. Then it was time to eat.

Myra was famished, hungrier than she could ever remember being. Flesh sizzled on the barbecues. Samuel handed her a plate heaped with meats. Myra hesitated, but soon lost control. Maureen must have been some carnivore because she could do nothing to keep drumsticks and hot dogs from squirming their way between her teeth and racing down her gullet. She consumed three hamburgers, two hot dogs, a steak and half a chicken. She put away enough for a large man, and Sarah Johnson, Doc Johnson's girl, amazed by the volume disappearing into Maureen's mouth asked her if she wanted to join in the cake eating contest. Myra, her face shiny with grease, could tell by the expectant looks from everyone that Maureen had never been a participant in this, if in anything, and decided to salvage a little of her reputation by demurring.

The meat bloated her and she suffered grossly from something she'd once heard called 'meat sweats.' She mopped her brow. Her dress clung moistly to her. She swore her skin smelled like a greasy hamburger and spent the rest of the evening just trying to keep it all down.

On the drive home, Samuel wanted to stop off in a cornfield and take advantage of the empty back seat of his dad's car, but Myra told him she still wasn't feeling well and wanted to go home. Samuel was disappointed.

"With the way you were putting that food away, I thought you were feeling just fine," he said. "You sure were sweaty."

"That was weird."

"It sure was."

Unable to sleep well with all the meat shoving itself through her body, she got up very early the next morning. She was most unhappy with the quality of her bowel movement. She wandered the quiet house looking for a newspaper, but this was apparently a non-reading family. Snatching a few coins from a cookie jar, she went out to buy a paper, walking along a curved street of houses similar to Maureen's, each with slightly different versions of white picket fencing. At a small pharmacy on the corner, she found a *Big City Chronicle* amongst the smaller local papers. The skinny balding clerk handed her the change with amused surprise.

"Maureen? Are you going to make paper mache?"

Myra glared at him. "I might."

As she left, the clerk said, "The comics are on page twenty-three."

She found herself angry and insulted, even though it was not actually she who was being insulted. She was developing a sort of ownership of Maureen. *If this is Heaven,* she thought, *it's a pretty screwed up place.* At *home,* she curled up on the couch to read. France had fallen to the Nazis, signing their surrender in the same rail car in which Germany had surrendered to France in 1918. Hitler had attended the event personally, trailed by a marching band and strutting before the cameras like a movie star. On page two there was an article that practically drained the fluids from her body. A hometown boy had been killed in the line of duty. The tone of the article was reverential. A legend was being made.

> Hitching up his wagaon and doing the "Westward, ho!"
> during the early stages of the great depression follow-
> ing the failure of his family's grocery business, this
> local hero found his fortunes under the bright lights of
> Hollywood, California. His name was Gaston Pulaski
> and his duty was movie producer.

A bit of drool soaked into the newspaper as Myra read the account of her own demise, her body seemingly lost forever at sea.

"I *am* dead," she said to herself. "Oh, poor Edison."

From upstairs a toilet flushed. She heard the low rumblings of a male throat clearing its morning phlegm. She still had yet to run into her *father*.

Oh, I hope that's not God.

The stairs quaked with the footfalls of a heavy body reluctant to be moving. Her *father*, big-eyed and pudgy-cheeked, passed through the living room, mumbled "G'mornin'," then froze, gawking at the newspaper in her hand. He shook his head—dislodging a chuckle—and continued on to the kitchen. A few minutes later she heard him go out to the garage. The sound of hammering followed, mixing with a knock on the front door.

Samuel again. He was horny this time and wanted her to come out and play.

"We could go into the Miller's barn again," he said, sliding his hands along her waist. "No one will find us there." His fingers brushed lightly on her buttocks. Myra recoiled. She was pretty sure that Maureen would not have.

"Did you see here that France has been occupied?" she said, holding up the newspaper and trying to divert his digits.

With a little makeup, Samuel's comic look of disbelief could have found easy work with the circus. "Why are you troubling yourself with *those* things?" he said. "You should be looking at wedding gowns."

"I just think it's important to pay attention to world events."

"Since when?"

"Don't you think about the war, Samuel?"

"Not very much. Should I?"

"Well … yes."

"Oh, I see where this is going," he laughed. He cupped her face in his hands and pulled her close. "You're afraid that I'll go off to war and find some European girl, aren't you?"

"That's not what I meant."

"Well, don't you worry your pretty little head. President Roosevelt says it's not going to happen and I believe him. I'm not going anywhere. We couldn't be safer right where we are." His hands moved down to her waist again, giving her a little squeeze on the hips. "Very safe."

Part of her, the Maureen part, wanted to give in to him. She wanted to jump his bones and to have her bones jumped. The thought of rutting around in the hay with big strong Samuel, his mustache sweeping over her various body parts, sent shivers through her. The Myra part of her overruled this and she slipped out of his grasp.

"Samuel," she said. "I'm serious. What's happening in Europe is important."

Samuel grew troubled. His brow furrowed, as if he had unpleasant work ahead of him. He tightened his lips so that they disappeared beneath his mustache and took on an authoritative air, bracing himself. "I don't want you to read the newspaper anymore."

"You what?" said Myra. Cake, meat and now this—her beloved newspaper.

"I'm sorry, Maureen. It's for your own good. Newspapers will only confuse you."

"You're kidding, right?"

"I'm not kidding," said Samuel. "In fact—I forbid it. There, I've said it."

"Well, you can just un-say it. I won't take that crap."

"Maureen!"

"Oh, shock and horror. A woman speaks. Shutup and spread your legs, is that it? I'm not kidding, either, Samuel. If you think you can lead me around like a trimmed poodle, you have another thought coming."

Samuel shook his head vigorously, trying to make sense of the situation. "I don't understand, Maureen. What's happened to you? Who are you?"

Myra could see he was having a difficult time of it. It seemed unfair to throw so much at him at once, so she let it go a little. She sat on the couch and leaned her head back.

What would Maureen do?

"I'm sorry, Samuel. I feel like so much is happening so fast. The war … the marriage. I know that the war probably isn't coming here, not where we are." In Heaven. "I know that you just want us to be happy."

Samuel sat beside her on the couch. "That's okay, Maureen." He smiled tenderly and put his hand on her breast. His timing was way off. Myra pushed it away.

"Oh, for chrissakes," she said.

Samuel reacted like he'd been slapped. His mustache twitched. "How dare you talk to me that way."

"Wait a minute. You can put your hand on my breast without asking, but I can't say 'For chrissakes'?"

"There! You said it again. And … that other word."

"You mean breast?"

Samuel stood quickly, tall and very erect. "I won't have that kind of talk in my house."

"This is my house. Remember?"

"You mean … ?"

"What?"

"This is going to be *our* house. And I'm the man."

"You want to live with my parents?"

"Oh, now that hurts. That really hurts." Samuel stomped for the door, pausing briefly with pointed finger. "You'll regret this, Maureen!" He slammed the door behind him.

She heard her *father* coming back in the house. He lumbered up in front of her and lobbed her an I-told-you-so sneer.

"What just happened?" said Myra, as the room grew bright and transparent.

The Resurrection

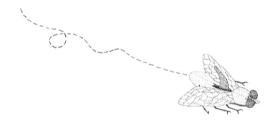

Myra's planned return to Los Angeles at the expiration of the 73.63754 hours of her first Glitch caused complications for the Time Flies. They were unsure as to exactly where Myra should return. When she disappeared, she had been rapidly leaving mid-air in an airplane about to slam into the concrete-like surface of the Pacific Ocean. Three days later, the airplane was now gone, smashed to smithereens, and placing Myra in mid-air didn't seem quite fair given the strictly enforced law regarding gravity. It would have been a watery death sentence and even considering that she would have died anyway had she not been tossed into middle America for three days, the Time Flies recognized this as their responsibility (without admitting any wrongdoing) and made partial amends by shipping her, instead, to the opposite end of the moisture spectrum—the desert. This had not been an easy decision. Debate had raged in Time Fly Court for nearly five days about what to do with her, with representatives of the court arguing windfully about the true meaning of the Time Fly Law. While this went on, Myra had hovered in a sort of nothingness, which, to her, felt like a few blank seconds. When the decision had finally been made and she had been plopped down under an angry desert sun, more than a week had passed since she'd been in Los Angeles. Or, to be exact: 192.45914 hours.

Myra went from the coolness of the bunny-patterned couch to a flank-burning sun-baked rock. At least the Time Flies had not set her upon a cactus. She looked around at the rocky outcroppings, the Joshua trees, the heat waves.

"Oh-oh." Desert. Heat. Pissing off Samuel. *You'll regret this, Maureen.* Had her eternity been relocated to that other place? Did Samuel send her here? Was *he* God?

She wasn't sure if freedom of movement was allowed just yet, but staying in one place didn't seem to have a future in it, and since there appeared to be no other sinners around, she began to walk. In the distance, she saw a car whizzing along and went toward it, cautiously skirting evil looking plants and possible rattlesnake hideaways, until she reached a ribbon of searing asphalt. There was a sign on the side of the road: *Los Angeles 162 miles.*

"Well, so much for Heaven. Those goddamned Time Flies."

She managed to hitch a ride with a musty-smelling chicken hauler who gave her a good once over as she climbed into the cab. Maureen's dress now hung loosely on her frame.

"So, what's your name?" he said.

Myra thought about it for a moment. "I'm not sure. Don't you know?"

"Oooh. Mystery woman," he said. He tried giving her The Look, but his leering was no match for her withering so it didn't go any further than that. It was a mostly silent drive back to LA except when the truck overheated just outside of Barstow and she got out to stretch her legs while the chicken hauler added water to the radiator.

"Where are you taking the chickens?" she asked.

"Market."

Myra walked around the truck lightly fingering the stacked cages. Chickens bobbed and clucked and pecked. She reminisced on eating all that meat last night as Maureen and worried that she was craving it again as Myra. While her eyes were on the chickens, Edison drove past in the Studebaker. Not knowing that Myra was on the far side of the truck, fingering chicken cages, nothing struck him as out of the ordinary and he passed without incident. By the time Myra looked down the highway to see the car receding, it was too far away for her to recognize. Opportunity missed.

The chicken hauler let her off near downtown and she walked the rest of the way home, arriving just after dark. The Three Bills were not on the sidewalk and Edison's car was gone. She was not seen by anyone she knew. She picked up the newspapers outside the apartment door and went inside.

She sat in Edison's favorite chair on the porch, cursing the Time Flies both silently and aloud for their flawed abilities to keep their prisoners in place. Why hadn't she told Edison that she was going flying with Pulaski? There hadn't been time, or at least it had seemed that way when Barthkowitz had told her to go. She saw the newspapers on the couch, opened to the story of the plane crash, and it reminded her that everyone must think she's dead. There was freedom in that.

But what about Edison? She didn't know that she had missed him by almost five days.

In the bathroom, she found drops of dried blood on the floor and a pink ring in the tub. Edison's bloody clothes were stuffed behind the toilet. She panicked briefly when she found her journal missing, but was touched that he had taken it with him.

She wondered where he had gone for those same days that she had been gone and why there had been bleeding involved. Did he fall in love with someone, too? She barely remembered Samuel now. He was just a memory of a silly boy. There was no more Maureen left in her, albeit for a vague craving for meat. She took off the dress and walked around the apartment naked, content with her body and all that gravity had done to it over the years. Her years. She felt beneath her breast and was glad to have her lump back, unchanged. She searched the rest of her body for signs that someone else had been using it in her absence, but found nothing obvious.

The apartment was so quiet. She looked out at Angels Flight, one car going up, the other one coming down, their parallelogram windows glowing peacefully in the darkness. Where was he now? The blood made her think of hospitals, but his missing things and no car out front didn't support that. It seemed he'd left of his own accord, without life-threatening injuries.

It was late and the trains were going to stop running soon. She decided to sleep.

In the morning, she packed her things—clothes, toiletries, the sanitary napkins that she still hadn't used but still felt she might. She followed the hum of the new refrigerator into the kitchen and placed the amputation kit on top where Dot would be sure to find it. She folded the Murphy bed into the wall, exposing the empty velvet covered eyeball tray beneath it, which she picked up and put with the amputation kit. She donned sunglasses and a green patterned scarf to cover her hair, so as not to be recognized on the street, a woman lugging her bag while being dead. Her whole life in a twenty-one pound bag. At the door, she paused to gaze over the bookshelves. Her eyes rested for a moment on the spine of *The Grapes of Wrath*. It was still hard to believe that it was only published a year ago and that even the movie had just finished its first run. It would be nice to leave a note for Dot, asking her to donate the books to the library, but dead women didn't do things like that. She tiptoed past Dot's apartment, snuck down the fire escape and hauled her bag up the utility stairs to Olive Street and hailed a taxicab.

Her scarf fluttered in the wind from the open window, the streets teeming with people she would never know. She asked the cabbie to wait at the bank, where she discovered that the account was at exactly half. Edison hadn't touched her half. That was reassuring. It meant that he still had hope, even if he didn't realize it himself. She knew that by closing the account she risked being recognized, but she needed the money, so did it anyway, under the name of Mrs. Edison Winslow, stuffing more than seven thousand dollars into her bag over the protests of the bank manager who begged and cajoled to no avail, leaving him bitter with her in the end.

She approached the gleaming white exterior of Union Station, skittering past idle taxis, Spanish arches and the coffee shop, glancing to and fro like a fugitive. Her footsteps echoed off the walls and ceilings. She stood looking across the lobby at the ticket window. Where to? It would be difficult to track Edison down. They weren't in any phone directory anywhere. There were no records of them. Edison Winslow and Myra Mix did not really exist.

She needed to walk. There was thinking to be done and walking was a good way to waste valuable time. She stowed her bag in a locker and walked until mid-afternoon, her head low and her mind reeling. As she strolled along Temple Street, a lady coming out of an apartment building carrying grocery bags reminded her of her mother. Through the smog, what may have been a lone cloud cruised slowly over city hall. Then it struck her—New York. They had talked about it. It was why he bought the car. It had to be. Yes, she would find Edison in New York City. She knew this.

"I'd like a ticket for the next train to New York, please."

"That would be the Super Chief, ma'am," said the man behind the ticket window. "It's a lovely train. Pullman sleepers. Gourmet dining. It's the Train of the Stars. Leaves in twenty minutes. You might even get lucky and see a movie star onboard."

Myra hesitated. "That's a little more than I had in mind. What else do you have?"

The clerk dropped his enthusiasm. "The El Capitan leaves tomorrow. All coach. No sleepers. Sandwiches."

"Nothing else today?"

She was considering her options when she turned and nearly yelped at the view before her. Barthkowitz, who was presently at Union Station to pick up his hypochondriac sister, Bertha, was about thirty yards away. His tie was knotted too short and he was holding two of Bertha's bags. He caught her eye at the same moment, dropping his jaw and letting his cigar fall. Sparks splayed across the floor.

"Oh, shit," said Myra.

"Pardon me?" said the clerk.

"Give me a ticket for the Chief. Quickly, please." She shoved money toward him and pushed her sunglasses tighter to her face.

"The Chief doesn't run until Thursday. Are you sure you don't mean the Super Chief?"

She leaned into the window. "Just give me a ticket for the next fucking train, will you, please?"

The clerk reared back, offended. "There's no need for that, ma'am."

"I'm sorry. I'm sorry. Please."

Satiated, the clerk readied her ticket, shaking his head over the crumbling of societal mores.

"Myra?" said Barthkowitz from behind her, cranking up little chainsaws of adrenaline in her veins.

"Hurry, please," she whispered harshly.

"Almost ready," said the clerk.

"Myra?" A little louder, a little closer. She ignored him.

"You'll switch to the 20th Century Limited in Chicago," said the clerk. "That's a lovely train, too. Red carpet service."

Myra snatched the ticket from the clerk's hand. "Done?"

"Don't forget your change."

"Thank you."

She spun around and landed in Barthkowitz's arms.

"Myra," he nearly shouted. "Myra. Where have you been?" His eyes were as wide as manhole covers. She struggled in his arms as he fawned minutely, sniffled lightly, but managed to hold off full-blown weeping. And before things went too far, he jammed a wedge into the gears of his brief dalliance with expressed emotions by dropping his arms and composing himself. "Why didn't you report to the studio that you were alive?"

Myra edged around him. "I'm sorry, sir," she said hoarsely, skirting him with her bag. "You must have me confused with someone else."

"The hell I do," he said. He reached for her arm, but she was too fast. "You're supposed to be dead. The papers said so," he called after her as she hustled toward her departure ramp. Curious heads turned his way, then hers.

Behind him, Bertha dropped her bag. "Reggie, my feet are sore." He tried to ignore her. "And I think my shingles are coming back. My face hurts."

Barthkowitz closed his eyes. "I'll be with you in a minute, Bertha." When he opened them again, Myra had disappeared. He grabbed Bertha's bags and followed, catching sight of Myra as she crested the ramp to the train platform. When he got to the top she was gone again. He waited. There were two trains, one on each side of the platform. He looked back and forth between them. Then he saw Myra sit down by a window. He could tell that she knew he was standing there, staring at her, but now he wasn't sure if it really was her. Damn, it seemed like her. When he'd held her in his arms, she'd felt like he had always imagined she would. Now, obscured by the window reflections, wearing a scarf and sunglasses, and her hand covering her jawline, he grew doubtful.

"You're still under contract!" he yelled, testing. Seconds later, she got up from the seat. Bertha caught up to him, rubbing her face, as he waited a few minutes more to see if Myra would return to the window. She didn't. And when Bertha's complaining finally started to earn its living, he picked up her bags and followed her out. He was long gone by the time the wheels of the train began to roll eastward.

Goodbye, For Now

Myra was not really convinced that Edison was on his way to New York City. Yes, they had talked about it and, yes, she wanted him to carry through with their plan. But she knew that it didn't make much sense. With her dead, Edison no longer had a reason to go to New York. He no longer had a reason to go anywhere.

Without Myra, it was like Edison had lost his compass, and, with it, his ability to navigate. His most likely course would be drifting. And with all those miles between the coasts, the chances of him turning his faulty rudder in the direction of New York City seemed remote.

As she watched the lights of Los Angeles recede into the past—replaced first by a craggy bulwark of mountains against the dusk, then by a vast stretch of desert, brilliantly bleached in the moonlight, lonely and freckled with sagebrush—Myra had the feeling that she may not see Edison for quite some time. It was even possible that she may not see him for the rest of their sentence, that she may only, finally, run into him on December 16, 1963, back in the Seattle house, in their living room, waiting to be returned to the future. Waiting to go home. But before that, he would have to make it through twenty-three more years of the past without getting himself killed. Unless she could find him first.

END OF BOOK I

Acknowledgements so far:

Although none of them would intentionally admit to having read this book, I'd like to expose a few of my friends by thanking them for responding so positively to my pestering and for providing such inspired feedback.

Trudy Love Tantalo, who stuck with me through a number of revisions, reading each one dutifully and giving me unvarnished feedback.

Sal Tonacchio, my former film instructor and current friend, who actually took notes and discussed them with me over cocktails, which is how all discussions should take place.

Christine Hernandez, who always wears a Bukowski t-shirt just for me whenever I see her, and who read this book twice in one weekend, took pages of notes, and spoke with such excitement that she almost had me convinced that the book is good.

Bob Anderton, a man who is never without a bicycle in his pocket, for all of his excellent feedback in the very early stages, when things were quite mucky and confusing. His repeated insistence that I stop calling a freeway a freeway and start calling it by its proper name, Interstate 5, was just irritating enough to make me change it. Thanks, Bob. You were correct.

Mark Powell, the man who swam the length of the polluted Duwamish River from mountain to ocean, for his thoughtful comments and for telling me to stop being so clever with the metaphors.

My stepdaughter, Lyla Irvine, who read this book because her mother made her, but nevertheless gave me extremely useful and honest feedback.

Wendy Gibson and Mariecris Gatlabayan, who mentally wrestled me to the ground and held me until I did something with this.

Emily Negley and Alisa Mowe, who lit the fuse and watched this rocket (book) launch. Their selflessness and generosity are unmatched. I'll never forget what they did for me.

Debbie Letterman (a real librarian!), for her continuing advice and assistive sarcasm.

Rob Siders at 52 Novels for his excellent ebook and print book interior production.

And to my beta readers—Sharon Elise Dunn, Melanie Erickson, Betsy Lawless, Patrick Turner, Peter Myers, Paul Johnson, Rowena Simoni, Lisa Rice, my sister, Patti Ciardi and my daughter, Taryn Ciardi—thank you all for reading this book and for then keeping our relationships alive by saying nice things about it, whether true or not.

Special thanks go to Gillianne Beyer for translating some parts of this into German (and for making it look like I actually did it myself, which I didn't, and couldn't), and to lawyer Lisa Lui, who, for the insane price of a bottle of bourbon, helped me decipher the contract with my first deadbeat agent (who promptly disappeared without a trace after signing).

Photo by Taryn Ciardi

About the Author

George Ciardi is a classic film buff with a bad memory, a published photographer and an incurable road tripper. He lives in Seattle with his wife, Sharon Elise Dunn, in an old house that has seasonal outbreaks of cluster flies. Much of this novel was originally written on Post-it notes.

https://georgeciardi.com/
http://www.commonmanstories.com/
https://www.facebook.com/GeorgeCiardiAuthor/
http://www.artificialdaylight.com/

Please rate this book from where you purchased it. Thank you.

Made in the USA
Columbia, SC
26 January 2018